Alan Furst has published five novels, most recently the highly regarded *Night Soldiers*. He has travelled widely in Europe, served as a Fulbright Teaching Fellow in southern France, and written extensively for *Esquire* magazine and for the *International Herald Tribune*. He lives in Paris.

DARK STAR

'Imagine discovering an unscreened espionage thriller from the late 1930s, a classic black-and-white movie that captures the murky allegiances and moral ambiguity of Europe on the brink of war. All the treasured cinematic touches that convey a mood of incipient danger are present – a dead Soviet agent in a waterfront brothel in Ostend, lonely footsteps muffled by the snow on a dark Berlin street, a worn leather satchel with a false bottom left in a Prague railway station. No, they do not make movies like that anymore. But in *Dark Star*, Alan Furst has replicated this idealized form, this image of Europe entwined in a web of malevolent ideology . . . What carries the book to a level beyond the cynicism of spy novels is its ability to carry us back in time. Nothing can be like watching *Casablanca* for the first time. But Furst comes closer than anyone has in years.'
Walter Schapiro, *Time*

'A rich, deeply moving novel of suspense that is equal parts espionage thriller, European history and love story. Furst has surpassed himself. The time-frame of the late 1930s on the continent was once the special property of Eric Ambler and Graham Greene; Furst has ventured into their fictional territory and brought out a story that is equally original a[illegible]ing.'
New York Times

By the same author

Shadow Trade
Night Soldiers

ALAN FURST

Dark Star

Grafton
An Imprint of HarperCollins*Publishers*

Grafton
An Imprint of HarperCollins*Publishers*
77–85 Fulham Palace Road,
Hammersmith, London W6 8JB

Special overseas edition 1992
This edition published by Grafton 1992
9 8 7 6 5 4 3 2 1

First published in Great Britain by
GraftonBooks 1991

Published by special arrangement with
Houghton Mifflin Company

The Author asserts the moral right to
be identified as the author of this work

ISBN 0 586 21318 X

Set in Times

Printed in Great Britain by
HarperCollinsManufacturing Glasgow

'You may not be interested in war,
but war is interested in you.'

– Lev Bronshtein, known as Leon Trotsky, June 1919

SWEDEN
DENMARK
Aarus
Copenhagen
BALTIC SEA
Lipāja
LIT
Memel
Königsberg
EAST
PRUSSIA
Kiel
Lübeck
Rostok
Hamburg
Danzig
Elbe R.
Oder R.
Berlin
Havil R.
Vistula R.
Bug R.
Warsaw
GERMANY
Neisse R.
Altenburg
POLAND
Czestochowa
Aussig
Prague
Cracow
Nürnberg
CZECHOSLOVAKIA
Nowy
Sącz
Krosn
Dukla Pass
Ulm
Munich
Danube R.
Vienna
HUNGARY
AUSTRIA
Budapest

P O L
and the Berlin-Mos

Riga
Jelgava
LATVIA
Moscow
UANIA
Vitebsk
Smolensk
RUSSIA
Kaunas
(Kovno)
Wilno
Minsk
Berezina R.
Mogilev
N
Bialystok
Gomel
Pripet Marshes
Pripet R.
MILES
0 100 200
0 100 200
KILOMETERS
Kovel
Kiev
Rovno
Zhitomir
Poltava
Brody
Berdichev
Lvov
Ternopol
Dnieper R.
PATHIAN MTS.
Dniester R.
ROUMANIA
Kishinev
Odessa
WARD

AND
cow Corridor, 1937

Silence in Prague

In the late autumn of 1937, in the steady beat of North Sea rain that comes with dawn in that season, the tramp freighter *Nicaea* stood at anchor off the Belgian city of Ostend. In the distance, a berthing tug made slow progress through the harbour swell, the rhythm of its engine distinct over the water, its amber running lights twin blurs in the darkness.

The *Nicaea*, 6,320 gross tonnes, of Maltese registry, had spent her first thirty years as a coastal steamer in the eastern Mediterranean, hauling every imaginable cargo from Latakia to Famagusta, back to Iskenderun, down to Beirut, north to Smyrna, then south to Sidon and Jaffa – thirty years of blistering summers and drizzling winters, trading and smuggling in equal proportion, occasionally enriching, more typically ruining, a succession of owner syndicates as she herself was slowly ruined by salt, rust, and a long line of engineers whose enthusiasm far exceeded their skill. Now, in her final years, she was chartered to Exportkhleb, the Soviet Union's grain-trading bureau, and she creaked and groaned sorrowfully to lie at anchor in such cold, northern seas.

Riding low in the water, she bore her cargo gracelessly – principally Anatolian wheat bound for the Black Sea port of Odessa, a city that had not seen imported grains for more than a century. She carried, as well, several small consignments: flax-seed loaded in Istanbul, dried figs from Limassol, a steel drum of Ammonal – a mining explosive made of TNT and powdered aluminium – en route to a sabotage cell in Hamburg, a metal trunk of engineering blueprints for an Italian submarine torpedo, deftly copied at a naval research station in Brindisi, and two passengers: a senior Comintern official using a Dutch passport with the alias Van Doorn, and a foreign correspondent of the newspaper *Pravda* travelling under his true name, André Szara.

Szara, hands thrust deep in pockets, hair blown about by the offshore gale, stood in the shelter of a passageway and silently cursed the Belgian tug captain who, from the methodical chug of the engine, was taking his own sweet time attending to the *Nicaea*. Szara knew harbourmen in this part of the world; stolid, reflective pipe smokers who were never far from the coffeepot and the evening paper. Unshakable in crisis, they spent the rest of their days making the world wait on their pleasure. Szara shifted his weight with the roll of the ship, turned his back to the wind, and lit a cigarette.

He had boarded the freighter nineteen days earlier, in Piraeus, having been assigned a story on *the struggle of the Belgian dockworkers*. That was one assignment; there was another. Killing time in a dockside tavern as the *Nicaea* was eased into moorage, he had been approached by the World's Plainest Man. Where, he wondered, did they find them? Russia marked people: deformed most, made some exquisite, at the very least burned itself deep into the eyes. But not this one. His mother was water, his father a wall. 'A small favour,' said the world's plainest man. 'You'll have a fellow passenger, he is travelling on Comintern business. Perhaps you will find out where he is stopping in Ostend.'

'If I can,' Szara had said. The word *if* could not really be used between them, but Szara pretended it could be and the NKVD operative – or GRU or whatever he was – graciously conceded his right to suggest he had a choice in the matter. Szara, after all, was an important correspondent.

'Yes. If you can,' he'd said. Then added, 'Leave us a little note at the desk of your hotel. To Monsieur Brun.'

Szara spelled it, to make sure he'd got it right. Defiance was over for the day.

'Just so,' said the man.

There was ample time to do the small favour; the *Nicaea* had been at sea for nineteen days, an eternity of icy, seawater showers, salt cod for dinner, and the smell of coal fumes from the freighter's rusting stack as she butted through the October seas. Squinting through the darkness at the lights of the wallowing tug, Szara ached for something sweet, sugar after salt, a cream cake, rain in a pine forest, a woman's perfume. He had, he thought, been too long at sea. An ironist, he heard the theatrical echo of the phrase and grinned privately. *La mélancolie des paquebots* – that said it better. He'd come across the phrase in Flaubert and it had stayed with him; it was all in those four words, the narrow cabin with a light bulb swaying on a cord, the seaweed reek of harbours, slanting rains, a column of black smoke from a funnel on the horizon.

The ship's bell sounded once. Four-thirty. The tug's amber lights grew brighter.

The Comintern man known as Van Doorn stepped from his cabin carrying a leather valise and joined Szara at the railing. He was swaddled in clothing like a child dressed for a winter day, woollen muffler crossed precisely at his throat, cap set low on his head, overcoat buttoned to the very top. 'One hour, eh? And we'll be down the gangplank. What is your view, André Aronovich?' Van Doorn was, as always, wryly deferential toward 'the famous journalist Szara.'

'If the port officer makes no difficulties, I would agree,' Szara said.

'That will not happen. He is *nash*.' The word meant *ours*, *we own him*, and the tone suggested Szara's great fortune in having such iron-fisted types as Van Doorn to watch out for him 'in the real world.'

'Well, then . . .' Szara said, acknowledging superior strength.

It happened that Szara knew who Van Doorn was; one of his friends in the Foreign Department of the NKVD had once pointed him out, with a sneer, at a party in Moscow. Szara's NKVD friends were, like himself, Russified Polish Jews or Latvians, Ukrainians, Germans, all sorts, and typically intellectuals. They constituted his *khvost* – the word fell somewhere between clique and gang. Van Doorn, in fact Grigory Khelidze, was from a different crowd: Georgians, Armenians, Russified Greeks and Turks, a *khvost* with roots in the southeast corner of the empire led by Beria, Dekanozov, and Alexei Agayan. It was a smaller group than the Poles and Ukrainians but easily its equal in power. Stalin came from down there; they knew what he liked and how he thought.

From the tugboat's silhouette, a high shape against the rain-softened glow of the city, a blinkered signal light began to operate. This was progress. Khelidze rubbed his hands to warm them up. 'Not long now,' he said merrily. He gave Szara a lecher's grin; in no time at all he'd be with his 'perfect dumpling.'

Thank heaven for the dumpling, Szara thought. Without her he might never have managed the small favour. Khelidze wasn't much to look at, a fattish man in his forties with pale hair worn well brushed and pomaded. His hands were small and chubby, endlessly fussing with a pair of silver-rimmed spectacles of which he was very proud. But he fancied himself a ladies' man. 'I envy you, André Aronovich,' he'd said one night when they were alone in the ship's wardroom after dinner. 'You move in exalted circles. The way it is with my job, well, the best I can hope for is the frau of some German shop steward, a big Inga with red hands, and then, likely as not, all a man gets is an extra potato and a stolen cuddle in the kitchen. Ah, but a man in your position – for you it's professors' daughters and lawyers' wives; those hot, skinny bitches that can't leave a journalist alone. Isn't it so?'

Szara had brought vodka to the feast, also brandy. The vast, green ocean rolled beneath them, the *Nicaea*'s engines coughed and grumbled. Khelidze rested his elbows on the faded oilcloth and leaned forward in expectation, a man who wanted to hear every detail.

Szara obliged. His talent, set alight by alcohol, burned and flamed. A certain lady in, ah, Budapest. Gold earrings like a Gypsy – but no Gypsy, an aristocrat who affected British tweeds and wore a silk scarf, the colour of a cloud, knotted at her throat. Hair dark red, like autumn, Magyar cheekbones, long, delicate fingers. Szara, a good storyteller, took his time. He cast about for a name, came up with Magda, thought it commonplace, but could do no better. Magda, then. The husband was a lout, ignorant, *nye kulturny* – a man of no culture who exported wool. So Szara had the wife. Where? In the stables? On straw? No, in the apartment, a *cinq-à-sept affaire* by lamplight. The husband was . . . hunting wild boar. Szara watched the level in the brandy bottle on the table. As it descended, so did the pants. And there, the most delicate little triangle, also dark red, like autumn. And fine blue veins beneath the milky skin. The green silk divan was ruined. Khelidze's ears were scarlet. Later it came to Szara that he'd been describing his private musings on a particular secretary he sometimes encountered at the Yugoslav Ministry of Posts and Telegraph.

Khelidze was drunk. He polished his glasses with a

handkerchief, his eyes watery and vague. Yes well, he said, one sometimes imagined. For himself, well it was all a matter of taste in this life wasn't it? He had, in all confidence, 'a perfect dumpling' in Ostend, resident at the Hotel Groenendaal in the street of the same name. 'A fat little thing. They dress her up like a child, with a bow and a party dress of white satin. My God, André Aronovich, how we carry on! Such a grand little actress she is, pouting, sulking, tossing her curls about, whining for biscuits and milk. But she can't have them. No, definitely not! Because, well, there's something she must do first. Oh no, she wails. Oh yes.' Khelidze sat back in his chair, put his glasses on, and sighed. 'A marvel,' he said. 'She'll suck ten years off a man's life.'

By the time they went singing off to bed, holding each other upright in the passageway that rolled with the motion of the ship, the dark surface of the sea was turning grey with dawn.

Szara's hotel in Ostend was all flowers: on the wallpaper, heavy cabbage roses on a sombre field; on the bedspread, a jungle of vines and geraniums; and in the park below his window, frostbitten asters, dusty purple and faded pink. And the place was called the Hotel Blommen. *Ignore this stern, northern, Flemish light, here we have flowers.* Szara stood at the window and listened to the foghorns from the harbour and the rattle of dead leaves as the wind swept them through the deserted park. He folded the note and creased it between thumb and index finger: 'M. Van Doorn will be visiting the Hotel Groenendaal.' He put it in an envelope, licked and sealed it, and wrote 'M. Brun' on the front. He didn't know what it meant, why a journalist was asked to report on a Comintern operative. But there was a reason, a single reason that lately explained anything you wanted explained: the purge had shuddered to a halt in '36, now another had begun. The first had taken politicians, Stalin's opposition, and more than a few journalists. This one, it was said, had gone to work on the intelligence services themselves. Szara, beginning in 1934, had learned to live with it: he was careful what he wrote, what he said, who he saw. Not yet what he thought – *not yet*, he told himself now and then, as though it needed to be said. He took the note down to the reception desk and handed it to the old man behind the counter.

The knock on the door was discreet, two taps with a knuckle. Szara had fallen asleep, still wearing shirt and trousers, on top of the bedspread. He sat up and pulled the damp shirt away from his back. It was a grey dawn outside the window, fog hanging in the tree branches. He looked at his watch – a little after six. The polite knock came a second time and Szara felt his heart accelerate. A knock at the door meant too much, nobody did that in Moscow anymore, they phoned first. 'Yes, a moment,' he said. Somewhere within, a small, urgent voice: *out the window*. He took a breath, staggered to his feet, and opened the door. It was the old man from the hotel desk, holding a coffee and a newspaper. Had he left a call to be woken up? No.

'Good morning, good morning,' said the old man tartly. It never really was, but one had to pretend. 'Your friend was kind enough to leave you the newspaper,' he added, putting it at the foot of the bed.

Szara fumbled for change and handed over a few coins. Drachmas, he thought. He'd bought Belgian francs in Athens; where were they? But the old man seemed happy enough, thanked him and left. The coffee was cooler than he would have liked, the boiled milk a little sour, but he was grateful for it. The front page of the newspaper was devoted to anti-Jewish riots that had broken out in Danzig, with a photo of shouting, black-shirted Nazis. In Spain the Republican government, under pressure from Franco's columns, had fled from Valencia to Barcelona. On page six, the misfortunes of Ostend's soccer team. Printed down the margin in pen, in a fine Cyrillic hand, were detailed instructions for a noon meeting. The 'small favour' had started to grow.

Szara walked down the hall, locked the door of the bathroom, and started to wash. The instructions in the newspaper frightened him; he was afraid of being forced into a car and taken away. The purge sometimes worked like that – the security *apparat* worked quietly when it took public figures. Senior NKVD officers were called to meetings in small towns just outside Moscow, then arrested as they got off the train, a tactic that kept friends and family from trying to intervene. A foreign country, he reasoned, would be even more convenient. Should he run? Was now the time? There was a part of him that thought so. *Go to the British consulate*, it said. *Fly for your life. Call the friends in Moscow who protect you. Buy a gun*. Meanwhile, he shaved.

Then he sat in the park, where a nursemaid with a baby carriage flirted with him. *Go with her*, he told himself, *hide in her bed. She will do anything you want*. Perhaps it was true. He very well knew, at the age of forty, somewhat past illusion, what she saw. The longish black hair he combed back with his fingers, the tight line of the jaw, a concentration of personality in the eyes. These were hooded, knowing, of a grey-green sea colour that women had more than once called 'strange,' and often read as both expectant and sorrowful, like dogs' eyes. His features were delicate, skin colourless, made to seem pallid by a permanent beard shadow. It was, taken altogether, a sad, attentive presence, anxious for happiness, certain of disappointment. He dressed the role of worldly intellectual, favouring soft clothing: thick grey cotton shirts, monochromatic ties in the sombre tones of basic colours. He was, in the world's mirror, a man you could take seriously, at least for a time. Then, later, there would be affection or intense dislike, a strong reaction whichever way it went.

The nursemaid, in a starched cap, plain, hand mindlessly rocking the carriage where some other woman's baby slept, had no doubts at all. He need only rescue her, from boredom, servitude, chapped hands, and she would do whatever was necessary. Below a broad forehead her eyes were frank. *Don't be frightened. I can fix anything.*

Just before ten-thirty he stood, pulled his raincoat tightly about him, and walked away. Glancing back, he easily read her expression: *Then no? Stupid man.*

A series of tram lines took him to a neighbourhood of worker tenements, the narrow streets smelled like fish, urine, fried onions. The November day was cool in the shadow of the buildings. Was he followed? He thought not. They had something better, a kind of invisible cable, the method the psychologist Pavlov used with laboratory animals. It was called – he had to look for the word – conditioning. His last day on earth, yet he did what he was told. His mind stood off and watched the scene: a man of intellect, independence, delivering himself to the *apparat*. Pitiful. Contemptible. Szara glanced at his watch. He didn't want to be late.

At a small market he stopped and bought fruit, then paid a few sous extra for a paper bag. The market woman wore a shawl over her head; her glance was suspicious. What was he, a foreigner, doing in this part of the city? Szara walked another block, made sure nobody was watching, and left most of the fruit in an alley. He watched the street behind him in a shop window where wooden soldiers were for sale. Then he moved off again, entering a small square lined by plane trees cut back to rounded pollard shapes for the coming winter. A driver slept in a parked taxi, a man in *bleu de travail* sat on a bench and stared at his feet, the war memorial fountain was dry: the square at the end of the world. A small brasserie, Le Terminus, had no patrons on its glassed-in *terrasse*.

Szara, more and more now the critic of his own abduction, was struck by the normalcy of the scene. What a placid, ordinary place they'd chosen. Perhaps they liked the name of the brasserie, Le Terminus – the terminal, the end of the line. Was the choice ironic? Were they that clever? Perhaps Pavlov was not, after all, the day's guiding spirit; perhaps that honour belonged to Chekhov, or Gorky. He searched for a terminal, for tramways, a railway station, but there was nothing he could see.

The interior of the brasserie was enormous and silent. Szara stood in the foyer as the door behind him bumped back and forth until it came to rest. Behind the zinc bar a man in a white shirt with cuffs turned back was aimlessly stirring a coffee, a few patrons sat quietly with a glass of beer, one or two were eating. Szara felt himself swept by intuition, a sense of loss, a conviction that this still life of a brasserie in Ostend was a frozen image of what had been and would now vanish forever: amber walls, marble tables, a wooden fan slowly turning on the smoke-darkened ceiling, a florid-faced man with a handlebar moustache who rattled his newspaper into place, the scrape of a chair on the tile floor, the cry of a seagull from the square, the sound of a ship's horn from the harbour.

There was an old weather glass on one wall, beneath it sat a woman in a brown, belted raincoat with buttoned epaulettes on the shoulders. She glanced at him, then went back to eating, a plate of eels and *pommes frites;* Szara could smell the horse fat the Belgians used for frying. A red wool scarf was looped over the top of an adjacent chair. The glass and the scarf were the recognition signals described in the margin of the newspaper.

The woman was perhaps in her late thirties. She had strong hands with long fingers – the knife and fork moved gracefully as she ate. She wore her chestnut hair cut close and short, a strand or two of grey caught the light when she moved. Her skin was pale, with the slight reddening at the cheekbones of a delicate complexion chapped by a sea breeze. *An aristocrat*, he thought. *Once upon a time*. Something fine and elegant in her had been discouraged, she wished to be plain, and almost was. Russian she was not, he thought. German perhaps, or Czech.

When he sat down across from her he saw that her eyes were grey and serious, with dark blushes of fatigue beneath them. The nonsense greetings of the *parol*, the confirmation passwords, were exchanged, and she lowered the edge of the paper bag he'd carried to make sure there was an orange inside.

Isn't this all absurd, I mean, oranges and a red scarf and . . . But these were words he never got to say. Just as he leaned toward her, to make contact, to let her know that they were the sort of people who could easily bridge the nonsense a foolish world imposed on them, she stopped him with a look. It made him swallow. 'I am called Renate Braun,' she said. *Called* meant what? An alias? Or simply a formal way of speaking. 'I know who you are,' she added. The notion *and that will suffice* was unstated but clear.

Szara liked women and they knew it. All he wanted to do, as the tension left him, was chatter, maybe make her laugh. They were just people, a man and a woman, but she wasn't buying. Whatever this was, he thought, it was not an arrest. Very well, then a continuation of the business he did with the NKVD from time to time. Every journalist, every citizen outside the Soviet Union, had to do that. But why make it into a funeral? Internally, he shrugged. She was German, he thought. Or Swiss or Austrian – one of those places where position, station in life, excluded informality.

She put a few francs on the waiter's saucer, retrieved her scarf, and they went outside into a hard, bright sky and a stiff wind. A boxy Simca sedan was now parked by the brasserie. Szara was certain it hadn't been there when he'd gone into the place. She directed him into the passenger seat and positioned herself directly behind him. If she shot him in the back of the neck, he thought, his dying words would be *why did you go to all this trouble?* Unfortunately, that particular wound didn't allow for last words, and Szara, who had been on battlefields in the civil war that followed the revolution, knew it. All he'd manage was *why – za chto?* what for? – but everyone, all the victims of the purge, said that.

The driver turned on the ignition and they drove away from the square. 'Heshel,' said the woman behind him, 'did it . . .?'

'Yes, missus,' the driver said.

Szara studied the driver as they wound through the cobbled streets of the city. He knew the type, to be found among the mud lanes in any of the ghettos in Poland or Russia: the body of a gnome, not much over five feet tall, thick lips, prominent nose, small, clever eyes. He wore a tweed worker's cap with a short brim tilted down over one eyebrow, and the collar of his old suit jacket was turned up. The man was ageless, and his expression, cold and humorous at once, Szara understood perfectly. It was the face of the survivor, whatever survival meant that day – invisibility, guile, abasement, brutality – anything at all.

They drove for fifteen minutes, then rolled to a stop in a crooked street where narrow hotels were jammed side by side and women in net stockings smoked lazily in doorways.

Renate Braun climbed out, Heshel waited. 'Come with me,' she said. Szara followed her into the hotel. There was no desk clerk to be seen, the lobby was empty except for a Belgian sailor sitting on the staircase with his head in his hands, a sailor cap balanced on his knee.

The stairway was steep and narrow, the wooden steps dotted with cigarette burns. They walked down a long corridor, then stopped in front of a door with 26 written on it in pencil. Szara noticed a tiny smudge of blue chalk at eye level on the door frame. The woman opened her shoulder bag and withdrew a ring of keys – Szara thought he saw the crosshatched grain of an automatic pistol grip as she snapped the bag closed. The keys were masters, with long shanks for leverage when the fit wasn't precise.

She unlocked the door and pushed it open. The air smelled like overripe fruit cut with ammonia. Khelidze stared at them from the bed, his back resting against the headboard, his pants and underpants bunched around his knees. His face was spotted with yellow stains and his mouth frozen in the shape of a luxurious yawn. Wound within the sheets was a large, humped mass. A waxy leg had ripped through the sheet; its foot, rigid as if to dance on point, had toenails painted baby pink. Szara could hear a fly buzzing against the windowpane and the sound of bicycle bells in the street.

'You confirm it is the man from the ship?' she said.

'Yes.' This was, he knew, an NKVD killing, a signed NKVD killing. The yellow stains meant hydrocyanic acid used as a spray, a method known to be employed by the Soviet services.

She opened her bag, put the keys inside, and took out a white cotton handkerchief scented with cologne. Holding it over her nose and mouth, she pulled a corner of the sheet free and looked underneath. Szara could see curly blond hair and part of a ribbon.

The woman dropped the sheet and rubbed her hand against the side of her raincoat. Then she put the handkerchief away and began to go through Khelidze's trouser pockets, tossing the contents onto the end of the bed: coins, rumpled notes of various currencies, a squeezed-out tube of medication, the soft cloth he'd used to polish his glasses, and a Dutch passport.

Next she searched the coat and jacket, hung carefully in a battered armoire, finding a pencil and a small address book that she added to the pile. She took the pencil and poked through the items on the bed, sighed with irritation, and searched in her bag until she found a razor blade with tape along both edges. She peeled off one of the tapes and went to work on the jacket and the coat, slicing open the seams and splitting the pads in the shoulders. This yielded a Soviet passport, which she put in her bag. Taking hold of the cuffs, she removed the trousers and methodically took them apart. When she let out the second cuff, a folded square of paper was revealed. She opened it, then handed it to Szara.

'What is it, please?'

'The printing is Czech. A form of some kind.'

'Yes?'

He studied the paper for a moment. 'I think it is a baggage receipt, from a shipping company. No, for the railway station. In Prague.'

She looked the room over carefully, then walked to the tiny, yellowed sink in the corner and began to wash her hands. 'You will collect the parcel,' she said, drying herself with her handkerchief. 'It is for you.'

They left the room together; she did not bother to lock the door. In the lobby she turned to him and said, 'Of course you'll be leaving Ostend immediately.'

He nodded that he would.

'Your work is appreciated,' she said.

He followed her out of the hotel and watched her get into the Simca. He crossed the narrow street and turned to look back. Heshel was watching him through the window of the car and smiled thinly as their eyes met. *Here is the world*, said the smile, *and here we are in it*.

Arriving in Antwerp at dusk, and adding two hours to local time for Moscow, he called his editor at home. From Nezhenko, who handled foreign assignments, he expected no trouble. This would not normally be the case, given a three-week lapse in communication, but when he was asked to do 'favours' for the *apparat*, someone stopped by the *Pravda* office for a cup of tea. 'That André Aronovich, what fine work he does! He must take endless time and pains in writing his dispatches. Your patience is admirable.' Enough said. And just as well, for Viktor Nezhenko smoked sixty cigarettes every day and had a savage temper; he could, if he chose, make life miserable for his staff.

Szara booked his call from a hotel room, it went through an hour later. Nezhenko's wife answered the phone, her voice bright and shrill with feigned insouciance.

When Nezhenko came to the phone, he offered no patronymic and no greeting, just, 'Where have you been?'

'I'm in Antwerp.'

'Where?'

Szara repeated himself. Something had gone wrong – Nezhenko had not been 'advised' of his assignment.

'So good of you to call,' Nezhenko said.

Szara hunted desperately for water to put out the fire. 'I'm doing a piece on dockworkers up here.'

'Yes? That will be interesting.'

'I'll wire it tomorrow.'

'Send it by mail if you like. Third class.'

'Did Pavel Mikhailovich cover for me?'

'Pavel Mikhailovich isn't here anymore.'

Szara was stunned. *He isn't here anymore* was code. When heard from friends, family, landladies, it meant that the person had been taken away. And Pavel Mikhailovich was – had been – a decent little man without enemies. But none of Szara's reactions, to ask questions, to show even the most civilized grief, was permissible on a telephone line.

'And people have been asking for you,' Nezhenko added. This too was code, it meant the *apparat* was looking for him.

Szara felt as though he'd walked into a wall. Why were they looking for him? They knew very well where he was and what he was doing – the world's plainest man had not been a mirage, and Renate Braun and her helper were realler yet. 'It's all a misunderstanding,' he said after a moment. 'The right hand doesn't tell the left hand . . .'

'No doubt,' Nezhenko said. Szara could hear him lighting a cigarette.

'I want to go down to Prague after I finish the piece on the dockworkers. There's the reaction to the Anti-Comintern Pact, views on the Sudetenland, all sorts of things. What do you think?'

'What do I think?'

'Yes.'

'Do as you like, André Aronovich. You must please yourself in all things.'

'I'll file on the dockworkers tomorrow,' Szara said.

Nezhenko hung up.

Writing the story of the Belgian dockworkers was like eating sand.

Once upon a time he'd persuaded himself that technical facility was its own reward: a sentence singing hymns to the attainment of coal production norms in the Donets Basin was, nonetheless, a sentence, and could be well rendered. It was the writer's responsibility in a progressive society to inform and uplift the toiling masses – word had, in fact, reached him that the number one toiler himself had an eye for his byline – so when some demon within wanted to write dark fables of an absurd universe, he knew enough to keep that imp well bottled up. To stay alive, Szara had taught himself discretion before the *apparat* had a chance to do the job for him. And if, by chance, an intransigent pen stubbornly produced commissar wolves guarding flocks of worker sheep or Parisian girls in silk underwear, well, then the great characteristic of paper was the ease with which it burned.

And these were, had to be, private fires. The world didn't want to know about your soul, it took you for who you said you were. The workers in the dark little hiring hall by the Antwerp docks were impressed that anybody cared enough to come around and ask them how they felt. 'Stalin is our great hope,' one of them said, and Szara sent his voice around the world.

He sat in yet one more hotel room as the Atlantic fog came curling up the streets and wrote these men into the brutal drama being played out in Europe. He caught the strength in their rounded shoulders and brawlers' hands, the way they quietly took care of one another, the granite decency of them. But for the wives and children who depended on them they would fight in Spain – some of the younger ones in fact were there – would fight in the worker suburbs of Berlin, would yet, families or not, fight from behind the cranes and sheds of their own docks. It was true, and Szara found a way to make it true on the page.

Stalin *was* their great hope. And if Khelidze mocked this with the yawn on his yellow-stained face, that was Szara's private problem. And if the 'small favour' was now a large favour, that, too, was Szara's private problem. And if all that made it hard to write, made writing the story like eating sand, who really could he blame? He could always say no and take the consequences. The Russian proverb had it just right: *You said you were a mushroom, now jump into the basket.*

And people have been asking for you.

Nezhenko's phrase rode the cadence of the train over the rails from Antwerp all the way to Paris. Much for the best, he calculated, to rush into their arms and find out what they wanted. He hadn't the courage to stand coolly apart from it all, whatever it was, so he did the next best thing. Checked in with the large *Pravda* bureau in Paris and asked the secretary to book him on the Paris-Prague express for the following day. He looked into her eyes, saw ball bearings, swore he could hear her lift the phone before the door was properly latched.

He stopped back that evening, picked up the ticket and drew both salary and expense funds, then went early to the Gare d'Austerlitz the following day in case they wanted to talk to him there. He did not precisely fear abduction, he was simply more comfortable in an open, public space with crowds of people about. He dawdled over coffee at a café by the departure platform, gazed mindlessly at the sullen Parisian sky above the glass roof on its vast iron fretwork, read *Le Temps*, found himself quoted in the Communist daily, *L'Humanité* – 'as *Pravda* correspondent André Szara has pointed out, bilateral relations between France and the USSR can only proceed once the Czechoslovakian question has been . . .' – and watched the appetizing French women sweep past, their heels clattering on the cement, their animation seemingly inspired by a grave sense of mission.

He had made himself available, but no contact was

made. When his train was announced and the engine vented plumes of white steam on the platform, he climbed aboard and found himself alone in a first-class compartment. *Pravda* did not buy whole compartments – only the *apparat* did that. Clearly, something was planned. *Perhaps in Nancy*, he thought.

He was wrong. Spent the afternoon staring through the rain at the low hills of eastern France and watching the names of battlefields glide past on the railroad stations. At the Strasbourg border control, just on the other side of the Rhine, a trio of German passport officials, two soldiers and a civilian in streaming black rubber raincoats, entered the compartment. They were cold-eyed and courteous, and his Soviet passport produced no evident reaction. They asked him a question or two, apparently just to hear his voice. Szara's German was that of someone who'd spoken Yiddish as a child, and the civilian, a security type, made clear that he knew Szara was a Jew, a Polish Jew, a Soviet Bolshevik Jew of Polish origin. He probed efficiently through Szara's travelling bag without removing his black gloves, then examined press and travel documents and, when he was done, stamped the passport with a fat swastika in a circle and handed it back politely. Their eyes met for just a moment: this business they had with each other would be seen to in the future, that far they could agree.

But Szara travelled too much to take the hostility of border police to heart and, as they gained speed leaving Stuttgart station, he fell into the rhythm of the tracks and the dense twilight of Germany: smoking factories on the horizon, fields left to the November frost.

He touched the baggage receipt in the inside pocket of his jacket for the tenth time that day; he might have taken yet one more look at the thing, but the sound of the train was suddenly amplified as the door to his compartment swung open.

On first glance, an ordinary businessman of Central Europe in dark overcoat and soft-brimmed hat, carrying a buckled briefcase of the kind that is held under one arm. Then, recognition. This was a man to whom he had been briefly introduced, perhaps a year earlier, at some Moscow function he couldn't recall. His name was Bloch, a lieutenant general of the GRU, military intelligence, and recently, according to rumour, the illegal – clandestine – *rezident* operating GRU and NKVD networks based in Tarragona. Thus a very senior member of the Soviet cadre involved in the Spanish Civil War.

Szara was immediately on his guard; powerful people in Moscow were afraid of this man. It was nothing specific. Those who knew the details didn't tell war stories, but they veered away from his name when it came up in conversation, looked around to see who might be listening, made a certain gesture of the face that meant *stay away*. What little was said about Bloch implied an insatiable appetite for success – an appetite gratified by means of ferocious tyranny. Life for those assigned to work for him was said to be a nightmare.

Yaschyeritsa, they called him behind his back, a kind of lizard. Because he had the look of the basilisk: a sharp triangular face, stiff hair combed back flat from the forehead, thin eyebrows angled steeply toward the inner corners of his eyes, which, long and narrow, were set above hard cheekbones that slanted upward.

André Szara, like everyone who moved in those circles known as the *nomenklatura*, the elite, was an adroit reader of faces. You had to know who you were dealing with. A Byelorussian? An Armenian? A native Russian? With Jews, it was often difficult because Jewish women had for centuries borne the children of their tormentors and thus carried the genes of many races. God only knew, Szara thought, what brutal band of marauders had forced themselves on Bloch's female ancestor to make him look as he did. Did evil, he wondered, travel in the blood as well?

Bloch nodded a greeting, sat down across from Szara, leaned over and locked the compartment door, then turned off the lamps on the wall around the window. The train was moving slowly through a village, and from the darkened compartment they could see that a local festival was in progress; a bonfire in the public square, cattle wearing garlands, Hitler Youth in shorts holding swastika banners hung lengthwise down long poles, like Roman fasces.

Bloch stared intently at the scene. 'At last,' he said pensively, 'they are back in the Middle Ages.' He turned his attention to Szara. 'Forgive me, comrade journalist, I am General Y. I. Bloch. I don't think we've ever spoken, but I read your work when I have a moment, so I know who you are. Do I need to tell you who I am?'

'No, comrade General. I know you are with the special services.'

Bloch acknowledged Szara's awareness as a compliment: a knowing smile, a brief inclination of the head, *at your service*.

'Tell me,' the general said, 'is it true you've been away from Moscow for a time? Several months?'

'Since late August,' Szara said.

'No easy life – trains and hotel rooms. Slow steamships. But foreign capitals are certainly more amusing than Moscow, so there are compensations. No?'

This was a trap. There was a doctrinal answer, something to do with *building socialism*, but Bloch was no fool and Szara suspected a pious response would embarrass them both. 'It's true,' he said, adding, 'though one gets tired of being the eternal stranger,' just in case.

'Do you hear the Moscow gossip?'

'Very little,' Szara said. A loner, he tended to avoid the Tass and *Pravda* crowd on the circuit of European capitals.

Bloch's face darkened. 'This has been a troubled autumn for the services, surely you've heard that much.'

'Of course I see the newspapers.'

'There is more, much more. We've had defections, serious ones. In the last few weeks, Colonel Alexander Orlov and Colonel Walter Krivitsky, who is called general in the European press, have left the service and sought refuge in the West. The Krivitsky matter has been made public, also the flight of the operative Reiss. As for Orlov, we'll keep that to ourselves.'

Szara nodded obediently. This had quickly become a very sensitive conversation. Orlov – a cover name within the service, he was in fact Leon Lazarevich Feldbin – and Krivitsky – Samuel Ginsberg – were important men, respectively NKVD and GRU officials of senior status. The Ignace Reiss affair had shocked him when he read about it. Reiss, murdered in Switzerland as he attempted to flee, had been a fervent idealist, a Marxist-Leninist in his bones.

'Friends?' Bloch raised an eyebrow.

'I knew Reiss to say hello to. No more than that.'

'And you? How does it go with you?' Bloch was concerned, almost fatherly. Szara wanted to laugh, had the services been panicked into *kindness?*

'My work is difficult, comrade General, but less difficult than that of many others, and I am content to be what I am.'

Bloch absorbed his answer and nodded to himself. 'So you march along,' he said. 'There are some,' he continued pensively, 'who find themselves deeply disturbed by the arrests, the trials. We cannot deny it.'

Oh cannot we? 'We've always had enemies, within and without. I served in the civil war, from 1918 to 1920, and fought against the Poles. It isn't for me to judge the operations of state security forces.'

Bloch sat back in his seat. 'Very well put,' he said after a time. Then his voice softened, just barely audible above the steady rumble of the train. 'And should it come your turn? Then what?'

Szara could not quite see Bloch's face in the shadow of the seat across from him, the countryside was dark, the light from the corridor dim. 'Then that is how it will be,' Szara said.

'You are a fatalist.'

'What else?' They lingered there a moment too long for Szara. 'I have no family,' he added.

Bloch seemed to nod at that, a gesture of agreement with a point made or a confirmation of something he believed. 'Not married,' he mused. 'I would have guessed otherwise.'

'I am a widower, comrade General. My wife died in the civil war. She was a nurse, in Berdichev.'

'So you are alone,' Bloch said. 'Some men, in such circumstances, might be careless of their lives, since nothing holds them to the world. Unconcerned with consequence, such men rise to an opportunity, sacrifice themselves, perhaps to cure their nation of a great evil. And then we have – why not say it? A hero! Do I have it right? Is this your view?'

A man and a woman – she had just said something that made him laugh – went by in the corridor. Szara waited until they passed. 'I am like everybody else,' he said.

'No,' Bloch said. 'You are not.' He leaned forward, his face taut, concentrated. 'To be a writer, that requires work. Work and sacrifice. And the determination to follow a certain road, wherever it may lead. Remember that, comrade journalist, whatever might happen in the days ahead.'

Szara started to reply, to fend off a version of himself he found grandiose, but Bloch raised a hand for silence. The gesture was casual enough, but it struck Szara dumb.

The general stood and unlatched the door, stared at Szara a moment, a look that openly weighed and calculated, then left the compartment abruptly, closing the door firmly behind him and disappearing down the passageway.

Some time later, the train halted at Ulm. The station platform was a lacework of shadows, and raindrops refracted trails of light as they rolled down the compartment window. A figure with a hat and an underarm briefcase hurried across the platform and entered the passenger door of a black Grosser Mercedes – an automobile often used by Reich officials – which sped away from the railroad station and was soon lost in the darkness.

A hero?

No, Szara thought. He knew better. He'd learned that lesson in war.

At the age of twenty-three, in 1920, he had campaigned with Marshal Tukachevsky, writing dispatches and inspirational stories for the home front, much as the writer Babel – a Jew who rode with Cossack cavalry – had served General Budenny. In the midst of the war against Poland, the Soviet forces had been driven back from Warsaw, from the banks of the Vistula, by an army commanded by General Pilsudski and his adviser, the French general Weygand. Szara's squadron, during the retreat, had been set upon by Ukrainian bandits, a remnant of the Petlyura army that had occupied Kiev. Attacked from the ridge of a hillside, and outnumbered, they had fought like men possessed, all of them – cooks, clerks, wagonmasters, and military correspondents. For the previous day they'd come upon the body of a Polish colonel, stripped bare, tied by one foot to a high tree branch, the impaling stake protruding from between his legs. The Ukrainian bands fought both sides, Poles and Russians, and God help anyone they took alive.

From horseback, Szara had ridden down one man,

slashed at another with his sabre. In the next instant he and his horse were down in the dust, the horse whinnying in pain and terror, its legs thrashing. Szara rolled frantically away from the animal, then a smiling man walked towards him, a small dagger in his hand. Horses galloped past them, there were shots and screams and pointless shouted commands, but this man, in cap and overcoat, never stopped smiling. Szara crawled on all fours, a horse leapt over him and its rider cursed, but he could gain no ground. The battle that raged around them mattered not to Szara nor, apparently, to his good-humoured pursuer. The smile was meant, he understood, to be reassuring, as though he were a pig in a sty. As the man closed on him he made a cooing sound and Szara came suddenly to his senses, fumbled his revolver loose of its holster, and fired wildly. Nothing happened. The smile broadened. Then Szara took hold of his fear, as though he could squeeze it in his fist, aimed like a marksman on a target range, and shot the man in the eye.

What he remembered later was not that he had fought bravely, he had simply decided that life mattered more than anything else in the world and had contrived to cling to it. In those years he had seen heroes, and how they went about their work, how they did what had to be done, and he knew he was not one of them.

The train was late getting into Prague. A Jewish family had attempted to board at Nürnberg, the last stop on German soil. Jews had been strongly 'encouraged' to emigrate from Germany – not least by a hundred and thirty-five racial decrees, together entitled 'The Law for the Protection of German Blood and German Honour' – to whatever country would accept them. But the situation, Szara knew, was not unlike that under the czar: a bureaucratic spider's web. While you could get Paper A stamped at the local police station, the stamp on Paper B, received from the

Economic Ministry, was now out of date and would have to be applied for all over again. Meanwhile, Paper A ran its term and automatically revoked itself.

The Jewish family at Nürnberg simply attempted to board the train, a pointless act of desperation. Thus young children, grandparents, mother and father, scampered in terror all around the station while policemen in leather coats chased them down, shouting and blowing whistles. Meanwhile, the passengers peered curiously from the train windows. Some, excited by the chase, tried to help, calling out, 'There, under the luggage compartment!' or 'She's crossed the tracks!'

Just after midnight it was cold in Prague, there were frost flowers on the paving stones, but the hotel was not far from the station, and Szara was soon settled in his room. He stayed up for hours, smoking, writing notes on the margin of *Le Temps*, studying the luggage ticket he'd been given. He was being drawn into something he did not understand, but he had a strong intuition about what awaited him at the end of it.

This extramarital affair with the services had been simple in the beginning, five or six years earlier, for they'd used him as an intellectual, an agent of influence, and he'd liked it, found it flattering to be trusted. Now he had got in over his head, and he had no doubt it would kill him. They were using him for something important, an official operation of the *apparat* or, and here was the death sentence, the plotting of a cabal within it. He only knew it was very dark and very serious. Soviet generals of military intelligence did not board German trains to chat with writers.

Nonetheless, he refused to blind himself to the possibility of exits. He would die, he thought, but did not want to discover as he died that there had been, after all, a way out. *That is the difference, comrade General, between the hero and the survivor*. The hours of reflection revealed nothing, but did serve to dissipate tension and tire him out. He crawled into bed and slept without dreams.

He woke to a day of light snow and subtle terror in Prague. He saw nothing, felt everything. On the fifth of November, Hitler had made a speech once again declaring the urgency, for Germany, of *Lebensraum*, the acquisition of new territory for German growth and expansion, literally 'room to live.' Like an operatic tenor, singing counterpoint to Hitler's bass, Henlein, the leader of the Sudeten Germans, pleaded publicly in an open letter carried by Czech newspapers the following day for a halt to Czech 'persecution' of German minorities in the Sudetenland, the area bordering southern Germany. On 12 November the countertenor, Reich Interior Minister Wilhelm Frick, said on the radio: 'Race and nationality, blood and soil, are the principles of National Socialist thought, we would be acting in contradiction if we attempted to assimilate a foreign nationality by force.'

This may have sounded warm and comforting in France, but the Sudeten Germans were not a foreign nationality, and neither were the Austrians – not according to German diplomatic definitions. Sudeten German representatives next staged a mass exodus from parliament, informing reporters waiting outside that they had been physically abused by Czech police.

Everybody in Prague knew this game – incidents, provocations, speeches – it meant that the German tank divisions sitting up on the border were coming down. Today? Tomorrow? When?

Soon.

On the surface, there was nothing to see. But what they felt here made itself known in subtle ways: the way people looked at each other, a note in a voice, the unfinished sentence. Szara took the receipt he'd been given in Ostend to the central railway station. The attendant shook his head, this was from a smaller station, and gestured toward the edge of the city.

He took a taxi, but by the time he arrived, the left-luggage room of the outlying station was closed for lunch. He found himself in a strange, silent neighbourhood with signs in Polish and Ukrainian, boarded windows, groups of tieless men with buttoned collars gathered on street corners. He walked along empty streets swept by wind-driven swirls of dust. The women were hidden in black shawls, children held hands and kept close to the buildings. He heard a bell, looked down a steep lane, and saw a Jewish pedlar with a slumped, starved horse, plumes of breath streaming from its nostrils as it attempted to pull a cart up a hill.

Szara found a tiny café; conversation stopped when he walked in. He drank a cup of tea. There was no sugar. He could hear a clock ticking behind a curtained doorway. What was it in this place? A demon lived here. Szara struggled to breathe, his persona flowed away like mist and left a dull and anxious man sitting at a table. The clock behind the curtain chimed three and he walked quickly to the station. The left-luggage clerk limped painfully and wore a blue railway uniform with a war medal pinned on the lapel. He took the receipt silently and, after a moment of study, nodded to himself. He disappeared for a long time, then returned with a leather satchel. Szara asked if a taxi could be called. 'No,' the man said. Szara waited for more, for an explanation, something, but that was it. *No*.

So he walked. For miles, through zigzag streets clogged with Saturday life, where every ancient stone leaned or sagged; past crowds of Orthodox Jews in caftans and curling sidelocks, gossiping in front of tiny synagogues;

past Czech housewives in their print dresses, carrying home loaves of black bread and garlic sausages from the street markets; past children and dogs playing football on the cobblestones and old men who leaned their elbows on the windowsills and smoked their pipes and stared at the life in the street below. It was every quarter in every city in Europe in the cold, smoky days of November, but to Szara it was like being trapped in the dream where some terrifying thing was happening but the world ignored it and went blindly about its business.

Reaching the hotel, he trudged upstairs and hurled the satchel onto the bed. Then he collapsed in a chair and closed his eyes in order to concentrate. Certain instincts flared to life: he must write about what he'd felt, must describe the haunting of this place. Done well, he knew, such stories spread, took on a life of their own. The politicians would do what they did, but the readers, the people, would understand, care, be animated by pity to speak out for the Czech republic. How to do it? What to select? Which fact really *spoke*, so that the writer could step aside and allow the story to tell itself. And if his own dispatch did not appear in other countries, it most certainly would run in the Communist party press, in many languages, and more foreign journalists than cared to admit it had a glance at such newspapers. Editorial policy said *anything to keep the peace*, but let the correspondents come here and see it for themselves.

Then the satchel reminded him of its presence. He examined it and realized he'd never seen one like it: the leather was dense, pebbled, the hide of a powerful, unknown animal. It was covered with a thick, fine dust, so he wet his index finger and drew a line through it, revealing a colour that had once been that of bitter chocolate but was now faded by sun and time. Next he saw that the seams were hand-sewn; fine, sturdy work using a thread he suspected was also handmade. The satchel was of the portmanteau style – like a doctor's bag, the two sides opened evenly and were held together by a brass lock. Using a damp towel, he cleaned the lock and found a reddish tracery etched into the metal surface. This was vaguely familiar. Where had he seen it? In a moment it came to him: such work adorned brass bowls and vases made in western and central Asia – India, Afghanistan, Turkestan. He tried to depress the lever on the underside of the device, but it was locked.

The handgrip bore half a label, tied on with string. Peering closely, he was able to make out the date the satchel had been deposited as left luggage: 8 February 1935. He swore softly with amazement. Almost three years.

He put one finger on the lock. It was ingenious, a perfectly circular opening that did not suggest the shape of its key. He probed gently with a match, it seemed to want a round shaft with squared ridges at the very end. Hopefully, he jiggled the match about but of course nothing happened. From another time the locksmith, perhaps an artisan who sat cross-legged in a market stall in some souk, laughed at him. The device he'd fashioned would not yield to a wooden match.

Szara went downstairs to the hotel desk and explained to the young clerk on duty: a lost key, a satchel that couldn't be opened, important papers for a meeting on Monday, what could be done? The clerk nodded sympathetically and spoke soothingly. Not to worry. This happens here every day. A boy was sent off and returned an hour later with a locksmith in tow. In the room the locksmith, a serious man who spoke German and wore a stiff, formal suit, cleared his throat politely. One didn't see this sort of mechanism. But Szara was too impatient to make up answers to unasked questions and simply urged the man to proceed. After a few minutes of meditation, the locksmith reluctantly folded up his leather tool case, put it away, and, reddening slightly, drew a set of finely made burglar's picks from the interior pocket of his jacket. Now the battle between the two technicians commenced.

Not that the Tadzik, the Kirghiz, the craftsman of the Bokhara market – whoever he'd been – didn't resist, he did, but in the event he was no match for the modern Czech and his shining steel picks. With the emphatic *snick* of the truly well made device the lock opened, and the locksmith stood back and applied an immaculate grey cloth to his sweaty forehead. 'So beautiful a work,' he said, mostly to himself.

So beautiful a bill, as well, but Szara paid it and tipped handsomely besides, for he knew the *apparat* could eventually find out anything, and he might have signed this man's death warrant.

At dusk, André Szara sat in his unlit room with the remnants of a man's life spread out around him.

There wasn't a writer in the world who could resist attributing a melancholy romance to these artifacts, but, he argued to his critical self, that did not diminish their eloquence. For if the satchel itself spoke of Bokhara, Samarkand, or the oasis towns of the Kara Kum desert, its contents said something very different, about a European, a European Russian, who had travelled – served? hidden? died? – in those regions, about the sort of man he was, about pride itself.

The objects laid out on the hotel desk and bureau made up an estate. Some clothing, a few books, a revolver, and the humble tools – thread and needle, digestive tea, well-creased maps – of a man on the run. On the run, for there was equal clarity, equal eloquence, in the items *not* found. There were no photographs, no letters. No address book, no traveller's journal. This had been a man who understood the people he fled from and protected the vulnerability of those who may have loved him.

The clothing had been packed on top, folded loosely but perfectly, as though by someone with a long history of military service, someone to whom the ordered neatness of a footlocker was second nature. It was good clothing, carefully preserved, often mended but terribly worn, its wear the result of repeated washings and long use in hard country. Cotton underdrawers and wool shirts, a thick sailor's sweater darned at the elbows, heavy wool socks with virtually transparent heels.

The service revolver dated from prerevolutionary days, a Nagant, the double-action officer's model, 7.62mm from a design of 1895. It was well oiled and fully loaded. From certain characteristics, Szara determined that the sidearm had had a long and very active life. The lanyard ring at the base of the grip had been removed and the surface filed flat, and the metal at the edges of the sharp angles, barrel opening, cylinder, the trigger itself, was silvery and smooth. A look down the barrel showed it to be immaculate, cleaned not with the usual brick dust – an almost religious (and thereby ruinous) obsession with the peasant infantry of the Great War – but with a scouring brush of British manufacture folded in a square of paper. Not newspaper, for that told of where you had been and when you were there. Plain paper. A careful man.

The books were also from the time before the revolution, the latest printing date 1915; and Szara handled them with reverence for they were no longer to be had. Dobrilov's lovely essays on noble estates, Ivan Krug's *Poems at Harvest*, Gletkhin's tales of travel among the Khivani, Pushkin of course, and a collection by one Churnensky, *Letters from a Distant Village*, which Szara had never heard of. These were companions of journey, books to be read and read again, books for a man who lived in places where books could not be found. Eagerly, Szara paged through them, looking for commentary, for at least an underlined passage, but there was, as he'd expected, not a mark to be found.

Yet the most curious offering of the opened satchel was its odour. Szara could not really pin it down, though he held the sweater to his face and breathed in it. He could identify a hint of mildew, woodsmoke, the sweetish smell of pack animals, and something else, a spice perhaps, cloves or cardamom, that suggested the central Asian marketplace. It had been carried in the satchel for a long time, for its presence touched the books and the clothing and the leather itself. Why? Perhaps to make spoiled food more palatable, perhaps to add an ingredient of civilization to life in general. On this point he could make no decision.

Szara was sufficiently familiar with the practices of intelligence services to know that chronology meant everything. 'May God protect and keep the czar' at the end of a letter meant one thing in 1916, quite another in 1918. With regard to the time of 'the officer,' for Szara discovered himself using that term, the satchel's contents offered an Austrian map of the southern borders of the Caspian Sea dated 1919. The cartography had certainly begun earlier (honorary Bolshevik names were missing), but the printing date allowed Szara to write on a piece of hotel stationery 'alive in 1919.' Checking the luggage label once again, he noted 'tentative terminal date, 8 February 1935.' A curious date, following by two months and some days the assassination of Sergei Kirov at the Smolny Institute in Leningrad, 1 December 1934, which led to the first round of purges under Yagoda.

A terminal date? *Yes*, Szara thought, *this man is dead*.

He simply knew it. And, he felt, much earlier than 1935. Somehow, another hand had recovered the satchel and moved it to the left-luggage room of a remote Prague railway station that winter. Infinite permutations were of course possible, but Szara suspected that a life played out in the southern extremity of the Soviet empire had ended there. The Red Army had suppressed the pashas' risings in 1923. If the officer, perhaps a military adviser to one of the local rulers, had survived those wars, he had not left the region. There was nothing of Europe that had not been packed on some night in, Szara guessed, 1920.

That the satchel itself had survived was a kind of miracle, though presently Szara came upon a rather more concrete possibility – the stitching on the bottom lining. This was not the same hand that had lovingly and expertly crafted the seams. The reattachment had been managed as best it could be done, with waxed thread sewn into a cruciform shape anchoring each corner. So, the officer carried more than books and clothes. Szara remembered what Renate Braun had said in the lobby of Khelidze's hotel: 'It is for you.' Not old maps, books, and clothing certainly, and not a Nagant pistol. What was now 'his' lay beneath the satchel's false bottom in a secret compartment.

Szara called the desk and had a bottle of vodka sent up. He sensed a long, difficult night ahead of him – the city of Prague was bad enough, the officer's doomed attempt to survive history didn't make things any better. He must, Szara reasoned, have been a loyal soldier in the czar's service, thus fugitive after the revolution in 1917. Perhaps he'd fought alongside White Guardist elements in the civil war. Then flight, always southeast, into central Asia, as the Red Army advanced. The history of that place and time was as evil as any Szara knew – Basmatchi, the marauding bandits of the region, Baron Ungarn-Sternberg, a sadist and a madman, General Ma and his Muslim army; rape, murder, pillage, captives thrown into locomotive boilers to die in the steam. He suspected that this man, who carried a civilized little library and carefully darned the elbows of his sweater, had died in some unremembered minor skirmish during those years. There were times when a bullet was the best of all solutions. Szara found himself hoping it had been that way for the officer.

The vodka helped. Szara was humming a song by the time he had his razor out, sawing away at the thick bands of crisscrossed thread. The officer was no fool. Who, Szara wondered, did he think to deceive with this only too evident false bottom contrivance? Perhaps the very densest border patrolman or the most slow-witted customs guard. The NKVD workshops did this sort of thing quite well, leaving only the slimmest margin for secreting documents and disguising the false bottom so that you really could not tell. On the other hand, the officer had likely done what he could, used the only available hiding place and hoped for the best. Yes, Szara understood him now, better and better; the sewn-down corners revealed a sort of determination in the face of hopeless circumstances, a quality Szara admired above all others. Having cut loose the final corner, he had to use a nail file to pry up the leather flap.

What had he hoped to find? Not this. A thick stack of greyish paper, frayed at the edges, covered with a careful pen scrawl of stiff Russian phrases – the poetry of bureaucrats. It was official paper, a bluntly printed letterhead announcing its origin as Bureau of Information, Third Section, Department of State Protection (Okhrannoye Otdyelyenye), Ministry of the Interior, Transcaucasian District, with a street address in Tbilisi – the Georgian city of Tiflis.

A slow, sullen disappointment drifted over Szara's mood. He carried the vodka bottle over to the window and watched as a goods train crawled slowly away from the railway station, its couplings clanking and rattling as the cars jerked into motion. The officer was not a noble colonel or a captain of cavalry but a slow-footed policeman, no doubt a cog in the czar's vast but inefficient secret police gendarmerie, the Okhrana, and this sheaf of misery on the hotel desk apparently represented a succession of cases, a record of *agents provocateurs*, payments to petty informers, and solemn physical descriptions of Social Revolutionary party workers in the early days of the century. He'd seen this kind of report from time to time, soul-destroying stuff it was, humanity seen through a window by the dim glow of a street lamp, sad and mean and obsessed with endless conspiracies. The thought of it made you want to retire to the countryside with a milk cow and a vegetable patch.

Not a military officer, a police officer. Poor man, he had carried this catalogue of small deceits over mountain and across desert, apparently certain of its value once the counterrevolution had succeeded and some surviving spawn of the Romanovs once again sat upon the Throne of All the Russias. In sorrow more than anger Szara soothed his frustrated imagination with two tiltings of the vodka bottle. *A paper creature*, he thought. *A uniform with a man in it.*

He walked back to the desk and adjusted the gooseneck lamp. The organization Messame Dassy (Third Group) had been founded in 1893, of Social Democratic origin and purpose, in political opposition to Meori Dassy (Second Group) – Szara sighed at such grotesque hair-splitting – and made its views known in pamphlets and the newspaper *Kvali (The Furrow)*. Known principals of the organization included N. K. Jordania, K. K. Muridze, G. M. Tseretelli. The informant DUBOK (it meant 'little oak' and had gone on to become the name for a dead-drop of any kind) enrolled and became active in 1898, at age nineteen.

Szara flipped through the stack of pages, his eye falling randomly on summaries of interviews, memoranda, alterations in handwriting as other officers contributed to the record, receipts for informer payments signed with cover names (not code names like DUBOK; one never knew one's code name, that belonged to the Masters of the File), a change to typewriter as the case spanned the years and reports were sent travelling upward from district to region to central bureau to ministry to Czar Nicholas and perhaps to God Himself.

Szara's temples throbbed.

Serves you right! What in the name of heaven had he expected? Swiss marks? Perhaps he had, deep down. Those exquisitely printed passports to anywhere and everything. *Idiot!* Maybe gold coins? The molten rubies of children's books? Or a single pressed rose, its last dying fragrance only just discernible?

Yes, yes, yes. Any or all of it. His eye fell in misery on the false plate lying on the floor amid a tangle of cut-up thread. He'd learned to sew as a child in Odessa, but this was not the sort of job he could do. How was he to put all this back together again? By employment of the hotel seamstress? *The guest in Room 35 requires the false bottom sewed back on his suitcase – hurry woman, he must cross the Polish frontier tonight!* A victim of betrayed imagination, Szara cursed and mentally called down the *apparat* as though summoning evil spirits. He willed Heshel with his sad little smile or Renate Braun with her purse full of skeleton keys, or any of them, grey shapes or cold-eyed intellectuals, to come and take this inhuman pettifoggery away from him before he hurled it out of the window.

In fact, where were they?

He glanced at the bottom of the door, expecting a slip of paper to come sliding underneath at that very moment, but all he saw was worn carpet. The world suddenly felt very silent to him, and another visit with the vodka did not change that.

In desperation he shoved the paper to one side and replaced it with sheets of hotel stationery from the desk drawer. If, in the final analysis, the officer did not deserve this vodka-driven storm in the emotional latitudes, the anguished people of Prague most assuredly did.

It was midnight when he finished, and his back hurt like a bastard. But he'd got it. The reader would find himself; *his* street, *his* neighbourhood, *his* nation. And the hysteria, the nightmare, was where it belonged, just below the horizon so you felt it more than saw it. To balance a story on 'the people' he'd have to do one on 'the ministry': quote from Beneš, quote from General Vlasy, something vicious from Henlein, and the slant – since the country had been created a parliamentary democracy in 1918 and showed no sign of yearning to become a socialist republic – would have to serve Soviet diplomatic interests by fervid anti-Hitlerism. No problem there. He could file on ministries with one eye shut and the pencil in his ear, and it would mean just about that much. Politicians were like talking dogs in a circus: the fact that they existed was uncommonly interesting, but no sane person would actually believe what they said.

Then, as always happened after he wrote something he liked, the room began to shrink. He stuffed some money in his pocket, pulled up his tie, threw on his jacket, and made his escape. He tried walking, but the wind blowing down from Poland was fierce and the air had the smell of winter, so he waved down a taxi and gave the address of the Luxuria, a *nachtlokal* where the cabaret was foul and the audience worse, thus exactly where he belonged in his present frame of mind.

* * *

Nor was he disappointed. Sitting alone at a tiny table, a glass of flat champagne at his elbow, he smoked steadily and lost himself in the mindless fog of the place, content beneath the soiled cutout of yellow paper pinned to a velvet curtain that served as the Luxuria's moon – a thin slice, a weary old moon for nights when nothing mattered.

Momo Tsipler and his Wienerwald Companions.

Five of them, including the oldest cellist in captivity, a death-eyed drummer called Rex, and Momo himself, one of those dark celebrities nourished by the shadows east of the Rhine, a Viennese Hungarian in a green dinner-jacket with a voice full of tears that neither he nor anyone else had ever cried.

'*Noch einmal al Abscheid dein Händchen mir gib*,' sang Momo as the cello sobbed. 'Just once again give me your hand to press' – the interior Szara was overjoyed, this horrid syrup was delicious, a wicked joke on itself, an anthem to Viennese love gone wrong. The title of the song was perfect: 'There Are Things We Must All Forget.' The violinist had fluffy white hair that stood out in wings and he smiled like Satan himself as he played.

The Companions of the Wienerwald then took up a kind of 'drunken elephant' theme for the evening's main attraction: the enormous Mottel Motkevich, who staggered into the spotlight to a series of rimshots from the drummer and began his famous one-word routine. At first, his body told the story: I just woke up in the maid's bed with the world's worst hangover and someone pushed me out onto the stage of a nightclub in Prague. What am I doing here? What are *you* doing here?

His flabby face sweated in the purple lights – for twenty years he'd looked like he was going to die next week. Then he shaded his eyes and peered around the room. Slowly, recognition took hold. He knew what sort of swine had come out to the *nachtlokal* tonight, ah yes, he knew them all too well. '*Ja*,' he said, confirming the very worst, his thick lips pressed together with grim disapproval.

He began to nod, confirming his observation: drunkards and perverts, dissolution and depravity. He put his hands on his broad hips and stared out at a Yugoslav colonel accompanied by a well-rouged girl in a shiny feather hat that hugged her head tightly. '*Ja!*' said Mottel Motkevich. There's no doubt about you two. Likewise to a pair of pretty English boys in plus fours, then to a Captain of Industry caught in the act of schnozzling a sort of teenage dairymaid by his side.

Suddenly, a voice from the shadows in the back of the room: 'But Mottel, why not?' Quickly the audience began to shout back at the comedian in a stew of European languages: 'Is it bad?' 'Why shouldn't we?' 'What can be so wrong?'

The fat man recoiled, grasped the velvet curtain with one hand, eyes and mouth widening with new understanding. '*Ja?*' You mean it's really all right after all? To do just every sort of thing we all know about and some we haven't figured out yet?

Now came the audience's great moment. '*Ja!*' they cried out, again and again; even the waiters joined in.

Poor Mottel actually crumpled under the assault. A world he presumed to love, of order and rectitude, had been torn to shreds before his very eyes and now the truth lay bare. With regret, he bade all that fatuous old nonsense adieu. '*Ja, ja*,' he admitted ruefully, so it has always been, so it will always be, so, particularly so, will it be tonight.

Just then something extremely interesting caught his eye, something going on behind the curtain to his right, and, eyes glittering like a love-maddened satyr, he bequeathed his audience one final, drawn-out *jaaa*, then stomped off the stage to applause as the Companions struck up a circus melody and the zebras ran out from behind the curtain, bucking and neighing, pawing their little forehooves in the air.

Naked girls in papier-mâché zebra masks, actually. Prancing and jiggling among the tables, stopping now and again to stick their bottoms out at the customers, then taking off again with a leap. After a few minutes they galloped away into the wings, the Companions swung into a sedate waltz, and the dancers soon reappeared, without masks and wearing gowns, as *Animierdamen* who were to flirt with the customers, sit on their laps, and tickle them into buying champagne by the bottle.

Szara's was heavy-hipped, with hair dyed a lustrous, sinister black. 'Can you guess which zebra was me? I was so very close to you!'

Later he went with her. To a secret room at the top of a cold house where you walked upstairs, then downstairs, across two courtyards where cats lived, finally to climb again, past blind turns and dark passageways, until you came to a low corridor under the roof gables.

'Zebra,' he called her; it made things simpler. He doubted he was the originator of the idea, for she seemed quite comfortable with it. She cantered and whinnied and shook her little white tummy – all for him.

His spirit soared, at last he'd found an island of pleasure in his particular sea of troubles. There were those, he knew, who would have found such sport sorrowful and mean, but what furies did they know? What waited for them on the other sides of doors?

The Zebra owned a little radio; it played static, and also a station that stayed on the air all night long, playing scratchy recordings of Schumann and Chopin from somewhere in the darkness of Central Europe, where insomnia had become something of a religion.

To this accompaniment they made great progress. And delighted themselves by feigning shock at having tumbled into such depths where anything at all may be found to swim. 'Ah yes?' cried the Zebra, as though they'd happened on some new and complex amusement, never before attempted in the secret rooms of these cities, as though their daring to play the devil's own games might stay his hand from that which they knew, by whatever obscure prescience, he meant to do to them all.

Warm and exhausted at last, they dozed off in the smoky room while the radio crackled, faded in and out, voices sometimes whispering to them in unknown languages.

The leaders of the Georgian *khvost* of the NKVD usually met for an hour or two on Sunday mornings in Alexei Agayan's apartment on Tverskaya street. Beria himself never came – he was, in some sense, a conspiracy of one – but made his wishes known through Dershani, Agayan, or one of the others. Typically, only the Moscow-based officers attended the meeting, though comrades from the southeast republics stopped by from time to time.

They met in Agayan's kitchen, large, dilapidated, and very warm, on 21 November at eleven-thirty in the morning. Agayan, a short, dark-skinned man with a thick head of curly grey hair and an unruly moustache, wore an old cardigan in keeping with the air of informality. Ismailov, a Russified Turk, and Dzakhalev, an Ossete – the Farsi-speaking tribe of the north Caucasus from whom Stalin's mother was said to be descended – were red-eyed and a little tender from Saturday-night excesses. Terounian, from the city of Yerevan in Armenia, offered a small burlap sack of ripe pears brought to Moscow by his cousin, a locomotive engineer. These were laid out on the table by Stasia, Agayan's young Russian wife, along with bowls of salted and sugared almonds, pine nuts, and a plate of Smyrna raisins. Agayan's wife also served an endless succession of tiny cups of Turkish coffee, *sekerli*, the sweetest variety, throughout the meeting. Dershani, a Georgian, the most important among equals, was also the last to arrive. Such traditions were important to the *khvost* and they observed them scrupulously.

It was altogether a traditional sort of gathering, as though in a coffeehouse in Baku or Tashkent. They sat in their shirt-sleeves and smoked, ate, and drank their coffees and took turns to speak – in Russian, their only common language – with respect for one another and with a sense of ceremony. What was said mattered, that was understood, they would have to stand by it.

Agayan, squinting in the rising smoke of a cigarette held in the centre of his lips, spoke solemnly of comrades disappeared in the purges. The Ukrainian and Polish *zhids*, he admitted, were getting much the worst of it, but many Georgians and Armenians and their allies from all over (some *zhids* of their own, for that matter) had also vanished into the Lubyanka and the Lefortovo. Agayan sighed mournfully when he finished his report, all the eulogy many of them would ever have.

'One can only wonder . . .' Dzakhalev said.

Agayan's shrug was eloquent. 'It's what he wants. As for me, I was not asked.' The nameless *he* in these conversations was always Stalin.

'Still,' Dzakhalev said, 'Yassim Ferimovich was a superb officer.'

'And loyal,' Terounian added. At thirty-five, he was by far the youngest man in the room.

Agayan lit a new cigarette from the stub of the old one. 'Nonetheless,' he said.

'You have heard what he said to Yezhov, in the matter of interrogation? "Beat and beat and beat."' Terounian paused to let the felicity of that phrasing hang in the air, to make sure everyone understood he honoured it. 'Thus anyone will admit anything, will surely name his own mother.'

'Yours too,' Ismailov said.

Dershani raised his right hand a few inches off the table; the gesture meant *enough* and stopped Ismailov dead in his tracks. Dershani had the face of a hawk – sharp beak, glittering, lifeless eyes – thin lips, high forehead, hair that had gone grey when he was young – some said in a single night when he was sentenced to die. But he'd lived. Changed. Into something not quite a man. A specialist at obtaining confessions, a man whose hand was rumoured to have 'actually held the pliers.' Ismailov's tone of voice was clearly not to his taste.

'His thinking is very broad,' Dershani said. 'We are not meant to understand it. We are not meant to comment upon it.' He paused for coffee, to permit the atmosphere in the room to rise to his level, then took a few pine nuts. 'These are delicious,' he said. 'If you look at our history – the history of our service, I mean – his hand may be seen to have grasped the tiller just at the crucial moment. We began with Dzerzhinsky, a Pole of aristocratic background from Vilna. Catholic by birth, he shows, early in life, a great affection for Jews. He comes to speak perfect Yiddish, his first lover is one Julia Goldman, the sister of his best friend. She dies of tuberculosis, in Switzerland, where he had placed her in a sanatorium, and his sorrow is soothed by a love affair with a comrade called Sabina Feinstein. Eventually he marries a Polish Jewess, from the Warsaw intelligentsia, named Sophie Mushkat. His deputy, the man he depends on, is Unshlikht, also a Polish Jew, also an intellectual, from Mlawa.

'When Dzerzhinsky dies, his other deputy, Menzhinsky, takes over. No Jew, Menzhinsky, but an *artiste*. A man who speaks Chinese, Persian, Japanese, in all twelve languages and who, while doing our work in Paris, is a poet one day, a painter the next, and lies around in silk pyjamas, smoking a perfumed cigarette in an ivory holder, the leader of a, a salon. Lenin dies. This young state, troubled, gravely threatened, thrusts itself at our leader, and he agrees to take its burdens upon his shoulders. He seeks only to continue the work of Lenin but, in 1934, the Trotskyite centre begins to gather power. Something must be done. In Lenin's tradition he turns to Yagoda, a Polish Jew from Lodz, a poisoner, who eliminates the writer Gorky through seemingly natural means. But he is too clever, keeps his own counsel, and by 1936 he is no longer the right sort of person for the job. Now what is the answer? Perhaps the dwarf, Yezhov, called familiarly "the blackberry," which his name suggests. But this one is no better than the other – not a Jew this time but a madman, truly, and malicious, like a child of the slum who soaks cats' tails in paraffin and sets them alight.'

Dershani stopped dead, tapping four fingers on the kitchen table. A glance at Agayan's wife, standing at the stove in the far part of the kitchen, brought her swiftly with a fresh little cup of coffee.

'Tell us, Efim Aleksandrovich, what will happen next?' Ismailov thus declared himself suitably chastened, symbolically sought Dershani's pardon for his momentary flippancy.

Dershani closed his eyes politely as he drank off his coffee, smacked his lips politely in appreciation. 'Stasia Marievna, you are a jewel,' he said. She nodded silently to acknowledge the compliment.

'It evolves, it evolves,' Dershani said. 'It is beautiful history, after all, and guided now by genius. But he must move at the proper speed, certain matters must be allowed to play themselves out. And, I tell you in confidence, there are many considerations that may elude our vision. These *zhids* from Poland cannot just be swept away wholesale. Such cleaning, no matter how appropriate, would draw unwelcome attention, might alienate the

Jews of America, for instance, who are great idealists and do our special work in their country. Thus Russians and Ukrainians, yes, and even Georgians and Armenians must leave the stage along with the others. This is necessity, historical necessity, a stratagem worthy of Lenin.'

'Then tell us, Efim Aleksandrovich,' said Agayan, not unconsciously echoing Ismailov's phrasing, 'if today we are not in fact privileged to hear the views of our comrade in Tbilisi?' He referred to Lavrenty Pavlovich Beria, presently first secretary of the Georgian Communist party and previously head of the Georgian NKVD. The modest bite in the question suggested that Dershani should perhaps not call his wife a jewel in front of his colleagues.

Dershani took only the smallest step backwards. 'Lavrenty Pavlovich might not disagree with the drift of what I am saying. We both believe, I can say, that we will win this battle – though there are actions which must be taken if we intend to do so. Most important, however, to perceive his, *his*, wishes and to act upon them with all possible measures.'

This opened a door. Agayan tapped his cup on the saucer and his wife brought him a fresh coffee. Dershani had cited *all possible measures*, and form now decreed that Agayan seek to discover what they were. Once described, they had to be undertaken.

Dershani glanced at his watch. Agayan leapt at the possibility. 'Please, Efim Aleksandrovich, do not permit us to detain you if duty calls elsewhere.'

'No, no,' Dershani said dismissively, 'I'm simply wondering what's become of Grigory Petrovich – he was specifically to join us this morning.'

'You refer to Khelidze?' Ismailov asked.

'Yes.'

'I'll call his apartment,' Agayan said, rising quickly, delighted with the interruption. 'His wife will know where he's got to.'

Dzakhalev snickered briefly. 'Not likely,' he said.

Monday morning, striding through a fine, wet mist that made the streets of Prague even greyer than usual, Szara went early to the SovPressBuro, which handled all Soviet dispatches, and filed the story he'd written on Saturday night. It had taken him some twenty-eight tries to get a title that settled properly on the piece. His initial instinct led down a path marked 'Prague, City in –.' He tried 'Peril,' 'Sorrow,' 'Waiting,' 'Despair,' and, at last, in fury that it wouldn't work, 'Czechoslovakia.'

At the end of patience the rather literal 'Silence in Prague' took the prize, a title, on reflection, that turned out to be a message from the deep interior where all the work really went on. For those who read with both eyes, the melodramatic heading would imply a subtle alteration of preposition, so that the sharper and truer message would concern silence *about* Prague – not the anguished silence of a city under political siege but the cowardly silence of European statesmen, a silence filled with diplomatic bluster that nobody took seriously, a silence that could be broken only by the sputter of tank ignitions as armoured columns moved to reposition themselves on the borders of Germany.

There was, in fact, another zone of silence on the subject of Prague, to the east of Czechoslovakia, where Stalin's Franco-Russian alliance specified that the USSR would come to the aid of the Czechs if Hitler attacked them, but only after the French did. Thus the USSR had positioned itself to hide behind the promises of a regime in Paris that compromised on every issue and staggered from scandal to catastrophe and back again. Yes, Stalin's Red Army was in bloody disarray from the purges of June '37, but it was sorrowful, Szara thought, that the Czechs would get the bill for that.

And there was, unknown to Szara, some further silence to come.

The dispatch clerk at the bureau near the Jiráskův bridge, a stern, full-breasted matron with mounds of pinned-up grey hair, read 'Silence in Prague' sitting in front of her typewriter. 'Yes, comrade Szara,' she breathed, 'you have told the truth here, this is just the way this city feels.' He accepted the compliment, and more than a little adoration in her eyes, with a deflective mumble. It wouldn't do to let her know just how much such praise meant to him. He saw the story off, then wandered along the streets that ran next to the Vltava and watched the barges moving slowly up the steel-coloured November river.

Szara returned to the press bureau on Tuesday morning, meaning to wire Moscow his intention to travel up to Paris. There was always a story to be found in Paris, and he badly needed to breathe the unhealthy, healing air of that city. What he got instead, as he came through the door, was a pitying stare from the maternal transmission clerk. 'A message for the comrade,' she said, shaking her head in sympathy. She handed him a telegram, in from Moscow an hour earlier:

> CANNOT ACCEPT SILENCE/PRAGUE IN PRESENT FORM STOP BY 25 NOVEMBER DEVELOP INFORMATION FOR PROFILE OF DR JULIUS BAUMANN, SALZBRUNNER 8, BERLIN, SUCCESSFUL INDUSTRIALIST STOP SUBMIT ALL MATERIAL DIRECTLY TO SOVPRESS SUPERVISOR BERLIN STOP SIGNED NEZHENKO

He saw that the clerk was waiting for him to explode but he shut his emotions down at once. He was, he told himself, a big boy, and shifts of party line were nothing new. His success as a correspondent, and the considerable freedom he enjoyed, were based equally on ability and a sensitivity to what could and could not be written at any given moment. He was annoyed with himself for getting it wrong, but something was brewing in Moscow, and it was not the moment for indignation, it was the moment for understanding that political developments excluded stories on Prague. For the clerk's benefit, he nodded in acceptance: Soviet journalism worker accepts criticism and forges ahead to build socialism. Yes, there was an overflowing wastebasket at his feet, and yes, he yearned to give it a mighty kick that would send it skittering into the wall, but no, he could not do it. 'Then it's to be Berlin,' he said calmly. He folded the telegram and slid it into the pocket of his jacket, said good-bye to the clerk, smiled brightly, and left, closing the door behind him so softly it made not a sound.

That night he was early for the Berlin express and decided to have a sandwich and coffee at the railway station buffet. He noticed a group of men gathered around a radio in one corner of the room and wandered over to see what was so interesting. It was, as he'd supposed, a political speech, but not in Czech, in German. Szara recognized the voice immediately – Adolf Hitler was born to speak on the radio. He was a brilliant orator to begin with, and somehow the dynamics of wireless transmission – static, the light hiss of silence – added power to his voice. Hitler teased his audience, tiptoeing up to a dramatic point, then hammering it home. The audience, tens of thousands by the sound of it, cheered itself hoarse, swept by political ecstasy, ready to die then and there for German honour.

Szara stood at the outer fringe of the group and listened without expression or reaction, pointedly ignoring an unpleasant glance of warning from one of the Czechs – Slovakians? Sudeten Germans? – gathered around the radio. The voice, working toward a conclusion, was level and sensible to begin with:

> Then the final aim of our whole party is quite clear for all of us. Always I am concerned only that I do not take any step from which I will have to retreat, and not to take any step that will harm us.
>
> I tell you that I always go to the outermost limits of risk, but never beyond. For this you need to have a nose [laughter; Szara could imagine the gesture], a nose to smell out, more or less, 'What can I still do?' Also, in a struggle against an enemy, I do not summon an enemy backed by a fighting force, I do not say 'Fight!' because I want to fight. Instead I say 'I will destroy you' [a swell of voices here, but Hitler spoke through it]. And now, Wisdom, help me. Help me to manoeuvre you into a corner where you cannot fight back. And then you get the blow, right in the heart. That's it!

The crowd roared in triumph and Szara felt his blood chill. As he turned to walk away there was a blur of motion to his right, the side of his head exploded, then he found himself sprawled on the filthy tiles of the restaurant floor. Looking up, he saw a man with a twisted mouth, his upper body coiled like a spring, his right fist drawn back over his left shoulder in order to hit a second time. The man spoke German. 'Jew shit,' he said.

Szara started to get up, but the man took a step toward him so he stayed where he was, on hands and knees. He looked around the restaurant; people were eating soup, blowing on their spoons before sipping it up. On the radio, a commentator's voice sounded measured and serious. The other men around the radio did not look at him, only the man with his fist drawn back – young, ordinary, broad, in a cheap suit and a loud tie. Szara's position seemed to mollify the man, who pulled a chair toward him and sat back down with his friends. He placed a metal salt shaker next to the pepper.

Slowly, Szara climbed to his feet. His ear was on fire, it throbbed and buzzed and he could hear nothing on that side. His vision was a little fuzzy and he blinked to clear it. As he walked away he realized that there were tears in his eyes – *physical, physical*, he told himself – but he was in many kinds of pain and he couldn't sort it out at all.

The Prague-Berlin night express left the central station at 9:03 P.M., due in at Berlin's Bahnhof am Zoo station at 11:51, stopping only at the Aussig border control post on the east bank of the Elbe. Szara now travelled with two bags, his own and the leather satchel. The train was cold and crowded and smoky. Szara shared a compartment with two middle-aged women he took to be sisters and two teenage boys whose windburned faces and khaki shorts suggested they'd been on a weekend mountain-climbing holiday in Czechoslovakia and had stayed on until Tuesday before returning to school in Germany.

Szara had some anxiety about the German customs inspection, but the officer's revolver now lay at the bottom of the Vltava and he doubted that a file written in Russian – something it would be normal for him to have – would cause any difficulty. Border inspections concentrated on guns, explosives, large amounts of currency, and seditious literature – the revolutionary toolkit. Beyond that, the inspectors were not very interested. He was taking, perhaps, a small chance, that a Gestapo officer would be in attendance (not unlikely) and that he would know enough Russian to recognize what he was looking at (very unlikely). In fact, Szara realized he didn't have much of a choice: the file was 'his,' but not his to dispose of. Sooner or later, *they* would want to know what had become of it.

As the train wound through the pine forests of northern Czechoslovakia, Szara's hand rose continually to his ear, slightly red and swollen and warm to the touch. He'd been hit, apparently, with the end of a metal salt shaker enclosed in a fist. As for other damage – heart, spirit, dignity; it had a lot of names – he finally managed to stand off from it and bring himself under control. *No*, he told himself again and again, you *shouldn't* have fought back. The men listening to the radio would've done far worse.

The border control at Aussig was uneventful. The train slowly gained speed, ran briefly beside the Elbe, shallow and still in the late autumn, and soon after passed the brown brick porcelain factories of Dresden, red shadows from the heating kilns flickering on the train windows. The track descended gradually from the high plain of Czechoslovakia to sea-level Germany, to flat fields and small, orderly towns, a stationmaster with a lantern standing on the platform at every village.

The train slowed to a crawl – Szara glanced at his watch, it was a few minutes after ten – then stopped with a loud hiss of decompression. The passengers in his compartment stirred about irritably, said '*Wuss?*' and peered out the windows, but there was nothing to see, only farm fields edged by woodland. Presently, a conductor appeared at the door to the compartment. An old gentleman with a hat a size too large for him, he licked his lips nervously and said, 'Herr Szara?' His eye roamed among the passengers, but there was really only one possible candidate.

'Well?' Szara said. *Now what?*.

'Would you be so kind as to accompany me, it's just . . .'

Entirely without menace. Szara considered outrage, then sensed the weight of Teutonic railway bureaucracy standing behind this request, sighed with irritation, and stood up.

'Please, your luggage,' the conductor said.

Szara snatched the handles and followed the man down the corridor to the end of the car. A chief conductor awaited him there. 'I am sorry, Herr Szara, but you must leave the train here.'

Szara stiffened. 'I will not,' he said.

'Please,' said the man nervously.

Szara stared at him for a moment, utterly confounded. There was nothing outside the open door but dark fields. 'I demand an explanation,' he said.

The man peered over Szara's shoulder and Szara turned his head. Two men in suits stood at the end of the corridor. Szara said, 'Am I to walk to Berlin?' He laughed, inviting them to consider the absurdity of the situation, but it sounded false and shrill. The supervisor placed a tentative hand above his elbow; Szara jerked away from him. 'Take your hands off me,' he said.

The conductor was now very formal. 'You must leave.'

He realized he was going to be thrown off if he didn't move, so he took his luggage and descended the iron stairway to the cinderbed on which the rails lay. The conductor leaned out, was handed a red lantern from within, and swung it twice towards the engine. Szara stepped away from the train as it jerked into motion. He watched it gather momentum as it rolled past him – a series of white faces framed by windows – then saw it off into the distance, two red lamps at the back of the guard's van fading slowly, then blackness.

* * *

The change was sudden, and complete. Civilization had simply vanished. He felt a light wind against his face, the faint rime of frost on a furrowed field sparkled in the light of the quarter moon, and the silence was punctuated by the sound of a night bird, a high-low call that seemed very far away. He stood quietly for a time, watched the slice of moon that dimmed and sharpened as haze banks drifted across it in a starless sky. Then, from the woodland at the near horizon, a pair of headlights moved very slowly toward a point some fifty yards up the track. He could see strands of ground mist rising into the illumination of the beams.

Ah. With a sigh Szara hefted the two bags and trudged towards the lights, discovering, as his eyes adjusted to the darkness, a narrow country lane that crossed the railway tracks. *General Bloch*, he thought. *Doing tricks with the German rail system*.

The car reached the crossing before he did and rolled gently to a stop. Somehow, he'd missed a signal – this meeting had the distinct feel of an improvised fallback. He was, on balance, relieved. The heart of the *apparat* had skipped a beat but now returned to form and required the parcel from Prague. Well, thank God he had it. As he approached the car, its outline took shape in the ambient glow of the headlamps. It was not the same Grosser Mercedes that had carried General Bloch away from the station at Ulm, but the monarchs of the *apparat* changed cars about as casually as they changed mistresses and tonight had selected something small and anonymous for the *treff*, clandestine meeting, in a German beet field.

The middle-aged sisters in the train compartment that Szara had recently occupied were amused, rather sentimentally amused, at the argument that now began between the two students returning from their mountain-climbing exertions in the Tatra. Sentiment was inspired by the recollection of their own sons; wholesome, Nordic youths quite like these who had, from time to time, gone absolutely mulish over some foolery or other, as boys will, and come nearly to blows over it. The sisters could barely keep from smiling. The dispute began genially enough – a discussion of the quality of Czech matches made for woodcutters and others who needed to make outdoor fires. One of the lads was quite delighted with the brand they'd purchased, the other had reservations. Yes, he'd agree that they struck consistently, even when wet, but they burned for only a few seconds and then went out: with damp kindling, clearly a liability. The other boy was robust in defence. Was his friend blind and senseless? The matches burned for *a long time*. No, they didn't. *Yes*, they did. Just like miniature versions of their papas, weren't they, disputing some point in politics or machinery or dogs.

As the train approached the tiny station at Feldhausen, where the track crosses a bridge and then swings away from the river Elster, a bet of a few groschen was struck and an experiment undertaken. The defender of the matches lit one and held it high while the other boy counted out the seconds. The sisters pretended not to notice, but they'd been drawn inexorably into the argument and silently counted right along.

The first boy was an easy winner and the groschen were duly handed over – offered cheerfully and accepted humbly, the sisters noted with approval. The match had burned for more than thirty-eight seconds, from a point just outside Feldhausen to the other end of the station platform and even a little way out into the countryside. The point was made: those were excellent matches, just the thing for woodsmen, mountain climbers, and any others who might need to light a fire.

* * *

As Szara approached the car, the man next to the driver climbed out, held the back door open and said, 'Change of travel plans,' with a smile of regret.

His Russian was elementary but clear, phrased in the slow cadence characteristic of the southeastern reaches of the country, near the Turkish border. 'It won't be so inconvenient.' He was a dark man with a great belly; Szara could make out a whitening moustache and thinning grey hair spread carefully over a bald head. The driver was young – a relative, perhaps even a son of the passenger. For the moment he was bulky and thick, the extra chin just beginning, the hair at the crown of his head growing sparse.

Szara settled himself in the back seat and the car moved forward cautiously through the night mist. 'You tried to contact me in Prague?' he asked.

'Couldn't get your attention, but no matter. Which one do we want?'

Szara handed the satchel over the seat.

'Handsome old thing, isn't it,' said the man, running an appreciative hand over the pebbled hide.

'Yes,' Szara said.

'All here?'

'Except for a pistol. That I dared not take through German border control. It's at the bottom of the river.'

'No matter. It's not pistols we need.'

Szara relaxed. Wondered where and how he'd be put back on his way to Berlin, knew enough about such *treffs* not to bother asking. The Great Hand moved everyone about as it would.

'Must keep to form,' said the man, reaching inside his coat. He brought out a pair of handcuffs and held them out to Szara over the back of the seat. The car entered a farming village, every window dark, thatched-roof stone barns, then they were again among the fields.

Szara's heart pumped hard; he willed his hand not to rise and press against his chest.

'What?' he said.

'Rules, rules,' said the fat man disconsolately. Then, a bit annoyed: 'Always something.' He shook the handcuffs impatiently. 'Come, then . . .'

'For what?' *Za chto?*

'It isn't *for* anything, comrade.' The man made a sucking noise against his tooth. He tossed the handcuffs into Szara's lap. 'Now don't make me irritable.'

Szara held the cuffs in his hand. The metal was unpolished, faintly oily.

'You better do what we say,' the young driver threatened, his voice uncertain, querulous. Clearly he wanted to give orders but was afraid that nobody would obey him.

'Am I arrested?'

'Arrested? *Arrested?*' The fat man had a big laugh. 'He thinks we're arresting him!' The driver tried to laugh like the other man but he didn't have the voice for it.

The fat man pointed a blunt index finger at him and partly closed one eye. 'You put those on now, that's plenty of discussion.'

Szara held his wrist up to the faint moonlight in the back window.

'In back – don't you know anything?' He sighed heavily and shook his head. 'Don't worry, nothing will happen to you. It's just one of those things that has to be done – you're certainly aware, comrade, of the many things we all must do. So, humour me, will you?' He turned back around in his seat, dismissively, and peered through the ground mist rising from the road. As he turned, Szara could hear the whisper of his woollen coat against the car upholstery.

Szara clicked the handcuff around his left wrist, then put it behind his back and held the other cuff in his right hand.

For a time, the men in the front seat were silent. The road moved uphill into a wood where it was very dark. The fat man leaned forward and peered through the window. 'Take care,' he said. 'We don't want to hit an animal.' Then, without turning around, 'I'm waiting.'

Szara closed the cuff on his right wrist.

The car left the forest and headed down a hill. 'Stop here,' the fat man said. 'Turn on the light.' The driver stared at the dashboard, twisted a button; a windshield wiper scraped across the dry glass. Both men laughed and the driver turned it off. Another button did nothing at all. Then the dome light went on.

The fat man leaned over and rummaged through the open satchel between his feet. He drew out a sheet of paper and squinted at it. 'I'm told you're sly as a snake,' he said to Szara. 'Haven't been hiding anything, have you?'

'No,' Szara said.

'If I have to, I'll make you tell.'

'You have all of it.'

'Don't sound so miserable. You'll have me weeping in a minute.'

Szara said nothing. He shifted in the seat to make his hands more comfortable and looked out the side window at the cloudy silhouette of the moon.

'Well,' the fat man said at last, 'this is just the way life is.' A shrill whine reached them from around a bend in the road and the single light of a motorcycle appeared. It shot past them at great speed, a passenger hanging on to the waist of the driver.

'Crazy fools,' the young man said.

'These Germans love their machines,' the fat man said. 'Drive on.'

They went around the bend where the motorcycle had come from. Szara could see more woodland on the horizon. 'Slowly, now,' said the fat man. He reached over and turned off the dome light, then stared out the side window with great concentration. 'I wonder if it's come time for eyeglasses?'

'Not you,' the driver said. 'It's the mist.'

They drove on, very slowly. A dirt track for farm machines broke away from the road into a field that had been harvested to low stubble. 'Ah,' the fat man said. 'You better back up.' He looked over the seat at Szara as the car reversed. 'Let's see those hands.' Szara twisted around and showed him. 'Not too tight, are they?'

'No.'

'How far?' said the driver.

'Just a little. I'm not pushing this thing if we get stuck in a hole.'

The car inched forward down the dirt path. 'All right,' said the fat man. 'This will do.' He struggled out of the car, walked a few feet, turned his back, and urinated. Still buttoning his fly, he walked to Szara's door and opened it. 'Please,' he said, indicating that Szara should get out. Then, to the driver: 'You stay here and keep the car running.'

Szara shifted himself along the seat, swung his legs out, and, leaning forward in a crouch, managed to stand upright.

'Let's walk a little,' said the fat man, positioning himself just behind Szara and a little to his right.

Szara walked a few paces. As the car idled he could hear that one cylinder was mistimed and fired out of rhythm. 'Very well,' said the fat man. He took a small automatic pistol from the pocket of his coat. 'Is there anything you would like to say? Perhaps a prayer?'

Szara didn't answer.

'Jews have prayers for everything, certainly for this.'

'There's money,' Szara said. 'Money and gold jewelry.'

'In your valise?'

'No. In Russia.'

'Ah,' said the fat man sorrowfully, 'we're not in Russia.' He armed the automatic with a practised hand, the wind gusted suddenly and raised a few strands of stiff hair so that they stood up straight. Carefully, he smoothed them back into place. 'So . . .' he said.

The whine of the motorcycle reached them again, growing quickly in volume. The fat man swore softly in a language Szara didn't know and lowered the pistol by the side of his leg so that it was hidden from the road. Almost on top of them, the cyclist executed a grinding speed shift and swung onto the farm track in a shower of dirt, the light sweeping across Szara and the fat man, whose mouth opened in surprise. From somewhere near the car an urgent voice called out, 'Ismailov?'

The fat man was astonished, for a moment speechless. Then he said, 'What is it? Who are you?'

The muzzle flare was like orange lightning – it turned the fat man into a photographic negative, arms spread like the wings of a bird as a wind swept him into the air while down below a shoe flew away. He landed like a sack and hummed as though he'd hit his thumb with a hammer. Szara threw himself onto the ground. From the car, the young driver cried out for his father amid the flat reports of a pistol fired in the open air.

'Are you hurt?'

Szara looked up. The little gnome called Heshel stood over him, eyes glittering in the moonlight above his hooked nose and knowing smile. His cap was pulled down ridiculously over his ears and a great shawl was wound around his neck and stuffed into his buttoned jacket. Three shotgun shells were thrust between the fingers of his right hand. He broke the barrel and loaded both sides. A voice from near the car said, 'Who's humming?'

'Ismailov.'

'Heshie, please.'

Heshel snapped the shotgun back together and walked towards the fat man. He fired both barrels simultaneously and the humming stopped. He returned to Szara, reached down, thrust a small hand into Szara's armpit, and tugged. 'Come on,' he said, 'you got to get up.'

Szara managed to scramble to his feet. At the car, the second man was hauling the driver out by his ankles. He flopped onto the ground. 'Look,' said the man who had pulled him out. 'It's the son.'

'Ismailov's son?' Heshel asked.

'I think so.'

Heshel walked over and stared down. 'From this you can tell?'

The other man didn't answer.

'Maybe you better start the machine.'

While Heshel retrieved the key and unlocked the handcuffs, the other man took a crank that clamped behind the rider's seat and locked it onto a nut on the side of the engine. He turned it hard a few times and the motorcycle coughed, then sputtered to life. Heshel made a hurry-up motion with his hand, the man climbed on the motorcycle and rode away. As the noise faded, they could hear dogs barking.

Heshel stood silently for a moment and stared at the front seat of the car. 'Look in the trunk,' he told Szara. 'Maybe there's a rag.'

In Berlin, it was raining and it was going to rain – a slow, sad, persistent business shining black on the bare trees and polishing the soot-coloured roof tiles. Szara stared out a high window, watching umbrellas moving down the street like phantoms. It seemed to him the city's very own, private weather, for Berliners lived deep inside themselves – it could be felt – where they nourished old insults and humiliated ambitions of every sort, all of it locked up within a courtesy like forged metal and an acid wit that never seemed meant to hurt – it just, apparently by accident, left a little bruise.

Late Tuesday night, Heshel had driven Szara to the terminus of a suburban branch line where he'd caught a morning train into Berlin. Once aboard, he'd trudged to the WC and, numb with resignation, forced himself to look in the mirror. But his hair was as it had always been and he'd barked a humourless laugh at his own image. *Still vanity, always, forever, despite everything*. What he'd feared was something he had seen, and more than once, during the civil war and the campaign against Poland: men of all ages, even in their teens, sentenced to die at night, then, the next morning, marched to the wall of a school or post office with hair turned, in the course of one night, a greyish white.

He took a taxi to an address Heshel had given him, a tall, narrow private house on the Nollendorfplatz in the western part of Berlin, not far from the Holländische Taverne, where he'd been told he could take his meals. A silent woman in black silks had answered his knock, shown him to a cot in a gabled attic, and left him alone. He supposed it to be a safe house used by the Renate Braun faction, but the ride in Ismailov's car and a few, apparently final moments in a stubbled wheat field had dislocated him from a normal sense of the world and he was no longer sure precisely what he knew.

Heshel, driving fast and peering through the steering wheel – there were bullet holes in the driver's side of the window and the glass had fractured into frosted lace around each of them – had signalled with his headlights to two cars and another motorcycle racing down the narrow road. So Szara gained at least a notion of the sheer breadth of the operation. Yet Heshel seemed not to know, or care, why Szara was headed into Berlin, and when Szara offered him the satchel he simply laughed. 'Me?' he'd said, heeling the car through a double-S curve in the road, 'I don't take nothing. What's yours is yours.'

What did they want?

To use the material in the satchel that rested between his feet. To discredit the Georgians – Ismailov and Khelidze had only that connection, as far as he knew. And *they* were? Not his friends in the Foreign Department. Who then? He did not know. He only knew they'd stuck him with the hot potato.

The kids in the Jewish towns of Poland and Russia played the game with a stone. If the count reached fifty and you had it, well, too bad. You might have to eat a morsel of dirt, or horse pie. The forfeit varied but the principle never did. And there was always some tough little bastard like Heshel around to play enforcer.

Heshel was a type he'd always known, what they called in Yiddish a *Luftmensch*. These *Luftmenschen*, it meant men of the air or men without substance, could be seen every morning but the Sabbath, standing around in front of the local synagogue, hands in pockets, waiting for a day's work, an errand, whatever might come their way. They were men who seemed to have no family or village, a restless population of day labourers that moved through eastern Poland, the Ukraine, Byelorussia, all over the Jewish districts, available to whoever had a few kopecks to pay them. The word had a second, ironic, meaning that, like many Yiddish expressions, embellished its literal translation. *Luftmenschen* were also eternal students, lost souls, young people who spent their lives arguing politics in cafés and drifting through the student communities of Europe – gifted, bright, but never truly finding themselves.

Yet Szara knew that he and Heshel were perhaps more similar than he wanted to admit. They were both citizens of a mythical country, a place not here and not there, where national borders expanded and contracted but changed nothing. A world where *everyone* was a *Luftmensch* of one kind or another. The Pale of Settlement, fifteen provinces in southwest Russia (until 1918, when Poland sprang back into national existence) ran from Kovno in the north, almost on the shores of the Baltic, to Odessa and Simferopol in the south, on the Black Sea; from Poltava in the east – historic Russia – to Czestochowa and Warsaw in the west – historic Poland. One had also to include Cracow, Lvov, Ternopol, and such places, part of the Austro-Hungarian empire until 1918. Add to this the towns of other off-and-on countries – Vilna in Lithuania and Jelgava in Latvia – throw in the fact that people thought of themselves as having regional affiliations, believing they lived in Bessarabia, Galicia (named for the Galicia in Spain from which the Jews were expelled in 1492), Kurland, or Volhynia, and what did you have?

You had a political landscape best understood by intelligence services and revolutionary cadres – fertile recruiting either way it went and often enough both and why not?

What can be so bad about a cover name or a *nom de révolution* if your own name never particularly meant anything? The Austro-Hungarian bureaucracy in the nineteenth century gave the Jews the right to call themselves whatever they liked. Most chose German names, thinking to endear themselves to their German-speaking neighbours. These names were often transliterated back into, for example, Polish. Thus some version of the German for *sharer* (and why that? nobody knew) became Szara, the Polish *sz* standing in for the German *s*, which was sounded *sch*. Eventually, with time and politics and migration, it changed again, this time to the Russian Ш. And, when Szara was born, his mother wanted to emphasize some quietly cherished claim to a distant relation in France, so named him not the Polish Andrej or the Russian Andrei, but André.

A man invented. A man of the air. Just how would such a man's allegiance be determined? In a land of, at best, shifting political loyalties often well leavened with fumes of Hasidic mysticism, a land where the name Poland was believed by many to be a version of the Hebrew expression *polen*, which meant *Here ye shall remain!*, and was thus taken to be good news direct from heaven.

The czar's Okhrana was recruiting in the Pale as early as 1878, seeking infiltrators – Jews *did* wander, turning up as pedlars, merchants, auction buyers, and what have you, just about anywhere – for their war against Turkey. Thus, when the operatives of the Okhrana and the Bolshevik faction went at each other, after 1903, there were often Jews on both sides: men of both worlds and none – always alien, therefore never suspected of being so.

They tended to show up somewhere with a business in one pocket. Szara's father grew up in Austro-Hungarian Ternopol, where he learned the trade of watchmaker, eventually becoming nearly blind from close work in bad light. As a young man, seeking a better economic climate in which to raise his family, he moved to the town of Kishinev, where he survived the pogrom of 1903, then fled to the city of Odessa, just in time for the pogrom of 1905, which he did not survive. By then, all he could see were grey shadows and was perhaps briefly surprised at just how hard shadows punched and kicked.

His death left Szara and his mother, and an older brother and sister, to get along as best they could. Szara was, in 1905, eight years old. He learned to sew, after a fashion, as did his brother and sister, and they survived. Sewing was a Jewish tradition. It took patience, discipline, and a kind of self-hypnosis, and it provided money sufficient to eat once a day and to heat a house for some of the winter.

Later, Szara learned to steal, then, soon after, to sell stolen goods, first in Odessa's Moldavanka market, then on the docks where foreign ships berthed. Odessa was famous for its Jewish thieves – and its visiting sailors. Szara learned to sell stolen goods to sailors, who told him stories, and he grew to like stories more than almost anything else. By 1917, when he was twenty years old and had attended three years of university in Cracow, he was a confirmed writer of stories, one of many who came from Odessa – it had something to do with seaports: strange languages, exotic travellers, night bells in the harbour, waves pounding into foam on the rocks, and always distance, horizon, the line where sky met water, and just beyond your vision people were doing things you couldn't imagine.

By the time he left Cracow he'd been a socialist, a radical socialist, a communist, a Bolshevik, and a revolutionary in all things – whatever one might become to oppose the czar, for that mattered above all else.

After Kishinev, where, as a six-year-old, he'd heard the local citizens beating their whip handles on the cobblestones, preparing their victims for a pogrom, after Odessa, where he'd found his father half buried in a mud street, a pig's tail stuffed in his mouth – *thus we deal with Jews too good to eat pork* – what else?

For the pogroms were the czar's gift to his peasants. There was little else he could give them, so, when they were pressed too hard by misery, when they could no longer bear their fate in the muddy villages and towns at the tattered edges of the empire, they were encouraged to seek out the Christ-killers and kill a few in return. Pogroms were announced by posters, the police paid the printing bills, and the money came from the Interior Ministry, which acted at the czar's direction. A pogrom released tension and, in general, evened things up: a redistribution of wealth, a primitive exercise in population control.

Thus the Pale of Settlement produced a great number of Szaras. Intellectuals, they knew the capitals of Europe and spoke their languages, wrote fiercely and well, and had a great taste and talent for clandestine life. To survive as Jews in a hostile world they'd learned duplicity and disguise: not to show anger, for it made the Jew-baiters angry, even less to show joy, for it made the Jew-baiters even angrier. They concealed success, so they would not be seen to succeed, and learned soon enough how not to be seen at all: how to walk down a street, the wrong street, in the wrong part of town, in broad daylight – invisible. The czar was in much more trouble than he ever understood. And when his time came, the man in charge was one Yakov Yurovsky, a Jew from Tomsk, at the head of a Cheka squad. Yurovsky who, while an émigré in Berlin, had declared himself a Lutheran, though the czar was in no position to appreciate such ironies.

Having lived in a mythical country, a place neither here nor there, these intellectuals from Vilna and Gomel helped to create another and called it the Union of Soviet Socialist Republics. Such a name! It was hardly a union. The Soviets – workers' councils – ruled it for about six weeks; socialism impoverished everybody, and only machine guns kept the republics from turning into nations. But to Szara and the rest it didn't matter. He'd put his life on the line, preferring simply to die at the wrong end of a gun rather than the wrong end of a club, and for twelve years – until 1929, when Stalin finally took over – he lived in a kind of dream world, a mythical country where idealistic, intellectual Jews actually ran things, quite literally a country of the mind. Theories failed, peasants died, the land itself dried up in despair. Still they worked twenty hours a day and swore they had the answer.

It could not last. Who *were* these people, these Poles and Lithuanians, Latvians and Ukrainians, these people with little beards and eyeglasses who spoke French down their big noses and read books? asked Stalin. And all the little Stalins answered. *We were wondering that very thing, only nobody wanted to say it out loud.*

The steady rain beat down on Berlin; somewhere in the house the landlady's radio played German opera, the curtains hung limp by the window and smelled of the dead air in a disused attic room. Szara put on his belted raincoat and walked through the wet streets until he found a telephone box. He called Dr Julius Baumann and managed to get himself invited to dinner. Baumann sounded suspicious and distant, but Nezhenko's telegram had been specific: the information was wanted by 25 November. There was no Soviet press bureau in Berlin, he'd have to file through the press office at the embassy, and 25 November was the next day. So he'd given Baumann a bit of a push – sometimes fincssc was a luxury.

He walked slowly back to the tall house and spent the afternoon with the Okhrana, DUBOK, the Caspian Oil Company, and thirty-year-old *treffs* in the back streets of Tbilisi, Baku, and Batum. They wanted him to be an intelligence officer and so he was. Fearless, heroic, jaw set with determination, he read reports for five hours in an anonymous room while the rain drummed down and he never once dozed off.

The Villa Baumann stood behind a high wall at the edge of the western suburbs, in a neighbourhood where gardeners pruned the shrubbery to sheer walls and flat tabletops and architects dazzled their clients with turrets and gables and gingerbread that made mansions seem colossal dollhouses. A yank at the rope of a ship's bell by the gate produced a servant, a stubby man with immense red hands and sloping shoulders who wore an emerald green velvet smoking jacket. Mumbling in a dialect Szara could barely understand, he led the way down a path that skirted the Villa Baumann and ended at a servant's cottage at the rear of the property, then tramped off, leaving Szara to knock at the door.

'I take it Manfred showed you the way,' Baumann said dryly. 'Of course this used to be his' – the cottage was small and plain, quite pleasant for a servant – 'but the new regime has effected a more, ah, even-handed approach to domicile, who shall live where.'

Baumann was tall and spare, with thin, colourless lips and the face, ascetic, humourless, of a medieval prince or monastic scholar. His skin was white, as though wind or sun had never touched it. Perhaps fifty, he was hairless from forehead to crown, which drew attention to his eyes, cold and green, the eyes of a man who saw what others did not, yet did not choose to say what he saw. Whatever it was, however, faintly displeased him, that much he showed. To Szara, German Jew meant mostly German, a position of significant hauteur in the Central European scheme of things, a culture wherein precise courtesies, intellectual sophistication, and quiet wealth all blended to create a great distance from Russian Jews and, it was never exactly expressed, most Christians.

Yet Szara liked him. Even as the object of that jellyfish stare down a long, fine, princely nose – *who are you?* – even so.

They were four for dinner: Herr Doktor and Frau Baumann, a young woman introduced as Fräulein Haecht, and Szara. They ate in the kitchen – there was no dining room – at a rickety table covered by a dazzling white damask cloth embroidered with blue and silver thread. The porcelain service showed Indian princes and thick-lipped, gold-earringed princesses boating on a mountain lake, coloured tomato red and glossy black with gold filigree on the rims. At one point, the tines of Szara's fork scraped across the scene and Frau Baumann closed her eyes to shut out the sound. She was a busy little pudding of a woman. A princess with a dowry? Szara thought so.

They ate poached salmon fillets and a rice and mushroom mixture in a jellied ring. 'My old shop still serves me,' Frau Baumann explained, the unspoken *of course* perfectly audible. 'During the hours of closing, you understand, Herr Szara, at the door in the alley. But they still do it. And they do cook the most lovely things and I am enough the domestic to reheat them.'

'A small premium is entailed,' Baumann added. He had a deep, hollow voice that would have been appropriate for the delivery of sermons.

'Naturally,' Frau Baumann admitted, 'but our cook . . .'

'A rare patriot,' said Baumann. 'And a memorable exit. One would never have supposed that Hertha was capable of giving a speech.'

'We were so good to her,' said Frau Baumann.

Szara sensed the onset of an emotional flood and rushed to cut it off. 'But you are doing so very well, I haven't eaten like this . . .'

'You are not wrong,' said Baumann quietly. 'There are bad moments, too many, and one misses friends. That more than anything. But we, my family, came to Germany over three hundred years ago, before there was even such a thing as Germany, and we have lived here, in good times and bad, ever since. We are German, is what it amounts to, and proud to be. That we proved in peace and war. So, *these people* can make life difficult for us, Jews and others also, but they cannot break our spirit.'

'Just so,' Szara said. Did they believe it? Perhaps Frau Doktor did. Had they ever seen a spirit broken? 'Your decision to stay on is, if I may say it, courageous.'

Baumann laughed by blowing air through his nose, his

mouth deformed by irony. 'Actually, we haven't the choice. You see before you the Gesellschaft Baumann, declared a strategically necessary enterprise.'

Szara's interest showed. Baumann waved off dinnertime discussion of such matters. 'You shall come and see us tomorrow. The grand tour.'

'Thank you,' Szara said. There went filing on time. 'The editors at *Pravda* have asked for material that could become a story. Would it be wise for a Jew to have attention called to him in that way? In a Soviet publication?'

Baumann thought for a moment. 'You are frank, Herr Szara, and it is appreciated. Perhaps you'll allow me to postpone my answer until tomorrow.'

Why am I here? 'Of course, I understand perfectly.'

Frau Baumann was breathless. 'We must stay, you see, Herr Szara. And our position is difficult enough as it is. One hears frightful things, one sees things, on the street –'

Baumann cut his wife off. 'Herr Szara has kindly consented to do as we wish.'

Szara realized why he liked Baumann – he was drawn to bravery.

'Surely, Herr Szara, a little more rice and mushroom ring.'

This from his left, Fräulein Haecht, obviously invited to balance the table. At first, in the little whirlpool of turmoil that surrounds the entry of a guest, her presence had floated by him; a handshake, a polite greeting. Obviously she was nobody to be interested in, a young woman with downcast eyes whose role it was to sit in the fourth chair and offer him rice and mushroom ring. Hair drawn back in a maiden's bun, wearing a horrid sort of blue wool dress with long sleeves – somehow shapeless and stiff at once – with a tiny lace collar tight at the throat, she was the perennial niece or cousin, invisible.

But now he saw that she had eyes, large and soft and

brown, liquid, and intense. He knew her inquiring look to be a device, worked out, practised at length in front of a dressing table mirror and meant to be the single instant of the evening she would claim for herself.

Said Frau Baumann: 'Oh yes, please do.'

He reached for the platter, held delicately in a small hand with bitten nails, set it beside him, and served himself food he didn't want. When he looked up she was gone, back into cover. It was the sort of skin, olive toned, that didn't exactly colour, yet he thought he saw a shadow darken above the lace collar.

'. . . just the other day . . . the British newspapers . . . simply cannot continue . . . friends in Holland.' Frau Baumann was well launched into an emotional appraisal of the German political situation. Meanwhile, Szara thought, *How old are you? Twenty-five?* He couldn't remember her name.

'Mmm!' he said, nodding vigorously at his hostess. How true that was.

'And one does hear such excellent news of Russia, of how it is being built by the workers. War would be such a waste.'

'Mm.' He smiled with enthusiasm. 'The workers . . .'

Finished eating, the Fräulein folded her little hands in her lap and stared at her plate.

'It cannot be permitted to happen, not again,' said the Herr Doktor. 'I believe that support for the present regime in the senior civil service and the army is not at all firm, *that man* does not necessarily speak for all of Germany, yet the European press seems blind to the possibility that –'

'And now,' the Frau Doktor cried out and clapped her hands, 'there is crème Bavarienne!'

The girl stood up quickly and assisted in clearing the table and making coffee while the Herr Doktor rumbled on. The blue dress descended to midcalf; white ribbed stockings rose to meet it. Szara could see her lace-up shoes had got wet in the evening rain.

'The situation in Austria is also difficult, very complex. If not handled with delicacy, there could be instability . . .'

By a cupboard in the far corner of the kitchen, Frau Baumann laughed theatrically to cover embarrassment. 'Why no, my dearest Marta, the willow pattern for our guest!'

Marta.

'. . . there must be rapprochement and there must be peace. We are neighbours, all of us here, there is no denying it. The Poles, the Czechs, the Serbs, they wish only peace. Can the Western democracies be blind to this? Yet they give in at every opportunity.' He shook his head in sorrow. 'Hitler marched into the Rhineland in 1936, and the French sat behind their Maginot Line and did nothing. Why? We cannot understand it. A single, determined advance by a French company of infantry – that's all it would have taken. Yet it didn't happen. I believe – no, frankly, I know – that our generals were astounded. Hitler told them how it would be, and then it was as he said, and then suddenly they began to believe in miracles.'

'And now this terrible politics must be put aside, Herr Szara,' said Frau Baumann, 'for it is time to be naughty.' The Bavarian cream, a velvety mocha pond quivering in a soup plate, appeared before him.

As the evening wore on, with cognac served in the cramped parlour, Dr Julius Baumann became reflective and nostalgic. Recalled his student days at Tübingen, where the Jewish student societies had taken enthusiastically to beer drinking and fencing, in the fashion of the times. 'I became a fine swordsman. Can you imagine such a thing, Herr Szara? But we were obsessed with honour, and so we practised until we could barely stand up, but at least one could then answer an insult by challenging the offender to a match, as all the other students did. I was tall, so our president – he is now in Argentina, living God only knows how – prevailed on me to take up the sabre. This I declined. I most certainly did not want one of these!' He drew the traditional sabre scar down his cheek. 'No, I wore the padded vest and the full mask – not the one that bares the cheek – and practised the art of the épée. Lunge! Guard. Lunge! Guard. One winter's day I scored two touches on the mighty Kiko Bettendorf himself, who went to the Olympic games the following year! Ach, those were wonderful days.'

Baumann told also of how he'd studied, often from midnight to dawn, to maintain the family honour and to prepare himself to accept the responsibility that would be passed down to him by his father, who owned the Baumann Ironworks. Graduating with a degree in metallurgical engineering, he'd gone on to convert the family business, once his father retired, to a wire mill. 'I believed that German industry had to specialize in order to compete, and so I took up that challenge.'

He had always seen his life in terms of challenge, Szara realized. First at Tübingen, then as an artillery lieutenant fighting on the western front, wounded near Ypres and decorated for bravery, next in the conversion of the Baumann business, then survival during the frightful inflations of the Weimar period – 'We paid our workers with potatoes; my chief engineer and I drove trucks to Holland to buy them!' – and now he found himself meeting the challenge of remaining in Germany when so many, 150,000 of the Jewish population of 500,000, had abandoned everything and started all over as immigrants in distant lands. 'So many of our friends gone away,' he said sorrowfully. 'We are so isolated now.'

Frau Baumann sat attentively silent during the discourse, her smile, in time, becoming a bit frozen – *Julius, my dearest husband, how I love and honour you but how you do go on.*

But Szara heard what she did not. He listened with great care and studied every gesture, every tone of voice. And a certain profile emerged, like secret writing when blank paper is treated with chemicals:

A courageous and independent man, a man of position and influence, and a patriot, suddenly finds himself bitterly opposed to his government in a time of political crisis; a man whose business, whatever it really was, has been officially designated *a strategically necessary enterprise*, who now declares himself, to a semiofficial representative of his nation's avowed enemy, to be *so isolated*.

This added up to only one thing, Szara knew, and the rather dubious assignment telegram from Nezhenko began to make sense. What he'd written off as a manifestation of some new, hopelessly convoluted political line being pursued in Moscow now told another story. The moment of revelation would come, he was virtually certain, during his 'grand tour' of the Baumann wire mill.

The dance of departure began at ten o'clock precisely, as Frau Baumann accepted with courteous despair the inevitability of Szara's return to his lodgings and instructed her husband to walk Fräulein Haecht back to her family's house. Ah but no – Szara fought back – Herr Doktor must in no way discommode himself, this was an obligation he insisted on assuming. What? No, it was unthinkable, they could not let him do that. Why not? Of course they must allow him to do that very thing. No, yes, no, yes, it went on while the girl sat quietly and stared at her knees as they fought over her. Szara finally prevailed – becoming emotional and Russian in the process. To dine so splendidly, then drive one's host out into the night? Never! What he needed was a good long walk to punctuate the pleasure of the meal. This proved to be an unanswerable attack and carried the day. Arrangements to meet the following morning were duly made, and Szara and Fräulein Haecht were ceremoniously walked to the gate and waved out into the night.

The night made over into something very different.

Sometime after dusk the rain of the afternoon had turned to snow – soft, feathery stuff, nighttime snow, that floated down slowly from a low, windless sky. They were startled, it simply wasn't the same city, they laughed in amazement. The snow crunched beneath their shoes, covered tree branches and roof-tops and hedges, changed the streets into white meadows or into silvered crystal where street lamps broke the shadow. Suddenly the night was immensely silent, immensely private; the snow clung to their hair and made their breaths into mist, surrounded them, muffled the world, cleaned it, buried it.

He had no idea where she lived and she never suggested one street or another, so they simply wandered. Walking together made it easy to talk, easy to confide, easy to say whatever came to you, because the silence and the snow made careful words seem empty. In such a moment one couldn't be hurt, the storm promised that among other things.

Some of what she said surprised him. For instance, she was not, as he'd thought, a cousin or a niece. She was the daughter of Baumann's chief engineer and longtime friend. Szara had wondered why she'd remained in Germany but this was simply answered: she was not Jewish. Thus her father would, she explained, almost certainly become the Aryan owner of the business – new laws decreed that – but he had already arranged for Baumann's interest to be secretly protected until such time as events restored them all to sanity. Was her father, then, a progressive? A man of the left? No, not at all. Simply a man of great decency. And her mother? Distant and dreamy, lived in her own world, who could blame her these days? She was Austrian, Catholic, from the South Tyrol down near Italy; perhaps the family on that side had been, some time in the past, Italian. She looked, she thought, a little Italian. What did he think?

Yes, he thought so. That pleased her; she liked being so black-haired and olive-skinned in a nation that fancied itself frightfully Nordic and blond. She belonged to the Italian side of Germany, perhaps, where romance had more to do with Puccini than Wagner, where romance meant sentiment and delicacy, not fiery Valhalla. Such private thoughts – she hoped he didn't mind her rambling.

No, no he didn't.

She knew who he was, of course. When Frau Baumann had asked her to make a fourth for dinner she hadn't let on, but she'd read some of his stories when they were translated into German. She very much wanted to meet the person who wrote those words, yet she'd been certain that she never would, that the dinner would be called off, that something would go wrong at the last minute. Generally she wasn't lucky that way. It was people who didn't care much who were lucky, she thought.

She was twenty-eight, though she knew she seemed younger. The Baumanns had known her as a little girl and for them she had never grown up, but she had, after all, one did. One wound up working for pfennigs helping the art director of a little magazine. Wretched things they printed now, but it was that or shut the doors. Not like him. Yes, she had a little envy, how he went the world over and wrote of the people he found and told their stories.

She took his hand – leather glove in leather glove down some deserted street where a crust of snow glittered on a wall. He wanted, now and then, to cry out that he was forty years old and scarred so badly he could not feel and that snow melted or changed back to rain, but of course he didn't. He knew every bad thing about the Szaras of the world, their belted raincoats and reputations, and their need to plunder innocence in girls like this. For, twenty-eight or lying, she was innocent.

They walked endlessly, miles in the snow, and when he thought he recognized the name of a street near the house where he was staying, he told her. She looked at him for the first time in a long while, her face lit up by walking in the night, wisps of hair escaped from the dreadful bun, and took off her glove, so he took his off, and they froze in order to touch. She told him he mustn't worry, her parents thought that she was staying with a girlfriend. Later they kissed, dry and cold, and he felt a taut back beneath the damp wool of her coat.

In his room, she was suddenly subdued, almost shy. Perhaps it was the room itself, he thought. Perhaps to her it seemed mean and anonymous, not the surroundings she would have imagined for him. Understanding, he smiled and shrugged – *yes, it's how my life is lived, I don't apologize* – hung up their coats, put the wet shoes by the hissing radiator. The room was dark, lit only by a small lamp, and they sat on the edge of the bed and talked in low voices and, in time, recaptured some part of the nameless grace they had discovered in the falling snow. He took her hands and said that their lives were different, very different. He'd be leaving Berlin almost immediately, was never in one place for very long, might not come back for a long time. Soon, even writing to someone in Germany might be difficult for somebody like him. It *was* a magic night, yes, he would never forget it, but they'd stolen it from a twilight world, and soon it would be dark. He meant . . . He would walk her home now. It might be better. She shook her head stubbornly, not meeting his eyes, and held his hands tightly. In the silence they could hear the snow falling outside. She said, 'Is there a place I may undress?'

'Only down the hall.'

She nodded, let go of his hands, and walked a little way off from the bed. He turned away. He heard her undoing buttons, the sliding of wool over silk as she pulled her dress over her head, and silk on silk as she took off her slip. He heard her roll down her white stockings, the shift of weight from foot to foot, the sound of her unhooking her brassiere, the sound of her lowering her underpants and stepping out of them. Then he couldn't keep his eyes away. She undid her hair and it hung loose about her face, crimped where she'd pinned it up. She was narrow-waisted, with pale, full breasts that rose and fell as she breathed, broad hips, and strong legs. Unconsciously, he sighed. She stood awkwardly in the centre of the room, olive skin half-toned in the low light, the tilt of her head uncertain, almost challenging. Was she desirable?

He stood and turned back the covers and she padded past him, heavy-footed on the bare wooden boards, and slid herself in carefully, staring at the ceiling as he undressed. He got in next to her, lying on his side, head propped on his hand. She turned toward him and started to tell him something, but he had guessed and stopped her from saying it. When, almost speculatively, he touched her nipples with his flattened palm, she drew a sharp breath through closed teeth and squeezed her eyes shut, and if he'd not been who he was, had not done everything he'd done, he would have been stupid and asked her if it hurt.

He was too excited to be as clever as he wanted to be; it was the nature of her, generosity and hunger mixed, heat and warmth at once, the swollen and smooth places, pale colours and dark, the catch of discovery in her breathing, and the way she abandoned not innocence – he'd been wrong; she had never been innocent – but modesty, the way she crossed her barriers.

'Lift up a little,' he said.

For a time he was afraid to move, her hands trembling against his back, then, when he did, he was in anguish when it ended. A little later she got out of bed to go down the hall, not bothering to put anything on, a pretty wobble in the way she walked, *I know you're watching*.

When she returned, she took the cigarette away from him and stubbed it out in the ashtray. So many things she had thought about for such a long time.

Thursday morning was cold and windy under dirty skies of shattered grey cloud. The streets to the factory district, at the northern reaches of the city, were banked by soot-stained hills of snow. Szara's taxi was driven by a meat-coloured giant with crossed swastika flags bound to his sunvisor with ribbon, and, as they drove through the Neukolln district, where miles of factories mixed with workers' flats, he hummed beer songs and chattered on about the virtues of the New Germany.

The Baumann wire mill proved hard to find. High, brown brick walls, name announced by a small, faded sign, as though anybody who mattered should know where it was. Szara was amused by the driver, whose face twisted with near-sighted effort as he looked for the entry gate.

A business-day Baumann awaited him in a cluttered office that looked out on the production lines. Szara found him edgy, over-active, eyes everywhere at once, and not at all stylish in a green V-neck sweater worn beneath a sober suit to keep out the chill of the factory. The narrative of the tour was delivered in a shout that was barely audible above the noise of the machinery.

Szara was a little dazed by it all. He'd arrived still in a lover's state of being, sensual, high strung, and the roaring hearth fires and clattering belt drives pounded at his temples. Steel was really the last thing in the world he wanted to think about.

One bad moment: he was introduced to Herr Haecht, a dour man in a smock, distracted from tally sheets on a clipboard when Baumann yelled an introduction. Szara managed a smile and a limp handshake.

Chicken sandwiches and scalding coffee were served in the office. When Baumann slammed the glass-panelled door, the racket of the place diminished sufficiently that a conversation could be held in almost normal tones.

'What do you think of it?' said Baumann, eager for his visitor to be impressed.

Szara did his best. 'So many workers . . .'

'One hundred and eight.'

'And truly on a grand scale.'

'In my father's day, may he rest in peace, no more than a workshop. What he didn't make wasn't worth mentioning – ornamental fence palings, frying pans, toy soldiers.' Szara followed Baumann's eyes to a portrait on the wall, a stern man with a tiny moustache. 'And everything by hand, work you don't see anymore.'

'I can only imagine.'

'One naturally cannot compare systems,' Baumann said diplomatically. 'Even our largest mills are not so grand as the Soviet steel works at Magnitogorsk. Ten thousand men, it's said. Extraordinary.'

'Each nation has its own approach,' Szara said.

'Of course here we specialize. We are all *nichtrostend*.'

'Pardon?'

'One says it best in English – austenitic. What is known as stainless steel.'

'Ah.'

'When you finish your sandwich, the best is yet to come.' Baumann smiled conspiratorially.

The best was reached by way of two massive doors guarded by an elderly man seated on a kitchen chair.

'Ernest is our most senior man,' Baumann said. 'From my father's time.' Ernest nodded respectfully.

They stood in a large room where a few workers were busy at two production lines. It was much quieter and colder than the other part of the factory. 'No forging here,' Baumann explained, grinning at the chill overtaking Szara. 'Here we make swage wire only.'

Szara nodded, drew a pencil and a notebook from his pocket. Baumann spelled the word for him. 'It's a die process, steel bars forced through a swage, a grooved block, under enormous pressure, which produces a cold-worked wire.'

Baumann took him closer to one of the production lines. From a table he selected a brief length of wire. 'See? Go ahead, take it.' Szara held it in his hand. 'That's 302 you've got there – just about the best there is. Resists atmosphere, doesn't corrode, much stronger than wire made from molten steel, this is. Won't melt until around twenty-five hundred degrees Fahrenheit, and its tensile strength is greater than that of annealed wire by a factor of approximately one third. Hardness can be figured at two hundred and forty on the Brinnell scale as opposed to eighty-five. Quite a difference all round, you'll agree.'

'Oh yes.'

'And it won't stretch – that's the really crucial thing.'

'What is it for?'

'We ship it to the Rheinmetall company as multiple strands twisted into cable, which increases its strength by a considerable factor but it remains flexible, to pass under or around various barriers, yet extremely responsive, even at great length. That's what you need in control cable.'

'Control cable?'

'Yes, for aircraft. For instance, the pilot sets his flaps by controls in his cockpit, but it's Baumann swage wire that actually makes the flaps go down. Also the high-speed rudder on the tail, and the ailerons on the wings. These are warplanes! They must bank and dip, dive suddenly. Response is everything, and response depends on the finest control cables.'

'So you are very much a factor in Luftwaffe rearmament.'

'In our own specialty, one could say preeminent. Our contract with Rheinmetall, which installs control cable on all heavy bombers, the Dornier 17, the Heinkel 111, and the Junkers 86, is exclusive.'

'All the swage wire.'

'That's true. A third production line is contemplated here. Something around four hundred and eighty feet per aircraft – well, it's quite a heavy demand.'

Szara hesitated. They were on the brink now; it was like sensing the tension of a diver at the instant preceding a leap into empty air. Baumann remained supremely energetic, expansive, a businessman proud of what he'd accomplished. Did he understand what was about to happen? He had to. He had almost certainly contrived this meeting, so he knew what he was doing. 'It's quite a story,' Szara said, stepping back from the edge. 'Any journalist would be delighted, of course. But can it be told?' *A door*, he thought. *Will you walk through it?*

'In the newspaper?' Baumann was puzzled.

'Yes.'

'I hardly think so.' He laughed good-naturedly.

Amen. 'My editor in Moscow misinformed me. I'm normally not so dense.'

Baumann clucked. 'Not so, Herr Szara, you are not anything like dense. Of Soviet citizens who might turn up in Germany, outside diplomatic staffs or trade missions, your presence is quite unremarkable. Surely not liked by the Nazis, but not unusual.'

Szara was a little stung at this. *So you know about clandestine life, do you?* 'Well, one could hardly expect your monthly production figures to be published in trade magazines.'

'Unlikely.'

'It would be considerable.'

'Yes it would. In October, for example, we shipped to Rheinmetall approximately sixteen thousand eight hundred feet of 302 swage wire.'

Divide by four hundred and eighty, Szara calculated, and you have the monthly bomber production of the Reich. Though tanks would be of great interest, no number could so well inform Soviet military planners of German strategic intentions and capabilities.

Szara jotted down the number as though he were making notes for a feature story – *our motto has always been excellence, Baumann claims*. 'Substantial,' he said, tapping his pencil against the number on the page. 'Your efforts must surely be appreciated.'

'In certain ministries, that's true.'

But not in others. Szara put the notebook and pencil in his pocket. 'We journalists don't often meet with such candour.'

'There are times when candour is called for.'

'Perhaps we'll be meeting again,' Szara said.

Baumann nodded his assent, a stiff little bow: a man of dignity and culture had made a decision, taken honour into account, determined that greater considerations prevailed.

They went back to the office and chatted for a time. Szara restated his gratitude for a delightful evening. Baumann was gracious, saw him to his taxi when it arrived, smiled, shook hands, wished him safe journey home.

The taxi rattled along past brown factory walls. Szara closed his eyes. She stood at the centre of the room, olive skin in half tones, pale breasts that rose and fell as she breathed. *Marta Haecht*, he thought.

Fate rules our lives. So the Slavs seemed to believe, and Szara had lived among them long enough to see the sense of the way they thought. One simply had to admire the fine hand of destiny, how it wove a life, tied desire to betrayal, ambition to envy, added idealism, love, false gods, missed trains, then pulled sharply on the threads, and behold! – there a human danced and struggled.

Here, he thought, was that exquisite deployment of fate known as *the coincidence*.

A man goes to Germany and is offered, simultaneously, both salvation for his aching soul and a guarantee of life itself. Amazing. What should such a man believe? For he can see that a clandestine affiliation with Dr Baumann and his magic wire will make him so appetizing a fellow to the special services that they will keep him alive if the devil himself tries to snatch his ankle. As for his soul, well, he'd been having rather a bad time with it lately. A man whose friends are vanishing every day must learn to nuzzle death in order to keep his sanity – didn't a kind of affection always take root in proximity? This is a man in trouble. A man who sits in a park in Ostend, offered, at least, a possibility of salvation, then stands and walks away in order to keep a timely appointment with those he has every reason to believe mean to abduct him – this man must need a reason to live. And if the reason to live is in Berlin? Tightly locked to the very means that will ensure survival?

Oh, a glorious coincidence.

In a vast and shifting universe, where stars glitter and die in endless night, one may choose to accept coincidence of every sort. Szara did.

There remained, amid such speculation, one gravely material difficulty, the Okhrana document, and the need to satisfy what he now believed to be a second group of masters – Renate Braun, General Bloch – within the intelligence *apparat*. For the Baumann assignment came, he was almost positive, from his traditional, longtime friends in the NKVD – the Foreign Department crowd, Abramov and others, some known, some forever in shadow.

Now, to stay alive, he would have to become an intelligence officer: an NKVD of one.

On the morning of 26 November, Szara filed as instructed at the Soviet embassy in Berlin. Not a dispatch, but the development of information that Nezhenko's telegram had specified: Baumann's age and demeanour, his wife, how they lived, the factory, the proud history. Not a word about swage wire, only 'plays a crucial part in German rearmament production.'

And there had been only three for dinner. Marta Haecht he would not give them.

Had the *apparat* known what it was getting, Szara reasoned, they'd have sent real officers. No, this was somebody who'd been informed of a potential opportunity in Berlin, somebody who'd told his assistant, *Oh send Szara up there*, figuring he'd let them know if he came across something useful. That was the nature of the intelligence landscape as he understood it: in a world of perpetual night, a thousand signals flickered in the darkness, some would change the world, others were meaningless, or even dangerous. Not even an organization the size of the NKVD could examine them all, so now and then it called on a knowledgeable friend.

The people at the embassy had been told to expect him, they took his report without comment. Then they informed him he was to return to Moscow. On the Soviet merchant vessel *Kolstroi*, departing Rostock, on the Bay of Pomerania, at five in the afternoon on 30 November. That was four days away. *Recall to Moscow*. Szara had to fight for equilibrium. The phrase sometimes meant arrest; the request to return was polite enough, but once they had you back in the country . . . *No*. Not him, and not now. He could anticipate some fairly uncomfortable interrogations. By 'friends' who would show up at his apartment bringing vodka and food – that was, at least, the usual method: *so glad to have you back, you must tell us everything about your trip*.

You really must.

He calmed himself down, decided not to think about it, and left the embassy with a pocket full of money and a determined heart, the twin pillars of espionage.

Were they watching him? The Foreign Department group? The Renate Braun group? He assumed they were – they'd certainly, thank God, been with him on the journey from Prague to Berlin. A lot of them.

He knew just enough, he thought, to lose a surveillance. Three hours it took – museums, train stations, department stores, taxis, trams, and restaurants with back doors. At last arriving, alone as far as he could tell, at an antique shop. Here he bought a painting, oil on canvas, dated 1909, in a heavy gilt frame. By one Professor Ebendorfer, the proprietor rather haughtily informed him, of the University of Heidelberg. A four-by-three-foot rectangle, the painting was executed in the Romantic style: a Greek youth, a shepherd, sat cross-legged at the foot of a broken column and played his pipe whilst his flock grazed nearby, a rich blue sky was studded with fleecy clouds, snow-capped mountains rose in the distance. *Huldigung der Naxos*, it was called – *Homage to Naxos* – and Professor Ebendorfer had signed it artfully in the lower right corner, on a laurel bush beset by a nibbling ram.

Back in the room at the narrow house, Szara went seriously to work, as he should have done all along.

And since he was not looking for anything in particular, simply performing a mechanical task that left his mind in a rather listless, neutral state, he eventually found everything. He immediately wished he hadn't. It was poison he found: the knowledge that kills. But there it was. He'd meant only to leave the original dossier, which would not pass a Russian border inspection, in Berlin, and carry with him to Moscow a condensed document, in a personal shorthand, of facts and circumstances. Using a cipher of contemporary dates and meaningless cities for the ones in the dossier, he believed he could get it past the NKVD border guards as 'journalist's notes.' These guards were not at all the NKVD types who worked in foreign political affairs – they were thorough, uncorruptible, and dull. He could handle them.

The job he set himself was like adding columns of figures – but it was this very exercise in brainless transposition that raised the answer above the horizon. Szara was accustomed to writer's thinking: the flash of insight or the revealing perspective produced by the persistent mind. Copying, he'd thought, was idiot's work. So now he learned a lesson.

To organize the effort he began at the beginning and proceeded, in a table of events, week by week, month by month. Without really meaning to, he'd fashioned what intelligence officers called a chron, short for chronology. For in that discipline *what* and *who* were of great interest, but it was often *when* that produced usable information.

Before the revolution, Bolshevik contact with the Okhrana

was common enough. Between revolutionaries and government special services there is almost always a relationship, sometimes covert, sometimes not. It might be said that they spend so very much time thinking and scheming about each other that it becomes their inevitable destiny to meet, and both write such connections off to intelligence gathering. The illusion of virginity is thereby maintained.

But DUBOK far exceeded the bounds of normalcy in this relationship, bought his safety with his comrades' lives, and was nurtured by the Okhrana like the most tender sprout imaginable. For him they duplicated the grim reality of the revolutionary experience but took care to buffer it, to draw its teeth. He went, like all the underground operatives, to jail and, like many others, escaped. But duration told the tale. They put him in Bailov prison, in Baku (he spent his time learning German), but had him out four months later. Exile, too, he had to experience, but it was to Solvychegodsk they sent him, in the north of European Russia, and not to Siberia. And he 'escaped' after only four months. Lucky, this DUBOK. Two years later he was 'caught' again, then sent back to finish his term in Solvychegodsk but tired of it after six months: long enough to hear what other exiles had to say, long enough to maintain his credibility as a Bolshevik operative, then, a man on a string, home again.

DUBOK, it became clear, was a criminal, was possessed of a criminal mind. His method never varied: he softened those around him by saying what they wanted to hear – he had a superb instinct for what that might be – then sacrificed them as necessary. He exploited weakness, emasculated strength, and never hesitated to indulge his own substantial cowardice. The Okhrana officer, Szara came to realize, manipulated DUBOK effortlessly because of a lifetime spent in the company of criminals. He understood them, understood them so well that he'd come to feel a sort of sorrowful affection for them. With time he developed the instincts of a priest: evil existed; the task was to work productively within its confines.

The officer, if one read between the lines, was profoundly interested in DUBOK'S effect on Bolshevik intellectuals. These men and women were often brilliant, knew science, languages, poetry, philosophy. DUBOK, for them, was a kind of symbol, a beloved creature from the lower depths, an enlightened thug, and their comradeship with him confirmed them as members of a newly reordered society. A political scientist, a philosopher, an economist, a poet, could only make revolution if they shared their destiny with a criminal. He was the official representative of *the real world*. Thus they advanced his standing at every opportunity. And DUBOK knew it. And DUBOK loathed them for it. Understanding condescension with every bone in his body, taking revenge at his leisure, proving that equality was in their minds, not his, as he obliterated them.

Now Szara had known from the beginning he had in his hands a Georgian and, when his perfectly capable mind finally bothered to do arithmetic, a Georgian at least fifty-five years old with a history of revolutionary work in Tbilisi and Baku. It could have been any one of a number of candidates, including the leaders of the Georgian *khvost*, but, as Szara worked laboriously through the dossier, these were eliminated by DUBOK himself. For the benefit of the Okhrana, DUBOK had written out a description of his friend Ordjonikidze. Eighteen months later he mentioned the Armenian terrorist Ter Petrossian, seen taking part in a bank 'expropriation' in Baku; referred, a few pages later, to the good-natured Abel Yenukidze; and spoke harshly against his hated enemy, Mdivani. In May of 1913, he was pressed to organize a situation in which the revolutionary Beria might be compromised, but DUBOK never quite managed to do more than talk about that.

After a day and a half, André Szara could no longer avoid the truth: this was Koba himself, Iosif Vissarionovich Dzhugashvili, son of a savage, drunken cobbler from Gori, the sublime leader Stalin. For eleven years, from 1906 to 1917, he had been the Okhrana's pet pig, snouting up the most rare and delicious truffles that the underground so thoughtlessly hid from its enemies.

This room, Szara thought, staring out at the grey sky over Berlin, *too much happens in it*. He rose from the desk, stretched to ease his back, lit a cigarette, walked to the window. The lady in silks was rustling about downstairs, doing whatever mysterious things she did all day. Below, on the pavement, an old man was holding the leash of a grizzled Alsatian dog while it sprayed the base of a street lamp.

Szara spent part of Sunday morning removing a soiled sheet of cotton cloth that sealed the back of *Huldigung der Naxos*, then distributing the sheets of the Okhrana dossier across the back of the painting itself, securing them with brown cord tied off to the heads of tiny nails he pounded in with a tack hammer. The cotton cloth he refitted with great care, the bent nails installed by the original framer repositioned in the dents and rust tracks they'd formed over the years. The weight of the heavy gilded frame concealed the presence of the paper, he thought, and *a hundred years from now, some art restorer . . .*

On Monday he was, for the first time, on stage as a German, speaking with slow deliberation, purging the Yiddish lilt from his accent, hoping to pass for a mildly unusual individual born somewhere far away from Berlin. He found that if he combed his hair straight back off his forehead, tied his tie very tight, and carried his chin in a position that, to him, felt particularly high, the disguise was credible. He took the name Grawenske, suggesting distant Slavic or Wendish origins, not at all uncommon in Germany.

He telephoned the office of an auctioneer and was given the name of a warehouse that specialized in the storage of fine art ('Humidity is your enemy!' the man told him). Herr Grawenske appeared there at eleven promptly, explained that he was joining the accounting staff of a small Austrian chemical company in Chile, muttered about his wife's sister who would be occupying his residence, and left Professor Ebendorfer's masterpiece in their care, to be crated, then stored. He paid for two years, a surprisingly reasonable amount of money, gave a fictitious address in Berlin, and was handed a receipt. The remainder of the officer's effects, and the fine satchel, were distributed to shops that supported charity missions.

Marta Haecht had given him the phone number at the little magazine where she 'helped out the art director.' Szara tried to call several times, chilled to the bone as the flat Berlin dusk settled down on the city. The first time, she'd gone on an errand to the printers. The second time, somebody giggled and said they didn't know where she'd got to. On the third try, close to quitting time, she came to the phone.

'I'm leaving tomorrow,' he said. 'May I see you tonight?'

'There is a dinner. My parents' wedding anniversary.'

'Then late.'

She hesitated. 'I'll be returning home . . .'

What? Then he understood there were people near the telephone. 'Home from a restaurant?'

'No, it isn't that.'

'Home to sleep.'

'It would be better.'

'What time is the dinner over?'

'One can't rush away. I hope you'll understand. It is a, it is an occasion, festive . . .'

'Oh.'

'Do you have to go away tomorrow?'

'It can't be helped.'

'Then I don't see how . . .'

'I'll wait for you. Maybe there's a way.'

'I'll try.'

Just after eleven the doorbell rang. Szara raced downstairs, hurried past the landlady's door – opened the width of an eye – and let her in. In the little room, she took off her coat. An aura of the cold night clung to her skin, he could feel it. She was wearing a midnight blue party dress, taffeta, with ruffles. The back was all tiny hooks and eyes. 'Be careful,' she said as he fumbled. 'I mustn't stay too long. Here it is not done to leave a party.'

'What did you tell them?'

'That a friend was going away.'

It was not a magic night. They made love, but the tension in her did not break. Afterwards she was sad. 'Maybe I shouldn't have come. Sweeter to have a memory of the snow.' With the tips of his fingers he pushed the hair back off her forehead. 'I'll never see you again,' she said. She bit her lip to keep from crying.

He walked her home, almost to the door. They kissed good-bye, dry and cold, and there was nothing to say.

In the late November of 1937, the Soviet merchant vessel *Kolstroi* shipped anchor in the port of Rostock, moved slowly up the Warnemünde inlet into Lübeck bay and, swinging north into the Baltic and setting a north-by-easterly course to skirt the Sasenitz peninsula and pass south of the Danish isle of Bornholm, made for Leningrad harbour, some eight hundred and forty nautical miles away.

The *Kolstroi*, heavily laden with machine tools, truck tyres, and bar aluminium loaded at the French port of Boulogne, docked at Rostock only to complete its complement of eleven passengers bound for Leningrad. Moving up the Warnemünde in gathering darkness, the *Kolstroi* sounded its foghorn continually, joining a chorus of in- and outbound freighters as it reached Lübeck bay, where the Baltic fogbanks rolled in toward shore in the stiff northerly winds. André Szara and the other passengers were not allowed the freedom of the deck until the ship was beyond the German territorial limit. When Szara did seek the air, after the close quarters of the ship's lounge where they were fed supper, there was little visibility, nothing of the lights on the German coast, only black water heaving in November swells and a building gale that drove iced salt spray onto the metal plates of the deck, where it froze into a lead-coloured glaze. He bore it as long as he could, staring into the fog whipping past the ship's lights, unable to see land.

The *Kolstroi* was Soviet territory; he'd bowed under the vast weight of it before they ever sailed, his possessions spread out on a table under the cold eyes of a security officer. *The journalist Szara* meant nothing to this one, *Homo Staliens*, a clock disguised as a human. He was thankful he had disposed of the Okhrana dossier before he left Berlin – memory itself was frightening in the atmosphere aboard the freighter.

The passengers were a mixed group. There were three English university students, with creamy skins and bright eyes, terribly earnest young men on a dream voyage to what they believed to be their spiritual homeland. There was one middle-aged trade representative, suffering from an illness – attempted escape, Szara thought – who was dragged on board by NKVD operatives. The tips of his shoes scraped the wooden gangplank as they carried him onto the ship – obviously he had been drugged senseless. He was not the only passenger going home to die. They were a strange brotherhood, silent, self-contained, having abandoned themselves to a fate they deemed inevitable; the man who'd been dragged on board proved the futility of flight. They rarely slept, greedy for their remaining hours of introspection, pacing about the deck when they could stand the cold, their lips moving as they rehearsed imagined conversations with their interrogators.

Mostly they avoided one another. A conversation with a tainted diplomat or scientist would be reported by the attentive security men and, how was one to know, might be made evidence in the cases against them, telling evidence, uncovered only in the last hours of the journey home – *we thought you were clean until we saw you talking to Petrov* – and dangerously sweet to the NKVD appetite for the fatal irony.

Szara spoke to one of them, Kuscinas, in younger days an officer in the Lettish rifle brigades that supported Lenin when he overthrew the Kerensky government, now an old man with a shaved head and a face like a skull. Yet there was still great strength in Kuscinas; his eyes glittered from deep in their sockets, and his voice was strong enough to hear above the gale. As the *Kolstroi* rose and crashed into the heavy seas off the Gulf of Riga, on the second day of the voyage, Szara found shelter under a stairway where they could smoke cigarettes and shield themselves from the bitter wind. Kuscinas never said exactly what he did, simply waved his hand when Szara asked, meaning that such things didn't matter. As for what was about to happen to him, he seemed to be beyond caring. 'For my wife I'm sorry, but that's all. Foolish woman, and stubborn. Unfortunately she loves me and this will break her heart, but there's nothing to be done about it. My sons they've turned into snakes, all the better for them now, I think, and my daughter married some idiot who pretends to run a factory in Kursk. They'll find a way to disown me, if they haven't done it already. I'm sure they will sign anything put before them. My wife, though . . .'

'She'll have to go to friends,' Szara said.

The old man grimaced. 'Friends,' he said.

The *Kolstroi*'s steel plates creaked as the ship pitched particularly high, then slammed down into the trough, sending aloft a huge explosion of white spray. 'And fuck you too,' Kuscinas said to the Baltic.

Szara steadied himself against the iron wall and closed his eyes for a moment.

'You're not going to give it up, are you?'

He flicked his cigarette away. 'No,' he said, 'I'm a sailor.'

'Will they arrest you?'

'Perhaps. I don't think so.'

'You have the right friends, then.'

Szara nodded that he did.

'Lucky. Or maybe not,' Kuscinas said. 'By the time you get to Moscow they may be the wrong friends. These days you can't predict.' For a time he was silent, eyes inward, seeing some part of his life. 'You're like me, I suppose. One of the faithful ones, do what has to be done, don't ask to see the sense of it. Discipline above all.' He shook his head sorrowfully. 'And in the end, when it's our turn, and somebody else is doing what has to be done, somebody else who doesn't ask to see the sense of it, the discipline of the executioner, then all we can say is *za chto?* – why? What for?' Kuscinas laughed. 'A sorry little question,' he said. 'For myself, I don't mean to ask it.'

That night, Szara couldn't sleep. He lay in his bunk and smoked, the man across from him mumbling restlessly in his dreams. Szara knew the history of that question, *Za chto?* Rumour attributed its initial use to the Old Bolshevik Yacov Lifschutz, a deputy people's commissar. His final word. Szara remembered him as a little man with wild eyebrows, the obligatory goatee, and a twinkling glance. Shuffling down the tile corridor in the basement of the Lubyanka – you got it on the way, nobody ever reached the end of that corridor – he stopped for a moment and turned to his executioner, an officer he happened to have known in childhood, and said, '*Za chto?*'

Along with the purge, the word spread everywhere; it was scrawled on the walls of cells, carved in the wooden benches of the Stolypin wagons that hauled prisoners away, scratched into planks in transit camps. Almost always the first words spoken to the police who came in the night, then again the first words of a man or a woman entering a crowded cell. 'But why? Why?'

We are all alike, Szara thought. We don't offer excuses or alibis, we don't fight with the police, we don't look for compassion, we don't even plead. We don't fear death; we always counted on it – in the revolution, the civil war. All we ask, rational men that we are, is to see the sense of the thing, its meaning. Then we'll go. Just an explanation. Too much to ask?

Yes.

The savagery of the purge, Szara knew, gave them every reason to believe there was, must be, a reason. When a certain NKVD officer was taken away, his wife wept. So she was accused of resisting arrest. Such events, common, daily, implied a scheme, an underlying plan. They wanted only to be let in on it – certainly their own deaths bought them the right to an answer – and then they'd simply let the rest of it happen. What was one more trickle of blood on a stone floor to those who'd seen it flow in streams across the dusty streets of a nation? The only insult was ignorance, a thing they'd never tolerated, a thing they couldn't bear now.

In time, the cult of *Za chto* began to evolve a theory. Particularly with the events of June 1937, when the only remaining alternative to the rule of the dictator was ripped to shreds. That June came the turn of the Red Army and, when the smoke cleared, it was seen to be headless, though still walking around. Marshal Tukachevsky, acknowledged as Russia's greatest soldier, was joined in his disappearance by two of four remaining marshals, fourteen of sixteen military commanders, eight of eight admirals, sixty of sixty-seven corps commanders, on and on and on. All eleven vice-commissars of defence, seventy-five of the eighty members of the Supreme Military Soviet. All of this, they reasoned – the shootings, the icebound mining camps, an army virtually destroyed by its own country – could have only one intention: Stalin simply sought to removc any potential opposition to his own rule. That was the way of tyrants: first eliminate enemies, then friends. This was an exercise in consolidation. On a rather grand scale, ultimately counted in millions – but what was Russia if not a grand scale?

What was Russia, if not a place where one could say, down through the centuries, times and men are evil, and so we bleed. This, for some, concluded the matter. The Old Bolsheviks, the Chekists, the officer corps of the Red Army – these people *were* the revolution but now had to be sacrificed so that the Great Leader could stand unthreatened and supreme. Russia's back was broken, her spirit drained, but at least for most the question had been answered and they could get on with the trivial business of execution with acceptance and understanding. A final gesture on behalf of the party.

But they were wrong, it wasn't quite that simple.

There were some who understood that, not many, only

a few, and soon enough they died and, in time, so did their executioners, and, later, theirs.

The following day, Szara did not see Kuscinas. Then, when the *Kolstroi* steamed up the Gulf of Finland, the first ice of the season pinging against the hull, the lights of the fortress at Kronstadt twinkling in the darkness, the security men and sailors began a frantic search, combing the ship, but Kuscinas had gone, and they could not find him.

8, rue Delesseux

The OPAL Network – 1938 – Brussels/Paris/Berlin

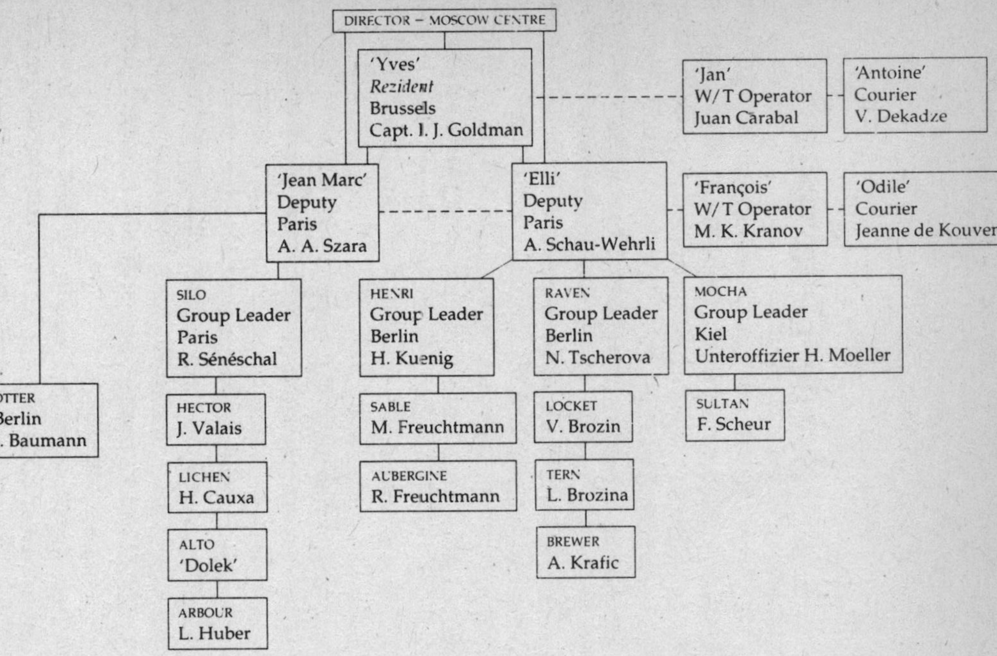

'André Aronovich! Over here!'

An urgent female voice, cutting through the uproar of a densely packed crowd in the living room of an apartment in the Mochovaya district. Szara peered through the smoke and saw a hand waving at him. 'Pardon,' he said. 'So sorry. Excuse me.' He chose an indirect route toward the hand and voice, swinging wide to avoid the dangerous elbows of those who had managed to break through to the buffet. Moscow was ravaged by shortages of nearly everything, but here there was black Servuga, grilled lamb, pirozhki, salted peas, stacks of warm blini, and platters of smoked salmon. What you had, then, was desperation: a roomful of *apparatchiks*, mandarins of agriculture and road planning, timber and foreign policy, as well as the security services, trying to feed themselves for the week to come. More than one pocket was stuffed with meat, smoked fish, even butter – whatever one could swipe.

For an instant, Szara caught sight of a vaguely familiar face that appeared over the shoulder of a naval officer, then vanished in the crowd. A sophisticated woman, lightly made up, with simple but stylishly managed hair and dangling silver earrings.

He figured it out just about the time they found each other: a curiously altered Renate Braun, wearing a full blouse of lime-coloured silk and the modestly coquettish smile one saw in films of cocktail parties. 'Heavens, what a crowd!' she said, brushing his cheek with hers – a dear friend one simply doesn't see often enough. Last seen slicing up a dead man's trouser cuffs with a razor blade in an Ostend whorehouse, here was an entirely different version of the woman.

'You must meet Mr Herbert Hull,' she gushed, speaking in German-accented English.

Now Szara noticed that she had in tow a tall, sandy-haired man with a weather-beaten face and wildly over-grown eyebrows. He was perhaps in his late forties and, from his casual, loose-jointed posture, evidently American. He was smoking, with difficulty, a poorly rolled *makhorka* cigarette, a self-conscious attempt to be part of the local scenery, Szara thought. 'Herb Hull,' he said. He had a powerful grip and sought something in Szara's eyes when they shook hands.

'Herb has been so anxious to meet you,' Renate Braun said.

'We all know André Szara,' Hull said. 'I'm a great fan of your work, Mr Szara.'

'Oh but you must call him André.'

'Yes. Please.'

Szara's English was at best uncertain. He was going to sound awful, hesitant and somehow importunate – an impression often created when Slavs spoke English. He already felt a hatefully ingratiating smile creeping over his face.

'Herb's an editor with a new American magazine. A very important undertaking. You'll know him, of course, from when he was with the *Nation* and the *New Republic*.'

'Ah yes.' Szara knew the names, prayed he wouldn't be questioned about specific articles. The anxious smile grew. 'Of course. Importantly.'

Szara saw Renate Braun wince, but plunged ahead. 'You are liking Russia?'

'Never the same place two days in a row, things go wrong, but there's a strength in the people that's irresistible.'

'Ach!' – mock horror from Renate Braun – 'he knows us too well.'

Hull smiled and shrugged. 'Trying to learn, at any rate. That's what we need. Firsthand knowledge, a feel for the real Russia.'

'I am certain that André can help you with that, Herb. Positive.'

'Yes?' Szara said.

'Why not?' Hull's eyebrows rose. 'After all, I'm an editor, you're a writer. For a new magazine, well, a Russian writer speaking about the USSR would be a change, change for the better I'm inclined to think. No?'

'Ah, but my English.'

'No problem, André. We'd be happy to do the translation, or it could be done here. Won't be perfect, but we'll guarantee to preserve the sense of it.'

'I am honoured,' Szara said. He was. The thought of appearing in a respected journal before an American audience, not the usual *Daily Worker* crowd, was immensely pleasing. Ilya Ehrenburg, *Pravda*'s number one correspondent, had done it, occupying the journalistic territory in the Spanish Civil War so effectively that Szara was virtually restricted to other parts of Europe.

Hull let the offer sink in, then went on. 'Renate tells me you're working on a historical piece that might be right up our alley. I won't kid you, running something like that would get us the attention we need. And we'll pay for it. Won't be Hollywood, of course, but I think you'll find us competitive in the New York market.'

Renate Braun seemed quite excited by the prospect. 'We've even discussed a title, André Aronovich.'

Szara stared at her. What was she talking about?

'Just discussed,' Hull broke in. He knew what a certain look on a writer's face meant. 'Working title is all it is, but I can tell you it caught my attention.'

'Title?'

Renate Braun said, 'The piece must be exciting – our plan fulfilment norms won't do, I suspect. It must have . . .' She looked at Hull for the word.

'Intrigue?'

'Yes. That's it. Intrigue! A story of Russia's revolutionary past, its secret history. We aren't completely sure what it is you're working on – you writers keep close with ideas – but we thought perhaps something on the order of "The Okhrana's Mysterious Man."' She turned to Hull. 'Yes? It's good English?'

'Yes indeed. Good enough to put on the cover, I'd say.'

Szara repeated the title in Russian. Renate Braun nodded vigorously. 'Your English is better than you think, André Aronovich.'

'Of course,' Hull said, 'you can always use a pen name if you like, I'm not unaware how easy it is to get into trouble these days. We'd rather have your name, of course, but we'll protect your identity if that makes you more comfortable.'

Szara just stared. How much did this man know? Did he have any idea what happened to people who played such games? Was he brave? Stupid? Both?

'Well, André, would you consider it?' Hull asked, eyes keen, head tilted inquiringly to one side, gauging his quarry.

'How could he not?' Renate Braun said. 'Such an opportunity!'

Szara walked for a long time that night. His tiny apartment in Volnitzky Alley wasn't far from the house where the party had been given, so he circled the centre of the city, crossing the icebound river, a lone, January figure in fur hat and overcoat. He kept an eye out for *bezprizorniye*, bands of children orphaned by the purge who attacked and robbed solitary walkers of their money and clothing – you might just as easily freeze to death if your head wasn't bashed in – but it was evidently too cold for hunting.

Sooner or later, he thought, *things fall into place and, often as not, you'd rather they hadn't*. Now the long leash in Prague and Berlin made sense. They were letting him have his time with the dossier, counting on the fact that he'd stick his curious writer's nose into the business. Seen externally, a well-known journalist had sniffed out a big story which, in the normal way of things, he'd tell the world. They'd protected him when the Georgian *khvost* operatives had him taken off the train, then left him free to work.

And now they were rather casually asking him to commit suicide.

Was it too much to ask? That one life should be sacrificed so that hundreds, perhaps thousands, might survive? All he need do was practise his natural trade. Who was the Okhrana's mysterious man? Well, we know a few small details. A, B, C, and D. A new and provocative enigma from enigmatic Russia. Perhaps, someday, we'll learn his real identity. Yours truly, André Szara. (Please omit flowers.)

Or, oh yes, the pen name. *Boris Ivanov has served in the Soviet diplomatic corps*. That would surely throw the NKVD off the scent. For perhaps a month. Or maybe a year. Not much longer.

Still, it would certainly communicate a point of view:

We know what you did and we can prove it, now stop killing us or we'll finish you. Blackmail. Plain old-fashioned politics. Ancient as time.

He admired the plan, though he felt more than a little chagrin over his apparently boundless capacity for self-deception. Certain things now made sense. On the train to Prague, General Bloch had told him, albeit obliquely, just what they had in mind for him. Szara had triumphantly misunderstood him, of course, taking delicately phrased information to be some sort of pompous philosophy, a homily.

With some difficulty Szara won back from his memory the general's statements: 'Some men, in such circumstances, might be careless of their lives. Such men rise to an opportunity. And then we have a hero!' In an empty street coated with grey ice, Szara laughed out loud. Bloch had said something about Szara's attitude toward himself after pointing out, dextrously enough, that he had neither wife nor children. What else? Oh yes. 'To be a writer requires work and sacrifice, to follow any road wherever it may lead.'

Yes. Well. Now one knew where it led. Just as one knew in 1917 when one was twenty and what did death matter. From the beginning, in the park in Ostend, Szara had sensed his fate. He'd dodged a time or two, yet here it was, back again. The Szara that Bloch found on the train was, like his revolutionary brethren, a man who had no business being alive, a man who had evaded the inevitable just long enough.

Suddenly, the walls of his irony collapsed and real anguish struck his heart. He stopped cold, his face twisted with pain and anger; a sob rose to the base of his throat and stuck there – he had to bite his lip to keep from howling the dreaded question directly at God and the streets of Moscow:

Why now?

Because *now* everything was different. Bloch had met a certain kind of man on the train to Prague but *now* he was not that man. He was instead that man who presses his face against the skin of a woman to inhale such fragrance as makes him want to cry out with joy. He was that man who spins between tenderness and raging lust like a helpless top, who wakes up on fire every morning, who spends his hours thinking of only one thing – yet how brilliantly he thinks of it!

He recovered. Regained himself, breathed deeply, resumed walking. The wall inside him must not be breached: it kept in, it kept out. He had to have it to survive.

He realized that the frost had stolen the feeling from his face and he turned towards home, walking quickly. Later he scalded his mouth with tea while sitting in his overcoat and fur hat at the table his wife, only a few months before she died, had insisted he put by the kitchen window. It had been a lovely table, an absurdly ornamental cherrywood thing with heavy, scrollworked legs. Using it in the kitchen they'd ruined it, of course. Now it was a place to watch the white dawn come up over the chimneys of Moscow, thin smoke standing motionless in the dead, frozen air.

Szara's interrogation – a form of debriefing for those cooperating with the special services – was the province of his official 'friend' in Moscow, Abramov. Nonetheless, an interrogation. And the fact that it was supervised by a friend made it, as the *apparat* intended, worse not better – a system that turned friends into hostages held against the subject's honesty. If you lied, and your interrogator believed it, and then they caught you lying, you were both finished: de facto conspirators. Maybe you didn't care to save your own miserable life, but perhaps you'd think twice about murdering a friend.

Szara lied.

Sergei Abramov lived in the higher reaches of the NKVD Foreign Department, a confidant of the godlings Shpigelglas and Sloutsky if not officially their equal. He would arrive at Szara's apartment every day at about eleven with egg sandwiches wrapped in newspaper, a paper sack of tea, sometimes vodka, occasionally little almond cakes with a sticky coating of honey that had you licking your fingers while you answered questions. He was a thickset, bulky man, handsome in his bulk, in a much-worn blue pinstripe suit, the jacket buttoned across his belly over a rippling vest with a gold watch chain stretched from pocket to pocket. Abramov had sharp eyes that caught the light, a broken nose, a black homburg that he never removed, and a full black beard that gave him the air of a successful operatic baritone – an artist used to getting his own way and certain to create havoc if he didn't. He would sit on a kitchen chair with his knees apart, place a cigarette between his lips, light it with a long, wooden match, then half close his eyes as he listened to you, apparently on the verge of sleep. Often he made a small noise, a grunt that might mean all sorts of things: sympathy – *what a time you've had of it* – or disbelief, perhaps an acknowledgment that what you said was true, perhaps the groan of a man too often deceived. It was in fact a stratagem, meant nothing, and Szara knew it.

Abramov spoke in a low, hoarse rumble, a voice rich with sorrow at having found all humankind to be the most absurd collection of liars and rogues. Posing a question, his face was filled with gloom. Like a teacher who knows his hopeless pupils will offer only wrong answers, Abramov was an interrogator whose subjects never told the truth. The method was ingenious. Szara understood and admired it but nevertheless felt the powerful undertow it created: he found himself wanting to please Abramov, to offer such resoundingly honest statements that the man's sour view of the world would be swept away by idealism reborn.

Alert to Abramov's dangerous gift, the ability to stimulate the essential human desire to please, Szara laid out his defences with care. To begin with, resistance. Later, a strategic submission, giving up everything but that which mattered most: Marta Haecht and all the signposts that pointed to her existence. Thus Szara's description of dinner

Ab[illegible]

Bloch and [illegible] the confessional, sta[illegible] of the interrogation to writing [illegible] Antwerp, an uneventful journey to Prag[illegible] in that city, and his rejected dispatch on the p[illegible] abandonment of Czechoslovakia. Baumann's revelation on the manufacture of swage wire he reported in perfect detail and was rewarded by a series of appreciative grunts. This ground was then covered a second time – Abramov's probing was artful, ingenious, a series of mirrors revealing every possible surface of the exchange. As for Khelidze, Szara described the conversations aboard the *Nicaea*, omitting their final confrontation in Ostend.

Until Monday of the second week, when Abramov began to show signs of restlessness. Interrogations always revealed something, something even better than a little orgy with a nightclub *animateur*. So? Where was it? Had he at last met a true saint? Szara caved in, warned elliptically that he now needed to say things that could not be said in a Moscow apartment. Abramov nodded sorrowfully, a physician coming at last upon the feared diagnosis, and touched his lips with his index finger. 'You've done well today, André Aronovich,' he said for the benefit of the listeners. 'Let us adjourn to the Metropol for a change of scenery.'

But, crunching through the fresh snow on Kusnetzki Most, they passed the Hotel Metropol and its popular café – where *apparat* operatives were in abundance – and entered instead a grimy hole-in-the-wall on a side street.

Abramov ordered *viesni*, parfaits ... pt,
chipped, greyish coffee cups but ... American
Szara told stage two: the ... ute discomfort.
the satchel, General Blo... per into the affair and
magazine editor. Abr... with pain, the encouraging
Every word of Sz... of horror, he signalled for more
he knew it – ... Yiddish, drummed his thick fingers on
grunts be... *viesni* ... op. When Szara finally wound down he sighed.
the ... 'André Aronovich, what have you done.'

Szara shrugged. How was he to have known that his orders did not come from Abramov or his associates? The second group based their play on that very assumption.

'I absolve you,' Abramov rumbled. 'But I am the least of your problems. I doubt the Georgians will shoot you in Moscow, but it would be wise to watch what you eat here, and stay away from high windows. It's a commonplace of ours; anyone can commit a murder, but suicide requires an artist. They have such artists. However, the fact that they've left you alone this long means they're scheming. This too they do very expertly. After all, they are our Sicilians, these southerners, and their feuds end only one way. Apparently, they have their own plans for the Okhrana material, and have not informed the Great Leader or his official toads; thus you remain alive. Of course, if you were to publish such an article . . .'

'Then what shall be done?'

Abramov rumbled.

'Nothing?'

Abramov thought for a moment, spooned the last of his *viesni* from the coffee cup. 'This *khvost* business is a little more complicated than meets the eye. Yes, things *have* happened, but. Instance: two years ago, at the trial of Lev Rosenfeld and Grigory Radomilsky – "Kamenev" and

"Zinoviev" – the prosecutor Vyshinsky, in his summation to the judges, said an odd thing, something that sticks in the mind. He called them "men without a fatherland." He would claim that he meant they'd betrayed, as Trotskyites, their country. But we've heard that kind of thing before, and we know what it means, just as it's said very openly in Germany, not so quietly in Poland, and has been said in all sorts of places for a very long time.

'Still, if somebody simply yearned to believe Vyshinsky, and such people exist, let them consider the case of the diplomat Rosengolts. They played with him like a cat with a mouse: released him from all official positions and let him stew for many weeks. He knew what was coming, for a certainty, but the *apparat* let it fester so that every day became a hundred hours long. This was hardest on his wife, a happy sort of person, not worldly, not so educated, from a typical *shtetl* somewhere in the Pale. Over a period of months, the waiting destroyed her, and when the NKVD searched Rosengolts after they finally got around to arresting him, they found she'd written out a charm against misfortune, the Sixty-eighth and Ninety-first psalms, secreted it within a piece of dry bread, wrapped it in a cloth, then sewed it into his pocket.

'At the trial, Vyshinsky made much humour of this pathetic little piece of paper. He read the psalms, such as, "For He shall deliver thee from the snare of the hunter: and from the noisome pestilence. He shall defend thee under his wings and thou shalt be safe under His feathers: His faithfulness and truth shall be thy shield and buckler. Thou shalt not be afraid for any terror by night: nor for the arrow that flieth by day." You see what she'd done. Vyshinsky spoke these words in a tone of savage contempt, then asked Rosengolts how the paper had got into his pocket. He admitted his wife put it there and told him it was for good luck. Vyshinsky pressed him on the point, mentioning "good luck" again and again, until the spectators in the court-room were roaring with laughter and Vyshinsky turned and winked at them.

'Very well, you'll say, the case is made. The purge is really a pogrom. But is it? Is this really true? Maybe not. The Section for Extraordinary Matters is headed by I. I. Shapiro – so if Jews are being purged, the purge is, often, guided by Jews. Now we come to the people who've involved you in their operation. General Bloch is a Jew, granted, though I should mention he is in military intelligence, the GRU, and not the NKVD – a fact you might keep in mind. Renate Braun is a German, likely from one of the Protestant sects, and she has nothing to do with the NKVD. She is a *spez* – a foreign specialist – employed by Mezhdunarodnaya Kniga, the State Publishing House, where she works on the publication of German texts to be smuggled into Germany. That clearly associates her with the Comintern.

'What I'm saying is this: consider the intelligence services as an ocean. Now consider the currents that might be found in it, some running one way, some another, side by side for a time, then diverging. So new? Nothing's new. It would be so at US Steel or the British telephone company. In work there is competition, alliance, betrayal. Unhappily, when an intelligence *apparat* plays these games, they are equipped with very sharp tools, vast and practical experience, and the level of play can be frightful. A journalist, any normal citizen, will simply be eaten alive. What do we have here? A political battle between nationalist interests? Or a pogrom? They're not the same thing.

'If a pogrom, a very quiet one. Of course Stalin cannot afford, politically, to estrange the Jews of the world because we have many friends among them. You know the old saying: *they join the ideology*. And now, with the birth of a hideous monster in Germany, they are mad to take action, any action, against fascism. This is, you understand, a useful circumstance for people in my profession. One can ask favours. Is Stalin capable of running a secret pogrom? Yes. And he would have to do it that way in the present political climate. Therefore, it's not so easy to pin down.

'Meanwhile, you. Drawn into an operation you cannot survive, yet I take it you wish to do so. You seem different, I might add. Changed. Not quite the cynical bastard I've known all these years. Why is that? All right, you had a close call; the Turk, Ismailov, almost did your business. Is that it? You looked death in the face and became a new man? Can happen, André Aronovich, but one sees that rarely, sometimes in a grave illness, where a man may ask a favour of his God, but less often in wet affairs. Still, it happened. I'm your friend. I don't ask why. I say what's to be done for poor André Aronovich?

'Now it would be normal to hand Baumann on to one of our operators in Germany – a thousand ways he can be run, even under present Jewish restrictions. He has a love affair, sees a dentist, goes to *shul*, takes a walk in the country and fills a dead-drop or visits his father's grave. Believe me, we can service him.

'On the other hand, we might make a case that he's skittish, nervous, not really committed, which in turn implies special needs in the selection of a case officer. What, in fact, are his motives? I might make a point of asking that question. Is he out to hurt Hitler? Or does he wish to feather a nest if things get worse in Germany? To aid the working classes? To get rich? *Mice*, we say of spies; the *m* stands for money, the *i* for ideology, the *c* for coercion, and the *e* for egotism. Which is it with Baumann? Or is there, we must ask, a fifth letter?

'Prove to me he's not the toy of the Abwehr, or worse, the Referat VI C of the Reichsicherheitshauptamt, the Main Security Office under that insufferable prick Heydrich. Referat VI C is Gestapo counterespionage both within and outside German borders, Walter Schellenberg's little shop, and Schellenberg is perfectly capable of this sort of dangle – he'll get hold of one end of the thread and pull so slowly and sweetly that you'll see an entire network unravel. Years of work wasted! And, in Moscow, careers destroyed. So I'm suspicious. My job depends on it. I'll surely point out that Szara can't be expected to know whether this is any good or it's the RSHA offering a temptation. What do we know? That a third secretary had a piece of paper slipped in his overcoat pocket while it was in the cloakroom of the opera house and he was suffering through three hours of Wagner. That a journalist had a dinner and heard a proposal and saw a piece of wire. What's that? That's nothing. We Russians have always favoured the *agent provocateur*, our intelligence history is crowded with them, and the Cheka learned the trick the hard way – from the Okhrana. Azeff, Malinovsky, maybe you-know-who himself. So, naturally, we fear it above all things for we know how well it works, how well it tickles our great vulnerability – intelligence officers are like men in love, they want to believe.

'What's the answer? What to do? Abramov is brilliant! *Let Szara do the work*, he says. Make him truly *nash*, our very own. He's been a journalist who does his patriotic duty and, from time to time, undertakes special work; now he'll be one of us, and now and then he'll write something. Kolt'sev, the editor of *Pravda*, is finished – sorry to tell you that, André Aronovich – and Nezhenko, the foreign editor, is no problem. We'll hook Szara up with one of the networks in Western Europe and let him play spymaster.'

Abramov settled back in his chair, put a cigarette in his mouth, and lit it with a long wooden match.

'Do you mean they won't find me in Europe?'

'They'll find you in *hell*. No, that's not what I mean. *We* become your protection, not this *khvost* and not that, the service itself. Your status will be adjusted and narrowly made known. I see Dershani every day, his office is down the hall from mine; we're both citizens of the USSR, we work in the same profession, and we don't shoot each other. I'll let him know, obliquely, that you're doing important work for us. So, hands off. That's an implicit promise from me, by the way, that you're going to be a good boy and not go off involving yourself in conspiracies and pranks. Understood?'

He did understand. Suddenly he stood on the threshold of a new life. One where he'd have to follow orders, trade freedom for survival, and live in a completely different way. Yes, he'd seen this opening after receiving information from Baumann, and quite smug he'd been about it. But the reality tasted awful, and Abramov laughed at his evident discomfort.

'This is a web you climbed into all by yourself, my friend; now don't go cursing the spider.'

'And shall I write for the American magazine?'

'After *I* have protected you? Well, that would be gratitude, wouldn't it. No good deed goes unpunished, Abramov, so here's a knife in the back for you. André Aronovich, you are forty years of age, perhaps it's time you grew up. Ask yourself: why have these people chosen me to do their dirty work? What will it accomplish? If the game is entirely successful and Soso – Joe – hurls himself out a Kremlin window, what is gained? Who takes over? Are you expecting some sort of Russian George Washington to appear? Are you? Look in your heart. No, forget your heart, look in your mind! Do you want to make Adolf Hitler happy? Why do you think anything will happen? Molotov will say "more imperialist lies" and the world will yawn, all except for one journalist, floating face down in a swamp somewhere so that nobody can see what a noble and superior smile he wore when he died.'

Szara felt miserable.

Abramov sighed. 'For the moment,' he said kindly, 'why not just do what everybody else in the world does. Try to get along, do the best you can, hope for a little happiness.' Abramov leaned across the table and patted him reassuringly on the cheek. 'Go to work, André Aronovich. Be a mensch.'

March 1938.

Winter would not go. At night the air froze and the stars did not shimmer, but stood as cold, steady lights in the distance. In the wind, the eyes ran, then tears turned to ice. Indoors it was not much better – when Szara woke in the morning his breath was a white plume against the dark blanket.

It was warmer in Central Europe: Hitler marched into Austria, France and Britain protested, crowds cheered in the Vienna streets, Jews were dragged from hiding, humiliated, and beaten. Sometimes they died from the beatings, sometimes from the humiliation. In Moscow, a new trial: Piatakov, Radek (Sobelsohn), Krestinsky, Yagoda, and Bukharin. Accused of conspiring with Nazi intelligence agents, accused of entering into secret agreements with the German government. The final sentence of Vyshinsky's summation had remained constant for three years: 'Shoot the mad dogs!' And they did.

Szara dragged himself through his days and drank all the vodka he could find, craving anaesthesia that eluded him; only the body went numb. He wanted to call Berlin but it was impossible – no words could leave Moscow. Slowly, the images of the attic room in the narrow house, too often summoned, lost reality. They were now too perfect, like mirages of water in the desert. Angry, lonely, he decided to make love to any woman who came along, but when he met women the signal system went awry and nothing happened.

At Abramov's direction, he attended a series of training schools – an endless repetition of dead-drops, codes and ciphers, forgery, and the construction of false identities. It was all about paper, he realized, a world of paper. Identity cards, passports, embassy cables, maps of defensive positions, order-of-battle reports. A mirror image of a former life, when he'd also lived amid paper.

Sometimes he wrote for Nezhenko; Abramov insisted on that. Stories about progress, always progress; life was getting better and better. What did such drudgery do to the secret spirit that he imagined lived deep within him? Curiously, nothing. For an hour or two it did what it had to do, then returned to its hiding place. He tried a version of 'The Okhrana's Mystery Man' and surprised himself, it positively *blazed*. He burned it.

He did see friends from time to time, those who remained, but no honest thing could be said and the accumulated caution and reserve strangled affection. Still, they met. Sometimes, finding themselves alone and unobserved, they spoke of what they'd seen and heard. Horror stories; separations, disappearances, failures of nerve. The light had gone out, it seemed, the very notion of heroism excised, the world now filled with soft, bruised, frightened people scheming over a few lumps of coal or a spoonful of sugar. You caught fear from friends, like a malady, and they caught it from you, and nobody suggested a cure.

Abramov was a rock, and Szara clung to him like a drowning man. They would sit in a warm office in Dzerzhinsky Square and the officer would teach him what he had to know. The principles of the work couldn't be spelled out precisely, you had to listen to anecdotes until you had an intuitive feel for what was effective and what wasn't. They discussed cities – some operations in Germany were run from neighbouring countries, which meant cities like Geneva, Paris, Luxembourg, Amsterdam, Brussels. Prague was no longer a possibility. Warsaw was extremely dangerous; the Polish services were powerful and deft, had an astute understanding of Soviet operational habits. Brussels was best – espionage, as long as it wasn't aimed at the Belgian government, wasn't even illegal.

Sometimes Abramov took him to meet people; these were momentary, casual occasions, a handshake, a few minutes of conversation. He had the impression of individuals who instantly knew who you were, what you were. He met Dershani in his office: a plain desk, filing cabinets, a dead flower in a glass. The man himself was exceptionally polite; the thin lips smiled. 'I'm very pleased to meet you,' he said. Szara thought about that later. The face was memorable – like looking at a hawk, it was the quality of the eyes that held your attention, suggested a world where they had seen things you hadn't.

He kept busy in the daytime, but the nights were not good. When the icy March snow rattled on the window he'd bury himself in blankets and clothing and sometimes his dead wife would visit him, and he would talk to her. Out loud. Talk to an empty room, in a certain quiet, definite language they had devised, a language meant to exclude the world from the fortress of sanity they had built to protect themselves.

They had been married – some might say 'married' – by a Red Army major in 1918. 'Be as one with the new order' was the way he'd blessed the union. Three years later she was dead, and they'd often been separated during that period by the exigencies of civil war. Working as a nurse in the Byelorussian town of Berdichev, she'd written him every day – notes scrawled on newsprint or scraps of paper – then sent a packet through when the postal system functioned. Byelorussia and the Ukraine were then, as always, the storm centres of madness. During the civil war, Berdichev was taken fourteen times, by Petlyura's army, by Denikin's, by Bolshevik units, by Galician irregulars, Polish infantry, Tutnik's bands, Maroussia's rebels, the anarchists under the insane Nestor Makhno – whose cavalry favoured Jewish prayer shawls as saddlecloths – and by what the writer Grossman referred to as 'nobody's Ninth Regiment.' Eventually, somebody had killed her, exactly who or where or under what circumstance he'd never learned.

Despite the long separations, there had been an iron bond between them, as though they were twins. There was nothing he feared to tell her, and nothing she did not understand. In the Moscow nights that March he needed her desperately. It was insane to speak out loud in the empty little apartment – he feared the neighbours, denunciation, so he used his softest voice – but he could not stop doing it. He asked her what to do. She told him to live a day at a time, and to be kind. Somehow this eased his heart and he could fall asleep.

There was one event that month which was to mean a great deal to him later, though at the time it had no special significance. It seemed just one more manifestation of the Great Inexplicable that lay at the heart of Russia, something you had to get used to if you meant to hang on to your sanity in that place. Nezhenko invited him to a semiofficial evening at the Café Sport on Tverskaya street. This was principally a gathering of Moscow's foreign community, so there was plenty of food and plenty to drink. At the height of the evening, conversation was quieted by somebody banging a spoon on a glass, then a well-known actor rose to present a recitation. Szara knew him slightly, Poziny, a barrel-chested man with a deeply lined face who played character roles in the Moscow Art Theatre – Szara had seen him do a splendid Uncle Vanya that had brought the audience to its feet for the curtain call.

To cries of Oop-la! a grinning Poziny was hoisted atop a table by the wall. He cleared his throat, gathered the audience to him, then announced he would recite a work by Aleksandr Blok, written in the early days of the Revolution, called *The Scythians*. The Scythians, he explained for the benefit of foreign guests, were the earliest Russian tribe, one of the world's most ancient peoples, known for intricate goldworking and exemplary horsemanship, who inhabited a region north of the Black Sea. While Poziny introduced the poem, several young men and women distributed translations in French, English, and German so that the guests could read along.

Poziny held nothing back. From the first line on, his powerful voice burned with conviction:

> There are millions of you; of us,
> swarms and swarms and swarms.
>
> Try and battle against us.
> Yes, we are Scythians; yes, Asiatics,
> With slanting, greedy eyes.
> . . . Oh, old world
>
> Russia is a Sphinx. In joy and grief,
> And pouring with black blood,
> She peers, peers, peers at thee,
> With hatred and with love.
>
> Yes, love, as only our blood can love,
> You have forgotten there can be such love
> That burns and destroys.
>
> Come to our side. From the horrors of war
> Come to our peaceful arms;
> Before it is too late, sheathe the old sword.
> Comrades, let us be brothers.
>
> And if not, we have nothing to lose.
> We, too, can be perfidious if we choose;

And down all time you will be cursed
By the sick humanity of an age to come.

Before comely Europe
Into our thickets and forests we'll disperse,
And then we shall turn upon you
Our ugly Asiatic face.

But we ourselves henceforth shall be no
  shield of yours,
We ourselves henceforth will enter no battle.
We shall look on with our narrow eyes
When your deadly battles rage.

Nor shall we stir when the ferocious Hun
Rifles the pockets of the dead,
Burns down cities, drives herds into churches,
And roasts the flesh of the white brothers.

This is the last time – bethink thee, old world! –
To the fraternal feast of toil and peace,
The last time – to the bright, fraternal feast
The barbarian lyre now summons thee.

There were several very long seconds of silence; only Poziny's graceful inclination of the head summoned applause that resolved the tension in the room. Everyone there knew what the poem meant, in the early days of the revolution and in March of 1938. Or thought they knew.

The Austrian chemical engineer H. J. Brandt arrived in Copenhagen on the Baltic ferry *Krøn Lindblad* from Tallinn, Estonia, on 4 April 1938.

The school teacher E. Roberts, from Edinburgh, took the Copenhagen-Amsterdam train, arriving at Amsterdam's Central Station in the early evening of 6 April.

The naturalized Belgian citizen Stefan Leib, of Czechoslovakian origin, got off the Amsterdam train at Brussels toward noon on 7 April, going immediately to the shop called Cartes de la Monde – maps of the world; antique, old, and new – he owned in the rue de Juyssens, in the winding back streets of the old business district.

A serious man, Monsieur Leib, in his early thirties, quiet, somewhat scholarly in his tweed jacket and flannels, and notably industrious. He could be found, most nights, in the small office at the rear of the store at a large oak desk piled high with old maps – perhaps the Netherlands of the seventeenth century, decorated with curly-haired cherubs puffing clouds of wind from the cardinal points of the compass – as well as utilitarian road maps of the Low Countries, France, and Germany; tidal charts, Michelin and Baedeker guides, or the latest rendering of Abyssinia (important if you had followed the fortunes of Italian expeditionary forces), Tanganyika, or French Equatorial Africa. Whatever you might want in cartography, Monsieur Leib's shop was almost sure to have it.

On the evening of 12 April, those with an eye for moderately prominent journalists might have spotted Monsieur Leib out for dinner with A. A. Szara, recently assigned to the Paris bureau of *Pravda*. Spotted, that is, if one happened to visit a very dark and out-of-the-way Chinese restaurant, of dubious reputation, in the Asian district of Brussels.

In the end, Abramov and his associates had not made a choice of cities or networks for Dr Baumann's case officer. Life and circumstance intervened and chose for them. Even the multiple European networks of the Rote Kapelle – the Red Orchestra, as the German security services had nicknamed them – were not immune to the daily vicissitudes and tragedies that the rest of the world had to confront. In this instance, a deputy officer of the Paris-based OPAL network, work name Guillaume, was late for a clandestine meeting established in Lyon – one of his group leaders from Berlin was coming in by train under a cover identity – and drove recklessly to avoid having to wait for a fallback meeting three days later. His Renault sedan failed to make a curve on the N6 just outside Mâcon and spun sideways into a roadside plane tree. Guillaume was thrown clear and died the next day in the hospital in Mâcon.

Captain I. J. Goldman, *rezident* of OPAL under the painstakingly crafted cover of Stefan Leib, was brought back to Moscow by a circuitous route – 'using passports like straw,' grumbled one of the 'cobblers' who manufactured or altered identity papers at the NKVD Foreign Department – for lengthy consultations. Goldman, son of a Marxist lawyer from Bucharest, had volunteered for recruitment in 1934 and was, following productive service in Spain, something of a rising star.

Like all *rezidents*, he hated personnel problems. He accepted the complicated burdens of secrecy, a religion whose rituals demanded vast expenditures of time, money, and ingenuity, and the occasional defeat managed by the police and counterespionage forces that opposed him, but natural disasters, like road accidents or wireless telegraph breakdowns, seemed especially cruel punishments from heaven. When a clandestine operator like Guillaume met an accidental death, the first thing the police did was to inform, or try to, a notional family that didn't exist. Had Goldman himself not contacted hospitals, police, and mortuaries in the region, Guillaume might have been determined a defector or runaway, thereby causing immense dislocation as the entire system was hurriedly restructured to protect itself.

Next, Goldman had to assure himself, and his directorate in Moscow, that the accident *was* an accident, an investigation complicated by the need to operate secretly and from a distance. Goldman, burning a cover identity that had cost thousands of roubles to construct, hired a lawyer in Mâcon to make that determination. Finally, by the time he arrived in Moscow, he was able to defend himself against all accusations save one: his supervision had been lax to the degree that one of his staff drove in an undisciplined manner. On this point he criticized himself before his superiors, then described countermeasures – lectures, display of the autopsy report obtained by the Mâconnais lawyer – that would be undertaken to eliminate such events in the future. Behind their stone faces, the men and women who directed OPAL laughed at his discomfort: they knew life, love affairs, bizarre sexual aberrations, lost keys, gambling, petty jealousies; all the absurd human horseshit that network *rezidents* had to deal with. They'd learned to improvise, now it was his turn.

When they were done scowling, they gave him a choice: elevate the Paris group leader to Guillaume's position or accept a new deputy. This was no choice at all, group leaders were infamously difficult to replace. On their ability to stroke and soothe, wheedle, nag, or threaten, everything depended. He could, on the other hand, accept a new deputy, the journalist Szara, an amateur 'who had done a few things with fair success.'

Goldman would have preferred experienced help, perhaps transferred from what he believed to be less crucial networks, for OPAL ran some fourteen agents in France and Germany and would now service a fifteenth (Baumann, officially designated OTTER), but the purges had eaten down into the *apparat* from the top and operationally sophisticated staff simply wasn't available. It was arranged for him to meet with Szara, who would work with a co-deputy in OPAL but would essentially be on his own in Paris while Goldman, as 'illegal' *rezident*, worked in protective isolation in Brussels. In the end he put a good face on it and indicated he was pleased with the arrangement. Somewhere, operating deep within the committee underbrush, there was a big, important rat who wanted Szara in Paris – Goldman could smell him.

Then too, for Goldman, it was best to be cooperative; his rising star was lately a little obscured, through no fault of his own, by a dark cloud on the horizon. His training class, the Brotherhood Front of 1934 – in fact a fractious crowd recruited from every lost corner of the Balkans – was not turning out as senior *apparat* people thought it would. A distressing number of the 'brothers' had left home; some defected, harbouring far less fraternal affection than their Russian family had supposed. The undisputed leader of the class, a Bulgarian, had vanished from Barcelona and resurfaced in Paris, where he'd become entangled in émigré politics and got himself arrested by French internal security officers in July of '37. A Serbian had disappeared back into the mountains of his homeland after a very complex exfiltration from a Spanish prison – a dreadful instance of ingratitude, though it was the NKVD that had shopped him to Franco's military intelligence in the first place, expedient neutralization after he resisted an order to purge POUM members in his guerrilla unit. And a Hungarian from Esztergom, worthless to the *apparat* from day one, had also fled to Paris where, hiding out in a Montmartre hotel, he'd apparently been murdered by a merchant seaman. What had *he* been involved in? Nobody knew.

Given that chamber of horrors, Goldman would be saying *yes sir* to senior officers for the foreseeable future. Privately, he had grave misgivings about André Szara. The journalist seemed both arrogant and insecure – a normal enough combination but potentially lethal under the stresses of clandestine work. Goldman was familiar with Szara's writing, he thought it sometimes powerful, almost always informative. But Goldman had been in the business just long enough to fear the creative personality. He'd developed a taste for blunt, stolid types, unemotional, who worked day and night without coming down with fevers, men and women who didn't nurse grudges, who preferred verification to intuition, were endlessly dependable and there when you needed them, could think on their feet in a crisis, *recognized* a crisis when one developed, and had the sense to ask you what to do when they weren't sure. Careers were made with such people. Not with the André Szaras of the world. But he was stuck, in no position to argue, and so he'd do the best he could.

Over the ghastly chop suey in Brussels, Goldman told him, '*Be* a journalist!'

What?

'Well, you are one, of course, very good, yes, but you must now make a special effort to live the life, and to be seen to live the life, one would expect of such a person. Go about, seek out your colleagues, haunt the right cafés. No slinking around, is what I mean. Of course you'll see the necessity of it, yes?'

Goldman made him mad, pointing this out. It was true that he'd habitually avoided journalists' haunts and parties and gone off on his own. For one thing, it didn't pay to be too friendly with Western Europeans – the lead diva of the Moscow Opera had been sent to the camps for dancing at a party with the Japanese ambassador. For another, he forever had to accomplish some special little task for the *apparat*. Such things took time, care, patience. And you didn't want colleagues around when you did it. *So, General Vlasy, the tread problem on the new R-20 tank turns out to be no problem at all, eh?* and all that sort of thing, certainly *not* with some knowing fellow journalist suppressing a cackle in the background.

Szara never really did respond to Goldman's direction. He looked at the grey noodles on his plate for a moment, then went on with the conversation. Inside he was broiling. Wasn't he unhappy enough about mortgaging his soul to Abramov and secretly abandoning his profession? Apparently not. They now laid upon his heart a heaping tablespoon of Russian irony, directing him to act more like what he no longer was. All this from some snotty little Romanian who thought he spoke idiomatic Russian, was very much his junior in age, and looked like (and probably acted like) some kind of rodent. Small eyes that glittered, ears a little too big, features set close together. Like a smart mouse. Maybe too smart. Who the hell did he think he was?

Back in Paris the following day, however, he kept his opinions to himself. 'You've met Yves,' said his fellow deputy, using Goldman's work name. 'What do you think?'

Szara pretended to ponder the question. He did not want to commit himself, but neither did he want to seem like a spineless idiot – he was going to have to work closely with this woman. She was the sort of individual who, in the setting of a business office, might well be known as *a bit of a terror*. Abramov had warned him about her: work name – Elli, real name – Annique Schau-Wehrli, reputation – lioness. In person she turned out to be fiftyish, short, stout, with a thrust-out bosom like a pouter pigeon and glasses on a chain around her neck. She wore a built-up shoe on one foot and walked with a cane, having been born with one leg shorter than the other. Szara found himself drawn to her – she was magnetic, perceptive, and also rather pretty, with rosy complexion, light, curly hair, a screen siren's long eyelashes, and omniscient eyes lit by a brisk, cheerful hatred.

She was an ardent, blistering Marxist, a former pillar of the Swiss Communist party from a wealthy bourgeois (and long ago rejected) family in Lucerne. She had a tongue like a sword, spoke six languages, and feared absolutely nothing. In Paris, she worked as office manager and resident saint for a League of Nations satellite office, the International Law Institute, which issued oceans of studies attempting to encourage the countries of the world to normalize and standardize their legal codes. Wasn't the theft of a female ancestor's soul in Nyasaland much the same, when all was said and done, as a stock swindle in Sweden?

'Well?' she repeated. 'Don't tell me you have no opinion of the man. I won't believe you.'

They were in her living room, a typical Parisian concoction of rich red draperies, silk pillows, naked gold women holding ebony-shaded lamps above their heads, and little things – ashtrays, onyx inkwells, ivory boxes, Gallé bottles, and porcelain bull terriers – on every shelf and table. Szara kept his elbows jammed well against his sides.

'Young,' he said.

'Younger than you.'

'Yes.'

'Brilliant, my dear comrade.'

'Glib.'

'Boof!' she said, a Gailic explosion of incredulous air. 'But how can you be like this? Measured any way you like, brilliant. Against the norm? Genius. Recall the Russian operative who went to London last year, pockets just stuffed with British pounds. He is there two days, ventures from his hotel for the first time. Persuaded by Soviet propaganda, he actually believes that the English working classes are so poor they wear paper shoes. He suddenly spies a shop window full of leather shoes, not at all expensive. *Ah-ha*, says he, my lucky day, and buys ten pairs. Then, at another store, *look, they too have shoes today!* He thinks his dear departed mother is sending down gifts from heaven. Again, ten pairs. And so on, until the poor soul had over a hundred pairs of shoes, no money for party work, and the MI5 surveillance team is practically rolling on the pavement. Just wait and see what some of our people can do, then you'll change your tune.'

Szara pretended to be slightly abashed. He was the new boy in the office, he had to make a decent impression, but he'd known Goldman's type before: a genius all right, a genius for self-advancement. 'I suppose you're right,' he said amiably.

Friday, the last week in April, in a warm, gentle rain that shone on the spring leaves of the boulevard trees, Szara booked a telephone call to Marta Haecht's magazine office in Berlin.

Twenty minutes later he cancelled it.

The gospel according to Abramov: 'Look, you can never be sure what they know about you, just as they can never be sure what we know about them. In times of peace, the services do two things in particular, they watch and they wait. This is a war of invisibility, fought with invisible weapons: information, numbers, wireless telegraph transmissions, social acquaintance, political influence, entrée to certain circles, knowledge of industrial production or infantry morale. So, show me an infantry morale. You can't. It's intangible.

'Counterintelligence operations are the most invisible of all. The people who run them don't want to neutralize their opponents – not right away. Some boss is screaming *stop it! stop it!* and his operatives are pleading *no. We want to see what they do*. For you it means this: you have to assume you have typhoid, you're infectious, and anyone you meet or know gets the disease. Whether this meeting is innocent or not, they must fall under suspicion if a third party is watching. You wonder why we recruit friends, family, lovers? We might as well – they're going to be considered guilty anyhow.'

The seed Abramov planted in Moscow grew a frightful garden in Paris. It grew in Szara's imagination, where it took the form of a voice: a quiet, resourceful voice, cultured, sure of itself, German-speaking. It was the voice of presumed surveillance, and when Szara contemplated something foolish, like a telephone call to Germany, it spoke to him. *28 April. 16:25.* SZARA (the flat, official format would be similar to DUBOK's file and Szara imagined the German officer to be not unlike the author of the Okhrana dossier) *telephones* MARTA HAECHT *at Berlin 45.633; conversation recorded and currently under analysis for code or Aesopian language.*

Aesopian language suggested reality with symbolism or implication. Are you still studying French? I sent you a card from Paris – did you receive it? I'm writing a story about the workers who built the Gare du Nord. I don't know where the time goes, I have to finish the piece by noon on the fourth of May.

It fooled nobody.

Even if *the voice* did not yet speak, Szara feared discovery. By 1938, Germany had been converted into a counterespionage state. Every patriotic German took it as his or her duty to inform the authorities of any suspicious behaviour, denunciation had become a national mania – *strangers visited them, a curious sound from their basement, a printing press?*

Of course he considered using the network for communication. This would either evade all suspicion or end in absolute tragedy. A lover's choice, *nyet?* Passion or death. They had described to him the details of what the Gestapo actually did, *kaschumbo*, whips soaked in pails of water. The idea of exposing her to that . . .

He worked.

The Parisian spring flared to life – one hot morning and

all the women were dressed in yellow and green, on the café terraces people laughed at nothing in particular, aromas drifted through the open doors of bistros where the owner's briard flopped by the cash register, a paw over its nose, dreaming fitfully of stock bones and cheese rinds.

The OPAL network was run from a three-storey building near the quais of the canal Saint-Martin and the canal de l'Ourcq, at the tattered edge of the nineteenth arrondissement where the streets around the Porte de Pantin turned to narrow roads leading into the villages of Pantin and Bobigny. A pulsating, sleepless *quartier*, home to the city's slaughterhouses as well as the stylish restaurants of the avenue Jean-Jaurès, where partygoing swells often ventured at dawn to eat fillet of beef baked in honey and avoid the tourists and taxi drivers down at Les Halles. Paris put things out there she wasn't sure whether she wanted or not – the Hippodrome where they held bicycle races and boxing matches, an infamous *maison close* where elaborate exhibitions could be arranged. In spring and fall, fog rose from the canal in the evening, the blue neon sign of the Hôtel du Nord glowed mysteriously, slaughterhouse workers and bargemen drank *marc* in the cafés. In short, a *quartier* that worked all night long and asked no questions, a place where the indefatigable snooping of the average Parisian wasn't particularly welcome.

The house at 8, rue Delesseux was crumbling brown brick like the rest of the neighbourhood, dirty and dark and smelling like a *pissoir*. But it could be entered through a street-level door, through a rear entrance to the *tabac* that occupied its tiny commercial space, or through an alley strewn with rags and broken glass that ran at an angle to the rue des Ardennes. It was handy to barges, a cemetery, a park, nameless village lanes, a sports arena, restaurants crowded with people – just about every sort of place that operatives liked to use.

The top floor of the house provided living and working space for the OPAL encipherer and wireless telegraph operator, work name François, true name M. K. Kranov, an 'illegal' with Danish passport, suspected to hold NKVD officer rank and, likely, the *apparat* spy reporting secretly to Moscow on the activities and personnel of the network.

On the second floor lived 'Odile,' Jeanne de Kouvens, the network's courier who serviced both Goldman in Brussels and the networks in Germany, the latter a twice-monthly run into Berlin under the pretext of caring for a nonexistent mother. Odile was Belgian, a tough nineteen-year-old with two children and a philandering husband, not a bit beautiful but violently sexy, her hair cut in a short, mannish cap – the street kid look – her cleft chin, swollen upper lip, tip-tilted nose, and indomitable eyes tossing a challenge at any man in the immediate vicinity. Her husband, a working-class fop with bushy, fin de siècle muttonchop whiskers, ran a portable merry-go-round that circulated through the neighbourhood squares of Paris. The *tabac* on the ground floor was served by Odile's brother, twenty years older than she, who had been wounded at Ypres and walked with the aid of two canes. He spent his days and nights on a stool behind the counter, selling Gitanes and Gauloises, Métro tickets and postage stamps, lottery chances, pencils, commemorative key rings, and more, an astonishing assortment of stuff, to a steady trickle of customers who created camouflage for operatives entering and leaving the house.

The Moscow Directorate had shuffled assignments to make life a little easier for Szara, putting Schau-Wehrli in charge of the three German networks, HENRI, MOCHA, and RAVEN, which left him with SILO, assigned to attack elements of the German community in Paris, and Dr Julius Baumann.

* * *

Spring died early that year, soft rains came and went, the sky turned its fierce French blue only rarely, a mean little wind arrived at dusk and blew papers around the cobbled streets. The end of April was generally admitted to be *triste*, only the surrealists like such unhappy weather, then summer came before anybody was really ready for it. The rising temperature seemed to drive the politicians further from sanity than usual.

Nobody could agree about anything: the Socialists had blocked a rearmament programme in March, then the Foreign Office claimed the French commitment to Czechoslovakia to be 'indisputable and sacred.' One senator pleaded for pacifism in the morning, called for preservation of the national honour in the afternoon, then sued the newspaper that described him as ambivalent. Meanwhile, senior civil servants demanded things of their mistresses that caused them to raise their eyebrows when they had their girlfriends in for coffee. Nobody was comfortable: the rich found their sheets scratchy and carelessly ironed, the poor thought their *frites* tasted of fish oil.

On the top floor of the house at 8, rue Delesseux, the afternoons grew hot as the sun beat on the roof; the dusty window shades were never raised, no air stirred, and Kranov worked at a large table with his shirt off. He was a small, sullen man with curly hair and Slavic features who seemed, to Szara, to do nothing but work. All OPAL transmissions, incoming and outgoing, were based on one-time pads, encrypted into five-digit numerical groups, then transformed – using a changing mathematical key and 'false' addition (5 + 0 = 0) – by a second encryption. Brief, pro forma transmissions were fleshed out with null groups to avoid the type of message that had always been the cryptanalyst's point of attack. From Egyptian times to the present, the phrase used to break codes never varied: *nothing new to report today*.

Szara usually slipped into the house at night. In Kranov's transmitting room a blanket was nailed across the window, a tiny lamp used for illumination. Swirls of cigarette smoke hung in the air. Kranov's fingers jittered on the telegraph key, the dots and dashes flowing through the ether to a code clerk on Dzerzhinsky Square in Moscow:

91464 22571 83840 75819 11501

On other frequencies, a French captain in the Naval Intelligence section at Sfax, on the Tunisian coast, requested Paris to approve additional funds for Informant 22, the third secretary of the Czechoslovakian embassy in Vienna reported on private meetings held by the Sudeten leader Henlein with German diplomats in the spa town of Karlsbad, the Polish service in Warsaw asked an operative in Sofia to ascertain the whereabouts of the priest JOSEF. All night long the W/T operators *played their pianos*, not only for the Rote Kapelle, but in a hundred orchestras performing for scores of espionage *Konzertmeisters* from a dozen countries. Szara could hear it. Kranov let him put the earphones on and turn the dial. It was a theatre of sound, pitched treble or bass, quick-fingered or deliberate, an order to liquidate an informer or a request for the local weather forecast. Sometimes crackling with the static of an electrical storm in the Dolomites or the Carpathians, sometimes clear as a crystal chime, the nightlong symphony of numbers flew through the darkened heavens.

If there was no *critical/immediate* signal, Kranov broke out Moscow's transmissions after he woke from a few hours' sleep. Szara fancied it a kind of critical daylight that inevitably followed the coded mysteries of the night. Slowly, as May turned to June, and the sweat soaked through Kranov's undershirt in the morning heat, Szara began to gain a sharper appreciation of the interplay between OPAL and its masters, the simply phrased requests for information and the terse responses now resolved to a dialogue from which the mood of the Directorate could be read.

Moscow was restless. It had been so from the beginning. Abramov, sacrificing information in the hope of enforcing discipline, had let Szara know just exactly what he would be dealing with. Emphatically *not* Nezhenko – or any editor. Both Abramov and his *khvost* rival Dershani sat on the OPAL Directorate, as did Lyuba Kurova, a brilliant student in neuropathology in the years before the revolution, a ruthless Chekist in Lenin's terror campaign, now, in her forties, a friend of Poskrebyshev, Stalin's personal secretary; also Boris Grund, an *apparatchik*, an experienced technician, and a majority voter in every instance, and Vitaly Mezhin, at thirty-six years of age quite young for the work, a member of the generation of 'little Stalins' who crept into the power vacuum created by the purge, as the Big Stalin intended them to do. 'If you wilfully disobey an order,' Abramov said, 'this is who you disobey.'

Szara now saw that Dr Baumann made them uncomfortable: (1) He was a Jew in Germany, his future gravely insecure. (2) His motives were unknown. (3) His product was crucial. Szara could imagine them, seated at a table covered with a green baize cloth, flimsies of decrypted signals arranged at every place, smoking nervously at their stubby Troika cigarettes, speaking so very carefully, conscious of nuance in themselves and others, groping toward a protective consensus.

Swage wire figures for January, February, March, and April received, projections from orders on hand for May. Case officer asked to obtain listing of company personnel, especially in accounting office. Characterize: age, political affiliation, cultural level. They clearly wanted Baumann to get to work finding his own replacement. It was up to Szara to find some sort of honey to make him swallow that pill.

Of course they wanted more than that – Dershani in particular thought Baumann ought to be pumped dry, the quicker the better. He must know other subcontractors – who were they? Could they be approached? If so, how? What were their vulnerabilities? Then too – Mezhin now took his turn, you didn't want to be a wilting flower in this crowd – what of his association with senior officers of Rheinmetall? Might there not be something for them in that? Boris Grund thought this line productive. And what was Baumann paying for austenitic steel? Grund said his pals downstairs in the Economic Section were starving for such information, maybe we should toss them a bone.

Kurova didn't like the dead-drop. They'd got the Baumanns to buy a dog, a year-old schnauzer they named Ludwig, so that Baumann could be out on the street at night and use a stone wall near his house as a letter-box. This brought Odile, in a maid's uniform, into the neighbourhood two or three times a month to drop off mail and collect a response. A bent nail in a telephone pole was used as a signal: head turned up told Baumann to collect, head turned down confirmed that his deposit had been picked up. All according to standard form and practice, Kurova acknowledged. But Germans were naturally curious, they stared out their windows, and they had an insatiable appetite for detail. *Why does Dr Baumann reach behind the stone in Herr Bleiwert's wall? Look how poor little Ludwig wants only to play*. Kurova just didn't like it. Both operatives were too much in the open.

Dershani agreed. What about a restaurant, something in the industrial neighbourhood where the wire mill was located?

Abramov thought not. As a Jew, Baumann's activities were limited – he couldn't just go to a restaurant. This would be noticed.

The factory, then, Mezhin offered. Best of all, could

they reach the engineer Haecht, who would, according to Szara, be nominally in control of the business as new anti-Jewish statutes were promulgated. They looked in their dossiers. They had a blurry photograph of Haecht, taken by an officer from the Berlin embassy. University records. Exemplar of handwriting. Inventory of family: wife Ilse, son Albert a pharmaceutical salesman, daughter Hedwig married to an engineer in Dortmund, daughter Marta an assistant art editor at a literary magazine.

Literary magazine? Perhaps a friend of ours, Dershani wondered idly.

Perhaps, Kurova admitted, but nice German girls don't go to factories.

Slow and easy, Abramov counselled, we don't want to create a panic.

This is no time for caution, Dershani said.

That was true.

Baumann's product *was* crucial. They had other sources of information on the German aircraft industry, but none that determined the numbers quite so exactly. The Directorate that handled the product coming in from Burgess and Philby and others in Great Britain confirmed the OPAL Directorate's hypotheses, as did sources in the French services. The German industrial machine was building a nightmare.

Baumann had shipped 14,842 feet of swage wire in October; this meant a monthly bomber production rate of 31 planes. From there they could project, using range and load factors already in their possession. The German bomber force as constituted in a theoretical month – May of 1939, for instance – would be able to fly 720 sorties in a single day against European targets and deliver 945 tons of bombs, causing a projected 50 casualties per ton – a total of almost 50,000 casualties in a twenty-four-hour period. A million casualties every three weeks.

And the USSR, Great Britain, and France were in absolute harmony on one basic assumption: *the bomber would always get through*. Yes, antiaircraft fire and fighter planes would take their toll, but simply could not cause sufficient damage to bring the numbers down.

The Russians, using their British spies, had followed with interest developments in British strategic thinking in the last month of 1937. The RAF experts had urged building up the British aircraft industry to deliver heavy bombers to match the German numbers, ultimately to create a counterweight of terror: you destroy our cities, we'll destroy yours. But the cabinet had overruled them. Said Sir Thomas Inskip: 'The role of our air force is not an early knockout blow . . . but to prevent the Germans from knocking us out.' This was not the usual thinking, but the cabinet, in the end, had determined the defensive system a better option, and British industry began to build fighters instead of bombers.

In Germany, also, a strategic decision was made, though this one rested on Hitler's power. When the Reich marched into the Rhineland in 1936 and opposition did not materialize, the German General Staff lost credibility. Hitler was right. It was proven. Soon thereafter, he turned his attention to Hermann Göring's Luftwaffe. Where, Hitler wanted to know, are my aeroplanes? Göring felt the pressure, and took steps to protect himself. Germany stopped production of four-engined bombers, the Dornier Do-19 and the Junkers Su-89. Those planes could operate at greater distances, in England or the USSR, and stay longer over target, as well as extend the air cover provided to U-boat packs beset by sub chasers or destroyers, but they were not going to be built. Driven by Hitler's impatience, Göring directed the aircraft industry to build twin-engined bombers. 'The Führer,' Göring said, 'does not ask me *what kind* of bombers I have. He simply wants to know *how many*.' The comment was believed to be private.

It wasn't.

And that was the point. The Moscow Directorate had to know what Göring said, and what the British cabinet thought, and had to do whatever, *whatever*, had to be done in order to know. In the same complex of buildings where the OPAL Directorate met, other groups laboured to keep Germany and Great Britain from finding out what Stalin said, or what the Politburo thought. That work, though, was none of their business. Their business was *a million casualties every three weeks*. With a threat of that dimension, how carefully could Dr Julius Baumann be treated? They had to, as Dershani counselled, take their chances, and if the man went slack with terror or rigid with fury it was Szara's job to handle him. If Szara couldn't do it, they'd find somebody who could. They were not in a position to be gentle with spies, even less with case officers.

'Then we are agreed,' Kurova said. There were stern nods of assent around the table.

That night, the W/T operator in Dzerzhinsky Square settled in on his frequency at 1:33 A.M., Moscow time, as scheduled for that date. He discovered a neighbour, some plodding fool out there somewhere, sending five-digit groups as though he had all eternity to get the job done. The operator swore softly with irritation, caressed his dial until he found a private little band of silent air, then began a long signal to his nameless, faceless, yet very familiar colleague in Paris. *Paris*, he thought, *a city I'll never see*. But that was fate. So, instead, he put a bit of his soul into the telegraphy, flying ghostlike across the sleeping continent along with his secret numbers.

* * *

Goldman had said, '*Be* a journalist!' so Szara did what he asked, but he didn't like it. He found a large, gloomy room on the rue du Cherche-Midi (literally, the street that looked for the sun, which it rarely found), midway between brawling Montparnasse and fashionably arty Saint-Germain; coming out of his doorway he turned right to buy a chicken, left to buy a shirt. He drank wine and ate oysters at the Dôme, a noisy barnyard of artists and artistes, the people who came to look at them, predators scenting the money of the people who came to look at them, *petits-bourgeois* celebrating their anniversaries and saying 'Ah!' when the food came to the table, and – he only grew aware of them with time – a surprisingly large number of reasonably appealing and attractively dressed people of whom one couldn't say more than that they ate at the Dôme. Simply Parisians.

Szara attended the occasional session of the Senate, dropped in at the trial of this week's murderer, browsed the women in bookstores, and showed up at certain *salons*. Where journalists were, there was André Szara. He passed through the *Pravda* office from time to time, collected a phone message or two, and if with some frequency he disappeared completely from sight for a day or two, well, so did many people in Paris. Szara was running an espionage network, God only knew what the rest of them were doing.

On the days when Ilya Ehrenburg wasn't in town, André Szara was the preeminent Soviet journalist in Paris. The city's hostesses made this clear to him – 'It's terribly late, I know, but could you come? We'd so love to have you!' He went, and Ehrenburg was never there. Szara had been called in as a last-minute substitute, *the* Soviet Journalist in the room, along with the Tragic Ballerina, the Rich American Clod, the Knave of Attorneys, the Sexually Peculiar Aristocrat, the Cynical Politician, and all the rest – like a pack of tarot cards, Szara thought. He much preferred relaxed social evenings at friends' apartments, spontaneous gatherings rich with combative exchanges on politics, art, and life, at the Malrauxs' on the rue du Bac, sometimes at André Gide's place on the rue Vaneau, occasionally at Ehrenburg's apartment on the rue Cotentin.

He was jealous of Ehrenburg, who occupied a position above him in the literary and social order of things, and when they did meet, Ehrenburg's kindness and courtesy toward him only made it worse. Not the least of the problem was Ehrenburg's writing itself – not so much the diction, but the sharp eye for a detail that told a story. Reporting from the civil war in Spain, Ehrenburg had described the different reactions of dogs and cats to bombing attacks: dogs sought safety by getting as close to their masters as they could, while cats went out the window and as far from humans as possible. Ehrenburg knew how to capture the reader's emotions better than he did, and now that he'd effectively left the competition, such good Ehrenburg stuff as he saw in print depressed him. There were rumours that Ehrenburg did favours for the *apparat*, but if he did, Szara had no evidence of it; and suspected that Ehrenburg's contacts were up in the Central Committee, well beyond his own reach.

One Thursday night in May, Szara dropped around to Ehrenburg's apartment to discover André Gide, under full throttle in a lengthy discourse on some point of literary philosophy. To drive home his point, Gide picked up a dog biscuit from a plate on the kitchen table and used it to draw lines in the air. Ehrenburg's dog, a terrier-spaniel mix called Bouzou, studied the progress of the biscuit for a time, then rose in the air and snapped it neatly out of Gide's fingers. Unperturbed, Gide picked up another biscuit and continued the lecture. Bouzou, equally unperturbed, did it again. A girl sitting near Szara leaned over and whispered, '*C'est drôle, n'est-ce pas?*'

Oh yes. Very funny.

Upstaged by Ehrenburg's dog, he thought, and immediately hated himself for thinking such things. *Ingrate! Listen to what Gide is saying, how mankind thrashes amid life's futility; how his tragi-comic destiny is, may be described as, has always been, will always be . . . some French word I don't know. Ah, but everybody is smiling wisely and nodding, so it's evidently a stunning insight.*

Such evenings. Wine and oysters. Frosted cakes. Aromatic women who leaned close to say some almost intimate little thing and brushed one's shoulder. The old Szara would have been lighthearted with ecstasy. Not all was roses, of course. The city was famous for its artful, petty humiliations – had not Balzac fashioned a career from such social warfare? – and Szara knew himself to be the sort of individual who took it to heart, who let it get into his bloodstream where it created malicious antibodies. Nonetheless, he told himself, he was lucky. Two thirds of the Russian writers were gone in the purges, yet here he was in Paris. That all the world should have no more problems than the envy of a fellow journalist and the obligation to do a bit of nightwork!

He looked at his watch. Stood, smiled genially, and turned to go. 'The witching hour, and the mysterious Szara leaves us,' said a voice.

He turned and made a helpless gesture. 'An early day tomorrow,' he said. 'A scene observed at dawn.'

A chorus of good nights and at least one disbelieving snicker accompanied him out the door.

He strolled a few blocks toward the edge of the seventh arrondissement, idling, crossing and recrossing a boulevard, then flagged a cab from the line at the Duroc Métro and sped to the Gare Saint-Lazare. Here he rushed through the station – *late for a train* – then found another taxi at the rue de Rome exit and gave his destination as the Gare d'Austerlitz. 'No hurry,' he said to the driver. 'There's something extra for you if we just wander a bit.' A novel instruction, but heeded, and as the cab meandered eastward Szara slumped lazily in the back seat, a posture that allowed him to watch the street behind him in the driver's rearview mirror. He changed cabs again at the Austerlitz station, then paid off the new driver on the boulevard de la Gare and crossed the Seine, now at the eastern edge of Paris where the railway tracks ran south-east between the Gare de Lyon and the wine *commerçants'* warehouses in the Bercy district. He had become, in the course of these clandestine exercises, what he thought of as *the other Szara*, a midnight self, a figure in a raincoat on a bridge above the Bercy marshalling yards, avoiding the yellow flare of a street lamp. *And here*, he thought, *Monsieur Gide, Monsieur Ehrenburg, Master Bouzou, we have quite another sort of antidote to the futility of existence.* A goods train chugged slowly under the bridge, the white steam from its engine spilling over the rampart as it passed beneath him. He liked the burned smell of the railway yards, the distant crash of couplings, the bright steel maze of rails that merged and parted and merged again, the hiss of decompression from an idling locomotive. He glanced at his watch, one-twenty, strolled casually – a reflective man thinking things over – to the end of the bridge. Reached the street just as a boxy Renault puttered to a stop. The passenger door opened and he swung smoothly into the front seat, the car accelerating onto the empty boulevard as he closed the door. It was well timed, he thought, quite artistic in its own way.

'*Et bonsoir, mon cher*,' said the driver cheerfully. He was the SILO group leader, Robert Sénéschal, the very perfection of the young, French, communist lawyer. Like so many French men, he seemed theatrically suited to his role in life – the spiky hair, acerbic smile, pigskin gloves, and upturned raincoat collar would have quite pleased a film director. Szara was drawn to him. Sénéschal's charm, his throwaway courage, reminded him of his own style ten years earlier: committed, self-assured, amused by the melodrama of clandestine life yet scrupulously meeting its demands.

Szara reached into the glove compartment and withdrew a thick manila envelope. He unwound the string and riffled through a sheaf of paper, squinting in order to make out the writing in the glow of the boulevard street lamps. He held up a page with twelve words on it, enormous letters fashioned in a torturous scrawl. Slowly, he tried to decipher the German. 'Can you make any sense of this?'

'A letter from the sister, it seems.'

'He steals a bit of everything.'

'Yes. Poor ALTO. He takes whatever feels important to him.'

'What is *Kra . . . Krai . . .*'

'*Kraft*, I think. *Kraft durch Freude*. "Strength through Joy," the Nazi recreation clubs for workers.'

'What's it to do with anything?'

'I managed to work my way through all of it. The sister in Lübeck is taking a cruise to Lisbon on one of the chartered liners they have, it's only costing a few reichsmarks, how she looks forward to it after the demands of her job. ALTO offers as well the telephone numbers of procurement specialists in the attaché's office.'

'That they'll like. As for the letter . . .'

'I'm just the postman,' Sénéschal said. He turned into the traffic *ronde-point* at the place Nation. Even though the May night was chilly, the terraces of the brasseries were crowded, people drinking and eating and talking, a white blur of faces and amber lights as the Renault swept past. Sénéschal moved up on the bumper of a rattletrap market truck in front of him, preventing an aggressive Citroën from cutting in. 'So much for you,' he said triumphantly.

ALTO was a sixteen-year-old boy known as Dolek, a Slovak nickname. His mother, whom Sénéschal had secretly observed and termed 'ravishing,' lived with a German major who worked in the office of the military attaché. They'd begun their love affair when the major was stationed in Bratislava and stayed together when he was transferred to Paris. The child of a previous love affair, Dolek suffered from a disease of the nervous system: his speech was slurred and difficult to understand, and he hobbled along with one arm folded against his chest while his head rested on his collarbone. His mother and her lover, intoxicated by the physical perfection of their own bodies, were sickened by his condition and ashamed of him, and kept him out of sight as much as they could. They treated him as though he were retarded and did not understand what they said about him. But he was not retarded, he understood everything, and eventually a desperate anger drove him to seek revenge. Left alone in the apartment, he copied out, as best he could and with immense effort, the papers the major brought home and left in a desk drawer. He made no distinctions – thus the letter from the sister – if the major treated the paper as private, Dolek copied it. Some months after the move to Paris he'd been locked in the apartment while his mother and the major spent a weekend at a country house. He'd got the door open and dragged himself to Communist party headquarters, where a young nurse, busy making banners for a workers' march, had listened sympathetically to his story. Word of the situation had then reached Sénéschal, who'd visited the boy while the mother and her lover were at work.

Szara sighed and stuffed the paper back in the envelope. The Renault turned up a dark side street and he could see into an apartment with open drapes, lit in such a way as to make the room seem suffused with golden light. 'Are you still taking Huber to Normandy?' he asked.

'That's the plan,' Sénéschal said. 'To make love, and eat apples in cream.'

Szara reached into an inside pocket and handed a wad of fifty-franc notes across the gearshift. 'Go to a nice restaurant,' he said.

Sénéschal took the packet. 'I thank you,' he said lightly.

'We want you to know you're appreciated.' Szara paused. 'I don't suppose you actually have much feeling for her.'

'It's *curieux*, if you want the truth. The fat little Nazi maiden squirming away . . . one closes one's eyes with passion.'

Szara smiled. Sénéschal clearly didn't mind all that much, yet there was a melancholy note of martyrdom in his voice, *that the world should come to this*. 'The broad masses stand and applaud as you build socialism.'

Sénéschal laughed and Szara was gratified that the joke worked. Being funny was easily the most difficult trick of all in a foreign language, sometimes the French just stared at him in palpable confusion – what *did* this man mean?

Lötte Huber was a chubby German woman employed as a clerk at the German Trade Mission. Working with his lawyer friend Valais, who helped various German enterprises with residence permits and the infinite complexities of French bureaucracy, Sénéschal had 'met' Huber by sitting next to her and a girlfriend at the theatre. During the intermission the four of them got to talking, then went out for drinks after the play. Sénéschal had presented himself as a young man of wealthy and aristocratic family, seduced the clerk, eventually proposed marriage. To his fury, his unseen 'parents' categorically rejected the match. He then estranged himself from his family, abandoning the vast inheritance that awaited him, sacrificing all for his darling

Lötte. He determined, once the dust settled, to make his own way in life, supposedly obtaining employment as a minor functionary in the French Foreign Office. But they could only, he told her, afford to get married if he were able to advance himself, which he would certainly do if she would supply helpful information about German Trade Mission business and personnel. In love, she told him all sorts of things, more than she could have understood, for the Gestapo intelligence service, the SD, used jobs at the Mission as cover for operatives – individuals seen to have contacts well beyond the scope of commercial affairs.

When this information was added to what Valais supplied – new arrivals needing *cartes de sejours* – the *apparat* was able to track German intelligence officers with considerable efficiency, leading to knowledge of French traitors, operations run against third countries, and insights into German objectives both in France and several other countries in Europe. Sénéschal had more than earned his weekend in Normandy.

The money was not at all a bribe – Sénéschal was motivated by idealism – but rather recognition that a group leader simply hadn't the time to earn much of a living for himself.

Sénéschal rolled down the window of the Renault and lit a cigarette. Szara closed the envelope and checked the signs on corner buildings to see what street they were on – anywhere but the neighbourhood of the rue Delesseux base would serve his purposes. Sénéschal was essentially the cut-out; the people he worked with did not know of Szara's existence, and he himself knew Szara only as 'Jean Marc,' had no idea of his true name, where he lived or the location of radios or safe houses. Meetings were arranged at different sites every time, with fallbacks in case one party or the other failed to show up. If the network were closed down, Sénéschal would appear three times at various places, nobody would be there to meet him, and that would be the end of it. The *apparat* could, of course, find him again if they wanted to.

Preparing to disengage, Szara asked, 'Anything you want or need?'

Sénéschal shook his head. He seemed to Szara, at that instant, a man perfectly content, doing what he wished to do without reservations, even though he could not safely share this side of his life with anyone. There were moments when Szara suspected that many idealists drawn to communism were at heart people with an appetite for clandestine life.

Szara said, 'The LICHEN situation remains as before?' LICHEN was a prostitute, a dark, striking woman of Basque origin who had fled north from the civil war in Spain. The intention was to use LICHEN to entice low-level German staff into compromising situations, but she had yet to produce anything beyond free sexual entertainment for a few Nazi chauffeurs.

'It does. Madame has the clap and will not work.'

'Is she seeing a doctor?'

'Being paid to. Whether she actually does it or not I don't know. Whores do things their own way. The occasional dose gets them vertical for a while, and she really doesn't seem to mind.'

'Anything else?'

'A message for you was left at my law office. It's in with the reports.'

'For me?'

'It says Jean Marc on the envelope.'

This was unusual, but Szara did not intend to go burrowing for the message in front of Sénéschal. They drove in silence for a time, up the deserted boulevard Beaumarchais past the huge wedding cake of a building that housed the Winter Circus. Sénéschal flipped his cigarette out the window and yawned. The light changed to red and the Renault rolled to a stop beside an empty taxi. Szara handed over a small slip of paper with the location, time, and date of the next meeting. 'Enjoy your weekend,' he said, jumped out of the Renault, and slid neatly into the back of the taxicab, slightly startling the driver. 'Turn right,' he said as the light went green, then watched as Sénéschal's car disappeared up the boulevard.

It was a little after three in the morning when Szara slipped into the rue Delesseux house and climbed to the third floor. Kranov was done with his W/T chores for the evening and Szara had the room to himself. First he found the envelope with Jean Marc printed across the front. Inside was a mimeographed square of paper with a drawing of a bearded man in Roman armour, a six-point star on his shield and a dagger held before him. The ticket entitled the bearer to Seat 46 in the basement theatre at the Rue Muret Synagogue at seven-thirty in the evening of the eighteenth day of the month of Iyyar, in the year 5698, for the annual Lag b'Omer play performed by the synagogue youth group. The address was deep in the Marais, the Jewish *quartier* of Paris. For those who might need a date according to the Julian calendar, a rather grudging 18 May was written in a lower corner.

Szara tucked it in a pocket – really, what would they think of next. A communication travelling upward from a network operative to a deputy was something he'd never heard of, and he rather thought that Abramov would go a little pale if he found out about it, but he was becoming, over time, quite hardened to exotic manifestations, and he had no intention of permitting himself to brood about this one. He had a ticket to a synagogue youth play, so he'd go to a synagogue youth play.

A thin sheet of paper bearing decrypts from the previous night's Moscow traffic awaited his attention, and this he did find disturbing. The problem wasn't with the SILO net – some of the answers to the Directorate's questions were probably in the manila envelope he'd picked up from Sénéschal – but the transmission that concerned OTTER, Dr Baumann, worried him. Moscow wanted him squeezed. Hard. And right away. There was no misreading their intention, even in the dead, attenuated language of decoded cables. At first glance, it seemed as though they wanted to turn Baumann Milling into what the Russians called an *espionage centre* – why else show such a profound interest in personnel? Because, if you thought about it a moment, they expected a conflagration. Soviet intelligence officers were not queasy types. Disaster only made them colder – that he'd seen for himself. The Foreign Department of the NKVD – now called the First Chief Directorate – had a hundred windows on Germany. What did they see coming? Whatever it was, they didn't believe that Baumann would survive it.

With some effort he recaptured his mind and forced himself to go to work, emptying the manila envelope on the table. Valais's list of German applications for residence permits presented no problems, he simply recopied it. Sénéschal's material from ARBOUR, Lötte Huber, was brief and to the point, the lawyer had essentially synthesized what he got and in effect done Szara's job for him: the German Trade Mission was probing the French markets for bauxite (which meant aluminium, which meant airframes), phosphorus, (flares, artillery shells, tracer bullets), cadmium (which meant nothing at all to him), and assorted domestic products, notably coffee and chocolate. From ALTO, Dolek, he would pass on the revised telephone directory of the attaché's office but would eliminate the major's letter from his sister in Lübeck. For himself, he informed the Directorate that he'd met with the SILO group leader, disbursed funds, and learned that LICHEN was not functioning due to illness.

Next he tore up the SILO originals, burned them in a ceramic ashtray, then walked down the hall and flushed the ashes down the toilet. Almost anyone who came in contact with the espionage world was told the story of the beginner operative who'd been instructed to either burn his papers or tear them into bits and flush them down the toilet. An anxious sort, he'd become confused, crumpled up a large wad of paper and dropped it in the toilet, then put a match to it and watched, aghast, as the flames set the toilet seat on fire.

Back in the W/T office, the big alarm clock by Kranov's work area said it was four-fifteen in the morning. Szara sat at the table and lit a cigarette; the darkened window hid any change of light, but he could hear a bird start up outside. He thought of the hundreds of operatives all across Europe who had finished with their nightwork, as he had, and now fell prey to the same predawn malaise: useless white energy, a nagging sense of some nameless thing left undone, a mind that refused to disengage. Sleep was out of the question.

He squared up the pad of flimsy paper and began to doodle. The memory of Dolek's handwriting, the enormous letters painfully carved into the paper with successive jerks of the pencil, would not leave his mind. Nor would the substance of the letter, especially the Strength through Joy cruise. His imagination wandered, picturing the sort of German worker who would sail off for Lisbon.

Dearest Schätzchen – Little Treasure – he wrote. *I wish to invite you on a special outing arranged by my Kraft durch Freude club.*

He went on a bit with it, mawkish, blustering, then

signed it *Hans*. Changed that to *Hansi*. Then tried *Your Sweet Hansi*. No, too much. Just *Hansi* would do.

What would Marta do if she got such a letter? At first she'd think it was a practical joke, tasteless, upsetting. But what if he crafted it in such a way that he made it clear, to her, who was writing? Odile could drop it in a letter box in Hamburg, that would bypass the postal inspectors who processed all foreign mail. He could address it to her personally and sign with a meaningful alias. She could sail to Lisbon on such a cruise. He had to consider it carefully, a lot could go wrong.

But, in principle, why not?

The evening of 18 May was cool and cloudy, but the basement of the Rue Muret Synagogue was warm enough for the women in the audience to produce scented handkerchiefs from their shiny leather handbags. It was not, Szara discovered, an extremely Orthodox synagogue, nor was it quite as poor as it first seemed. Buried deep in the gloom of a twisting little street in the Marais, the building seemed to sag in every possible direction, its roofline jagged as though scribbled on paper. But the basement was packed with well-dressed men and women, probably parents of the children in the play, their relatives and friends. The women seemed more French than Jewish, and though Szara had taken the precaution of buying a yarmulke (let the Moscow Directorate reimburse him for *that*), there were one or two men in the audience with uncovered heads. Certain cars parked outside, half on the narrow pavement, indicated to Szara by their licence plates that some members of the congregation were now doing well enough to live just outside Paris, but retained a loyalty to the old synagogue on the rue Muret, a street that retained a distinct flavour, and aroma, of its medieval origins.

Szara expected to recognize the occupant of Seat 47 or

45, but the place to his right was more than filled by a bulky matron in diamond rings while to his left, on the aisle, sat a dark, teenage girl in a print dress. He had arrived early, been handed a playbill, and waited patiently for contact. But nobody showed up. Eventually, two droopy curtains creaked apart to reveal ten-year-old Pierre Berger, in cardboard armour, as Bar Kochba, the Jewish rebel of Judea in A.D. 132, in the act of recruiting his friend Lazar for service against the legions of the Emperor Hadrian.

BAR KOCHBA (pointing at the roof): Look, Lazar! There, in the east. There it is!
LAZAR: What do you see, Simon Bar Kochba?
BAR KOCHBA: I see a star. Brighter than all others. A star out of Jacob.
LAZAR: As in the Torah? 'A star out of Jacob, a sceptre out of Israel'?
BAR KOCHBA: Yes, Lazar. Can you see it? It means we shall free ourselves from the tyrant, Hadrian.
LAZAR: Always you dream! How can we do this?
BAR KOCHBA: By our faith, by our wisdom, and by the strength of our right hand. And you, Lazar, shall be my first recruit, but you must pass a test of strength.
LAZAR: A test?
BAR KOCHBA: Yes. Do you see that cedar tree over there? You must tear it from the earth to prove you are strong enough to join our rebellion.

As Lazar strode across the stage to a paper cedar pinned to a clothes tree, a grandmother's aside was stilled by a loud 'Shhh!' Lazar, a stocky, red-cheeked – the makeup artist had been a little overenthusiastic with the rouge – child in a dark blue tunic, huffed and puffed as he struggled with the clothes tree. Finally, he lifted it high, shook it at Bar Kochba, and laid it carefully on its side.

The play, *A Star out of Jacob*, proceeded as Szara, from his own days at the *cheders* in Kishinev and Odessa, knew it had to. A curious holiday, Lag b'Omer, commemorating a host of events all across the span of Jewish tradition and celebrated in a variety of ways. It was sometimes the Scholars' Festival, recalling the death of Rabbi Akiva's students in an epidemic, or the celebration of the first day of the fall of Manna as described in the Book of Exodus. It was a day when the three-year-old children of Orthodox Jews got their first haircuts or a day of weddings. But in Szara's memory of eastern Poland, it was particularly the day that Jewish children played with weapons. Toy bows and arrows long ago, then, during his own childhood, wooden guns. Szara perfectly remembered the Lag b'Omer rifle that he and his father had carved from the fallen branch of an elm tree. Szara and his friends had chased each other through the mud alleys of their neighbourhoods, street fighting, peering around corners and going 'Krah, krah' as they fired, a fairly accurate approximation by kids who had heard the real thing.

These children were different, he mused, more sophisticated, miniature Parisians with Parisian names: Pierre Berger, Moïse Franckel, Yves Nachmann, and, standing out sharply from all the others, the stunning Nina Perlemère, as Hannah, inspiring the Bar Kochba rebels when they are reluctant to creep through the underground passages of Jerusalem to attack the legionnaires, sweeping her cardboard sword into the sky and slaying Szara entirely with her courage.

HANNAH: Let there be no despair. First we will pray, then we will do what we must.

This one, pretty as she was, was the warrior: her lines rang out and produced a scattering of spontaneous applause, causing a Roman centurion in the wings to peer around the curtain through blue-framed eyeglasses. There was a slight disturbance to Szara's left as the dark girl in the print dress moved up the aisle and was replaced by General Yadomir Bloch. He reached over and took Szara's left hand in his right for a moment, then whispered, 'Sorry I'm late, we'll talk after the play.' This produced a loud 'Shh!' from the row behind them.

Through the dark streets of the Marais, Bloch led him to a Polish restaurant on the second floor of a building propped up by ancient wooden beams braced against the pavement. The tiny room was lit by candles, not for atmosphere but – Szara could smell the paraffin they were using for the stove – because there was no electricity in the building. Squinting at the menu written in chalk on the wall, they ordered a half bottle of Polish vodka, bowls of tschav – sorrel soup – a plate of radishes, bread, butter, and coffee.

'The little girl who played Hannah,' Bloch said, shaking his head in admiration. 'There was one like that in Vilna when I was a boy, eleven years old and she drew every eye. You didn't mind coming to the play?'

'Oh no. It brought back the past. Lag b'Omer, playing guns.'

'Perfect, yes, I intended it so. Soviet Man this, Soviet Man that, but we mustn't forget who we are.'

'I don't think I ever forget, comrade General.'

Bloch tore a strip of crust from the brown loaf, trailed it through his soup, leaned over his bowl to eat it. 'No? Good,' he said. 'Too many do. A little hint of pride in one's heritage and somebody screams *bourgeois nationalism! Take the Zionist away!*' Having finished the bread, he wiped his mouth with a small cloth napkin, then began an expedition through his pockets, finally retrieving a folded page torn from a journal, which he opened carefully. 'You know Birobidzhan?'

'Yes.' Szara smiled grimly. 'The Jewish homeland in Siberia – or so they insisted. Lenin's version of Palestine, to keep the Zionists in Russia. I believe some thousands of people actually went there, poor souls.'

'They did. A sad place, surely, but effective propaganda. Here, for instance, is a German Jew writing on the subject: "The Jews have gone into the Siberian forests. If you ask them about Palestine, they laugh. The Palestine dream will have long receded into history when in Birobidzhan there will be motorcars, railways and steamers, huge factories belching forth their smoke. . . . These settlers are founding a home in the taigas of Siberia not only for themselves but for millions of their people. . . . Next year in Jerusalem? What is Jerusalem to the Jewish proletarian? Next year in Birobidzhan!"'

Szara raised his glass in a mock Seder toast and drank off the vodka. Bloch folded his paper back up and put it in his pocket. 'It would be funnier if people didn't believe it,' Bloch said.

Szara shrugged. 'Bundists, communists, socialists left and right, three kinds of Zionists, and mostly, when all is said and done, people in the shtetls of the Pale who say *do nothing, wait for the Messiah*. We may not own anything to speak of, but we are wealthy when it comes to opinions.'

'So, you must have one too.'

Szara thought for a moment. 'For centuries we have run around Europe like scared mice, maybe it's time to at least consider a hole in the wall, especially lately, as the cat population seems to be on the rise.'

Bloch seemed satisfied. 'I see. Now, to a tender subject. You have, one is told, a splendid opportunity to write something for an American magazine, but nothing appears. Perhaps others counsel you not to do it. Maybe somebody like Abramov, a man you admire – admire, come to that – convinces you that it's r worth it. He takes you under his protection, he sol problems with the Georgians, he makes life possible. If it's that, well, you've made a decision and, really, what can I do about it. On the other hand, maybe there's something you need, maybe I can be of assistance. Or not. It's for you to say. At worst, a little play from the synagogue youth group and a plate of nice tschav – not a wasted evening at any rate.'

'Comrade General, may one ask a frank question?'

'Of course.'

'What, actually, is the nature of your business?'

'That's a good question, I'll try to answer it. The truth is I'm in several businesses. Like you, like all of us, I was in the paradise business. We got rid of the czar and his pogroms to make a place where Jews, where everyone, could live like human beings and not like slaves and beasts – that's one definition of paradise and not a bad one. This paradise, we soon saw, needed a few willing souls to serve as guardians. Isn't that always the way with paradise? So I offered my humble services. Thus my second business, one could say, became the GRU, the military intelligence business. In this choice I was guided by the example of Trotsky, who became a soldier when he had to and did pretty well at it. And yet, even so, paradise slipped away. Because now we have a new pogrom, run, like so many in history, by a shrewd peasant who understands hatred, who knows its true value and how to use it.

'There is a trick, André Aronovich, played on us through the centuries and now played again: the Jew is accused of being cunning, by someone a thousand times more cunning than any Jew has ever been. So, sorrowfully, this problem has become my third business, and now I'm taking you out to theatre and dinner in a businesslike sort of way and trying to interest you in becoming an associate. What do I offer my associates? A chance to save a few Jewish lives, never a commodity with much value, but then Jews have always found their way to such enterprises – they deal in cheap stuff: old rags, scrap metal, bones and gristle, whatever, like themselves, people don't really want. And that's all, frankly, that I can offer you. Is it dangerous? Oh yes. Could you die? It's likely. Will your heroism be known to history? Very doubtful. Now, have I successfully persuaded you to throw everything you value in life away and follow this peculiar, ugly man over the nearest horizon to some dreadful fate?'

General Bloch threw his head back and laughed – it was unfettered, infectious. Szara joined in, was then unable to stop. People at other tables turned to look at them, smiling nervously, a little frightened to be trapped in a tiny Polish restaurant with a pair of madmen. Neither of them could have explained it. They had, somehow, in this strange, hidden, broken building, caught the tail of absurdity, and the thrash of it made them laugh. 'God forgive me,' Bloch said, wiping his eyes with his hand, 'for enjoying such a life as much as I do.'

A good laugh. A successful laugh. For it prevented Szara from actually having to answer Bloch's question, from saying *no* immediately. Later they walked to the Métro together. Bloch kept coming back to the play. Oh the little girl who played the part of Hannah, what was her name? Perlemère? Yes, he was sure Szara had it right, a few months on the front lines and already he had the operative's trained memory. Perlemère, mother-of-pearl, like Perlmutter in German. Where did Jews get these names? But, under any name at all, wasn't she a treasure.

Weren't they all.

Even those in Russia. Not so quick and clever as these

children, perhaps, but bright and eager, little optimists, knock them down and they bounce. Szara surely knew them: the sons and daughters of the Jews in the universities, in the state bureaus and the diplomatic corps, yes, even in the security services.

Those children. The ones who no longer had homes or parents. The ones who ate from garbage cans in the darkness.

Long after Bloch left him, Szara continued the conversation with himself.

A writer once again, Szara sat at his kitchen table at noon; through the open window he could smell lunch being cooked in the other apartments on the courtyard. When it was served, he could hear the sounds of knives and forks on porcelain and the solemn lilt of conversation that always accompanied the midday meal.

He would write the story.

Then he would have to disappear. For, under NKVD scrutiny, a nom de plume would not protect him for long.

So, where did one disappear to these days? America. Shanghai? Zanzibar? Mexico?

No, America.

You met people in Moscow now and then who'd gone off to America – the ones who had come back to Russia. That little fellow who'd worked in a tie factory. What was his name? At some party somewhere they'd been introduced. Szara remembered a face soured by despair. 'Hat in hand,' he'd said. 'Always hat in hand.'

Szara was haunted by that image, and now it coloured his vision of the future. He saw himself with Marta Haecht, they were hand in hand like fugitives in a storybook. The mad run from Paris at midnight, the steamship boarded at Le Havre. Ten days in steerage, the Statue of Liberty, Ellis Island. New York! Vast confusion, adrift in a sea of hopes and dreams, the sidewalks jammed with his fellow adventurers, everybody could be a millionaire if they tried. The pennies scraped together for the new suit, the offices, editors, lunches, encouragements, high hopes, then, ultimately . . . a janitor.

A janitor with an alias. A *nom de mop*. A cartoon capitalist with a cigar loomed up before him: 'You, Cohen, you call this floor clean? Lookit here! And here!' Hat in hand, always hat in hand. The obsequious immigrant, smiling and smiling, the sweat running from his armpits.

But what would he do in Shanghai? Or Zanzibar? Where, in fact, *was* Zanzibar? Or did it exist only in pirate movies?

On the table before him sat a secondhand Underwood, bought at a junk shop, some vanished novelist's golden calf, no doubt. Poor thing, it would have to be left on a street corner somewhere; it too would have to run away once it wrote forbidden words in its own, very identifiable handwriting. Szara stabbed idly at the keyboard with his index fingers, writing in Polish, putting in accents with a sharp pencil.

To the musical clatter of lunchtime in the courtyard, André Szara wrote a magazine story. *Who was the Okhrana's mysterious man? Certain documents are said to exist . . . revolutionary times in Baku . . . intrigue . . . rumours that won't die . . . perhaps high in the Soviet government today . . . tradition of the agent provocateur, Roman Malinovsky who rose to be head of the Bolshevik party in the Russian Duma was known to have been an Okhrana agent and so was the engineer Azeff, who actually led the Battle Organization of the Socialist Revolutionary party and personally organized the bomb assassination of the minister of the interior, Plehve, in 1904 . . . banished to Siberia . . . records said to have been burned in 1917, but did they get them all? Will we ever know for certain*

. . . secrets have a way . . . once the identity is known . . . that the course of history will once again be altered, perhaps violently, by the Okhrana's mysterious man.

In personal code, Szara had the address in a little book. He found an envelope and typed across the front Mr Herbert Hull, Editor, and the rest of it. The following morning would be time enough to put it in the mail. One always liked to let these articles settle a bit, to see later on, with fresh eyes, what might need changing.

That evening he took a long walk. If nothing else, he owed himself some serious thinking. Perhaps he was letting fate decide, but, if he was, it did. Paris chose that night to be rather a movie of itself. An old man was playing a concertina and a few aristocrats were dancing in the street – the French were tight as fiddle strings until they decided to let loose, and then they could be delightfully mad. Or, perhaps, it was a day for some special little ritual – they arrived frequently and Szara never knew exactly what was going on – when everybody was expected to do the same thing: eat a particular cake, buy a prescribed bouquet, join open-air dancing on the boulevards. Some street corner toughs; wide jackets, black shirts, white ties, their shoulders hunched a certain way, beckoned him over, then stood him a Belgian beer at a corner bar. A girl with blond hair flowing like the wind floated by him and said some deliciously indecipherable thing. It made him want the girl in Berlin – to live such a night unshared was a tragedy. It stayed light forever, a flight of little birds took off from the steeple of a church and fled northwards past the red-stained clouds in a fading sky. So lovely it hurt. He walked past the Santé prison, looked up at the windows, wondered who might be watching this same sky, could taste the freedom in his own life. He stopped for a sausage in a small French loaf, bought from an old lady in a windowed booth. The old lady gave him a look, she knew life, she had him figured out, she knew he'd do the right thing.

Odile returned from her courier run on 12 June. The product generated by the Berlin networks, as well as OTTER material from Dr Baumann, was photographed on microfilm in the basement of a Berlin butcher shop; the spool was then sewn into the shoulder pad of Odile's suit jacket for the German border crossing and the train ride back to Paris. By the morning of 13 June the film had been developed, and Szara, working at the rue Delesseux house, had an answer to his carefully phrased – *peripheral data*, he'd been told to call it, as though nobody really cared – request for identification of Baumann Milling office workers and sketches of their personalities. Baumann's response was brusque:

> FINAL PRODUCTION FOR MAY WAS 17715. WE PROJECT JUNE AT 20588 BASED ON ORDERS AT HAND. THE OTHER DATA YOU REQUEST IS NOT PER OUR AGREEMENT. OTTER.

Szara was not pleased by this rejection but neither was he surprised. A week earlier, he'd made a day trip to Brussels and conferred with Goldman, a discussion that had prepared him for what the *rezident* suspected might happen, and set up his return message. This he wrote on a sheet of paper that would find its way to Baumann on Odile's next trip to Berlin:

> WE HAVE RECEIVED YOUR MAY/JUNE FIGURES AND ARE APPRECIATIVE AS ALWAYS. ALL HERE ARE CONCERNED FOR YOUR CONTINUED HEALTH AND WELL-BEING. THE ANNOTATED LIST IS NEEDED

TO ASSURE YOUR SECURITY AND WE URGE YOU STRONGLY TO COMPLY WITH OUR REQUEST FOR THIS INFORMATION. WE CAN PROTECT YOU ONLY IF YOU GIVE US THE MEANS TO DO SO. JEAN MARC.

Untrue, but persuasive. As Goldman put it, 'Telling somebody that you're protecting him is just about the surest way to help him see that he's threatened.' Szara looked up from his plate of noodles and asked if it in fact were not the case that Baumann was in peril. Goldman shrugged. 'Who isn't?'

Szara took another piece of paper and wrote a report to Goldman, which would then be retransmitted to Moscow. He assumed that Goldman would, in the particular way he chose to put things, protect himself, Szara, and Baumann, in that order. The message to Goldman went to Kranov for encryption and telegraphy late that night.

Szara checked his calendar, made a note of Odile's 19 June courier run, Moscow's incoming transmission, and his next meeting with Sénéschal – that afternoon, as it happened. He squashed out a cigarette, lit another. Ran his fingers through his hair. Shook his head to clear it. Times, dates, numbers, codes, schedules, and somebody might die if you made a mistake.

New piece of paper.

He'd acquired from the Lisbon port authority the expected arrival date, 10 July, of a Strength through Joy cruise from Hamburg. Figuring from Odile's 19 June courier mission, he saw that Marta could just make it if there was room on the boat. For an hour he worked on the letter. It had to be sincere; she had great respect for honesty of a certain kind, yet he knew he mustn't gush. She would hate that. He tried to be casual, *let's enjoy ourselves*, and romantic, *I do need to be with you*, at the same time. Difficult. Suddenly he sat bolt upright.

How on earth could he find a German stamp in Paris? He would have to ask Odile to buy one when she got off the train in Berlin. Should he confide in her? No, better not. He was the deputy director of the net, and this was simply another form of communication with an agent. Even love had become espionage, he thought, or was it just the times he lived in? That aside, when was his meeting with Sénéschal? Where was it? He had it written down somewhere. Where? Good God.

4:20 P.M. The racetrack at Auteuil. By the rail, facing the entrance to Section D. A well-conceived location for a *treff* – shifting crowds, anonymous faces – except if it was raining, which it was. Szara saw immediately that he and Sénéschal would wind up standing together, isolated, in the view of thousands of people with sense enough to move into the shelter of the grandstand.

Such tradecraft, he thought, whistling loudly to catch Sénéschal's attention as he emerged from the entry gate. Silently they climbed to the last row of the grandstand as a few horses splattered mud on each other at the far turn of the oval track. '*Allez* you shithead,' said a dispirited old man in an aisle seat.

Szara was by nature acutely aware of shifts in mood, and he sensed Sénéschal's discomfort right away. The lawyer's tousled hair was soaked, a damp cigarette hung from his lips – nobody liked getting wet, but there was more to it than that. His face was pale and tense, as though something had broken through his insouciant defences and drained his optimism.

For a time they watched galloping horses, a primitive loud-speaker system crackled and popped, the muffled voice of an excited Frenchman could just barely be made out as he called the race.

'A difficult weekend with Fräulein?' Szara asked, not

unsympathetically. He had a hunch that the romantic trip to Normandy had gone wrong.

A Gallic shrug, then, 'No. Not so bad. She gives herself like a woman in love – anything at all to please since nothing between lovers can be wrong. If she feels I'm not sufficiently passionate she gets up to tricks. You're a man, Jean Marc, you know.'

'It can't always be easy,' Szara said. 'Humans aren't made of steel, and that includes communists.'

Sénéschal watched eight new horses being led out into the rain.

'Shall we give you a little breathing space? Perhaps a notional journey, something to do with the Foreign Office. The crisis in Greece.'

'Is there one?'

'Usually.'

Sénéschal grunted, not terribly interested. 'She wants to get married. Immediately.'

'I can't believe you didn't use a . . .'

'No. It's not that. She thinks she's to be dismissed from her position, sent back to Germany in disgrace. Last weekend, after we'd done with all the little shrieks and gasps, there were tears. Floods. She turned bright red and puffed up. It rained like a bastard up there. All weekend the stuff ran down the windows. She bawled, I tried to comfort her but she was inconsolable. Now, she says, only marriage can keep her in France, with me. As for my job at the Foreign Office and the information she's provided, well, too bad. We will live on love, she says.'

'Did she explain?'

'She gabbled like a goose. What I can make of it is that her boss, Herr Stollenbauer, is under severe pressure. Lötte spent all last week running around Paris in taxis – and she claims she's frightened of Parisian cab drivers – because no Mission cars were available. She says she hunted through every fancy shop in the city, Fauchon, Vigneau, Rollet, the finest *traiteurs* you see, in search of what she calls Rote Grütze. Do you know what that is? Because I don't.'

'A sort of sweetened sauce. Made of red berries,' Szara said.

'Also, they're trying to rent a house, somewhere just outside Paris. In Suresnes or Maisons-Laffitte, places like that. According to her they're more than willing to pay, but French *propriétaires* take their time, want papers signed, bank guarantees, first this, then that. It's ceremonial, drives the Germans crazy; they just want to wave money about and get what they want. They think the French are venal – they aren't wrong but they don't understand how French people worry about their properties. From her stories I gathered, more or less, that this is what's going on. And the worse it gets, the more Stollenbauer feels the pressure, the more he shouts at her. She isn't used to that, so now the answer is to get married, she'll stay in France, and I suppose tell Stollenbauer off in the bargain.'

'*Somebody's* coming to Paris.'

'*Évidemment.*'

'Somebody with an aide to call up and say, "Oh yes, and make sure the man's Rote Grütze sauce is available when he eats his pfannkuchen."'

'Shall one go to the forest and pick red berries?'

To Szara's horror, Sénéschal was not at all sarcastic. 'Not to worry,' he said sternly. Sénéschal was clearly in the process of wilting. He was physically brave, Szara knew that for a fact, but the prospect of daily married life with Huber had unnerved him. Szara spoke with authority: 'It's the Frenchwoman of your dreams you'll marry, my friend, and not the Fräulein. Consider that an order.'

The new information was provocative. Szara's old instincts – the journalist happening on a story – were sharply aroused. Suddenly the horses churning through the mud seemed triumphant, images of victory: their nostrils flaring, flanks shining with kicked-up spray. The business with the Rote Grütze sauce was curious, but the search for a safe house, that was truly *interesting*. Trade Missions didn't acquire safe houses. That was embassy business, a job undertaken by resident intelligence officers. But the embassy was being circumvented, which meant a big secret, and a big secret meant a big fish, and guess who happened to be standing there with a net. *Cameras*, he thought, *just every kind of camera*.

He made a decision. 'Huber won't be fired,' he said. 'It's to be quite the opposite. Stollenbauer will be crawling at her feet. And as for you, your only problem will be a woman in triumph, a star of stage, screen, and radio, a princess. Demanding, I think, but not something you can't deal with.'

Fully mobilized, Szara's web of contacts had an answer within days.

An Alsatian *traiteur* was located; a smiling Lötte Huber left his shop trailed by a taxi driver struggling under the weight of two cases of Rote Grütze sauce in special crocks of the Alsatian's own design. He was also prepared to offer weisswurst, jaegerwurst, freshly cured sauerkraut subtly flavoured with juniper berries because – and here the rosy-cheeked *traiteur* leaned over the counter and spoke an exquisitely polite German – 'a man who favours Rote Grütze will always, *always*, madame, want a hint of juniper in his sauerkraut. This is an appetite for piquancy. And this is an appetite we understand.'

Schau-Wehrli dismissed the house dilemma with an imperious Swiss flick of the hand. Her progressive friends and colleagues at the International Law Institute were sounded out and a suitable property was soon located.

It was in Puteaux, a step or two from the city border, a dignified, working-class neighbourhood near the Citroën loading docks on the southwestern curve of the Seine: everywhere a grim, sooty brown, but boxes of flowers stood sentry at all the parlour windows, and the single step up to each doorway was swept before eight every morning. At the far edge of the district sat a three-storey, gabled brick residence – the home of a doctor now deceased and the subject of an interminable lawsuit – with a high wall covered in ivy and a massive set of doors bound in ironwork. A bit of a horror, but the ivied wall turned out to hide a large, formal garden. Sheets were removed from the furniture, a crew of maids brought in to freshen up. Terracotta pots were placed by the entryway and filled to overflowing with fiery geraniums.

Stollenbauer was, as Szara had predicted, magically relieved of much of his burden. The pending visit still made him nervous, much could go wrong, but at least he now felt he *had some support*. From chubby little Lötte Huber no less! Had he not always said that someday her light would shine? Had he not always sensed the hidden talent and initiative in this woman? She'd been so clever in finding the house – where his pompous assistants had shouted guttural French into the phone, cunning Lötte had taken the feminine approach, spending her very own weekend time wandering about various neighbourhoods and inquiring of women in the marketplace if they knew of something to rent, not too much legal foolishness required.

Meanwhile, Szara arrayed his forces and played his own office politics. Oh, Goldman was *informed*, he had to be, but the cable was a masterpiece of its genre – *Trade Mission apparently expecting important visitor sometime in near future*, item eight of seventeen items, not a chance under heaven that such a phrase would bring the greedy *rezident* swooping down from Brussels to snaffle up the credit.

Using a copy of the house key, Szara and Sénéschal had a look around for themselves one evening. Szara would have dearly loved to record the proceedings, but it would simply have been too dangerous, requiring a hidden operative running a wire recorder. Then too, important visitors usually had security men in attendance, people with a horror of unexplained ridges under carpets, miscellaneous wires, even fresh paint.

Instead they approached a birdlike little lady, the widow of an artillery corporal, who lived on the top floor of the house across the street and whose parlour window looked out over the garden. *A troublesome affair*, they told her; *a wayward wife, a government minister, the greatest discretion*. They showed her very official-looking identity documents with diagonal red stripes and handed over a crisp envelope stuffed with francs. She nodded grimly, perhaps an old lady but a little more a woman of the world than they might suppose. They were welcome to her window; it was a change to have something going on in this dull old street. And did they wish to hear a thing or two about the butcher's wife?

Stollenbauer summoned Lötte Huber to his office, sat her down on a spindly little chair, rested his long fingers lightly on her knee, and told her, in strictest confidence, that their visitor was an associate of Heydrich himself.

Sénéschal had walked Lötte Huber through the 'discovery' of the safe house and the Rote Grütze sauce and counselled how these successes should be explained. And what thanks did he get? The young woman's new sense of pride and achievement made her shut up like a clam. Under Szara's tutelage, he applied pressure every way he could. Told her *the big job* was now open at the Foreign Office – would he get it, or would his sworn enemy? Only she could help him now.

He took her to dinner at Fouquet's, fed her triangles of toast covered thickly with goose liver pâté and a bottle of Pomerol. The wine made her cute, funny, and romantic, but not talkative. Finally they fought. What use, she wanted to know, had the French Foreign Office for information that an associate of Heydrich's was coming to town for an important meeting? That was *the very sort of thing* that interested them, he said. The big cheese in his office was secretly a great admirer of Hitler and could be counted on to help, quietly, if any more problems developed with the meeting. But he had to be told exactly what was going on. No, she said, stop, you begin to sound like a spy. That made Sénéschal pale and Szara even paler when the conversation was reported. 'Apologize,' Szara said. 'Tell her you were overwrought and' – he reached into a pocket and came forth with francs – 'buy her jewelry.'

Szara accepted the inevitable. They weren't going to get the meeting date or the names of the other participants, surveillance was their only other option. He could not risk pressing Huber too hard and losing her as a source. It was the first time a wisp of regret floated across his view of the operation – it was not to be the last.

They drove to Puteaux in Sénéschal's car, parked in the narrow street, and watched the house – a surveillance technique that lasted exactly one hour and twelve minutes, perhaps a record for brevity. Children stared, young women pretended not to notice, an angry streetsweeper scraped the hubcap with his twig broom, and a drunk demanded money. *Discomfort* did not begin to describe how it felt; it just wasn't a neighbourhood where you could do something like that.

Odile returned from her courier run to Berlin on 22 June (Baumann wouldn't budge), so she, Sénéschal, and Szara took turns sitting in the old lady's parlour. The wisp of regret had by now become a smoky haze that refused to dissipate. Goldman had the people to do this kind of work; Szara had to improvise with available resources. As for surveillance from the apartment, the principle was one thing, the reality another. The building, cold stone to the eye, was alive, full of inquisitive neighbours you couldn't avoid on the stairs. Szara squared his shoulders and scowled – *I am a policeman* – and left the old lady to deal with the inevitable tongue-wagging.

For her part, she seemed to be enjoying the attention. What she did not enjoy, however, was their company. They were, well, *there*. If somebody read a newspaper, it rattled; if she wanted to clean the carpet, they had to lift their feet. Odile finally saved the situation, discovering that the old lady had a passion for the card game called bezique, a form of pinochle. So the surveillance evolved into a more or less permanent card party, all three watchers contriving to play just badly enough to lose a few francs.

The smoky haze of regret thickened to a fog. What point in having Sénéschal or Odile watch the house if Szara could not be reached when something finally happened – this was *his* operation. But the rules emphatically excluded contact with an agent-operator at his home or, God forbid, at the communications base. Thus he found a rooming house in Suresnes with a telephone on the wall in the corridor, gave the landlady a month's rent and an alias, and there, when he wasn't on duty in Puteaux, he stayed, waiting for Sénéschal or Odile to use the telephone in a café just down the street from the old lady's building.

Waiting.

The great curse of espionage: Father Time in lead boots, the skeleton cobwebbed to the telephone – any and all of the images applied. If you were lucky and good an opportunity presented itself. And then you waited.

July came. Paris broiled in the sun, you could smell the butcher shops half a block away. Szara sat sweating in a soiled little room, not a breath of air stirred through the window; he read trashy French novels, stared out at the street. *I dared to enter the world of spies*, he thought, *and wound up like the classic lonely-pensioner-alone-in-a-room of a Gogol story*. There was a woman who lived just down the hall, fortyish, dyed blond, and fleshy. Fleshy the first week, sumptuous the second, Rubenesque thereafter. She too seemed to be waiting for something or other, though Szara couldn't imagine what.

Actually he could imagine, and did. Her presence in the hallway was announced by a trail of scent called Cri de la Nuit, cheap, crude, sweet, which drove his imagination to absurd excesses. As did her bitter mouth, set in a permanent sneer that said to the world, and especially to him, 'Well?'

Before he could answer, the phone rang.

'Can you come to dinner?' Odile said. Heart pounding, Szara found a cranky old taxi at the Suresnes Mairie and reached the Puteaux house in minutes. Odile was standing well back from the window, looking through a pair of opera glasses. With a little grin of triumph she handed them over. 'Second floor,' she said. 'To the left of the entryway.'

By the time he focused, they weren't where she said they were, but had moved to the top floor, two colourless men in dark suits seen dimly through the gauze curtain shielding the window. They vanished, then reappeared for a moment when they parted the drapes in an adjoining room. 'A security check,' he said.

'Yes,' Odile said. 'Their car is parked well down the street.'

'What model?'

'Not sure.'

'Big?'

'Oh yes,' she said. 'And shiny.'

Szara felt his blood race.

* * *

The following afternoon, 8 July, they were back. This time it was Szara on duty. He'd moved the bezique table in front of the window and, having begged the old lady's pardon, removed his shirt, appearing in sleeveless undershirt, a cigarette stuck in his lips, a hand of playing cards held before him, a sullen expression on his face. This time a heavy man with a bow tie accompanied the other two and from the open gateway stared up at Szara, who stared right back. *A living Brassai*, he thought, *Card Player in Puteaux* – he lacked only a bandanna tied around his neck. The man in the bow tie broke off the staring contest, then slowly closed the door that concealed the garden from the street.

9 July was the day.

At 2:00 P.M. sharp, two glossy black Panhards pulled up at the gate. One of the security men left the first car and opened the gate as his partner drove off. The second car was aligned in such a way that Szara could identify the driver as the man with the bow tie. He also caught a glimpse of the passenger, who sat directly behind the driver and glanced out the window just before the Panhard swung through the gateway and the security man pushed the doors shut. The passenger was in his early forties, Szara guessed. The angle of sight, from above, could be misleading, but Szara took him to be short and bulky. He had thick black hair sharply parted, a swarthy, deeply lined face, and small dark eyes. For the occasion he wore a double-breasted suit, a shirt with a stiff high collar, a grey silk tie. *Gestapo*, Szara thought, dressed up like a diplomat, but the face read policeman and criminal at once, with a conviction of power that Szara had seen in certain German faces, especially – no matter how they preached the Nordic ideal – the dark men who ruled the nation. Important, Szara realized. The single glance out the window had asked the question *Am I pleased?*

'Ten of clubs,' said the old lady.

Fifteen minutes later, a grey Peugeot coasted to a stop in front of the house. A hawk-faced man got out on the side away from Szara and the car immediately left. The man looked about him for a moment, made certain of his tie, then pressed the doorbell set into the portal of the gateway.

Dershani.

Sénéschal knocked twice, then entered the apartment. 'Christ, the heat,' he said. He collapsed in an armchair, set a Leica down carefully among the framed photographs on a rickety table. His suit was hopelessly rumpled, black circles at the armpits, a grey shadow of newsprint ink darkening the front of his shirt. He had spent the last two hours lying on sheets of newspaper in a lead-lined gutter at the foot of the sloped roof. The building's scrollwork provided a convenient portal for photography.

Sénéschal wiped his face with a handkerchief. 'I took all the automobiles,' he said. 'The security man who worked the door – several of him. Tried for the second man, but not much there I'm afraid, perhaps a one-quarter profile, and he was moving. As for the face in the back seat of the Panhard, I managed two exposures, but I doubt anything will show up.'

Szara nodded silently.

'Well? What do you think?'

Szara gestured with his eyes toward the old lady, waiting not quite patiently to resume the card game. 'Too early to know much of anything. We'll wait for them to use the garden,' he said.

'What if it rains?'

Szara looked up at the sky, a mottled grey in the Paris humidity. 'Not before tonight,' he said.

They appeared just before five – *a break in the negotiation.* Odile had arrived at her usual time, Szara now used her opera glasses and stood well back from the window.

The man he took to be a German intelligence officer was short and heavy, as he'd supposed. Magnification revealed a thin white scar crossing his left eyebrow, a street fighter's badge of honour. The two men stood at the garden entrance for a moment, open French doors behind them. The German spoke a few words, Dershani nodded, and they walked together into the garden. They were the image of diplomacy, strolling pensively with hands clasped behind their backs, continuing a very deliberate conversation, choosing their words with great care. Szara studied their lips through the opera glasses but could not, to his surprise, determine if they were speaking German or Russian. Once they laughed. Szara fancied he could hear it, faintly, carried on the heated air of the late afternoon amid the sound of sparrows chirping in the trees of the garden.

They made a single circuit on the gravel path, stopping once while the German pointed at an apple tree, then returned to the house, each beckoning the other to enter first. Dershani laughed, clapping the German on the shoulder, and went in ahead of him.

At 7:20, Dershani left the house. He turned up the street in the direction his car had gone and disappeared from view. A few minutes later, the security man opened the gate and, after the car had passed through, closed it again. He climbed in beside the driver and the Panhard sped away. In the garden, the setting sun made long shadows on the dry grass, the birds sang, nothing moved in the still summer air.

* * *

'*Tiens*,' said the old lady. 'Will the government fall tomorrow?'

Sénéschal was grave. 'No, madame, I can in confidence inform you that, thanks to your great kindness and patience, the government will stand.'

'Oh, too bad,' she said.

Odile left first, to walk to the Neuilly Métro stop. Sénéschal disappeared into the old lady's closet and emerged a few minutes later smelling faintly of mothballs. He handed Szara a spool of film. Szara thanked the old lady, told her they might be back the following day, gave her a fresh packet of money, and went out into the humid dusk.

Sénéschal's car was parked several blocks away. They walked through streets deserted by the onset of the dinner hour; smells of frying onions and potatoes drifted through the open windows.

'Do we try again tomorrow?' Sénéschal asked.

Szara thought it over. 'I sense that they've done what they came together to do.'

'Can't be certain.'

'No. I'll contact you at your office, if you don't mind.'

'Not at all.'

'I should say, officially, that gratitude is expressed – charming the way they put these things. Personally, thank you for everything, and I'm sorry your shirt is ruined.'

Sénéschal inspected the front of his shirt. 'No. My little friend is a wonder. No matter what I get into she knows a way to take care of it. Nothing is to be thrown out, it can always last "a bit longer."'

'Is she aware of your, ah, love affair?'

'They always know, Jean Marc, but it's part of life here. It's what all those sad little café songs are about.'

'You are in love, then.'

'Oh that word. Perhaps, or perhaps not. She is my

consolation, however, always that, and doesn't she ever know it. *L'amour* covers quite some territory, especially in Paris.'

'I expect it does.'

'Have you a friend?'

'Yes. Or I should say "perhaps."'

'She's good to you?'

'Good for me.'

'*Et alors!*'

Szara laughed.

'Beautiful too, I'd wager.'

'You would win, eventually, but it's not the sort of dazzle that catches the eye right away. There's just something about her.'

They reached the car; the smell of overheated upholstery rushed out when Sénéschal opened the door. 'Come have a beer,' he said. 'There's plenty of time for your vanishing act.'

'Thank you,' Szara said.

Sénéschal turned the ignition, the Renault came reluctantly to life as he fiddled expertly with the choke. 'This whore drinks petrol,' he said sourly, racing the engine.

They wandered through the twisting streets of Puteaux, crossed the Seine on the pont de Suresnes – the tied-up barges had pots of flowers and laundry drying on lines – then the Bois de Boulogne appeared on their left, a few couples out strolling, men with jackets over their arms, an organ grinder. Sénéschal stopped by an ice cream seller. 'What kind?'

'Chocolate.'

'A double?'

'Of course. Here's a few francs.'

'Keep it.'

'I insist.'

Sénéschal waved the money away and bought the cones.

When he got back in the car he drove slowly through the Bois, steering with one hand. 'Watch, now I really will ruin the shirt.'

Szara's double cone was a masterpiece – he ate the ice cream and looked at the girls in their summer dresses.

But what he'd seen that afternoon did not leave him. His mind was flying around like a moth in a lamp. He didn't understand what he'd witnessed, didn't know what it meant or what, if anything, to do about it. He'd seen something he wasn't supposed to see, that much he did know. Maybe it meant nothing – intelligence services talked to each other when it was in the interest of both to do so, and Paris was a good, neutral place to do it.

'If you've the time, we'll find ourselves a brasserie,' Sénéschal said.

'Good idea. Is there a place you go?' Szara wanted the company.

Sénéschal looked at him oddly. Szara realized his error, they couldn't go to a place where Sénéschal was known. 'We'll just pick one that looks good,' he said. 'In this city you can't go too far wrong.'

They'd drifted into the fifteenth arrondissement, headed east on the boulevard Lefebvre. 'We're in the right place out here,' Sénéschal said. 'They have great big ones where the whole family shows up – kids, dogs. A night like this' – the Renault idled roughly at a red light; a fat man in suspenders was picking through books at a stall – 'the terraces will be . . .' The Panhard rolled to a gentle stop on Sénéschal's side of the car.

Seen from a window in the old lady's apartment, he'd been a colourless man in a suit. Now, looking through the Panhard's passenger window, he was much realer than that. He was young, not yet thirty, and very bright and crisp. His hair was combed just so, swept up into a stiff pompadour above his white forehead. 'Please,' he said in measured French, 'may we speak a moment?' He smiled. *What merry eyes*, Szara thought. For a moment he was unable to breathe.

Sénéschal turned to him for help, his knuckles white on the steering wheel.

'Please? Yes?' said the man.

The driver was older, his face a silhouette in the lights of the boulevard shops. 'Don't be so fucking polite,' he grumbled in German. He turned and looked at Sénéschal. It was the face of a German worker, blunt and stolid, with hair shaved above the ears. He was smoking a cigar, the tip reddened as he inhaled.

The light went green. A horn beeped behind them. 'Drive away,' Szara said. Sénéschal popped the clutch and the car stalled. Swearing under his breath, he twisted the ignition key and fumbled with the choke. The driver of the Panhard laughed, his partner continued to smile. *Like a clown in a nightmare*, Szara thought.

The engine caught and the Renault roared away from the light. Sénéschal cut into an angled street, took a narrow cobbled alley between high walls at full speed – the car bouncing and shimmying – tried to turn sharply back into the boulevard traffic, but the light had changed again and he had nowhere to go. The Panhard rolled up beside them. 'Whew,' said the smiling man. 'What a bumping!'

'Look,' the driver said in French, holding his cigar between thumb and forefinger, 'don't make us chase you around all night . . .'

Traffic started to move and Sénéschal forced his way between two cars. The Panhard tried to follow, but the driver of a little Fiat cut them off with a spiteful glare.

'Tell me what to do,' Sénéschal said.

Szara tried to think of something, as though he knew. 'Stay with the traffic,' he said. Sénéschal nodded vigorously, he would follow Szara's plan meticulously. He settled the Renault into traffic, which now began to thin out noticeably as they approached the eastern border of the city. At the next light, Szara leaned over in order to look in the rearview mirror. The Panhard was two cars back in the adjoining lane. The passenger saw what he was doing, stuck his arm out the window and waved. When the light changed, Sénéschal stamped the gas pedal against the floorboards, swerved around the car in front, changed lanes, turned off the headlights, and shot across the oncoming traffic into a side street.

Szara twisted around, but the Panhard was not to be seen. Sénéschal began to make lefts and rights, tearing through the darkness of deserted side streets while Szara watched for the Panhard. 'Any idea where we are?' he said.

'The thirteenth.'

A shabby neighbourhood, unlit; peeling wooden shutters protected the shopfronts. Up ahead, a broad boulevard appeared and Sénéschal pulled over and left the car idling as they both lit cigarettes. Szara's hands were trembling. 'The passenger was at the safe house,' Sénéschal said. 'You have his photograph. But the other one, with the cigar, where did he come from?'

'I never saw him.'

'Nazis,' Sénéschal said. 'Did you *see* them?'

'Yes.'

'What did they want?'

'To talk, they said.'

'Oh yes! I believe it!' He exhaled angrily and shook his head. 'Shit.'

'Their time will come,' Szara said.

'Did you hear him? That cunt? "Please, may we speak a moment."' Sénéschal made the man sound effeminate and mincing.

'That was a good idea, cutting across.'

Sénéschal shrugged. 'I just did it.' He flicked his cigarette out the window and eased the Renault into first gear, turning the headlights back on. He swung left onto the deserted boulevard. 'A bad neighbourhood,' he said. 'Nobody comes here at night.'

They drove for five minutes, Szara spotted a Métro station on the corner. 'Expect a contact by telephone. After that, our meetings will be as usual.'

'I'll be waiting,' Sénéschal said, voice mean and edgy. The brush with the Germans had frightened him. Now he was angry.

The car stopped in midblock and Szara got out and closed the door behind him. He thrust his hands in his pockets, squeezing the roll of film to make sure of it, and walked quickly toward the Métro entrance. He reached the grillwork arch above the stairway, saw it was the Tolbiac station, stopped dead as a metallic explosion echoed off the buildings followed by the sound of shattered glass raining on the pavement. He stared at the noise. Two blocks away the Renault was bent around the front of a car that had ploughed into the driver's door. The passenger door was jammed open and something was lying in the street a few feet away from it. Szara started to run. Two men got out of the black car that had struck the Renault. One of them held his head and sat on the ground. The other ran to the thing in the street and bent over it. Szara stopped dead and found the shadows next to a building. Lights began to go on, heads appeared in windows. The glow of the street lamps was reflected in the liquid running into the street from the two cars, and the smell of petrol reached him. The man who had been bending over the thing in the street squatted for a moment, seemed to be searching for something, then rose abruptly and kicked savagely at whatever it was that was lying there. People began to come out of their doorways, talking excitedly to each other. The man by the Renault now turned, took the other man under one arm and hauled him to his feet, pulling him forward, at last getting him to stumble along quickly. They disappeared up a side street across the boulevard.

Walking quickly toward the cars, Szara found himself amid a small crowd of people. The Panhard's windscreen was starred on the right side, and the driver's door on the Renault had been mashed halfway across the front seat by the impact. Sénéschal lay face down near the Renault's sprung passenger door, his jacket up over his head, shirttail pulled halfway out of his pants. A group of men stood around him, one bent down for a closer look, lifted the jacket, then straightened up, eyes shut in order not to see what he'd seen. He waved a dismissive hand across his body and said, 'Don't look.' Another man said, 'Did you see him *kick* him?' The voice was quivering. 'He kicked a dead man. He did. I saw it.'

TRANSMISSION 11 JULY 1938 22:30 HOURS

TO JEAN MARC: DIRECTORATE JOINS YOU IN REGRET FOR LOSS OF COMRADE SILO. INQUIRY TO BE UNDERTAKEN BY YVES WITH ASSISTANCE OF ELLI, A REPORT TO BE MADE TO DIRECTORATE SOONEST OF CIRCUMSTANCES PERTINENT TO THIS INCIDENT WITH SPECIAL REGARD TO PREVIOUS ACCIDENT INVOLVING FORMER DEPUTY. ESSENTIAL TO DETERMINE EXACT CIRCUMSTANCES OF BOTH THESE INCIDENTS WITH REGARD TO THEIR POSSIBLE INTENTIONAL ORIGIN. THE REMOTEST POSSIBILITY TO BE CONSIDERED. ALL OPAL PERSONNEL TO BE ON HIGHEST ALERT FOR HOSTILE ACTION AGAINST THE NETWORK.

THERE IS GRAVE CONCERN FOR THE CONTINUITY OF THE ARBOUR PRODUCT. SINCE HECTOR WAS PRESENT WHEN INITIAL CONTACT MADE BETWEEN ARBOUR AND SILO, AND HECTOR HAS BEEN PRESENTED AS THE FRIEND OF SILO, CAN HECTOR FIND MEANS TO OPERATE AS SILO'S REPLACEMENT IN THIS RELATIONSHIP? HECTOR TO SHOW CONCERN AS FAMILY FRIEND AND PROVIDE COMFORT AS HE IS ABLE. IT IS SUGGESTED THAT SILO'S FUNERAL IS THE LOGICAL SETTING FOR CONTACT BETWEEN HECTOR AND ARBOUR. ALTERNATIVELY, IF SILO'S TRUE POLITICAL AFFILIATION IS REVEALED, CAN PRESSURE BE BROUGHT TO BEAR ON ARBOUR? WILL ARBOUR COOPERATE IN THIS CONTEXT? RESPOND BY 14 JULY.

OTTER MUST BE PRESSED TO EXPAND HIS REPORTING. RECOMMEND NEW MEASURES TO BE TAKEN WITHIN 48 HOURS.

ACCOUNT NO. 414–223–8/74 AT BANQUE SUISSE DE GENEVE TO BE CLOSED. NEW ACCOUNT NO. 609–846 DX 12 AT CREDIT LEMANS OPERATIVE AS OF 15 JULY IN NAME COMPAGNIE ROMAILLES WITH CREDIT OF 50,000 FRENCH FRANCS. 10,000 FRANCS TO BE TAKEN BY COURIER TO YVES. DIRECTOR

Sitting in the hot, dirty room where Kranov transmitted and decoded, Szara tossed the message aside. The frantic endgame attempted by the Directorate, their shrill tone, and the certainty of failure he found faintly depressing. He perfectly remembered the André Szara who would have been enraged by the Directorate's calculating attitude, a man who, not so very long ago, believed passionately that the only unforgivable human sin was a cold heart. Now he was not that man. He understood what they wanted, understood them for wanting it, and knew the result: Lötte Huber was lost. Sénéschal's friend Valais, HECTOR, also a lawyer formerly active in the French Communist party, had been with Sénéschal the night they'd 'met' Huber and her friend at the theatre, and had been brought on stage as a confidant – *Lötte, he's so worried and upset, you must help him* – to move the operation along. But Huber would never accept him as a lover; this was *analyst's* thinking, a scheme created at a great distance from events and in breathtaking ignorance of the personalities involved. Valais was a ponderous, contemplative man, a fair-skinned Norman lacking entirely Sénéschal's Mediterranean intensity and charm.

And blackmail was absurd. Huber would go to pieces, bring the French police down on their heads. Moscow was clearly rattled: losing first the operative Szara had replaced, in a car accident outside Mâcon, and now Sénéschal in what had been presented to them as a second car accident, a hit-and-run tragedy.

For Szara had not told them otherwise.

A pawn in *khvost* politics had become an active participant.

Was he to inform the Directorate, and thus Dershani, of photographs taken in a Puteaux garden? A secret meeting of senior Soviet and German intelligence officers, perhaps of diplomatic importance, not so secret after all. Penetrated. Photographed. Maybe the Directorate knew of Dershani's contact with the Nazi service.

Maybe it didn't.

The Germans certainly wanted to keep the contact secret – they'd murdered Sénéschal on that basis. So what would the NKVD have in store for him? He chose not to find that out, instead undertook a damage control programme to protect himself, informing Schau-Wehrli that, according to Huber's final report to Sénéschal, the grand meeting had not yet taken place, and cabling both Goldman and Moscow to that effect.

Odile, of course, presented a very different problem and he'd had to approach her directly. He'd got her off by herself and placed his life in her hands: there will be an investigation; you must not tell the Brussels *rezident*, or anybody, what you were doing on the days leading up to 9 July. He'd watched her, a tough Belgian girl from the mining towns, raw, nineteen, and loyal to the death once she got it straightened out what was what. She'd thought it over for quite some time. Her face, usually flip and sexy and moody all at once, was closed, immobile, he couldn't read it. Finally, she'd agreed. She trusted him, instinctively, and perhaps she feared it was already too late to tell the truth. She also knew, from growing up within Communist party politics, that conspiracy was bread-and-butter to them all: you chose a side and lived with the result.

The photographs had turned out to be adequate. He'd had them developed by randomly choosing a little shop, assuming the technician would make no particular sense of the subjects. Picking them up in midafternoon, he'd found an empty booth in a deserted café and spent an hour turning them over in his hands, cloudy black and white impressions shot from above, eleven prints paid for with a life. The crisp, young security man opening a gate. Head and shoulders of a man at the wheel of a car. Car window with a faint blur behind it. Dershani and the Gestapo officer in a garden, the German speaking tentatively, left hand turned up to emphasize a point. There was no photograph of the man with the cigar who drove the Panhard, Sénéschal had not managed to record his own murderer.

Now, what to do with them. He'd thought about that for a long time, then decided that if Bloch didn't contact him he'd pass them to Abramov whenever an opportunity presented itself. Not officially, not through the system, friend to friend. Until then, he'd hide them in his apartment.

As he thought about the photographs, the blacked-out room began to feel claustrophobic. A few feet away, facing the opposite wall, Kranov worked like a machine. The rhythmic tapping of his wireless key grated across Szara's nerves, so he filed the Moscow cable in a metal box and left the house, walking out into the still night air and heading toward the canals. The slaughter-house workers were hard at it on the loading docks of the abattoirs, hefting bloody beef quarters on their shoulders, then swinging them in to butchers who waited in the backs of their trucks. They cursed and laughed as they worked, wiping the sweat from their eyes, brushing the flies off their spattered aprons. In a brightly lit café, a blind man played the violin and a whore danced on a table while the raucous crowd teased him with lurid descriptions of what he was missing, and he smiled and played in such a way as to let them know he saw more than they did. Szara walked on the cobbled pathway by the canal, then stood for a time and watched the reflections of the neon signs, bending and bowing with the motion of the black water.

To Sénéschal, dead because of his, Szara's, ignorance and inexperience, he could only give a place in his heart. He wondered if he'd ever learn how the Germans had managed it – the discovery of the surveillance, the tracking of the Renault while remaining invisible. Technically, they were simply more adept than he was – only the chance decision to use the Tolbiac Métro had saved his life – thus Sénéschal was gone, and he was the one left to stare into the dead waters of the canal and think about life. His sentence was to understand that, and to remember it. To remember also, forever, the driver of the Panhard, a dim shape seen at a distance, barely the form of a man, then the savage kick, a spasm of useless rage. *Sudden, without warning*; like the blow that had knocked him to the floor of a railway station buffet in Prague. He watched the wavering signs in the water, red and blue, recalled what Sénéschal had said about his girl-friend, the one who threw nothing away, the one for whom anything could be made to last a little longer.

8 July.

He took the night train to Lisbon.

Sat up in coach class, saving money, anticipating the cost of lovers' feasts: iced prawns with mayonnaise, the wine called Barca Velha, cool from the cellar of the *taberna*. Then too, he did not want to sleep. Somewhere out on the ocean, he imagined, Marta Haecht was also awake. Avoiding the ghastly end-of-voyage parties she would be standing at the rail, watching for a landfall glow in the distance, only dimly aware of the Strength through Joy revellers braying Nazi songs in the ship's ballroom. In her purse she would have the letter, carefully folded, something to laugh about in Portugal.

Nothing so good for a lover as a train ride through the length of the night, the endless click of the rails, the engine sometimes visible in the moonlight as it worked its way around a long curve. All night long he summoned memories – *Is there a place I may undress?* The train pounded through the vineyards of Gascony at dawn. He stood in the alcove at the end of the car, watched the rails glitter as they swept below the coupling, smelled the burnt cinder in the air. It was cold in the foothills of the Pyrénées; the scent of pine resin sharpened as the sun climbed the slopes. Falangist Guardia in leather hats checked the passports at the Hendaye border crossing, then they were in Franco's Spain all day long. They passed a burned-out tank, a raw lumber gallows standing at the edge of a town.

The haze shimmered in the hills north of Lisbon. The city itself was numb, exhausted in the faded summer light of evening. The carriage horses at the station barely bothered to flick their tails. Szara found a hotel called the Mirador, with Moorish turrets and balconies, and took a room above a courtyard where a fountain gushed rusty water over broken tiles and heavy roses lay sodden in the heat. He put his toothbrush in a glass, then went out for a long walk, eventually buying a pair of linen trousers, a thin white shirt, and a panama hat. He changed in the store and a Spanish couple asked directions of him on the way back to the hotel.

He spotted a Russian émigré newspaper at a kiosk, then spent the night reading to the whirr of cicadas and the splashing of the cracked fountain. *Stalin the Murderer! Prince Cheyalevsky Presents a Cheque to the Orphans' League. Mme Tsoutskaya Opens Milliner's Shop*. At dawn, he forced the ancient shutters closed, but he could not sleep. He had not asked Goldman's permission to leave Paris – he doubted it would have been granted; Sénéschal's death had everybody on edge – nor had he told Schau-Wehrli where he was going. Nobody knew where he was, and such freedom made it impossible to sleep. He wasn't seriously missing, not yet. He gave himself a week for that; then they'd panic, start calling the morgue and the hospitals.

Walking back to the hotel, he'd happened on a family of Jews: ashen faces, downcast eyes, dragging what remained of their possessions down the hill toward the docks. From Poland, he suspected. They'd come a long way, and now they were headed – where? South America? Or the United States?

Would *she* go? Yes, eventually she would. Not at first, not right away – one didn't just walk away from one's life. But later, after they'd made love, really made love, then she would go with him. He could see her: head propped on hand, sweat between her breasts, brown eyes liquid and intense; could hear the cicadas, the shutter creaking in the evening breeze.

He had money. Barely enough, but enough. They'd go to the American consulate and request visitors' visas. Then they would vanish. What else was America but that, the land of the vanished.

At ten the next morning he watched the docking of the liner *Hermann Krieg* – a Nazi martyr, no doubt. A crowd of German workers streamed down the gangplank, grinning at the brutal white sun they'd come to worship. The men leered at the dark Portuguese women in their black shawls, the wives took a firm grip on their husbands' arms.

Marta Haecht was nowhere to be seen.

That summer, the heat spared nobody.

And while London gardens wilted and Parisian dogs slept under café tables, New York positively steamed. ANOTHER SCORCHER, the *Daily Mirror* howled, while the *New York Times* said 'Temperatures Are Expected to Reach 98° Today.' It was impossible to sleep at night. Some people gathered on tenement stoops and spoke in low voices; others sat in the darkness, listened to Benny Goodman's band on the radio, and drank gallons of iced tea.

It was bad during the week, but the August heat wave seemed to save its truly hellish excesses for the weekends. You could take the subway to Coney Island or the long trolley ride to Jones Beach, but you could hardly see the sand for the bodies much less find a spot to spread out your towel. The ocean itself seemed warm and sticky, and a sunburn made everything worse.

About the best you could hope for on the weekends was to own a little house in the country somewhere or, almost as good, to have an invitation to stay with somebody who did. Thus Herb Hull, senior editor at the magazine trying to make space for itself between the *Nation* and the *New Republic*, was elated to receive a Tuesday morning telephone call from Elizabeth May, asking him to come down with them on Friday night to their place in Bucks County. Jack May ran one of the Schubert box offices in the West Forties theatre district, Elizabeth was a social worker at a Lower East Side settlement house. They were not Hull's close friends, but neither were they simply acquaintances. It was instead something in between, a sort of casual intimacy New Yorkers often fell into.

After the usual misadventures – a traffic jam in the Holland Tunnel, an overheating problem in the Mays' '32 Ford outside Somerville, New Jersey – they reached a sturdy little fieldstone house at the edge of a small pond. The house was typical: small bedrooms reached by a staircase with a squeaky step, battered furniture, bookcase full of murder mysteries left by former guests, and a bed in the guest room that smelled of mildew. Not far from Philadelphia, Bucks County had summer homes and artists' studios up every dirt road. Writers, painters, playwrights, editors, and literary agents tended to cluster there, as did people who worked at a great range of occupations but whose evenings were committed to books and plays and Carnegie Hall. They arrived on Friday night, unloaded the weekend groceries (corn, tomatoes, and strawberries would be bought at roadside stands), ate sandwiches, and went to bed early. Saturday morning was spent fussing at projects that never got done – you just weren't enjoying the country if you didn't 'fix' something – then the rest of the weekend drifted idly by in talking and drinking and reading in all their combinations. At Saturday night parties you'd see the same people you saw in Manhattan during the week.

Herb Hull was delighted to spend the weekend with the Mays. They were very bright and well read, the rye and bourbon flowed freely, and Elizabeth was a fine cook, known for corn fritters and Brunswick stew. That's what they had for dinner on Saturday night. Then they decided to skip the usual party, instead sat around, sipping drinks while Jack played Ellington records on the Victrola.

The Mays were charter subscribers to Hull's magazine and avid supporters of the causes it embraced. Not Party people but enlightened and progressive, fairly staunch for Roosevelt though they had voted for Debs in '32. The conversation all across Bucks County that night was politics, and the Mays' living room was no exception. In unison, the three lamented the isolationists, who wanted no part of 'that mess in Europe,' and the German-American Bund, which supported them, de facto encouragement to Hitler. Sorrowfully, they agreed that there was no saving the Sudetenland; Hitler would snap it up as he had Austria. There would eventually be war, but America would stay out. That was shameful, cowardly, ultimately frightening. What had become of American idealism? Had the grinding poverty of the Depression gutted the national values? Was the country really going to be run by Westbrook Pegler and Father Coughlin? Did the American people hate Russia so much they were going to let Hitler have his way in Europe?

'That's the crux of it,' Jack May said angrily, shaking his head in frustration.

Hull agreed. It was all pretty sad stuff: Henry Ford and his anti-Semite pals, plenty of people down in Washington who didn't want to get involved in Europe, the hate groups claiming that Roosevelt was 'Rosenfeld,' a Bolshevik Jew. 'But you know,' Hull said, 'Stalin isn't exactly helping matters. Some of the statements out of Moscow are pretty wishy-washy, and he's got Litvinov, the foreign minister, running all over Europe trying to play the same sort of diplomacy game as England and France. That won't stop Hitler, he understands the difference between treaties and tanks.'

'Ah for Christ sakes,' Jack May said. 'You know the situation in Russia. Stalin's got two hundred million peasants to feed. What's he supposed to do?'

'Herb, weren't you there this year?' Elizabeth asked.

'Last winter.'

'What was it like?'

'Oh, secret and strange – you get the sense of people listening behind the drapes. Poor. Just not enough to go around. Passionate for ideas and literature. A writer there is truly important, not just a barking dog on a leash. If I had to put it in two words, I guess one would be *inconvenient*. Why I don't know, but everything, and I do mean everything, is just so damn difficult. But the other word would have to be something like *exhilarating*. They're really trying to make it all work, and you can definitely feel that, like something in the air.'

Jack May looked at his wife, a mock-quizzical expression on his face. 'Did he have a good time?'

Elizabeth laughed.

'It was fascinating, that I can't deny.'

'And Stalin? What do they think about him?' she asked.

May took Hull's glass from the coffee table and splashed some bourbon over a fresh ice cube. Hull took a sip while May turned the record over. 'They certainly watch what they say. You never know who's listening. But at the same time they're Slavs, not Anglo-Saxons, and they want to open their heart to you if you're a friend. So you do hear stories.'

'Gossip?' May said. 'Or the real thing?'

'Funny, they don't gossip, not truly, not the way we do. They're instinctively restrained about love affairs and such.

As for "the real thing," yes, sometimes. I met one fellow who's got a story about how Stalin was secretly in cahoots with the Okhrana. Pretty good story, actually – lively, factual. I think we'll run it around Christmas.'

'Oh, that old red herring,' Elizabeth scoffed. 'That's been around for years.'

Hull chuckled. 'Well, there you have the magazine business. It'll make the Stalinists mad as hell, but they won't cancel their subscriptions, they'll just write letters. Then the socialists and the Trotskyites will write back, madder yet. We'll sell some newsstand copies in the Village. In the long run it's just dialogue, open forum, everyone gets to take their turn at bat.'

'But is this person actually in a position to know something like that?' Elizabeth was slightly wide-eyed at the possibility.

Hull thought for a time. 'Maybe. Maybe not. We'll acknowledge, implicitly, that we really don't know. "Who can say what goes on behind the walls of the Kremlin?" Not quite so obvious as that, but in that general direction.'

'What are you? *Time* magazine?' May was getting ready to argue.

Hull shrugged it off. 'I wish we had the Luces' money. But I'll tell you something, though it's never to leave this room. We're all of us, *Time* included, in the same boat. The editorial slant is different – is it ever – but we're nothing without the readership, and we've just got to come up with something juicy once in a while. But don't be alarmed, the rest of the issue will be as usual – plenty of polemic, snarling capitalists and courageous workers, a Christmas cry for justice. I think you'll like it.'

'Sounds pretty damn cynical to me,' May grumbled.

Elizabeth rushed in. 'Oh poo! Just think about the stuff they put on stage where you work. You're just being critical, Jack, admit it.'

May smiled ruefully. 'Democracy in action,' he said. 'Makes everybody mad.'

It certainly made somebody mad.

On the night of 14 September the editorial offices of Hull's magazine were burned, and 'Who Was the Okhrana's Mysterious Man?' went up with all the other paper, or was presumed to have, because all they ever found were grey mounds of wet ash that went into the East River along with the chairs and desks and typewriters and, in the event, the magazine itself.

It was certainly no accident – the petrol can was left right there on the floor of the editor-in-chief's office, where the arson investigators found it when they picked through what remained of the ceiling. Some of the newspaper beatmen asked the Fire lieutenant who'd done it, but all he gave them was an eloquent Irish smile: these little commie outfits, how the hell was anybody going to know what went on, maybe a rival, maybe they didn't pay the printer, the list was too long.

At first, the magazine's board of directors thought they intended to go forward bravely, but wisdom ultimately prevailed. The venture had already eaten one trust fund and ruined a marriage, maybe they'd best leave the field to the competition. Herb Hull was on the street for exactly three weeks, then signed on with a glossy, general readership magazine, a big one. His new job was to go up against *Collier's* and the *Saturday Evening Post*, which meant getting to know a whole new crowd of writers, but Hull, God help him, liked writers and soon enough he had the stories coming – 'Amelia Earhart, Is She Still Alive?' – and life for him was back to normal. He had a pretty good idea of why the magazine office burned up but he kept it to himself – martyrdom was not in his stars – though he did sometimes play a little game with four or five names he could have jotted down if he'd wanted to.

André Szara found out a few days later. Standing at a zinc bar in the rue du Cherche-Midi, drinking his morning coffee, he thumbed through one of the official newspapers of the French left and read about the fire, obviously set, said its American correspondent, by J. Edgar Hoover's FBI or its fascist stooges, as part of their hate campaign against the progressive and peace-loving workers of all nations.

Szara felt little enough on reading it, simply a sense of recognition. He turned the event over in his mind for a time, staring out at the street. The purge was slowly dying out, like a fire that has consumed everything in its path and at last consumes itself: one week earlier, Goldman had quietly informed him during a meeting in Brussels that Yezhov was on the way out. What had actually happened? The NKVD had surely learned of the article and prevented its publication. But just as surely Stalin had been told – or seen the article himself, since they had likely stolen it before they started the fire. Had he been influenced? Jogged just enough in a certain way at a certain time so that ending the purge now seemed preferable to continuing it? Or was it simply coincidence, a confluence of events? Or was there yet more to the story than he knew? There was an excellent possibility that he had not been the only one set in motion against the purge; intelligence operations simply did not work that way – one brave man against the world. The expectation of failure was too high in any individual case for the skilful operator not to have several attacks going at once.

Finally, he couldn't be sure of anything. *Perhaps this morning I have actually been victorious*, he thought. He could not imagine a greater absence of drums and trumpets. And he did not care. Since Sénéschal's death and his return from Lisbon he found he didn't particularly care about anything, and he found also that this made life, or his life anyhow, much simpler. He finished the coffee, left a few coins on the bar, and headed off to a press conference with the Swedish ambassador, first putting up his umbrella, for it had begun to rain.

The Iron Exchange

10 October 1938.

André Szara, as long as he lived, remembered that day as a painting.

A curious painting. Quite literal, in the style of the 1880s yet touched by an incongruity, something askew, that suggested the surrealism of a later period. The subject was a long, empty beach near the Danish city of Aarhus on the coast of Jutland; the time was late afternoon, beneath the mackerel sky of the Scandinavian autumn, rows of white scud shifting slowly toward a pale wash horizon. To the east lay an expanse of flat, dark water, then a cloud bank obscuring the island of Samsoe. Small waves lapped at the shore; pebbly, dark sand with a meandering tideline marked by a refuse of broken shells. Gulls fed at the water's edge, and on the dunes that rose behind the beach the stiff grass swayed in the offshore breeze. A common, timeless seascape caught at a common, timeless moment.

But the figures in the scene were alien to it. Sergei Abramov, in his dark blue suit and vest with watch chain, his black homburg and black beard and black umbrella – just there the painting had gone wrong. This was a city man who belonged to city places – restaurants, theatres – and his presence on the beach somehow denied nature. No less his companion, the journalist A. A. Szara, in a rumpled raincoat with a French newspaper rolled up in one pocket.

The final touch, which perfected the incongruity, was the stack of eleven photographs that Abramov held, studying them as people do, placing the topmost at the back when he was done with it, proceeding in turn until it reappeared, then starting over.

Could the artist have caught Abramov's mood? Only a very good artist, Szara felt, could have managed it. There was too much there. Drawn deep inside himself, impervious to the screaming gulls, to the gust of wind that toyed with his beard, Abramov wore the expression of a man whose brutal opinion of humankind has, once again, been confirmed. But, in the cocked eyebrow, in the tug of a smile at one corner of the mouth, there was evidence that he expected no less, that he was a man so often betrayed that such events now seemed to him little more than an inconvenience. Very deliberately he squared the stack of photographs, resettled them in an envelope, and slid them into the inside pocket of his jacket. 'Of course,' he said to Szara.

Szara's expression showed that he didn't understand.

'Of course it happened, of course it was Dershani who made it happen, of course the proof comes too late.' He smiled grimly and shrugged, his way of saying *udari sudbi*, the blows of fate, wasn't this exactly the way of the world. 'And the negatives?'

'Burned.'

'Sensible.'

'Will you burn these as well?'

Abramov thought a moment. 'No,' he said. 'No, I shall confront him.'

'What will he do?'

'Dershani? Smile. We will smile at each other: brothers, enemies, conspirators, fellow wolves. When we've got that over with, he'll inquire how I came to have such photographs.'

'And you'll tell him?'

Abramov shook his head. 'I will tell him some rich, transparent lie. Which he will acknowledge with one of his predatory stares. I'll stare back, though he'll know that's a bluff, and that will be that. Then, later, as if from nowhere, something may happen to me. Or it may not. Something may happen to Dershani instead – political fortune is a tide like any other. In any event, the photographs prove he was clumsy enough to get caught, perhaps a margin of vulnerability that will keep me alive a little longer. Or, perhaps, not.'

'I didn't know,' Szara apologized. 'I thought we'd caught him at it.'

'At what?'

'Collaboration.'

Abramov smiled gently at Szara's innocence. 'Such a meeting can be explained a thousand ways. For instance, one could say that Herr Joseph Uhlrich has now been brought under Soviet control.'

'You know him.'

'Oh yes, it's a small world. The SS Obersturmbannführer, to give him his proper rank, the equivalent of a lieutenant colonel in Russia, is an old friend. A brave, fighting street communist in his youth, then a Brown Shirt thug, eventually a spy for Hitler's faction, the Black Shirts, against Ernst Röhm. He took part in the Brown Shirt executions of 1934 and is now one of Heydrich's assistants in the Sicherheitsdienst, SD, Gestapo foreign intelligence. He works in the Unterabteilung subdivision that concerns itself with Soviet intelligence services. Perhaps Dershani has been brought under the control of the SD rather than the other way around.'

'Uhlrich had the security, the Germans planned the meeting, Dershani was essentially alone and unguarded. To me, it seemed a courteous welcome for a traitor.'

Abramov shrugged. 'I will find out.' He put his back to the wind, lit a cigarette, and put the extinguished match in his pocket. 'But, even so, doing something about it may be impossible. Dershani is now chairman of the OPAL Directorate. Abramov is demoted to simple membership. He may be demoted further, even much further – you understand – and Yezhov is no longer Dershani's superior. That position now belongs to the Georgian Beria, so the Georgian *khvost* is victorious. And they are cleaning house. A writers' conspiracy has been uncovered; Babel, too friendly with Yezhov's wife, has disappeared, and so has Kolt'sev. *Pravda* will soon have a new editor. Then there were others, many others: writers, poets, dramatists, as well as Yezhov's associates, every single one of them, seventy at last count.'

'And Yezhov?'

Abramov nodded. 'Ah yes, Yezhov himself. Well, I may inform you that Comrade Yezhov turned out to be a British spy. Imagine that! But, poor man, perhaps he was not fully aware of what he was doing.' Abramov closed one eye and tapped his temple with an index finger.

'Nicolai Ivanovich evidently went mad. For late one night an ambulance appeared at his apartment block, then two attendants, sturdy fellows, were seen to remove him in a straitjacket. He was taken to the Serbsy Psychiatric Institute and, regrettably, left alone in a cell, where he contrived to hang himself from the barred window by ingeniously fashioning his underpants into a noose. This would have required an extraordinary feat of acrobatics, and "the bloody dwarf" was never known as much of an athlete, but, who knows, perhaps madness lent him unimagined physical prowess. We all like to think so, at any rate.'

'I was told that Yezhov was in decline,' Szara said, 'but not this.'

'*Decline* could describe it, I suppose. Meanwhile, *bratets*' – the affectionate term meant 'little brother' – 'now more than ever, you better keep your nose clean. I don't know what actually happened to your agent SILO in Paris, but here I see these photographs and they tell me you've been meddling with Germans, and so to put two and two together doesn't take a genius.'

'But it was –'

'Don't tell me,' Abramov interrupted. 'I don't want to know. Just understand that, once again, it's a good time for Jews to be invisible, even in Paris. Beria is no *shabbos goy* – you know, a friend of the Orthodox Jews who turns the lights on and off on the sabbath so the prohibition against work is observed. Far from it. His most recent experience involved a man you may have known, Grisha Kaminsky, formerly people's commissar for health. He came forward at the February Plenum and made a most interesting speech, claiming that Beria once worked for the Transcaucasian Muslims, the Mussavat nationalists, at a time when the British controlled them during the intervention at Baku, just after the revolution. According to Kaminsky's speech, Beria was operating a Mussavatist counterintelligence network, and that made *him* a British spy. Needless to say, Kaminsky disappeared into thin air after the Plenum. So, you'll understand I'm in no hurry to run to Beria with a story, even an illustrated story, that his *khvost* pal Dershani is in contact with the fascist enemy.'

Abramov paused to let it all sink in, and the two men stood silently on the beach for a time.

In Szara's understanding, the ascendency of Beria, despite Kaminsky's near suicidal attack, confirmed what Bloch had said five months earlier: the purge, grinding, deliberate, somehow both efficient and random at once, was in effect a pogrom. He doubted that Abramov, as strong and as smart as he was, would survive it. And if Yezhov's allies were murdered, Abramov's friends would be treated no differently when the time came. 'Perhaps,

Sergei Jakobovich,' he said hesitantly, 'you ought to consider your personal safety. From Denmark, for instance, one can go virtually anywhere.'

'Me? Run? No, never. So far I'm just demoted, and I've absorbed that like a good ghetto *zhid* – eyes cast down, quiet as a mouse, no trouble from me, Gospodin, sir. No, what saves me is that with Hitler in the Sudetenland, Germany gains three and a half million people – all but seven hundred thousand of them ethnic Germans – easily four army divisions, the way we think, plus industrial capacity, raw materials, food, you name it. This adds up to one more big, strategic headache for Russia and, when all is said and done, that's my business, and I've been in that business since 1917 – it's what I know how to do. So they'll want to keep me around, at least for the time being.'

'And me too, they'll want to keep around.'

'Oh very definitely you. After all, you operate an important mine for us – without you and your brethren the Directorate can produce nothing. We manufacture precision tools, at least we try to, but where would we be without iron ore? Which brings me to what I came here to talk about, I didn't drag myself to some beach in Denmark just to get a pocketful of dirty pictures.

'The background is this: Hitler has the Sudetenland, we know he's going for all of Czechoslovakia, we think he wants more, a lot more. If the OTTER material was significant, it's now crucial, and the Directorate is going to have its way with this man whether he likes it or not. To that end, we've determined to send you to Berlin. This is dangerous, but necessary. Either you can talk OTTER into a more, ah, generous frame of mind or we're really going to put the screws on. In other words, patience now exhausted. Understood?'

'Yes.'

'Also, we want you to deliver money to the RAVEN

network, to RAVEN herself. Take a good look at her; you're going to be asked for your views when you return to Paris. The Directorate has faith in Schau-Wehrli, please don't misunderstand, but we'd like a second opinion.'

'Will Goldman supply passports for the trip?'

'What passports? Don't be such a noodle. You go as yourself, writing for *Pravda*, on whatever takes your fancy. Goldman will discuss with you the approach to OTTER and to RAVEN, and you'll work with him on questionnaires – we want you to guide OTTER into very particular and specific areas. Questions?'

'One.'

'Only one?'

'Why were you sent all this way? The "third country" meeting is usually reserved for special circumstances – you taught me that – and I haven't heard anything, anything official that is, that couldn't have been communicated by wireless. Am I missing something?'

Abramov inhaled deeply and acknowledged the impact of the question with a sigh that meant *look how smart he's getting*. 'Briefly, they're not so sure about you. You haven't made headway with OTTER, you lost an agent – even if that wasn't your fault, the Directorate doesn't excuse bad luck – and your one great triumph, which I now have in my pocket, is unknown to them. To be blunt, your credit is poor. So they wanted me to have a look at you, and make a decision about whether or not you should continue.'

'And if not?'

'That's not the decision, so don't be too curious. Now I used a car to get here, but I want you to leave first. You've got about a half-hour walk back into Aarhus, so you'll forgive me if I pass you on the road like I never saw you. Last word: again I remind you to be very careful in Berlin. Your status as a correspondent protects you, but don't go finding out how far. When you contact agents, follow procedure to the letter. As for all the chaos in Moscow, don't let it get you down. No situation is as hopeless as it appears, André Aronovich – remember the old saying: nobody ever found a cat skeleton in a tree.'

They said good-bye and Szara struggled up the soft sand to the top of the dunes. Looking back, the sense of the scene as a painting returned to him. Sergei Abramov, umbrella hooked on one forearm, hands thrust in pockets, stared out to sea. The autumn seascape surrounded him – crying gulls, incoming waves, the rustling beach grass, and pale-wash sky – but he was alien to it. Or, rather, it was alien to him, as though the idea of the painting was that the solitary figure on the shore was no longer part of life on earth.

27 October 1938.

Such visions did not leave him.

A fragment of bureaucratic language, *date of expiry*, the sort of phrase one saw on passports, visas, permits of every kind, became his private symbol for what was essentially a nameless feeling. *Europe is dying*, he thought. The most commonplace *good-bye* had an undertone of *farewell*. It was in the songs, in the faces in the streets, in the wild changes of mood – absurd gaiety one moment, desolation the next – he saw in friends and in himself.

The dining car on the Nord Express to Berlin was nearly deserted, the vibrations of stemware and china at the empty tables far too loud without the normal babble of conversation. An elderly waiter stood half asleep at his station, napkin draped over one arm, as Szara forced himself to eat a lukewarm veal chop. When the train approached the border, an officious porter came through the car lowering the window shades, presumably denying Szara and one other couple a view of French military fortifications.

And the passport control in Germany was worse than

usual. Nothing he could exactly put his finger on, the process was the same. Perhaps there were more police, their sidearms more noticeable. Or perhaps it was in the way they moved about, bumping into things, their voices a little louder, their intonations not so polite, something almost exultant in their manner. Or it might have been the men in suits, sublimely casual, who hardly bothered to look at his documents.

Or was he, he asked himself, merely losing his nerve? There had been no horrid Chinese food in Brussels this time. He'd spent hours in the back office of Stefan Leib's cartography shop, where Goldman had inflicted on him a series of exhausting, repetitious briefings that often lasted well past midnight. This was a different Goldman, leaning over a cluttered desk in the glow of a single lamp, voice tense and strained, breath sharp with alcohol, slashing pencil lines across a street map of Berlin or explaining, in sickening detail, the circumstances in which Dr Baumann now found himself.

The situation for German Jews had deteriorated, but far worse was the form the deterioration took. There was something hideously measured about it, like a drum, as some new decree appeared every month, each one a little worse than the last, each one inspiring, and clearly meant to inspire, its victims with a terrifying sense of orchestration. Whatever ruled their destiny simply refused to be placated. No matter how precisely and punctually they conformed to the minutiae of its rules, it grew angrier and more demanding. The more they fed it, the hungrier it got.

In April of 1938 only forty thousand Jewish firms remained in Germany; all others had passed to Aryan ownership, sometimes for a nominal fee, sometimes for nothing. Those businesses that remained under Jewish control either brought in foreign currency, which Germany desperately needed to buy war materials or, like Baumann Milling, were directly connected to rearmament efforts. In June, Jews had to provide an inventory of everything they owned, with the exception of personal and household goods.

In July, a glimmer of hope, a conference on Jewish emigration held at the French spa town of Évian, where representatives of the world's nations met to consider the problem. But they refused to take in the German Jews. The United States would accept only twenty-eight thousand, in severely restricted categories. Australia did not wish to import 'a racial problem.' South and Central American countries wanted only farmers, not traders or intellectuals. France had already accepted too many refugees. Britain claimed not to have space available, and immigration to British-controlled Palestine was sharply curtailed to a few hundred certificates a month since Arab riots and ambushes – beginning in 1936 – had created political difficulties for those who favoured letting Jews into the country. In addition, British access to oil in the Middle East was based on the maintenance of good relations with the Arab sheikdoms, and they were in general opposed to Jewish settlement in Palestine. Of all the nations convened at Évian, only Holland and Denmark would accept Jewish refugees who could leave Germany. By the end of the conference, most German Jews understood they were trapped.

The decrees did not stop. On 23 July, all Jews were required to apply for special identification cards. On 17 August it was ordered that Jews with German given names would have to change them – male Jews now to be known as Israel, females to be called Sarah. On 5 October, Jews were forced to hand in their passports. These would be returned, they were told, with an entry identifying the holder as a Jew.

As the train sped through the Rhine valley toward

Düsseldorf, Szara raised the window shade and watched the little clusters of village lights go by. He consciously tried to free his mind of Goldman's briefing and to concentrate on the likelihood of seeing Marta Haecht during his time in Berlin. But even in his imagination she lived in the shadow of her city, a very different Marta from the one he had believed was rushing to meet him in Lisbon. Perhaps she was nothing at all like his construction of her. Was it possible that she existed only in a fantasy world he'd built for himself? It did not matter, he realized, letting his head rest against the cold glass of the window. Whatever she might be, he ached for her presence, and this need was the single warmth that survived from the time when he'd believed the whole world lived for desire. Otherwise, there was only ice.

The journalist Szara got off the train at Potsdam station a few minutes after three in the morning, woke a taxi driver, and was taken to the Adlon, where all Russian journalists and trade delegations stayed. The hotel, musty and creaky and splendidly comfortable, was on Pariser Platz at the foot of the grandiose avenue Unter den Linden, next to the British embassy and three doors down from the Russian embassy. Trailing a sleepy porter down the long hall to his room, Szara heard exuberant, shouted Russian and the crash of a lamp. *Home at last*, he thought. The old man carrying his bag just shook his head sorrowfully at the uproar.

In the morning he saw them, groping toward coffee in the elegant dining room. Tass correspondents, officially, a range of types – from the broad-shouldered, fair-haired, and pale-eyed to the small, intense ones with glasses and beards and rumpled hair. Nobody he knew, or so he thought, until Vainshtok materialized at his table with a dish of stewed figs. 'So, now Szara arrives. Big news must be on the way.' Vainshtok, son of a timber merchant from Kiev, was infamously abrasive. He had wildly unfocused eyes behind round spectacles and a lip permanently curled with contempt. 'Anyhow, welcome to Berlin.'

'Hello, Vainshtok,' he said.

'So pleased you have chosen to honour us. I have to file on *everything*, up half the night. Now you're here maybe I get a break now and then.'

Szara gestured inquisitively toward the Tass reporters scattered about the dining room.

'Them? Ha!' said Vainshtok. 'They don't actually write anything. You and me, Szara, we have to do the work.'

After breakfast he tried to phone Marta Haecht. He learned she'd left the magazine two months earlier. He tried her home. Nobody answered.

The day before he left Paris, Kranov had handed him a personal message from Brussels:

> THE WORK HAS BEEN COMPLETED FOR YOUR ASSIGNMENT. HAVE A SAFE AND PRODUCTIVE JOURNEY. REZIDENT.

In Berlin, on the night of 28 October, André Szara understood what that message truly meant. Of those who undertook *the work*, he knew only one, Odile, whose 26 October dead-drop deposit for OTTER had warned of *a visit from a friend* who would arrive *at night*. The greatest part of the preparation, however, had been managed by nameless, faceless operatives – presumably stationed in Berlin, though he could not be certain of that. Perhaps some of the Tass reporters seen stumbling toward their morning coffee at the Adlon, perhaps a team brought in from Budapest; he was not to know. Once again, the unseen hand.

But the André Szara moving toward a clandestine meeting in Gestapo territory was more than grateful for it. He entered the Grunewald neighbourhood in the gathering dusk, leaving the Ringbahn tram stop with a few other men carrying briefcases and indistinguishable from them. Most of the residents of the Grunewald came and went by car, many of them chauffeured. But the evening return from business was as much cover as the operatives had been able to devise, and Szara was thankful for even that minimal camouflage.

The Baumann villa faced Salzbrunner street, but he was going in the back way. Thus he walked briskly up Charlottenbrunner, slowed to let one last returning businessman find his way home, crossed a narrow lane, then counted steps until he saw a rock turned earth side up. Here he entered a well-groomed pine wood – at the blind spot the operatives had discovered, away from the view of nearby houses – found the path that was supposed to be there, and followed it to the foot of a stucco wall that enclosed the villa adjoining the Baumann property.

Now he waited. The Berlin weather was cold and damp, the woods dark, and time slowed to a crawl, but they'd hidden him here to accommodate an early entry into the neighbourhood, at dusk, and now kept him on ice to await the magic hour of nine o'clock, when the servant couple who occupied the main residence on the Baumann property were known to go to sleep – or at least turn off their lights. At ten minutes after nine he set out, feeling his way along the wall and counting steps until, just where they said it would be, he found a foothold that an operative had dug into the stucco facing. He put his left foot into the small niche, drove his weight upward, and grabbed the tiled cap of the wall. He'd been told to wear rubber-soled shoes, and the traction helped him as he scrabbled his feet against the smooth surface. It wasn't graceful, but he eventually lay flat on the corner formed by the wall he'd climbed and that which divided the two properties.

Looking down to his left, he saw a woman in a flowered robe reading in a chair by the window. To his right, the servants' cottage had its blinds drawn. Just below, a garden shed stood against the wall – he cautiously lowered himself to its shingle roof, which gave unpleasantly under the strain but held until he hopped off. From the cottage came the high-pitched barking of a small dog – that would be Ludwig, the *apparat* mechanism for moving Baumann out into the neighbourhood at night – which was almost immediately calmed. Staying out of sight of the villa itself, he found the back door of the cottage and knocked lightly three times – not a signal, but a style recommended by Goldman as 'informal' and 'neighbourly.' The door opened quickly and Dr Baumann let him in.

The operatives had got him safely inside. Somebody, shivering in the Berlin mist at dawn, had dug a piece out of the wall with a clasp knife – or however it had been done, by twelve-year-olds for all he knew – anyhow, he was in. He had been manoeuvred, like a weapon, into a position where his light, his intellect, influence, craft, whatever it was, could shine.

They'd done their job. Pity he couldn't do his.

Oh, he tried. Goldman had said, 'You must control this man. You can be courteous, if you like, or lovable. Threats sometimes work. Be solemn, patriotic, or just phenomenally boring – this too has been done – but you must control him.' Szara couldn't.

Dr Julius Baumann was grey. The brutal, ceaseless pressure orchestrated by the Reich bureaucracies was proceeding quite successfully in his case. His face was ruined by tension and lack of sleep; he had become thin, stooped, old. 'You cannot know what it's like here.' This he said again and again, and Szara could find no way through it. 'Can we help you?' he asked. 'Do you need anything?' Baumann just shook his head, somehow closed off behind a wall that no such offer could breach.

'Be positive,' Goldman had said. 'You represent strength. Make him feel the power you stand for, let him know it supports him.'

Szara tried: 'There's little we can't do, you know. Your account with us is virtually unlimited, but you must draw on it.'

'What is there to want?' Baumann said angrily. 'What they've taken from me you cannot give back. Nobody can do that.'

'The regime is weakening. Perhaps you can't see it, but we can. There's reason to hope, reason to hang on.'

'Yes,' Baumann said, the man who will agree to anything because he finds the argument itself tiresome. 'We try,' he added. *But we do not succeed*, his eyes said.

Frau Baumann had changed in a different way. She was now more hausfrau than Frau Doktor. If in fact it was her pretensions – the desire for social prominence and the need to condescend – that had driven a nation of fifty million people into a blind fury, she had certainly been cured of all that. Now she fussed and fiddled, her hands never still. She had reduced her existence to a series of small, household crises, turned fear into exasperation with domestic life; thimbles, brooms, potatoes. Perhaps it was her version of the world in which the common German housewife lived, perhaps she hoped that by joining the enemy she could keep – they would allow her to keep – what remained of her life. When she left the room, Baumann followed her with his eyes. 'You see?' he whispered to Szara, as though something needed to be proved.

Szara nodded sorrowfully; he understood. 'And work?'

he asked. 'The business? What's it like there? How do they feel about you, your employees. Still faithful? Or do most of them follow the party line?'

'They look out for themselves. Everybody does, now.'

'No kindness? Not one good soul?'

Perhaps Baumann wavered for an instant, then realized what came next – just who is that good soul – and said, 'It doesn't matter what they think.'

Szara sighed. 'You refuse to help us. Or yourself.'

Something flickered in Baumann's eyes – a strange kind of sympathy? Then it was gone. 'Please,' he said, 'you must not ask too much of me. I am less brave every day. Going to the stone wall for the message is an agony, you understand? I make myself do it. I –'

The telephone rang.

Baumann was paralysed. He stared through the doorway into the kitchen while the phone rang again and again. Finally Frau Baumann picked up the receiver. 'Yes?' she said. Then: 'Yes.' She listened for a time, started to exclaim, was evidently cut off by the person at the other end of the line. 'Can you wait a moment?' she asked. They heard her set the receiver down carefully on a wooden shelf. When she entered the living room she was holding both hands lightly to the sides of her face.

'Julius, darling, do we have money in the house?' She spoke calmly, as though drawing on a reserve of inner strength, but her hands were trembling and her cheeks were flushed.

'Who is it?'

'This is Natalya. Calling on the telephone to say that she must return to Poland. Tonight.'

'Why would she . . .?'

'It has been ordered, Julius. The police are there and she is to be put on a train after midnight. They are being very polite about it, she says, and are willing to bring her here on the way to the station.'

Baumann did not react; he stared.

'Julius?' Frau Baumann said. 'Natalya is waiting to see if we can help her.'

'In the drawer,' Baumann said. He turned to Szara. 'Natalya is her cousin. She came here from Lublin six years ago.'

'There isn't very much in the drawer,' Frau Baumann said.

Szara took a thick handful of reichsmarks out of his pocket. 'Give her this,' he said, handing it to Baumann.

Frau Baumann returned to the telephone. 'Yes, it's all right. When are you coming?' She paused for the answer. 'Good, then we'll see you. I'm sure it will be straightened out. Don't forget your sweaters, Polish hotels . . . Yes . . . I know . . . Twenty minutes.' She hung up the phone and returned to the living room. 'All the Jewish immigrants from Poland must leave Germany,' she said. 'They are being deported.'

'*Deported?*' Baumann said.

His wife nodded. 'To a place called Zbąszyń.'

'Deported,' Baumann said. 'A sixty-three-year-old woman, deported. What in God's name will she do in Poland?' He stood up abruptly, then walked to a bookcase by the window, took a large book down and thumbed through the pages. 'What is it called?'

'Zbąszyń.'

Baumann moved the atlas under a lamp and squinted at the page. 'Warsaw I could understand,' he said. 'I can't find it.' He looked up at his wife. 'Did she think to call ahead for a room at least?'

Szara stood. 'I'll have to be going,' he said. 'The police will . . .'

Baumann looked up from the book.

'I think you should get out,' Szara said. 'This must involve thousands of people. Tens of thousands. Next they'll find someplace to send you, it's possible.'

'But we're not Polish,' Frau Baumann said. 'We're German.'

'We'll get you out,' Szara said. 'To France or Holland.'

Baumann seemed dubious.

'Don't answer now. Just think about it. I'll have you contacted and we'll meet again in a few days.' He put his raincoat on. 'Will you consider it?'

'I'm not sure,' Baumann said, evidently confused.

'We'll at least discuss it,' Szara said and, looking at his watch, headed for the door.

Outside, the still air was cold and wet. A rickety ladder got him to the roof of the shed; from there he mounted the wall, hung by his hands to decrease the distance, then dropped the few feet to the ground. His exfiltration time was 10:08, but the forced exit had made him early, so he waited in the woods as he'd done before. In the silence of the Grunewald neighbourhood, he heard what he took to be the brief visit of the cousin: opening and closing car doors, an idling engine, muffled voices, doors again, then a car driving away. That was all.

29 October.

Szara decided that calling Marta Haecht on the telephone was a bad idea; a conversation necessarily awkward, difficult. Instead he wrote, on a sheet of Adlon stationery, 'I've returned to Berlin on assignment from my paper. I would like, more than I can say in this letter, to be with you for whatever time we can have. Of course I'll understand if your life has changed, and it would be better not to meet. In any case your friend, André.'

He spent a listless day, trying not to think about the Baumanns. There was no Directorate plan to take them out of Germany, and he had no authorization to make such an offer, but Szara didn't care. *Enough is enough*, he thought.

The following morning, Szara had an answer to his letter, in the form of a telephone message taken at the Adlon desk.

An address, an office number, a date, a time. From Fräulein H.

31 October.

Szara stood by the open window and stared out into the Bischofstrasse, shiny with rain in midafternoon, wet brown and yellow leaves plastered to the pavements. The damp air felt good to him. He heard Marta's heavy tread as she moved across the room, then felt her warm skin against his back as she hid behind him. 'Please don't stand there,' she whispered. 'The whole world will see there's a naked man in here.'

'What will you give me?'

'Ah, I will give you that for which you dare not ask, yet want beyond all things.'

'Name it.'

'A cup of tea.'

They walked away from the window together and he sat at a table covered with an Indian cloth and watched as she made tea.

The room was a loft on the top floor of an office building, with large windows and a high ceiling that made it the perfect studio for an artist. *Benno Ault*. So the name read on a directory in the great, echoing marble lobby below, vestige of a lost grandeur. *Herr Benno Ault, Room 709*. And he was? According to Marta, 'a university friend. Dear, sweet, lost.' An artist who now lived elsewhere and rented her his studio as an apartment. His presence remained. Tacked to the walls – painted an industrial beige many years before, now water-stained and flaking – was what Szara took to be the oeuvre of Benno Ault. Dear, sweet, and lost he may well have been but also, from the look of the thing, mad as a hatter. The unframed canvases writhed with colour, garish yellows and greens. These were portraits of the shipwrecked and the damned, pink faces howled from every wall as saffron oceans pulled them under and they clawed at the air with grotesque hands.

She brought him tea in a steaming mug, standing by his chair and spooning in sugar until he told her to stop, the curve of her hip pressed against his side. 'It's sweet the way you like?' she said, innocent as dawn.

'Just exactly,' he said.

'Good,' she said firmly and arranged herself in a nearby armchair, a huge velvet orphan that had seen better times. She spread a napkin across her bare tummy – a pun on decorum, as though she were a Goya nude minding her manners. When she sipped her tea she closed her eyes, then wiggled her toes with pleasure. The background for this performance was provided by a giant radio with a station band lit up bright amber, which had played Schubert lieder since the moment he'd walked in the door. Now she conducted, waving a stern index finger back and forth. 'Am I,' she said suddenly, 'as you remember?'

'Am I?' he said.

'Actually, you are quite different.'

'You also.'

'It's the world,' she said. 'But I don't care. Your letter was sweet – a little forlorn. Did you mean it? Or was it just to make things easy? Either way it's all right, I'm just curious.'

'I meant it.'

'I thought so. But then I thought; after an hour, we'll see.'

'The hour's over. The letter stands.'

'Soon I must go back to work. Shall I see you again? Or will we wait another year?'

'Tomorrow.'

'I haven't said I would.'

'Will you?'

'Yes.'

She had answered his knock at the door in a short silk robe tied loosely at the waist – just purchased; the scent of new clothing lingered on it beneath her perfume – hair worn loose and brushed out, red lipstick freshly applied. A woman of the world now, looking forward to an assignation in the middle of the day. Seeing her like that, framed in the doorway, stunned him. It was too good to be true. When she lifted her face to him and closed her eyes he felt like a man suddenly and unexpectedly warmed by sunlight. He actually, for an instant as they embraced, felt her mouth smile with pleasure. But after that everything – being led by the hand to a sofa, pillows kicked off, robe flung away – happened too quickly. What he had imagined would be artful and seductive wasn't like that at all. It wasn't really like them. Two other people, then, very hungry, urgent, selfish people. They laughed about it later, but things were different and they knew it.

At one point she'd raised her head from the sofa and whispered delicately next to his ear. The words were familiar enough, a lover's request, but they had shocked him – because they were German words and the sound of them unlocked something inside him, something cold and strong and almost violent. Whatever it was, she felt it. She liked it. This was a very dangerous place to go, he sensed, but they went there just the same.

He had wondered, later on, drinking tea, how much she understood of what had happened. Was this *eternal woman*, accepting, absorbing? Or had she, for a moment, become his companion in decadence, playing her part in some mildly evil version of a lovers' game? He couldn't ask. She seemed happy, making jokes, wiggling her toes, content with herself and the afternoon.

Then she got dressed. This too was different. By degrees she became a working woman, a typical Berliner: the ingenuous, vaguely Bohemian Marta, adoring of Russian journalists, was no more. Garter belt, stockings, a crisp shirt with a rounded collar, a rusty tweed, mid-calf-length suit, then a small, stylish hat with a feather – the perfect disguise, ruined at the last when she made a little-girl brat face at him: what they called here *Schnauze*, literally snout, a way of telling the world to go to hell. She gave him a cool cheek to kiss on the way out – not to ruin the lipstick – and rumpled his hair.

He stayed for a time after she left, drinking tea, watching out of the window as a cloud of starlings swerved away through the rainy sky. The radio programme changed, to what he guessed was Beethoven – something dark and thoughtful at any rate. The city drew him into its mood; he found it almost impossible to resist, became autumnal and meditative, asked questions that really could not be answered. Marta Haecht, for instance: had she, he wondered, become so newly sophisticated at the hands of other lovers? Certainly, that was it. Who, he wondered. That was, in his experience of such things, always a surprise. *Him?*

With a Russian girl he would have known all. Every private thought would have been bashed about between them, plenty of tears to wash it all down with, then forgiveness, tenderness, and wild – likely drunken – lovemaking to paste everything back together again. Poles and Russians knew how hidden feelings poisoned life; in the end the vodka was just a catalyst.

But she wasn't Russian or Polish, she was German, like

this damned sorrowful music. The reality of that had come home to him when they were on the sofa. What was *that?* The Eastern conqueror takes the Teutonic princess? Whatever it was, it was no game.

Restless now, wishing that Marta hadn't gone back to work, Szara walked around the room as he got dressed, confronted by Ault's maniacal paintings. *Strange people*, he thought. *They make a virtue of anguish*. Nonetheless, he began counting the hours until he'd see her again and tried to shake off the sense of oppression gathering in his heart.

Perhaps it was the influence of the building itself. Dating from the early days of the century, its long hallways, set in tiny octagonal black and white tiles, echoed with every footstep and lived in perpetual dusk, a greyish light that spilled from frosted glass door panels numbered in Gothic script. Called Die Eisenbourse Haus, the Iron Exchange Building, it had certainly been some builder's cherished dream. There was no Iron Exchange, not that Szara knew about. Had one been planned, perhaps somewhere nearby? Only its adjunct had been built, in any case, seven storeys of elaborate brickwork with the name in gold script on the glass above the entryway. The lift would have been installed later, he thought. It was enormous, an anthill intended as home to every sort of respectable commerce. But the builder had raised it in the wrong place. Bischofstrasse was across the river Spree from the better part of Berlin, reached by the Kaiser Wilhelm bridge, on the edge of the ancient Jewish quarter. Had a commercial district once been planned here? The builder evidently thought so, locating just west of the Judenstrasse, across from Neue Markt, between Pandawer and Steinweg streets.

But it had not turned out that way. The building stood as a grand edifice among tenements and dreary shops, and its lobby directory told the story: piano teachers, theatrical agents, a private detective, a club for sailing instruction and a club for lonely hearts, an astrologer, an inventor, and Grömmelink the cut-rate denture man.

Szara rang for the lift, which wheezed ponderously to the top floor. The metal door slid open, then a soiled white glove slowly drew the gate aside. The operator was an old man with lank hair parted in the middle and swept back behind his ears, fine, almost transparent skin, and a face lined by tragedy. He was called Albert, according to Marta, who thought him an original, rather amusing, the ruling troll of the Castle Perilous, her moat-keeper. Szara, however, was not amused by Albert, who stared at him with sullen and intense dislike as he got on the elevator, then sniffed loudly as he slammed the gate. *I smell a Jew*, that meant. On the wall above the control handle were taped two curling photographs of serious young men in Landwehr uniform. Sons dead in the war? Szara thought so. As the floors bumped slowly past, Szara repressed a shiver. He never would have imagined Marta Haecht living in such a place.

But then there were all sorts of new things about Marta. Wandering about in the apartment, he'd found a wooden rack holding a further collection of Ault's paintings – these evidently not worthy of display. Idly curious, he'd looked through them, come upon a pink nude standing pensively, almost self-consciously, amid frantic swirls of green and yellow. Something familiar piqued his interest, then he realized he knew the model, knew her in that very pose. All sorts of things new about Marta.

The elevator came to a stop. Albert opened the gate, then the exterior door. 'Lobby,' he said harshly. 'Now you get out.'

* * *

Back in his room at the Adlon he closed the heavy drapes to shut out the dusk, locked the door, and lost himself in ciphering. Using the German railway timetable Goldman had handed him – a very unremarkable find if he were searched – he converted his plaintext into numerical groups. In his statement to the Directorate he'd been extremely cautious, in fact deceptive: the broken man in the Grunewald, described as he was, would set off alarms and excursions all over Dzerzhinsky Square. Dr Baumann was not under anyone's control, including his own, and Szara could only imagine what the Directorate might order done if they found that out, especially the Directorate as led by Dershani.

The report described an agent under stress yet operating efficiently. Stubborn, self-motivating, a prominent and successful businessman after all, thus not just somebody that could be ordered about. Szara strengthened the deception by implying, faintly, that the Directorate should soften its instinct for bureaucratic domination and acknowledge that it was dealing with a man to whom independence, even as a Jew in Germany, was instinctive, habitual. Baumann had to believe he was in control, Szara suggested, and to perceive the *apparat* as a kind of servant.

But if Baumann was steadfast, Szara continued, the situation as he found it in Germany was extremely unstable. He described the telephone call from the cousin forced to return to Poland, noted the disbursement of emergency funds, then went on to suggest that OTTER ought to be offered exfiltration – *if the time should ever come* – followed by resettlement in a European city. Against that day, Baumann Milling ought to hire a new employee, as designated by the case officer, who would remain in deep cover until activated. Szara closed with the statement that he would be remaining in Berlin for at least seven days, and requested local operative support in arranging a second meeting.

He grouped his numbers, did his false addition, counted letters in the timetable a second time, just to be sure. Garbled transmissions drove Moscow wild – *What's a murn? And why does he ask for raisins?* – and he urgently needed to have their trust and good faith if they were going to accept his analysis of the situation.

He walked the half block to the embassy, a place the journalist Szara would be expected to visit, found his contact, a second secretary named Varin, and delivered the cable. Then he disappeared into the Berlin night.

He had, oh, a little company, he thought. Nothing too serious. Nothing he couldn't deal with.

Said Goldman: 'There are two situations which, if I were you, would be of concern: (a) You find yourself truly blanketed – perhaps a moving box: one in front, one behind, two at three o'clock and nine o'clock, go down an alley and the whole apparatus shifts with you. Or maybe it's people in parked cars on an empty street, women in doorways. All that sort of thing, they're simply not going to let you out of their sight. Either they insist on knowing who you really are and where you're going, or they're trying to panic you, to see what you do. You'll break it off, of course. Go back to the hotel, use your telephone contact, the 4088 number. There'll be no answer, but one ring will do the job.

'Or, (b) you ought to be alarmed if there's absolutely no sign of surveillance. A Soviet journalist in Berlin must, *must*, be of interest at some level of the counterintelligence bureaux. The normal situation would be periodic, one or two men, probably detectives who'll look like what they are. They'll follow at a medium distance. Ideally, don't go showing them a lot of tradecraft – if you're too slick it will provoke their curiosity. If you can't dispose of them with a casual manoeuvre or two, give it up and try again later. A normal approach for the Germans would be to tag along at night, leave you free in the daytime. But if it's – what? the Sahara, then be careful. It may mean they're really operating – that is, they've put someone really good on you, and he, or she for that matter, is better than you are. In that case, see the second secretary at the embassy and we'll get you some help.'

Very well, he thought. This time the little genius in Brussels knew what he was talking about. *Out for a stroll*, Szara lit a cigarette on the Kanonierstrasse, standing in front of the vast gloomy facade of the Deutsche Bank, then, *stranger in your city*, he peered about him as though he were slightly at sea. The other man lighting a cigarette, about forty metres behind him, visible only as a hat and an overcoat, was company.

Not a good night for company. With ten thousand reichsmarks wadded up in his pockets he was headed toward the Reichshallen theatre for a meeting with Nadia Tscherova, actress, émigrée, RAVEN, and group leader of the RAVEN network. Tscherova would be available to him backstage – not at the grandiose Reichshallen but at a small repertory theatre in a narrow lane called Rosenhain Passage – after 10:40. Szara refused to hurry, wandering along, waiting until he reached Kraussenstrasse before making a move to verify the surveillance. If he didn't make the *treff* tonight, Tscherova would be available to him for three nights following. Run by Schau-Wehrli with a very firm hand, RAVEN was known to follow orders, so Szara relaxed, taking in the sights, a man with no particular place to go and all the time in the world to get there.

About Tscherova he was curious. Schau-Wehrli handled her with fine Swiss contempt, referring to her as *stukach*, snitch, the lowest rank of Soviet agents, who simply traded information for money. Goldman's view differed. He used the word *vliyaniya*, fellow traveller. This term was traditionally reserved for agents of influence, often self-recruited believers in the Soviet dream: typically academics, civil servants, artists of all sorts, and the occasional forward-looking businessman. In the sense that Tscherova moved in the upper levels of Nazi society, he supposed she was *vliyaniya*, yet she was paid, as were the brother and sister Brozin and Brozina and the Czech balletmaster Anton Krafic, the remainder of the RAVEN network. As for the highest-level agents, the *proniknoveniya* – penetration specialists serving under direct, virtually military discipline – Szara was not allowed anywhere near them, though he suspected Schau-Wehrli's MOCHA group might fall under that classification, and Goldman was rumoured to be running, personally, an asset buried in the very heart of the Gestapo.

Of course the system varied with the national point of view. Low-level agents for the French were called *dupeurs*, deceivers, and principally reported on the military institutions of various countries. *Moutons*, sheep, went after industrial intelligence while *baladeurs*, strolling players, took on free-lance assignments. The French equivalent of the *proniknoveniya*, highly controlled and highly placed, was the *agent fixe*, while the *trafiquant*, like Tscherova, handled a net of subagents.

At the corner of Kraussenstrasse Szara paused, studied the street signs, then hurried across the intersection, not running exactly, but managing in such a way that two speeding Daimlers went whizzing past his back. A tobacconist's shop window, briefly inspected, revealed his company peering anxiously from the other side of the street, then crossing behind him. Szara quickened his pace slightly, then trotted up the steps of the Hotel Kempinski, passed through the elegant lobby, then seated himself at a table in the hotel bar. This was sophisticated Berlin; a study in glossy black and white surfaces with chrome highlights, palm trees, a man in a white dinner-jacket playing romantic songs on a white piano, a scattering of well-dressed people, and the soothing, melodic hum of conversation. He ordered a schnapps, leaned back in a leather chair, and focused his attention on a woman who was alone at a nearby table – rather ageless, not unattractive, very much minding her own business; which was a tall drink with a miniature candy cane hung on the side of the glass.

Ten minutes later, company arrived. Sweaty, moon-faced, anxious; an overworked detective who'd evidently parked himself on a chair in the lobby, then got nervous being out of contact with his assignment. He stood at the bar, ordered a beer, counted out pocket change to pay for it. Szara felt sorry for him.

Meanwhile, the woman he'd picked out made steady progress with her drink. Szara walked over to her and, presenting his back to the detective, leaned over and asked her what time it was. She said, politely enough, that she didn't know, but thought it was getting on towards ten. Szara laughed, stood up, turned halfway back toward his table, thought better of it, looked at his watch, said something like 'I'm afraid my watch has stopped' in a low voice, smiled conspiratorially, then returned to his chair. Fifteen minutes later, she left. Szara checked his watch, gave her five minutes to get wherever she was going, then threw a bill on the table and departed. Out in the lobby, he hurried into an elevator just before the door closed and asked to be let off at the fourth floor. He walked purposefully down the hall, heard the door close behind him, then found a stairway and returned to the lobby. The detective was sitting in a chair, watching the elevator door like a hawk, waiting for Szara to return from his assignation. Szara left the hotel through a side entrance, made certain he had no further company, then hailed a cab.

* * *

Rosenhain Passage was medieval, a crooked lane surfaced with broken stone. Half-timbered buildings, the plaster grey with age, slanted backwards as they rose, and a cold smell of drains hung in the dead air. What had happened here? He heard water trickling from unmended pipes, all shutters were closed tight, the street was lifeless, inert. There were no people. In the middle of all this stood Das Schmuckkästchen – the Jewel Box – theatre, as though a city cultural commission had been told to *do something about Rosenhain Passage* and here was their solution, a way of brightening things up. A hand-painted banner hung from the handle of an old-fashioned coach horn announcing the performance of *The Captain's Dilemma* by Hans-Peter Mütchler.

Midway down an alley next to the theatre, a door had been propped open with a pressing iron. Szara shoved it out of the way with his foot, let the door close gently until the lock snapped. Behind a thick curtain he could hear a play in progress, a man and a woman exchanging domestic insults in the declamatory style reserved for historical drama – *listen carefully, this was written a long time ago*. The insults were supposed to be amusing, the thrust of the voice told you that, and someone in the theatre did laugh once, but Szara could feel the almost palpable discomfort – the shifting and coughing, the unvoiced sigh – of an audience subjected to a witless and boring evening.

As Goldman had promised, there wasn't a soul to be seen where he entered. He peered through the darkness, found a row of doors, and tapped lightly at the one marked C.

'Yes? Come in.'

He found himself in a small dressing room: mirrors, costumes, clutter. A woman with a book in her hand, place held with an index finger, was sitting upright on a chaise longue, her face taut and anxious. Goldman had shown him a photograph. An actress. But the reality left him staring. Perhaps it was Berlin, the grotesque weight of the place, its heavy air, thickly made people, the brutal density of its life, but the woman seemed to him almost transparent, someone who might float away at any moment.

She put her head to one side and studied him clinically. 'You're different,' she said in Russian. Her voice was hoarse, and even in two words he could hear contempt.

'Different?'

'They usually send me a sort of boar. With bristles.' She was tall and slight, had turned up the cuffs of a thick sweater to reveal delicate wrists. Her eyes were enormous, a blue so pale and fragile it reminded him of blindness, and her hair, worn long and loose, was the colour of an almond shell. It was very fine hair, the kind that stirred with the slightest motion. Also she had been drinking; he could smell wine. 'Sit down,' she said softly, changing moods.

He sat in a thronelike armchair, clearly a stage prop. 'Are you in the play?' She was wearing slacks and strapped shoes with low heels, the outfit didn't go with the old-fashioned bluster he could hear from the stage.

'Done for the night.' Her voice easily suggested quotation marks when she added, 'Beatrice, a maid.' She shrugged, a dismissive Russian gesture. 'It's my rotten German. Sometimes I play a foreigner, but mostly it's maids. In little maid costumes. Everybody likes little maid costumes. When I bend over you can almost see my ass. But not quite.'

'What play is it?'

'What? You don't know *The Captain's Dilemma?* I thought everybody did.'

'No. Sorry.'

'Mütchler suits the current taste – that is, Goebbels's taste. He's said to consider it quite excellent. The captain returns to his home ten years after a shipwreck; he finds his wife living beyond her means, a slave to foolish fashion, beset by sycophants and usurers. He, on the other hand, is a typical *Volk:* sturdy, forthright, honest, a simple man from Rostock with the pleasures of a simple man. Simple pleasures, you see – we play him as a turnip. So now we have *conflict*, and a kind of drawing room comedy, with all sorts of amusing character parts: hypocrites, fops, oily Jews.'

'And the dilemma?'

'The dilemma is why the playwright wasn't strangled at birth.'

Szara laughed.

'What are you? A writer? I mean beside the other thing.'

'How do you know I'm the other thing?'

'Cruel times for Nadia if you're not.'

'And why a writer?'

'Oh, I know writers. I have them in my family, or used to. Do you want some wine? Be careful – it's a test.'

'Just a little.'

'You fail.' She reached behind a screen, poured wine into a water glass, and handed it to him, then retrieved her own glass, hidden behind a leg of the chaise longue. '*Nazhdrov'ya*.'

'*Nazhdrov'ya*.'

'Phooey.' She wrinkled her nose at the glass. 'Your pretty little niece, who is no doubt dying to be an actress – tell her it all rests on a tolerance for atrocious white wine.'

'You are from Moscow?' he asked.

'No, Piter, St Petersburg. So sorry, I mean Leningrad. An old, old family. Tscherova is my married name.'

'And Tscherov? He's in Berlin?'

'Pfft,' she said, casting her eyes up at the ceiling and springing four fingers from beneath her thumb, flicking Tscherov's soul up to heaven. 'November 1917.'

'Difficult times,' he said in sympathy.

'A Menshevik, a nice man. Married me when I was sixteen and didn't I give him a hellish time of it. The last eight months of his life, too. Poor Tscherov.' Her eyes shone for a moment and she looked away.

'At least you survived.'

'We all did. Aristocrats and artists in my family, all crazy as bats; revolution was the very thing for us. I have a brother in your business. Or I should say had. He seems to have vanished. Sascha.' She laughed at his memory, a harsh cackle, then put her fingers to her mouth, as though it were a drunken sound and embarrassed her. 'Sorry. Colonel Alexander Vonets – did you know him?'

'No.'

'Too bad. Charming bastard. Ah, the elegant Vonets family – but see what they've come to now. Miserable *stukachi*, dealing in filthy Nazi gossip. "Oh, but my dear General, how absolutely fasss-cinating!"' She snickered at her own performance, then leaned toward him. 'You know what they say in Paris, that a woman attending a soirée needs only two words of French to be thought an elegant conversationalist? *Formidable* and *fantastique*. Well, it's the same here. You look up at them – you sit down if they're squatty little things; the eyes simply must look up at them – and they talk and talk, and you say – in German of course – *formidable*! after one sentence and *fantastique*! after the next. "Brilliant woman!" they say later.'

'So it's all nothing more than conversation.'

She studied him for a moment. 'You are very rude,' she said.

'Forgive me. It's just curiosity. I don't care what you do.'

'Well, as I'm certain you know, this wasn't my idea.'

'No?'

'Hardly. When they discovered I'd escaped from Russia

and was in Berlin, they sent some *people*, not like you, around.' She shrugged, remembering the moment. 'Offered a choice between death and money, I chose money.'

Szara nodded in sympathy.

'We go to . . . parties, my little troupe and I. Parties of a sort, you know. We're considered a terrific amount of fun. People drink. Lose their inhibitions. Shall you hear it all?'

'Of course not.'

She smiled. 'It isn't so bad as you think. I avoid the worst of it, but my associates, well. Not that I'm innocent, you understand. I've known a couple of them better than I should have.' She paused. Looked at him critically, closed one eye. 'You must be a writer – so serious. Everything *means* something, but for us . . . In the theatre, you know, we're like naughty children, like brothers and sisters playing behind the shed. So these things don't mean so much, it's a way to forget yourself, that's all. One night you're this person and the next night you're that person, so that sometimes you're no person at all. This profession . . . it deforms the heart. Perhaps. I don't know.'

She was lost for a moment, sitting on the edge of the chaise, weight borne by elbows on knees, glass held in both hands. 'As for the Nazis, well, they're really more like pigs than humans, if you think about it. The men – and the women – just like pigs, they even squeal like pigs. It's no insult to say this, it's literal. It isn't their "*Schweine!*" that I'm talking about but real pigs: pink, overweight, quite intelligent if you know anything about them, certainly smarter than dogs, but very appetitious, there the common wisdom has it just right. They do want what they want, and lots of it, and right away, and then, when they get it, they're happy. Blissful.'

'I thought you said the man who came to see you was like a boar.'

'I did say that, didn't I. I'm sure there's a difference, though. You just have to be much smarter than me to see it.'

From the stage Szara could hear the ringing tones of a soliloquy, a kind of triumphant anger shot through with blistering rectitude. Then a pause, then desultory applause, then the creak of an unoiled mechanism closing the curtain. This was followed by a heavy tread in the hallway, a man's gruff voice, '*Scheiss!*' and the emphatic slam of a door.

'There,' said Tscherova, switching into German, 'that's the captain now. A simple *Volk*.'

Szara reached into his pockets and withdrew the thick wads of reichsmarks. She nodded, took them from him, stood, and stuffed the pockets of a long wool coat hanging on a peg.

Szara now assumed their conversation to be perfectly audible to the 'captain' next door. 'You'll take care of your, ah, health. I really hope you will.'

'Oh yes.'

He stood in order to leave; in the small room they were a little closer together than strangers would normally have been. 'It's better,' he said quietly, 'not to find out how it would be. Yes?'

She smiled impishly, amused that the proximity affected him. 'You *are* different, you are. And you mustn't be too concerned.' Her slim hand brushed the waistband of her slacks, then held up a tiny vial of yellow liquid. Her eyebrow lifted, *see how clever?* 'End of story,' she said. 'Curtain.' Then she hid it behind her back, as though it didn't exist. She bent toward him, kissed him lightly on the mouth – very warm and very brief – and whispered good-bye, in Russian, next to his ear.

* * *

Szara walked east from the theatre, away from the Adlon, unconsciously following procedure. Balked by the Neu-Kölln Canal, he veered south to Gertraudten Bridge, lit a cigarette, watched orange peels and scrapwood drifting past on the black water. It was colder, the lamp lights had pale haloes as mist drifted off the canal.

The Directorate never knew their agents in person; Szara now saw the reason for that. Tscherova's vulnerability would not leave his mind. Caught between the Gestapo and the NKVD, between Germany and Russia, she lived by her wits, by looking as she did, by clever talk. But she would have to drink the yellow liquid eventually, maybe soon, and the idea of so much life – all the emotional weather that blew across her heart – winding up as a formless shape collapsed in a corner tormented him. Could a woman be too beautiful to die? Moscow wouldn't like his answer to that. Was he a little bit in love with her? What if he was. Was all her capering about, the way she worked on him with her eyes, meant to draw him to her? He was sure of it. How could that be wrong?

She'd have to drink the liquid because agents didn't survive. The result of all the elaborate defences, secrecy and codes and clandestine methods of every sort, was time gained, only that, against a known destiny. Things went wrong. Things always, eventually, went wrong. The world was unpredictable, inconsistent, volatile, ultimately a madhouse of bizarre events. Agents got caught. Almost always. You replaced them. That's what the *apparat* expected you to do: reorganize the chaos, mend the damage, and go on. There were ways in which he accepted that, but when women entered the equation he failed. His need was to protect women, not to sacrifice them, and he could not, would not, change. An ancient instinct, to stand between women and danger, sapped his will to run operations the way they had to be run and made him a bad intelligence officer – it was just that simple. And the worst part of it was that the yellow liquid wasn't part of some spy kit – the NKVD didn't believe in such things. No, Tscherova had obtained the liquid herself, because she knew what happened to agents just as well as he did and she wanted to have it over and done with when the time came. The idea made him ill, the world couldn't go on that way.

But they had a Jew up on the end of Brüderstrasse, where Szara turned north, a pack of drunken Hitlerjugend in their fancy uniforms, teenagers, forcing some poor soul on hands and knees to drink the black water in a gutter, and they were shouting and laughing and singing and having a tremendously good time at it.

Szara faded into a doorway. For a moment he thought he was having a stroke – his vision swam and a terrible force hammered against his temples like a fist. Steadying himself against a wall, he realized it wasn't a stroke, it was rage, and he fought to subdue it. For a moment he went mad, shutting his eyes against the pounding blood and pleading with God for a machine gun, a hand grenade, a pistol, any weapon at all – but this prayer was not immediately answered. Later he discovered a small chip missing from a front tooth.

Some time after midnight, having crept away into the darkness, walking through deserted streets toward his hotel, he made the inevitable connection: Tscherova, by what she did, could help to destroy these people, these youths with their Jewish toy. She could weaken them in ways they did not understand, she was more than a machine gun or a pistol, a far deadlier weapon than any he'd wished for. The knowledge tore at him, on top of what he'd seen, and there were tears on his face that he wiped off with the sleeve of his raincoat.

The following afternoon, he told Marta Haecht what he'd seen. Instinctively she reached for him, but when her hands flew to touch him he no more than allowed it, unwilling to reject an act of love, but equally unwilling to be comforted.

This was pain he meant to keep.

To maintain his cover, he had to write something.

'Nothing political,' Goldman had warned. 'Let Tass file on diplomatic developments; you find yourself something meaningless, filler. Just pretend that some ambitious editor has taken it into his head that *Pravda*'s view on Germany needs the Szara touch. Even with all the bad blood and political hostility, life goes on. A bad job but you're making the best of it; you want to lead the Reich press office to believe that, a little of their fine Teutonic contempt is the very thing for you. For the moment, let them sneer.'

Midmorning, in the dining room at the Adlon, Szara submitted himself to the tender mercies of Vainshtok. The little man ran his fingers through his hair and studied his list of possible stories. 'A Szara needs help from a Vainshtok?' he said. 'I knew the world was turning upside down, Armageddon expected any day now, but this!'

'What have you got?' Szara said. He caught the attention of a passing waiter: 'A Linzer torte for my friend, plenty of schlag on it.'

Vainshtok's eyebrows shot up. 'You're in trouble. That I can tell. My mama always warned me, "Darling son, when they put the whipped cream on the Linzer torte, watch out." What is it, André Aronovich? Have you fallen from favour at last? Got a girlfriend who's giving you a hard time? Getting older?'

'I can't stand Berlin, Vainshtok. I can't think in this place.'

'Oy, he can't stand Berlin. Last year they sent me to Madagascar. I ate, I believe I actually ate, a lizard. Did you hear the china breaking, Szara, wherever you were?

Eleven generations of Vainshtok rabbis were going wild up in heaven, breaking God's kosher plates, "*Gott im Himmel!* Little Asher Moisevich is eating a lizard!" Ah, here's something, how about weather?'

'What about it?'

'It's happening every day.'

'And?'

'Well, it's not especially cold, and it's not especially hot. But more than likely such a story won't stir up the Reichsministries. On the other hand, it might. "What do you mean, *normal?* Our German weather is clean and pure, like no other weather anywhere!"'

Szara sighed. He hadn't the strength to fight back.

'All right, all right,' Vainshtok said as his treat arrived, swimming in cream. 'You're going to make me cry. Take Frau Kummel, up in Lübeck. Actually she's called Mutter Kummel, Mother Kummel. It's a story you can write, and it gets you out of Berlin for the day.'

'Mutter Kummel?'

'I'll write down the address for you. Yesterday she turned a hundred years old. Born the first of November, 1838. Imagine all the exciting things she's seen – she may even remember some of them. 1838? Schleswig-Holstein still belonged to the Danes, Lübeck was part of the independent state of Mecklenburg. Germany – of course you'll have to say *Germany as we know it today* – didn't exist. You're to be envied, Szara. What a thrilling time that was, and Mutter Kummel somehow lived through every minute of it.'

He took the train that afternoon, a grim ride up through the flatlands of the Lüneberg Plain, through marshy fields where gusts of wind flattened the reeds under a hard, grey sky. He avoided Hamburg by taking the line that went through Schwerin, and outside a little village not far from the sea he spotted a traffic sign by a tight curve in the road: *Drive carefully! Sharp curve! Jews 75 miles an hour!*

Mutter Kummel lived with her eighty-one-year-old daughter in a gingerbread house in the centre of Lübeck. 'Another reporter, dear mother,' said the daughter when Szara knocked at the door. The house smelled of vinegar, and the heat of the place made him sweat as he scribbled in his notebook. Mutter Kummel remembered quite a bit about Lübeck: where the old butcher shop used to be, the day the rope parted and the tumbling church bell broke through the belfry floor and squashed a deacon. What Nezhenko would make of all this Szara could only imagine, let alone some coal miner in the Donbas, wrapping his lunch potato in the newspaper. But he worked at it and did the job as best he could. Toward the end of the interview the old lady leaned forward, her placid face crowned by a bun of white hair, and told him how *die Juden* were no longer to be found in Lübeck – yet one more change she'd witnessed in her many years in the town. Polite people when one met them in the street, it had to be admitted, but she wasn't sorry to see them go. 'Those Jews,' she confided, 'for too long they've stolen our souls.' Szara must have looked inquisitive. 'Oh yes, young man. It's what they did, and we here in Lübeck knew about it,' she said slyly. Szara, for a moment, was tempted to ask her to explain – for he sensed she'd worked it out – the mechanics of such a thing: how it was actually accomplished, where the Jews hid the stolen souls and what they did with them. But he didn't. He thanked the ladies and took the train back to Berlin and an evening with Marta Haecht, the promise of which had kept him more or less sane for another day.

* * *

Later on, he would have reason to remember that afternoon.

Later on, when everything had changed, he would wonder what might have happened if he'd missed the Berlin train, if he'd had to spend the night in Lübeck. But he knew himself, knew that he would have found some way to be with Marta Haecht that night. He considered himself a student of destiny, perhaps even a *connoisseur* – that obnoxious word – of its tricks and turns: how it hunted, how it fed.

He would see himself on the train to Berlin, a man who'd beaten his way across a lifeless afternoon by banking thoughts of the evening. And though the browns and greys of the German November flowed past the train window he was not there to see them; he was lost in anticipation, lost in lover's greed. In fact, he would ask himself, what *didn't* he want? He certainly wanted her, wanted her in the ways of a Victorian novel kept in a night table drawer – what magnificent fantasies he made for himself on that train! But that wasn't all. He wanted affection; kindness, refuge. He wanted to spend the night with his lover. He wanted to play. The game of temptations and surrenders, cunning noes and yesses. And then he wanted to talk – to talk in the darkness where he could say anything he liked, then he wanted to sleep, all wrapped and twined around her in a well-warmed bed. He even wanted breakfast. Something delicious.

And what he wanted, he got.

In its very own diabolical way, destiny delivered every last wish. Only it added a little something extra, a little something he didn't expect, buried it right in the midst of all his pleasures where he'd be sure to find it.

* * *

The Iron Exchange Building was even stranger at night: the long tile hallways in shadow, the frosted glass doors opaque and secretive, the silence broken only by an agonizing piano lesson in progress on the floor below and the echo of his footsteps.

But in low light the studio of the painter Benno Ault was agreeably softened. The shrieks and torments pinned to the wall faded to sighs, and Marta Haecht, at centre stage, appeared in short silk robe and Parisian scent, slid gracefully into his arms, and gave him every reason to hope that his thoughts on the train had not been idle fantasies.

They had their Victorian novel – in feeling if not in form – and wound up sprawled together across the sofa, for a moment stunned senseless. Then Marta turned the lamp off and they lay peacefully in the darkness for a time, sticky, sore, thoroughly pleased with themselves and the very best of friends. 'What was that you said?' she asked idly. 'Was it Russian?'

'Yes.'

'I wasn't sure, perhaps it was Polish.'

'No, Russian. Very much so.'

'Was it a sweet thing to say?'

'No, a rough thing. Common. A command.'

'Ah, a command. And I obeyed?' She was smiling in the darkness.

'You did. Somehow you understood.'

'And that you liked.'

'Couldn't you tell?'

'Yes. Of course.' She thought for a time. 'We are so different,' she mused.

'Not really.'

'You mustn't say that. Such a difference is a, a pleasure for me.'

'Oh. Day and night, then.'

She put a hand on his chest. 'Don't,' she said.

They were still for a while. He looked up at the large window, illuminated by the pale night sky of a city. A few snowflakes drifted against the glass and melted into droplets. 'It's snowing,' he said.

She turned halfway around to look. 'It's a sign,' she said.

'You mean the night we met, back again.'

'Yes, just so. I can still see you in Dr Baumann's kitchen, making small talk. You hadn't even noticed me. But I knew everything that would happen.'

'Did you truly?'

She nodded yes. 'I knew you would take me off somewhere, a hotel, a room. I thought, *a man like you can always have a woman like me*. It struck me, that thought, I was so surprised at myself. Because I was so *good*. I'd always known boys who wanted me, at the university and so forth, but I was such a little *Mädchen*, I wouldn't. I'd blush and push them away – they were so earnest! And then – this thing always happens when you aren't expecting it – the Baumanns, the stuffy old Baumanns, invited me to their house.' She laughed. 'I didn't want to go. My father made me.'

'But you said you knew who I was, that you wanted to meet me.'

'I know I said that. I lied. I meant to flatter you.'

'Ach!' He pretended to be wounded.

'But no, you should be flattered by such a lie, because the moment I saw you I wanted everything, to be made to do everything. Your dark shirt, your dark hair, the way you looked into me – it was so . . . Russian – I can't describe it. Something about you, not polite, not at all polite the way Germans are, but strong, intense.' She smoothed his hair back above his ear; the gesture seemed to last a long time and he could feel the heat of her hand.

'Isn't that what Germans always think of Russians, when they don't hate them?'

'It's true. Some hate, and are hateful. But for the rest of us it's complicated. We are all tied up inside ourselves, almost embarrassed at being in the world. It's our German culture I think, and we see Russians – Jews, Slavs, all the people in the East – as passionate and romantic, their feelings out for all to see, and deep in our hearts we're envious of them because we sense that they *feel*, whereas we just think about everything, think and think and think.'

'What about Dr Baumann? Passionate and romantic?'

'Oh, not him.' She laughed at the idea.

'But he's a Jew.'

'Yes of course he is. But here they're more like us than anything else, all tight and cold, self-conscious. That's the problem here in Germany; the Jews have become German, consider themselves German, just as good as any German, and there are many Germans who feel it is a presumption. They don't like it. Then, after the revolution in 1917 we had here in Berlin the Russian and Polish Jews, and they are really quite different from us – perhaps rude is the word, not cultured. Mostly they stay off by themselves, but when one sees them, for instance when they are on the trolley car and it is crowded, they stare, and one can smell the onions they eat.'

'The Jews from Poland have been sent back.'

'Yes, I know this and it's sad for them. But there were some who wanted to go back, and Poland would not let them in, and there are people who said why must this be always Germany's problem? So now they all have to go back, and for them I feel sad.'

'And Dr Baumann? Where can he go?'

'Why should he go anywhere? For most Jews it's terrible, a tragedy, they lose everything, but for him it's not like that. The Dr Baumanns of the world always find a way to get along.'

'Is this something your father tells you?'

'No. Something I know from my own eyes.'

'You see him?'

'Socially? Of course not. But I work for a man called Herr Hanau, a man from the little town of Greifswald, up on the Baltic. Herr Hanau has a small shipping company, one big ship and three little ones, and to receive consideration for government contracts he has moved his business to Berlin, and here I am his assistant. So, some weeks ago, we were awarded a small shipment of machine tools that goes up to Sweden, a great victory for us, and Herr Hanau invited me to lunch at the Kaiserhof, to celebrate. And there, large as life, is Dr Baumann, eating a cutlet and drinking Rhine wine. Life cannot be so bad for him after all.'

Puzzled, Szara stared at the window, watched the snowflakes drifting slowly downward on the still air. 'How could he do that?' he asked. 'Can a Jew, like Dr Baumann, walk into one of the better hotels in Berlin and just have lunch?'

'I think not. These waiters have a sense of propriety, alone he would not have been served or there might have been a scene. But he was with his protector, you see, and so everything just went along in the normal way.'

'Protector?'

'Naturally. Though my father stands ready to help him, to take over the ownership of the mill, Dr Baumann remains in charge. Baumann Milling does defence work, as you may have guessed, and so Dr Baumann is protected.'

'By whom?'

'It seemed strange to me, these two men having lunch. Dr Baumann and some very tall, reedy fellow, almost bald, with little wisps of blond hair. An aristocrat, I thought, that's what they look like: late thirties, no chin, and that hesitant little smile, as though somebody were about to break a priceless vase and they're afraid they'll let on that they're brokenhearted.'

Szara shifted his weight on the couch. 'I hope you don't describe me to anyone,' he said with mock horror.

She clucked. 'I don't tell secrets, *Liebchen*.'

'Who do you suppose he was?'

'I asked Herr Hanau. "Don't meddle," says he. "That's Von Polanyi from the Foreign Office, a clever fellow but not someone for you to know."'

'He sounds Hungarian.'

He felt her shrug. 'During the Austro-Hungarian time the noble families moved around, we have all sorts in Germany. In any event, don't be too concerned for Herr Doktor Julius Baumann, for it turns out he's rather comfortably situated.'

Szara was silent for a long time.

'Are you asleep?'

'No, dreaming.'

'Of me?'

He moved closer to her.

'Give me your hand,' she said.

And in the morning, when the light woke them up, after the Victorian novel, the affection, the honest talk in darkness, and, well, some condition of absence that at least imitated sleep, Marta Haecht tied the little silk robe at her waist and stood before the stove and made blini, thin ones like French crêpes, then spread them with strawberry jam from Berlin's finest store, folded them carefully, and served them on pretty plates and Szara realized, just about then, that had he been able to taste anything at all they would have been, as he'd imagined on the train to Berlin, delicious.

* * *

5 November.

A telephone message at the Adlon desk requested that he stop by the press office at the embassy. On the Unter den Linden, in a light, dry snowfall that blew about like dust, thousands of black-shirted Nazi party members were marching toward the Brandenburg Gate. They sang in deep voices, roared out their chants, and threw their arms into the air in fascist salutes. Amid the sea of black there were banners denouncing the Comintern and the Soviet Union, and the men marched by slamming their boots against the pavement; Szara could actually feel the rhythm of it trembling beneath his feet. He pulled his raincoat around him and pretended to ignore the marchers. This was what most Berliners did – glanced at the singing men, then hurried on about their business – and Szara followed their example.

The embassy was extremely busy. People were rushing about here and there, clerks ran by with armloads of files, and the tension could be easily felt. Varin, the second secretary, was waiting for him in the press office, rather pointedly not watching the parade below his window. He was a small, serious man, determined, and not inclined toward conversation. He handed over an envelope; Szara could feel the waxy paper of the folded flimsy inside. A radio was playing in the press office and when the news forecast came on at noon, all talk stopped. 'They have a big mess over at Zabąszyń,' Varin said when the commentator had finished. 'Fifteen thousand Polish Jews penned up in barbed wire at the border. Germany's thrown them out, but Poland won't let them in. There's not enough water, hardly any shelter, and it's getting colder. Everybody's waiting to see who gives in first.'

'Maybe I should go up there,' said the journalist Szara.

Varin closed his eyes for an instant and just barely

moved his head to indicate that he should do no such thing.

'Is that what the parade is all about?'

Varin shrugged, indifferent. 'They like to march, so let them. It's the weather – they always feel spirited when the winter comes.'

Szara stood to go.

'Watch yourself,' said Varin quietly.

For just a moment, Szara had been tempted to lay his troubles at Varin's door, but it was a temptation instantly dismissed. Still, as he walked back to the Adlon, the word *Funkspiele* drummed relentlessly in his consciousness. Playback, it meant, when a wireless was used. In general, the operation of a doubled agent. There might have been an innocent explanation for Baumann meeting with someone from the Foreign Office, but Szara didn't think so. The Directorate had been restless with Baumann from the very beginning; now he understood that they'd been right. People like Abramov had spent most of their lives in clandestine work – against the Okhrana before 1917, against the world after that. One developed sharpened instincts; on certain nights the animals are reluctant to approach the waterhole.

Suddenly there wasn't a choice, he had to be an intelligence officer like it or not. If Baumann was under German control, all the traditional questions bobbed up to the surface: From the beginning? Or caught, then turned? How accomplished? By coercion, clearly. Not money, not ego, and not, God forbid, ideology. A frightened Jew was appropriate to their purposes. Which were? Deceptive. In what way deceptive, toward what end? If the swage wire figures were high, that meant they wanted to scare the USSR into thinking they had more bombers than they did, a tactic of political warfare, the same method that had proved fatal for Czechoslovakia. If they were low, it was an attempt to lull the USSR into false strategic assumptions. And that meant war.

At the Adlon he knocked, harder than he meant to, at Vainshtok's door. The little man was in shirtsleeves, a cloud of cigarette smoke hung in the air, and a sheet of paper protruded from a typewriter on the desk. 'Szara? It better be important. You scared the shit out of my muse.'

'May I come in?'

Vainshtok beckoned him inside and closed the door. 'Don't knock like that, will you? Call from the lobby. These days, a knock on the door . . .'

'Thank you for the Mutter Kummel story.'

'Don't mention it. I thought you needed all the excitement you could get.'

'Do you know anything about the Reich Foreign Office?'

Vainshtok sighed. He went over to an open briefcase, dug around inside for a time, and emerged with a thin, mimeographed telephone directory. 'Oh the forbidden things we have here in the Adlon. I expect the Gestapo will set fire to it any day now. That'll be something to see – a hundred firemen, all wearing eyeglasses.' He cackled at the idea. 'What do you want to know?'

'Do you find a man called Von Polanyi?'

It took only a moment. 'Von Polanyi, Herbert K.L. Amt 9.'

'What is it?'

'I don't know. But then, that in itself is informative.'

'How so?'

'When you don't know, chances are they don't want you to know. So, they're not the people who keep track of the Bulgarian bean harvest.'

Back in his room, Szara drew the blinds, set out pencils and paper, propped up the railway timetable against the back of the desk, spread the code flimsy out under the lamp, and decrypted it.

TRANSMISSION 5 NOVEMBER 1938 04:30 HOURS
TO: JEAN MARC
A SECOND MEETING WITH OTTER IS APPROVED. FOR 10 NOVEMBER, 01:15 HOURS, AT 8 KLEINERSTRASSE, WITTENAU. YOU WILL BE TRANSPORTED TO THE TOWN OF WITTENAU, APPROXIMATELY 30 MINUTES FROM BERLIN, BY CAR. AT 12:40 HOURS BE AT THE KOLN FISCHMARKT, AT INTERSECTION OF FISCHERSTRASSE AND MUHLENDAMM, ASSIGNED TO COVER STORY OF FISH MARKET VISITED BY TOURISTS AT NIGHT. A MAN IN A TARTAN SCARF WILL APPROACH YOU. THE PAROL WILL BE: CAN YOU TELL ME WHAT TIME IT IS? THE COUNTERSIGN WILL BE: I'M SORRY. MY WATCH STOPPED ON THURSDAY.
8 KLEINERSTRASSE IS AN OLD WOODEN BUILDING FACING NORTH, AT THE EASTERN END OF THE STREET BORDERING PRINZALLEE. A SIGN ABOVE THE DOOR IDENTIFIES IT AS BETH MIDRESH, A SYNAGOGUE. APPROACH SUBJECT THROUGH DOOR AT THE END OF THE LEFT-HAND AISLE. YOU ARE TO SPEND NO MORE THAN THIRTY MINUTES WITH SUBJECT, THEN RETURN TO BERLIN BY CAR, HAVING ARRANGED MEETING WITH DRIVER.
NO OFFER OF FUTURE EXFILTRATION OR RESETTLEMENT IS TO BE MADE.
DIRECTOR

7 November.

He arrived at the loft just after nine, a little out of breath, his face cold from the night air, carrying a bottle of expensive wine wrapped in paper. A different mood for Marta: hair carefully pinned up, red Bakelite earrings with lipstick to match, tight sweater and skirt. She gave him a leather case holding a pair of gold cuff links set with tiny citrines, a faded lemon colour. His shirt had buttons, so she brought one of her own out of a bureau to show him what they looked like; he found them almost impossible to attach and fumbled grimly till she came to the rescue, grinning at his efforts. They drank the wine and ate biscuits from a box with a paper doily in it. He turned the radio to a different station – light Viennese froth that drew a sneer from Marta – but he'd come to associate the serious German composers with the mood of the city and he didn't want that in his sanctuary. They talked, aimless and comfortable; she picked candied cherries off the tops of the biscuits and put them in an ashtray. They would eat supper later, after they made love. But tonight they were in no hurry.

It had become, in just a few days, a love affair with rules of its own, a life of its own, a life that radiated from a bulbous old green sofa at its centre, an affair with ups and downs, rough moments smoothed over, and unimportant, courteous lies. Something between adults. Marta, a working woman, a sophisticated Berliner with a life of her own, accepted him for what she thought he was: a Soviet journalist who travelled constantly, a man to whom she was deeply, sexually, attracted, a man she'd encountered in the last days of girlhood who now loved her as a woman.

It was too bad they couldn't go out to restaurants or concerts, but the present reality was uncertain in that way and they agreed without discussion not to put themselves in a situation where unpleasantness might occur – life was too short for turmoil, it was best to float with the tide. Szara did not mention the Aesopic letter or the trip to Lisbon. He doubted she knew he'd written it. If she did, she'd also decided it would not bear discussion. They had negotiated a treaty, and now they lived by it.

The radio played 'Barcarole' from *The Tales of Hoffman*. She sat on his lap. 'This is pretty,' she said. 'Two lovers on a boat, drifting along a canal.' He slipped a hand under her sweater; she closed her eyes, leaned her head on his shoulder and smiled. The song ended and an announcer, rattling a paper into the microphone, stated that a special bulletin from Dr Joseph Goebbels would follow. 'Oh, that hideous man!' Marta said.

Goebbels's delivery was professional, but the nasal whine of his personality was more than evident. As he read, from an editorial that would appear the following day in the *Völkischer Beobachter*, a kind of choked-off rage thickened his voice. This news, the tone implied, was well beyond shouting. Ernst Vom Rath, third secretary at the German embassy in Paris, had been shot and gravely wounded by a seventeen-year-old Polish Jew named Hershl Grynszpan, a student whose parents had been deported from Germany to Poland, then held at the frontier town of Zbąszyń. Goebbels's point was clear: we try to help these people, by sending them away from a nation where they aren't wanted to a place where they will be more at home, and look what they do – they shoot German diplomats. And just how long shall we Germans be expected to put up with such outrages? The bulletin ended, a Strauss waltz followed. 'This world,' said Marta sadly, closing her eyes again and wriggling to get comfortable. 'We must be tender to one another,' she added, placing her warm hand over his.

10 November.

A German dearly loves his fish. Making a show of being a journalist, Szara jotted down impressions on a pocket notepad. *Herring and whitebait*, he wrote. *Flounder and haddock*. After midnight, the stalls of the Koln Fischmarkt began to fill with the day's catch trucked in from the coast: glistening grey and pink eels on chipped ice, baskets of whelks and oysters trailing seaweed, crayfish floating in a lead tank filled with cloudy brine. The sawdust underfoot was wet with blood and sea water, and the air, even in the cold November night, was rank – *the iodine smell of tidal pools*, Szara wrote, *barrels of cast-off fishheads. Stray cats*. There were plenty of people around; vendors shouted snappy fish jokes at their customers – a bit of psychology: lively talk implied fresh seafood. Some local swells and their girlfriends, faces bright with drinking, were waltzing around with half a dripping mackerel. There was even a bewildered British tourist, asking questions in slow, loud English, puzzled that he couldn't get an answer.

The operative was precisely on time, a heavy man with eyebrows grown together and red cheeks, hair sheared off in a military cut. After the parol was completed, they walked silently to the car, a black Humboldt parked a little way down the Muhlendamm. The operative was an expert driver, and cautious, squaring blocks and ceaselessly crossing back over his own tracks to make sure they weren't followed. They worked their way west through the Grunewald and eventually turned north on the near bank of the Havel, following a succession of little roads to avoid police on the main highways. 'I'm told to warn you there's some kind of trouble brewing,' the driver said.

'What kind of trouble?'

'*Aktionen*. Actions against the Jews. A monitoring unit at the embassy distributed a teleprinter message just as I was leaving; it was from Müller's office to all Gestapo headquarters. The timing was specified as "at very short notice." You'll probably get in and out without difficulties – but don't dawdle.'

'The *treff* takes place in a synagogue.'

'I know where it takes place. The point is, there won't be anyone around, and it's best for your contact, who comes from the east without going into the city. We got him in for Friday night services and he just didn't leave.'

The car slowed as they came to the outskirts of Wittenau. The street swung away from the Havel, and the sheds and low buildings of small industrial shops appeared on both sides. The driver pulled over and turned off the engine. The night was still, the air smelling faintly of coal smoke. The *apparat* had a genius, Szara thought, for finding such places; dead zones, nighttime deserts on the edges of cities.

'This is Prinzallee,' said the driver. 'Up ahead of you, about fifty paces, is the start of Kleinerstrasse. Your synagogue is on the corner. What time do you have?'

'Eight minutes after one.'

'It will take you only a minute to walk.'

Szara fidgeted in the front seat. A bird started up nearby, otherwise the silence was oppressive. 'Does anybody live here?' he asked.

'No more. It was a ghetto thirty years ago, then it turned into factories. Only the synagogue is left, and a few tenements with old Jews living in them – most of the young ones got out after '33.'

Szara kept looking at his watch.

'All right,' said the driver. 'Don't close the car door – it's a noise everybody knows. And please keep it short.'

Szara climbed out. The bulb had been removed from the roof light, so the interior of the car remained dark. He walked close to a board fence on a dirt pathway that muffled his footsteps, but the night was so quiet he became conscious of his own breathing.

The synagogue was very old, a two-storey wood frame structure with a sloping roof, built perhaps a century earlier for use as a workshop, possibly a carpentry workshop since it stood against the low shed of a neighbouring lumberyard.

A sign in Hebrew above the door said Beth Midresh, which meant House of Worship. That told Szara that it was being used by immigrant Jews from Poland and Russia – all synagogues in the Pale were identified that way. In France they used the name of the street, while the wealthy Jews of Germany often named their synagogues after a leader in the community – the Adler synagogue, for instance. Those were grand and glorious temples, nothing like what he approached. Seen in the light of a waning moon, the synagogue on Prinzallee might have stood in Cracow or Lodz, seemed to come from another time and place.

The impression held. The front door was unlocked, but the frame was warped and Szara had to pull hard to get it open. The interior took him back to Kishinev – the smell of sweat and urine in stale air, as though the windows were never opened. Behind the altar, above the double-doored ark that held the scrolls of the Torah, was a tiny lamp, the eternal light, and he could just make out two narrow aisles between rows of wooden chairs of several different styles. He took the aisle on the left and walked toward the front, the boards creaking softly under his feet. The door to one side of the altar was ajar; he gave it a gentle push and it swung open to reveal a man sitting slumped at a bare table. The room was narrow, perhaps serving at one time as a rabbi's study – there were empty book shelves built up one wall.

'Dr Baumann,' he said.

Baumann looked up at him; his collapsed posture didn't change. 'Yes,' he said in a low voice.

There was a chair directly across the table from Baumann's and Szara sat down. 'You're not sick, are you?'

'Tired,' Baumann said. He meant the word in both senses: exhausted, and tired of life.

'We have to discuss a few things, quickly, and then we can leave. You have a way to get safely home?'

'Yes. It isn't a problem.'

Perhaps he had a driver waiting or was driving his own car, Szara didn't know. 'We want to find out, first of all, if you've come under pressure from any of the Reichsministries. I don't mean having to hand in your passport, or any of the laws passed against the Jews in general, I mean you in particular. In other words, have you been singled out in any way, any way at all?'

Szara thought he saw the probe hit home. The room was dark, and the reaction was very brief, not much more than a pause, but it was there. Then Baumann shook his head impatiently, as though Szara was wasting his time with such foolish notions: this was not a question he wished to discuss. Instead, he leaned forward and whispered urgently: 'I'm going to accept your offer. Your offer to leave here, for my wife and I. The dog too, if it can be managed.'

'Of course,' Szara said.

'Soon. Maybe right away.'

'I have to ask . . .'

'We want to go to Amsterdam. It shouldn't be too hard; our friends say that the Dutch are letting us in, no questions asked. So the only difficulty is getting out of Germany. We'll take a suitcase and the little dog, nothing else, they can have it all, everything.'

'One thing we'll need to –' Szara stopped cold and leaned his head to one side.

Baumann sat up straight as though he'd been shocked. 'My God,' he said.

'Is it singing?'

Baumann nodded.

Szara instinctively looked at his watch. 'At one-thirty in the morning?'

'When they sing like that,' Baumann said, then paused,

his voice fading into silence as he concentrated on the sound.

Szara remembered the parade on the Unter den Linden. These were the same voices, deep and vibrant. Both of them sat still as the sound grew louder, then Baumann stood suddenly. 'They must not see us.' The beginning of panic was in his voice.

'Would we be better off out in the street?'

'They're coming here. *Here*.'

Szara stood. He remembered the road into Wittenau – there was nothing there. By now the words of the song were plainly audible; it was something they sang in the Rathskellers as they drank their beer: *Wenn's Judenblut vom Messer spritzt / Dann geht's nochmal so gut, dann geht's nochmal so gut*. When Jewish blood squirts under the knives / Then all is well, then all is well. Baumann turned away from the door and the two men stared at each other, both frightened, uncertain what to do and, suddenly, perfect equals.

'Hide.' Baumann spoke the word in a broken whisper, the voice of a terrified child.

Szara fought for control of himself. He had been through pogroms before – in Kishinev and Odessa. They always attacked the synagogue. 'We're getting out,' he said. It was an order. Whatever else happened, he wasn't going to end his life in dumb shock like an animal that knows it's going to die. He walked quickly out of the narrow room and had taken two steps back up the aisle when one of the dark windows flanking the entry door suddenly brightened; a golden shadow flickered against it for a moment, then the glass came showering in on the floor. The men outside sent up a great cheer and, simultaneously, Baumann screamed. Szara spun and clapped his hand over the man's mouth; he felt saliva on his palm but held on tight until Baumann made a gesture that he could control himself. Behind them, the other window exploded. Szara leaned close to Baumann. 'A stairway,' he whispered. 'There must be a stairway.'

'Behind the curtain.'

They ran up three steps onto the altar. Szara heard the stubborn door squeak at the other end of the building just as Baumann threw the curtain aside and they disappeared behind the ark. There was no banister on the stairs, just steps braced against the wall. He raced up, Baumann behind him, and tried the door. On the other side of the curtain he could hear chairs being kicked around and the other windows being broken to a chorus of laughter and cheers. 'Jews come out!' roared a drunken voice. Szara tore the door open with one hand and reached back for Baumann's sleeve with the other, pulling him into the upstairs room, then turning and kicking the door shut. The second storey was unused – a pile of drapes, cobwebbed corners, broken chairs, the smell of old wood . . . and something else. Burning. He turned to look at Baumann; his mouth was wide open, gasping for air, and his hand was pressed against the middle of his chest. 'No!' Szara said. Baumann looked at him strangely, then sank to his knees. Szara ran to the closest window, but there were torches below and dim shapes moving across the alley side of the synagogue. He crossed the room to a second window and saw that the upper storey was just above the roof of the lumberyard shed. It was a very old window, tiny panes of glass in wooden strips, and had not been opened for years. He strained at it for a moment, then drew his foot back and kicked out the glass and the bracing, kicking again and again, savagely, even though he felt the fabric of his trousers rip and saw blood droplets suddenly appear in the thick dust on the sill. When the opening was sufficiently wide, he ran to Baumann and took him under the armpits. 'Get up,' he said. 'Get up.'

There were tears on Baumann's face. He did not move.

Szara began dragging him across the floor until, at last, Baumann started crawling. Szara spoke to him like a child: 'Yes, that's it.' Somewhere close by he heard the splintering sound of a door being ripped off its hinges and he glanced, horrified, toward the stairway, then realized the noise came from below, that they were after the scrolls of the Torah in the ark. The smell of burning was getting stronger; a curl of smoke worked through the floorboards in one corner. He leaned Baumann against the wall below the window and spoke by his ear: 'Go ahead, I'll help you, it isn't far and then we'll be safe.' Baumann mumbled something – Szara couldn't understand what he said but it meant he wanted to be left to die. Infuriated, Szara pushed him aside and worked his way through the jagged circle of broken glass and wood, tumbling forward onto his hands on the tarred gravel surface of the roof of the lumberyard shed. He scrambled to his feet and reached back through the opening, getting a grip on the lapels of Baumann's jacket and hauling him forward. When Baumann's weight began to tilt over the sill, he thrust out his hands instinctively and the two of them fell together.

Szara lay stunned for a moment. Falling backwards and taking Baumann's weight had knocked the wind out of him. Then he began to breathe again and, in the cold air, became aware of a wet sock. He struggled away from Baumann and sat up to look at his ankle. Blood was welling steadily from a slash down his shin. He pressed the wound together for a moment, then remembered about silhouettes and threw himself on his stomach. Baumann's breathing distracted him – loud and hoarse, like sighing. He moved the man's hand, which lay flaccid against his chest, and felt for a heartbeat. What he found was a shock – a beating of such force and speed it frightened him. 'How is it?' he asked.

'My God in heaven,' Baumann said.

'We're going to be all right,' Szara said. 'I'll buy you a dinner in Amsterdam.'

Baumann smiled weakly, the wind blowing strands of his hair around, one side of his face pressed against the black surface of the roof, and nodded yes, that's what they would do.

Szara began to think about the operative and the car, then decided to try to get a look from the edge of the roof. Very carefully he moved forward, scraping his cheek against the surface, staying as flat as possible, gaining an inch at a time until he could just see over the end of the shed. He could not get a view of the path by the board fence where he'd left the car – the angle was wrong. But he was high enough to look out over part of Wittenau, the Havel, and an ancient stone bridge that crossed the river. His eyes were beginning to water from the smoke – the fire was taking hold; the old wood snapped and exploded as it caught – but what there was to see, he saw: a group of men with torches shifting restlessly in a knot at the centre of the bridge, an instant of motion in the darkness. Then there was a scream that carried perfectly on the night air, a white churning in the water at the foot of the bridge pier, a strangled cry for help, the yellow arc of a torch hurled into the water, then laughter and cheering as the men on the bridge headed back into Wittenau. Some of them began to sing.

As the fire swept up the front of the synagogue it illuminated the shed, and Szara scrambled backwards, afraid of being seen. Burning embers were all over the roof, producing, for the moment, only an oily black smoke from the tar surface. He realized it was only a matter of time before the shed, and the lumberyard, went up in flames. Just before he retreated, he saw fiery shapes flying into the street from the direction of the synagogue door

– long dowels on either side of thick, yellow parchment. The Nazis, not content to burn down the synagogue, were making a special, private bonfire of the Torah scrolls from the ark, first stripping off the ceremonial satin covers. *Now they'll have to be buried*, Szara thought. He wondered how he remembered that but it was true, it was the law: a burnt Torah had to be buried in the graveyard, like a dead person, there was a ceremony for it. It was part of growing up in the Pale of Settlement, knowing such lore – rituals for raped women and all sorts of useful knowledge – for these things had happened many times before.

It was another thirty minutes before they got away. After watching the fire for a time, the mob had gone off in search of further amusement. Szara and Baumann stayed where they were, lying flat to conceal themselves, brushing embers off their clothing with the sleeves of their jackets. From where they lay they could see the dancing orange shadows of other fires against the night sky, could hear the showers of falling glass, occasional shouts or cries, but no sirens. The lumberyard caught first – that was bad because of the burning creosote – and then the shed, an afterthought. Szara and Baumann worked their way backwards off the roof, dropping to the ground on the side away from the street. They circled behind the synagogue, now collapsed into itself around a column of fire that roared like a wind, and made a dash for the Humboldt.

They saw only one person, standing alone in the darkness: a town policeman, wearing the traditional high helmet with polished brasswork and short visor – something like the old-fashioned spiked *Pickelhaube* of the 1914 war – with a strap pulled up ferociously tight just under the chin. By the light of the flames Szara saw his face and was struck by a kind of anguish in it. Not sorrow for Jews or synagogues – it wasn't that. It had more to do with a life dedicated to perfect order, where no crime should ever go unpunished – a murder or a piece of paper tossed in the street, it was all the same to this face. Yet tonight the policeman had certainly seen arson – and perhaps murder, if he'd looked in the direction of the river – and had done nothing about it because he had been told to do nothing about it. Evidently, he had not really known what to do, so had stationed himself across the street from the fire, on the night when the firemen never came, and there he stood, rigid, anguished, in some sense ruined and aware of it.

The car was empty, the passenger door ajar as it had been left.

It would make, Szara thought, at least a hiding place, and he directed Baumann to lie flat on the floor below the back seat while he would do the same in front. As they entered the car, the operative materialized, gliding toward them from some shadow he'd used as cover while the mob roamed the streets. Not a mob, in fact, the operative told Szara later. Party men, some uniformed SS, an organized attack directed by the German state.

It was not the burning and the chaos that upset the operative, he was reasonably used to burning and chaos; it was Dr Julius Baumann, OTTER, an agent he was not supposed to know about, much less see, least of all to have in an automobile along with his case officer. This shattered unbreakable rules of every variety and set the man's face dancing with bureaucratic horror. He did the best he could under the circumstances: secreted Baumann in the trunk, first prying back a section of the metal jamb to make an air passage. Szara quietly protested as he slid into the front seat. 'Be glad I'm doing that much,' said the operative.

'He may have had a heart attack,' Szara said.

The operative shrugged. 'He will be cared for.'

They drove a little way back toward Berlin, crossed the

Havel on a narrow, deserted bridge, then turned north, swinging around Wittenau and moving east, through the back of the Berlin suburbs. It was artful navigation, evidently from memory, a slow but steady progress through the winding lanes of Hermsdorf, Lubans, Blankenfelde and Niederschonhausen, where villas and workshops faded into farmland or forest. It was almost four in the morning when they reached Pankow. And here the operative took a complicated route that brought them to the *Bahnhof*. He disappeared into the station for a few minutes and used the public telephone in the waiting room. Then east again, Weissensee and eventually Lichtenburg, where they drove through a very aristocratic part of town, swerving suddenly into the parklike courtyard of a private hospital, the gate closing automatically behind them. The operative opened the trunk and helped Baumann into the hospital. He would receive medical attention, the operative explained to Szara, but they'd decided to hide him there whether he needed it or not.

Heinrich Müller's teleprinter message had ordered, along with attacks on synagogues and Jewish businesses throughout Germany, the arrest of twenty to thirty thousand Jews: 'Wealthy Jews in particular are to be selected.' This meant money, which the Nazis especially liked. So, said the operative as they pulled away from the hospital, they needed to put OTTER somewhere he wouldn't be found, else he would be taken to Buchenwald or Dachau, stripped of all assets, and eventually deported.

As they turned back toward Berlin, they drove through streets that sparkled with shattered glass – Szara later learned that fifty per cent of the annual plate glass production of Belgium, the manufacturing centre for German glass, had been smashed. At times the traffic police, after checking their Russian identity papers, would steer them politely around the damage. And here and there they saw things: Jewish men and boys crawling around in the street or capering in the town pond, cheered on by hooting SS troopers and local Nazis. Szara knew them well enough; schoolyard bullies, beerhall fat boys, unpleasant little men with insulted faces, the same trash you would find in any town in Russia, or indeed anywhere at all.

The operative was no Jew. From his accent Szara guessed he might have origins in Byelorussia, where pogroms had been a way of life for centuries, but the events of 10 November had enraged him. And he swore. His thick hands gripped the wheel in fury and his face was red as a beet and he simply never stopped swearing. Long, foul, vicious Russian curses, the language of a land where the persecutors had always, somehow, remained just beyond the reach of the persecuted, which left you bad words and little else. Eventually, as a grey dawn lightened Berlin and ash drifted gently down on the immaculate streets, they reached the Adlon, where Szara was instructed to use a servants' entrance and a back stairway.

By then the operative had said it all, virtually without repeating himself, having covered Hitler, Himmler, Göring, and Heydrich, Nazis, Germans one and all, their wives and children, their grandparents and forebears back to the Teutonic tribes, their weisswurst and kartoffel, dachshunds and schnauzers, pigs and geese, and the very earth upon which Germany stood: urged to sow its fucking self with salt and burn fallow for eternity.

11 November.

By dusk the weather had turned bitter cold and it was like ice in Benno Ault's studio. There was little heat in the Iron Exchange Building at night; the owners maintained a certain commercial fiction, pretending that their tenants, like normal business people, hurried home after dark to the warmth of home and family. But Szara suspected that the blind piano tuner, the astrologer, in fact many of the resident shadows, both worked and lived in their offices.

Marta Haecht was asleep in the bed fitted into an alcove at one end of the studio, warm beneath a mound of feather quilts that rose and fell with her steady breathing. A dreamless sleep, he suspected. Untroubled. When he'd arrived, just after dusk, the street cleaners were still at it in the Bischofstrasse; he could hear them sweeping up the broken glass and dumping it in metal garbage cans.

A blanket pulled over his shoulders, he sat on the green sofa, smoked cigarettes, and stared out of the tall window. His ankle burned beneath the handkerchief he'd tied over the gash, but that wasn't what kept him awake. It was a coldness that had nothing to do with the building. He'd seen it that morning, in his room at the Adlon, when he'd looked in the mirror. His face seemed white and featureless, almost dead, the expression of a man who no longer concerns himself with what the world might see when it looked at him. Marta's breathing changed, the quilt stirred, then everything was again peaceful. *A healthy animal*, he thought. She'd been only briefly disturbed by the events of what they called Kristallnacht. Night of glass. A clever name, like the Night of the Long Knives, when Roehm and his Brown Shirts were murdered in 1934. Not just knives – those were for brawling sailors and thieves – but *long* knives. A mythic dimension. 'This is Goebbels's work,' she'd said, shaking her head at the sorry brutality of bad elements. Then she'd closed the door on it, coaxing him to her, twining herself around him, refusing to consider the possibility of the poison reaching either of them.

But it was Tscherova, the actress, who occupied his thoughts. The second secretary, Varin, and the nameless operative. The war they fought. He'd been contacted at the Adlon and told in no uncertain terms to get out of Germany and go back to Paris. His train left in the morning and he would be on it. He looked at his watch. After 2:30. It *was* the morning – in seven hours he'd be gone. He'd not told Marta Haecht, not yet, he didn't know why. He wouldn't be able to explain convincingly, but that was only part of it. He wished to keep her in his mind a certain way, without tears or, worse, dry-eyed and cool. He treasured the memory of her as she'd been – the girl who thought that deep down she was perhaps Italian, Mediterranean, softer and finer than the stiff, northern people she lived among. The girl in the falling snow.

He stood and walked to the window. By the light of the street lamps he could see a boarded-up shop window down Bischofstrasse; yesterday a toy shop, evidently a Jewish toy shop. In a nearby doorway he caught a momentary pinpoint of red. A cigarette. Was this for him? Some poor bastard freezing through a long night of surveillance? An SD operative? Or somebody from Von Polanyi's *Amt 9*, perhaps. Making sure their secret communication line into Dzerzhinsky Square came to no harm so that Moscow continued to believe whatever Berlin wanted it to believe. Or was it a Russian down there – or a German described as *nash* – some operative sent to make sure nothing happened to him on Berlin territory – *let him screw her, he leaves in the morning*.

Or was it just a man smoking a cigarette in a doorway.

'Can't you sleep?' She was propped on one elbow, hair thick and wild. 'Come and keep warm,' she pouted, folding back the quilts as an invitation.

'In a minute,' he said. He didn't want to be warm, to fold himself around her sweetly curved back; he didn't want to make love. He wanted to think. Like the self-absorbed man he knew he was, he wanted to stay cold and think. He remembered a nursemaid in a little park in Ostend. *Come escape with me*. Marta flopped over on one side and grumbled as she pulled up the bedding. Soon her breathing changed to the rhythm of sleep.

He didn't want her to know he was leaving – it was better simply to disappear. He saw a scrap of paper she used for a marker in the book she was reading – Saint-Exupéry, of all things; no, that was right – and retrieved a pen from the pocket of his jacket. *Dearest love*, he wrote, *I had to go away this morning*. Then he signed it *André*. He doubted he'd see her again, not while the war between Moscow and Berlin went on. He'd caught himself earlier in the evening in the midst of a certain kind of speculation: *Her boss, Herr Hanau, owns ships. What cargoes do they carry and where do they go?* No, he told himself; he wasn't going to let it come to that. Hard enough to report the truth about Baumann to Goldman or Abramov and keep her name out of it. Really very difficult, but he would find a way. Whether they loved each other or not they were lovers, and he was damned if he'd see her sucked into this brutal business.

'What are you writing?'

'Something to remember,' he said, and put the scrap of paper back in her book, hiding his hands behind a vase of flowers on the table. 'I thought you'd gone back to sleep,' he added.

'I fooled you,' she said.

11 November.
Strasbourg.
It was well after eleven A.M. – the official minute of the armistice of the 1914 war, the eleventh hour of the eleventh day of the eleventh month – when Szara's train crossed the border but the train's engineer was French, thus not a man to permit clocks to interfere with honour. Many of the passengers on the train got off when notified by the conductors that a three-minute observance would be held on French

soil. Szara left with them, stood beneath a rich blue sky in a fresh breeze, held his hand against his heart and meant it. A few kilometres of trees and fields, yet another world: the smell of frying butter, the sound of sputtering car engines, the look in women's eyes; France. Mentally, he was down on his knees at the foot of a wind-whipped Tricolor and kissing the earth. It was as though the passage across the border had severed a tangled knot in his heart and he could breathe again.

By the time he pushed open the shutters in his musty apartment and welcomed himself back to his courtyard – busy, loud, and smelly as always – Germany seemed like a land of apparitions, a dream, a play. It made no logical sense – truly he believed that people were people – but his instinctive sense of the world told a very different story. He leaned on the windowsill, closed his eyes, and let Paris wash over him.

The *apparat* did not leave him to his pleasures for long – an hour later Odile was at his door to tell him he was expected at Stefan Leib's shop in Brussels that same night. Dutifully he took the train up to Belgium. Goldman shook his hand, welcomed him back like a hero, locked the door, and pulled down the shades.

If they'd given him a little room to breathe, things might have turned out differently; he would have shaped and crafted a functional deception and told them the part of the truth they needed to know: they had a compromised agent in Berlin. Not necessarily – Baumann and Von Polanyi could, at the Kaiserhof, have been discussing the price of pears, or Amt 9 might be the section of the Foreign Office that ordered clothes hangers from wire manufacturers.

But as a rule what you got in the intelligence business was a protruding corner, almost never the whole picture. That nearly always had to be inferred. But it was enough of a corner and Szara knew it. Von Polanyi was an intelligence officer; Herr Hanau seemed to have said so, Vainshtok had more or less confirmed it, and that was certainly more than enough to set the dogs running. Other sources would be tapped – you had the corner, somebody else had the top of the frame, a file already held the name of the artist, a local critic would be sent in to steal the dried paint off the palette. Result: full portrait with provenance. *Funkspiele*. Playback.

He had quite a bit, actually. For instance, the Germans were playing Dr Baumann in a very effective way. They didn't have him sneaking around dead-drops at midnight or playing host to journalists who climbed over his garden wall; they took him for an excellent lunch at the best hotel. Really, there was a lot Szara could have told them, more than enough. From there, they could have either declared Baumann innocent or turned the game back around on the Germans.

But he would not give them Marta Haecht, he would not compromise himself, he would not permit them to own him that completely. And if you were going to report pillow talk, because that's exactly what they called it and that's exactly what it was, you had to put a name and address to the head on the pillow.

So Szara lied. A lie of omission – the hard kind to discover. And in a way Goldman abetted the lie. With the death of Sénéschal, one of the Paris networks wasn't all that productive, because there was no realistic way to regain control of Lötte Huber, and she'd been the star of the show. This had the effect of expanding Baumann's importance to the stature of the OPAL network itself, and Goldman as *rezident* was neither more nor less important than the network he ran. There was competition anywhere you cared to look; hundreds of networks spread out all over Europe, Asia, and America, every one of them run by an officer of the GRU or the NKVD who wanted success, promotion, the usual prizes. So Goldman wanted to hear everything – especially everything good for Goldman.

Szara described Baumann truthfully: grey, suddenly old, under frightful tension.

'It could not be otherwise,' Goldman said sympathetically.

'He almost died at the second meeting,' Szara pointed out.

'Do you know that for a fact?'

'No. It was my impression.'

'Ah.'

This information produced from Goldman a reminiscence of Spain. Some poor soul infiltrated into the Falange in 1936, when the Republican side still had a chance to win the war. 'He too was grey,' Goldman mused. 'He too suffered. The pressure of living a double life consumed him – the Bulgarian case officer watched it happen – and he died in Paris a year later.' Of what? Nobody was really sure. But Goldman and others believed it was the strain and constant danger of duplicity that finished him. And Baumann was not *proniknoveniya*, an agent in the heart of the enemy camp, as the man in Spain had been. 'I appreciate the problem, really I do,' Goldman said. 'Just servicing a drop is enough to make some men quake with terror. From one personality to the next, courage is eternally a variable, but it is our job, André Aronovich, to make them heroes, to give them heart.'

Thus Goldman.

An attitude sharply confirmed when Szara offered warm news of Tscherova. 'She is for the cause,' Szara said. 'I know she was coerced, originally – induced and threatened and paid and what you like. Things have changed, however. An émigrée from Russia she may be, but she is no émigrée from human decency. And the Nazis themselves, by being as they are, have made us a gift of her soul.'

'What did she look like, exactly?' Goldman asked.

But Szara wasn't falling for that. 'Tall and thin. Plain – for an actress. I suppose the greasepaint and the stage lighting might make her attractive to an audience, but up close it's another story.'

'Does she play the romantic lead?'

'No. Maids.'

'Aside from the work, do you suppose she's promiscuous?'

'I don't believe so, she's not really the type. She claims to have had a lover or two in Berlin, but I believe most of that has actually been done by her associates. She is constantly around it, and she is no saint, but neither is she the devil she pretends to be. If I were you, I'd direct Schau-Wehrli to handle her carefully and to make sure nothing happens to her. She's valuable, and certainly worth protection, whatever it takes.'

Goldman nodded appreciatively. He seemed, Szara thought, more and more like Stefan Leib as time went by: hair a little too long, corduroy jacket shapeless and faded, the introverted cartographer, absentminded, surrounded by his tattered old maps. 'And Germany?' he asked.

'In a word?'

'If you like.'

'An abomination.'

Goldman's mask slipped briefly and Szara had a momentary view of the man beneath it. 'We shall settle with them this time, and in a way they will not forget,' he said softly. 'The world will yet thank God for Joseph Stalin.'

With Kristallnacht, a kind of shiver passed through Paris. The French had their own problems: communists and the Comintern, the fascist Croix de Feu, conspiracy and political actions among the various émigré groups, strikes and riots, bank failures and scandals – all against a deafening drumbeat from the Senate and the ministries. Stripped of all the rhetoric, it came out *trouble in Germany and Russia, now what?* They'd not really got over the Great War – there was a political sophism afoot that the French did not die well, that they loved life a little more than they should. But in the 1914 war they had died anyhow, and in great numbers. And for what? Because now, twenty years later, the trouble was back, three hundred miles east of Paris.

Troubles from the east were nothing new. Napoleon's experiment in Russia hadn't gone at all well, and with the defeat at Waterloo in 1815, Russian squadrons, among them the Preobajansky Guard, had occupied Paris. But the French were never quite as defeated as you thought they were; the Russians had, in time, gone home, bearing with them various French maladies of which two proved ultimately to be chronic: unquenchable appetites for champagne and liberty, the latter eventually leading to the Decembrist uprising of 1825 – the first in a series of revolutions ending in 1917.

But the present trouble from the east was German trouble, and the French could think of nothing worse. Burned in 1870 and scorched in 1914, they prayed it would go away. Hitler was such a *cul*, with his little moustache and his little strut; nobody wanted to take him seriously. But Kristallnacht was serious, broken glass and broken heads, and Frenchmen knew in their stomachs what that meant no matter what the politicians said. They had tried to manoeuvre diplomatically with Stalin, figuring that with an alliance on either side of Hitler they could crush the shitty little weasel between them. But, manoeuvring with Stalin . . . You thought you had it all agreed and then something always just seemed to go wrong.

The days grew shorter and darker but the bistros did not grow brighter – not this year they didn't. The fog swirled along the rue du Cherche-Midi and Szara sometimes went home with the carefree girls from the cafés, but it never made him all that happy. He thought it would, each time – oh, that strawberry blond hair and those freckles – but only the usual things happened. He missed being in love – definitely he missed that – but winter 1938 didn't seem to be the season for it. So he told himself.

Life ground on.

Baumann reported obediently, milling more swage wire every month as the bombers rolled out of the Reich factories.

Or maybe didn't.

Or maybe did even more than Moscow knew.

The lawyer Valais, HECTOR, picked up a new agent, a mercenary Bavarian corporal called Gettig who assisted one of the German military attachés. Odile's husband ran off with a little Irish girl who worked in a milliner's sewing room. Kranov now wore a thick sweater in the cold upstairs room on the rue Delesseux and stolidly punched away at the W/T key: the eternal Russian peasant in the technological age. To Szara he became a symbol, as the journalist for the first time saw OPAL clearly for what it was: a bureaucratic institution in the business of stealing and transmitting information. It was Kranov who handed Szara the decoded flimsy announcing the accession of Lavrenti Beria to the chairmanship of the NKVD. The official triumph of the Georgian *khvost* meant little to Szara at the time; it was simply one more manifestation of a bloody darkness that had settled on the world. When Beria cleaned the last of the Old Bolsheviks out of high positions in the intelligence *apparat*, the purge ended.

In the middle of December they came at him again – this time from a different angle, and this time they meant it.

A stiff, creamy envelope addressed to him, by hand, at

the *Pravda* bureau, the sort of thing journalists sometimes got. *Le Cercle Rénaissance invites you* . . . A square of clear cellophane slipped from within the card and floated to the floor at his feet. He didn't bite the first time so they tried him again – just before Christmas when nobody in Paris has enough invitations – and this time somebody took a Mont Blanc pen and wrote *Won't you please come?* below the incised lettering.

It meant the barber and it meant the dry cleaner and it meant a white shirt laundered to the consistency of teak – expensive indignities to which he submitted in the vain, vain hope that the invitation was precisely what it said it was. He checked the organization, the Renaissance Club; it did exist, and it was extremely exclusive. One of the excluded, a guest at a gallery opening, shot an eyebrow when he heard the name and said, 'You are very fortunate to be asked there,' with sincere and visible loathing in his expression.

The address was in Neuilly, home to some of the oldest and quietest money in France. The street, once the frantic taxi driver managed to find it, was a single row of elegant three-storey houses protected by wrought-iron palings, discreetly obscured by massed garden foliage – even in December – and bathed in a satin light by Victorian street lamps. The other side of the street was occupied by a private park, to which residents received a key, and beyond that lay the Seine.

A steward collected Szara's dripping umbrella and showed him up three flights of stairs to a small library. A waiter appeared and set down an ivory tray bearing a Cinzano apéritif and a dish of nuts. Abandoned to a great hush broken only by an occasional mysterious creak, Szara wandered along the shelves, sampling here and there. The collection was exclusively concerned with railways, and it was beautifully kept; almost all the books had been rebound. Some were privately printed, many were illustrated, with captioned sepia prints and daguerreotypes:

On the platform at Ebenfurth, Stationmaster Hofmann waits to flag through the Vienna-Budapest mail.

Flatcars loaded with timber cross a high trestle in the mountains of Bosnia.

The 7:03 from Geneva passes beneath the rue Lamartine overpass.

'So pleased you've come,' said a voice from the doorway. He was rather ageless, perhaps in the last years of his fifties, with faded steel-coloured hair brushed very flat against the sides of his head. Tall and politely stooped, he was wearing a formal dinner jacket and a bow tie that had gone slightly askew. He'd evidently walked a short distance through the rain without coat or umbrella and was patting his face with a folded handkerchief. 'I'm Joseph de Montfried,' he said. He articulated the name carefully, sounding the hard *t* and separating the two syllables, the latter lightly emphasized, as though it were a difficult name and often mispronounced. Szara was amused – a cultured Frenchman would as likely have got the Baron de Rothschild's name wrong. This family too had a baron, Szara knew, but he believed that was the father, or the uncle.

'Do you like the collection?' said with sincerity, as though it mattered whether Szara liked it or not.

'It's yours?'

'Part of mine. Most of it's at home, up the street, and I keep some in the country. But the club has been indulgent with me, and I've spared them walls of leatherbound Racine that nobody's ever read.' He laughed self-consciously. 'What've you got there?' Szara turned the book's spine toward him. 'Karl Borns, yes. A perfect madman, Borns, had his funeral cortege on the Zürich local. The local!' He laughed again. 'Please,' he said, indicating that Szara should sit down at one end of a couch. De Montfried took a club chair.

'We'll have supper right here, if you don't mind. Do you?'

'Of course not.'

'Good. Sandwiches and something to drink. I've got to meet my wife for some beastly charity thing at ten – my days of eating two dinners are long over, I'm afraid.'

Szara did mind. Going upstairs, he'd caught a glimpse of a silk-walled dining room and a glittering array of china and crystal. All that money invested at the barber and the dry cleaner and now sandwiches. He tried to smile like a man who gets all the elaborate dinners he cares to have.

'Shall we stay in French?' de Montfried asked. 'I can try to get along in Russian, but I'm afraid I'll say awful things.'

'You speak Russian?'

'Grew up speaking French *en famille* and Russian to the servants. My father and uncle built much of the Russian railway system, then came the revolution and the civil war and most of it was destroyed. Very entrepreneurial place – at one time anyhow. How's it go? "Sugar by Brodsky, Tea by Vysotsky, Revolution by Trotsky." I suppose it's aimed at Jews, but it's reasonably faithful to what happened. Oh well.' He pressed a button on the wall and a waiter appeared almost instantly. De Montfried ordered sandwiches and wine, mentioning only the year, '27. The waiter nodded and closed the door behind him.

They chatted for a time. De Montfried found out quite a bit about him, the way a certain kind of aristocrat seemed able to do without appearing to pry. The trick of it, Szara thought, lay in the sincerity of the voice and the eyes –

I am so very interested in you. The man seemed to find everything he said fascinating or amusing or cleverly put. Soon enough he found himself trying to make it so.

There was no need for Szara to find out who de Montfried was. He knew the basic outline: a titled Jewish family, with branches in London, Paris, and Switzerland. Enormously wealthy, appropriately charitable, exceptionally private, and virtually without scandal. Old enough so that the money, like game, was well cured. Szara caught himself seeking something Jewish in the man, but there was nothing, in the features or the voice, that he could identify; the only notable characteristics were the narrow head and small ears that aristocrats had come to share with their hunting dogs.

The sandwiches were, Szara had to admit, extremely good. Open-faced, sliced duck or smoked salmon, with little pots of flavoured mayonnaise and cornichons to make them interesting. The wine, according to its white and gold label, was a *prémier cru* Beaune called Château de Montfried – it was easily the best thing Szara had ever tasted.

'We've my father to thank for this,' de Montfried said of the wine, holding it up against the light. 'After we were tossed out of Russia he took an interest in the vineyards, more or less retired down there. For him, there was something rather biblical in it: *work thy vines*. I don't know if it actually says that anywhere, but he seemed to think it did.' De Montfried was hesitantly sorrowful; the world would not, he understood, be much moved by small tragedies in his sort of family.

'It is extraordinary,' Szara said.

De Montfried leaned toward him slightly, signalling a shift in the conversation. 'You are recommended to me, Monsieur Szara, by an acquaintance who is called Bloch.'

'Yes?'

De Montfried paused, but Szara had no further comment. He reached into the inside pocket of his dinner jacket, withdrew an official-looking document with stamps and signatures at the bottom, and handed it to Szara. 'Do you know what this is?'

The paper was in English, Szara started to puzzle through it.

'It's an emigration certificate for British Palestine,' de Montfried said. 'Or Eretz Israel – a name I prefer. It's valuable, it's rare, hard to come by, and it's what I want to talk to you about.' He hesitated, then continued. 'Please be good enough to stop this discussion, now, if you feel I'm exceeding a boundary of any kind. Once we go further, I'm going to have to ask you to be discreet.'

'I understand,' Szara said.

'No hesitation? It would be understandable, certainly, if you felt there were just too many complications in listening to what I have to say.'

Szara waited.

'According to Monsieur Bloch, you were witness to the events in Berlin last month. He seems to feel that you might, on that basis, be willing to provide assistance for a project in which I take a great interest.'

'What project is that?'

'May I pour you a little more wine?'

Szara extended his glass.

'I hope you'll forgive me if I work up to a substantive description in my own way. I don't want to bore you, and I don't want you to think me a hopeless naïf – it's just that I've had experience of conversations about the Jewish return to Palestine and, well, it can be difficult, even unpleasant, as any political discussion is likely to be. Polite people avoid certain topics, experience shows the wisdom in that. Like one's dreams or medical condition – it's just better to find something else to talk about.

Unfortunately, the world is now acting in such a way as to eliminate that courtesy, among many others, so I can only ask your forbearance.'

Szara's smile was sad and knowing, with the sort of compassion that has been earned from daily life. He was that listener who can be told anything without fear of criticism because he has heard and seen worse than whatever you might contrive to say. He withdrew a packet of Gitanes, lit one, and exhaled. *I cannot be offended*, said the gesture.

'At the beginning of the Great War, in 1914, Great Britain found itself fighting in the Middle East against Turkey. The Jews in Palestine were caught up in the Turkish war effort – taxed into poverty, drafted into the Turkish armies. A certain group of Jews, in the town of Zichron Yaakov, not far from Haifa, believed that Great Britain ought to win the war in the Middle East, but what could they do? Well, for a small, determined group of people arrayed against a major power there is only one traditional answer, other than prayer, and that is espionage. Thus a botanist named Aaron Aaronson, his sister Sarah, an assistant called Avshalom Feinberg, and several others formed a network they called NILI – it's taken from a phrase in the Book of Samuel, an acronym of the Hebrew initials for *The Eternal One of Israel will not prove false*. The conspiracy was based at the Atlit Experimental Station and was facilitated by Aaron Aaronson's position as chief of the locust control unit – he could show up anywhere, for instance at Turkish military positions, without provoking suspicion. Meanwhile Sarah Aaronson, who was ravishing, became a fixture at parties attended by high-ranking Turkish officers. The British at first were suspicious – the Aaronsons did not ask for money – but eventually, in 1917, NILI product was accepted by British officers stationed on ships anchored off Palestine. There were – it's a typical problem, I understand – communications difficulties, and

Avshalom Feinberg set out across the Sinai desert to make contact with the British. He was ambushed by Arab raiders and murdered near Rafah, in the Gaza strip. Local legend has it that he was buried in the sand at the edge of the town and a palm tree grew up from his bones, seeded by dates he carried in his pockets. Then the spy ring was uncovered – too many people knew about it – and Sarah Aaronson was arrested by the Turks and tortured for four days. At that point she tricked her captors into letting her use the washroom, unsupervised, where she had secreted a revolver, and took her own life. All the other members of the network were captured by the Turks, tortured and executed, except for Aaron Aaronson, who survived the war only to die in a plane crash in the English Channel in 1919.

'Of course the Arabs fought on the side of the British as well – they too wished an end to Turkish occupation – and their revolt was led by skilled British military intelligence officers, such as T. E. Lawrence and Richard Meinertzhagen. The Arabs believed they were fighting for independence, but it did not quite turn out that way. When the smoke cleared, when Allenby took Jerusalem, the British ruled Mandate Palestine and the French held Syria and the Lebanon.

'But the NILI network was not the only effort made on Britain's behalf by the Jews. Far more important, in its ultimate effect, was the contribution of Dr Chaim Weizmann. Weizmann is well known as a Zionist, he is an articulate and persuasive man, but he is also known, by people who have an interest in the area, as a biochemist. While teaching and doing research at the University of Manchester, he discovered a method of producing synthetic acetone by a process of natural fermentation. As Great Britain's war against Germany intensified, they discovered themselves running out of acetone, which is the solvent that must be used in the manufacture of cordite, a crucial explosive in artillery shells and bullets. In 1916 Weizmann was summoned before Winston Churchill, at that time first lord of the Admiralty. Churchill said, "Well, Dr Weizmann, we need thirty thousand tons of acetone. Can you make it?" Weizmann did not rest until he'd done it, ultimately taking over many of Britain's large whisky distilleries until production plants could be built.

'Did Weizmann's action produce the Balfour Declaration? It did not hurt, certainly. In 1917 Balfour, as foreign secretary, promised that the British government would "use their best endeavours to facilitate the establishment in Palestine of a national home for the Jewish people." The League of Nations and other countries supported that position. It would be pleasant to think Weizmann had a hand in that, but the British are a wonderfully practical people, and what they wanted at that moment was America's entry into the war against the Germans, and it was felt that Lord Balfour's declaration would mobilize American Jewish opinion in that direction. But Weizmann played his part.'

De Montfried paused, refilled Szara's glass, then his own. 'By now, Monsieur Szara, you likely see where this is headed.'

'Yes and no,' Szara said. 'And the story isn't over.'

'That's true, it continues. But this much can be said: the survival of Jewish Palestine depends on the attitude of the British, and from that perspective, the Chamberlain government has been a disaster.'

'The Czechs would certainly agree.'

'No doubt. When Chamberlain, after giving in to Hitler in September, asked why Great Britain should risk war for the sake of what he called "a far-away country of which we know very little and whose language we don't understand," people who share my views were horrified.

If he perceived the Czechs in that way, what does he think about the Jews?'

'You see Munich as a moral failure, then.'

De Montfried teetered on the edge of indignation, then asked quietly, 'Don't you?'

He wasn't precisely angry, Szara thought. Simply, momentarily, balked. And he wasn't used to that. His life was ordered to keep him clear of uncertainties of any kind, and Szara had, rather experimentally, said something unexpected. To de Montfried it was like being served cold coffee for breakfast – it wasn't wrong, it was unthinkable.

'Yes, I do,' Szara said at last. 'But one ought to wonder out loud what Chamberlain was hearing from the other end of the conference table – from the generals, and the discreet gentlemen in dark suits. But then, after they made their case, he had the choice to believe them or not. And then to act. I can theorize that what he heard concerned what might happen to England's cities, particularly London, if they started a war with Germany – bombers and bomb tonnage and what happened in Guernica when it was bombed. People get hurt in war.'

'People get hurt in peace,' de Montfried said. 'In Palestine, since 1920, Arab mobs have murdered hundreds of Jewish settlers, and the British Mandate police haven't always shown much interest in stopping them.'

'Great Britain runs on oil, which the Arabs have and it doesn't.'

'That's true, Monsieur Szara, but it's not the whole story. Like Lawrence, many officials in the British Foreign Service idealize the Arabs – the fierce and terrible purity of the desert and all that sort of thing. Whereas with the Jews, well, all you get is a bunch of Jews.'

Szara laughed appreciatively and de Montfried softened. 'For a moment,' he said, 'I was afraid we were very far apart in the way we see these things.'

'No. I don't think so. But your Château de Montfried gives one an elevated view of existence, so I'm afraid you're going to have to be very direct with me.'

Szara waited to see what that might produce. De Montfried thought for a time, then said, 'The Arabs have made it clear they don't want Jewish settlement in the Middle East. Some are more hostile than others – several of the diplomats, in person, are more than decent in their understanding of our difficulties and not insensible to what we have to offer them. The German migration brought to Palestine a storehouse of technical information: medicine, engineering, horticulture; and they are people for whom the sharing of knowledge is instinctive, second nature. But Rashid Ali in Iraq is a creature of the Nazis and so is the mufti of Jerusalem. They've chosen the German side; other Arabs may join them if they don't get what they want. England is in a difficult position: how to retain the good will of the Arab nations without alienating America and other liberal countries. So they've adopted, on the subject of the Jewish question, a regime of conferences and more conferences. Instead of actually doing something, they have taken refuge in deciding what to do. I'll grant it's a legitimate diplomatic manoeuvre, one way to simply avoid trouble: thus the Peel Report and the Woodhead Commission and the Évian Conference, and next we're to have, in February, the St James's Conference, after which a White Paper will be issued. Meanwhile, Kristallnacht . . .'

'That was not a conference,' Szara said.

'Hitler spoke to the world: Jews may not live in Germany any longer, this is what we intend to do to them. A hundred dead, thousands beaten, tens of thousands locked up in the Dachau and Buchenwald camps. The German and Austrian Jews certainly understood; they're fighting to get out any way they can. But the problem is, they can't just get out, they have to go somewhere, and there is nowhere for them to go. I happen to have a rather accurate forecast of the White Paper that's going to be written after the St James's Conference. You, ah, journalists will understand how one comes upon such things.'

'One is never entirely without friends. One had better not be, at any rate.'

'Just so. We hear that emigration to Mandate Palestine is going to be limited to fifteen thousand Jews a year for five years, then it stops dead. At the moment, there are still three hundred thousand Jews in Germany, another sixty-five thousand remain in Austria, and only fifteen thousand of them can get into Palestine. And, if this thing were somehow to spread to Poland – and the way Hitler talks about Poland is the way he used to talk about the Sudetenland – then what? That's three million three hundred thousand more.'

'What is being done?'

De Montfried leaned back in his chair and stared. His eyes were dark, difficult to read, but Szara sensed a conflict between mistrust – the natural, healthy sort – and the need to confide.

'Beginnings,' he said finally. 'From all points on the political compass, the established groups have been fighting this battle for years – the labour people in the Histadrut, Vladimir Jabotinsky's New Zionists and the organization they call Betar. David Ben-Gurion and the Jewish Agency. And others, many others, are doing what they can. It is a political effort – letters written, favours called in, donations given, resolutions passed. It all creates a kind of presence. Also, in Palestine there is the Haganah, a fighting force, and its information bureau, known as Sherut Yediot, generally called Shai, its first initial. But it is all they can do to keep the Jews of *Palestine* alive.

'Then, just lately, there is something more. As you know, emigration to Palestine is called by the name Aliyah.

The word has the sense of *return*. The British entry certificates permit a few thousand people a year into the country, and there is a Jewish organization to administer the details – travel, reception, and so on. But there exists within that group, in its shadow, another. There are only ten of them at the moment, nine men and a very young woman, who call themselves the Mossad Aliyah Bet, that is, the Institute for Aliyah B – the letter indicates illegal, as opposed to legal, emigration. This group is now in the process of leasing ships – whatever derelict hulk can be found in the ports of southern Europe – and they intend to bring Jews out of danger and effect clandestine landings on the coast of Palestine.'

'Will they succeed?'

'They will try. And I am in sympathy with them. A moment comes and if you wish to look upon yourself as human you must take some kind of action. Otherwise, you can read the newspapers and congratulate yourself on your good fortune. Weizmann, however, makes an interesting point. After Kristallnacht he said to Anthony Eden that the fire in the German synagogues may easily spread to Westminster Abbey. So the self-congratulatory souls may one day have their own moment of reckoning, we shall see.'

'And you, Monsieur de Montfried, what is it that you do?'

'I invite you to the Renaissance Club of Neuilly, among other things. I somehow happen to meet Monsieur Bloch. I have a few friends, here and there; we try to spend money wisely, in the right places. When I can, I tell important people those things I believe they ought to know.'

'A group of friends. It has, perhaps, a name?'

'No.'

'Truly?'

'The less official the better, is what we think. One can

be without structure of any kind and still be of enormous help.'

'What kind of help, Monsieur de Montfried?'

'There are two areas in which we have a very special interest. The first is simple: legitimate emigration certificates above and beyond the publicly stated number allowed by the British foreign office. Each one represents several lives saved, because they can be used by families. The second area is not simple, but can be of far greater impact. Shall we call it a demonstration? As good a word as any. A demonstration that groups sympathetic to Jewish settlement in Palestine are a source of assistance that the British cannot ignore. It's a way of buying influence – as NILI did, as Weizmann did, by serving the interests of the governing nation. It's what, finally, the British understand. Quid pro quo. The White Paper will be debated in Parliament, where there are those who want to help us; we'd like to make it easier for them. The only way to accomplish that is with concrete acts, something definite they can point to. Not in public. Nothing happens in public. But in the halls, in the cloakrooms, the gentlemen's clubs, the country houses – that's where the serious business is done. That's where we must be represented.'

'Can the emigration certificates be produced privately?'

'Forged, you mean.'

'Yes.'

'Of course it's tried, and if one can be proud of forgers, Jewish forgers are among the best, though they have been known to go off on their own and produce the occasional Rembrandt.

'Unfortunately, the British have a tendency to count. And their colonial bureaucracy is efficient. The weakness in the system is that the civil servants in their passport offices are underpaid, a situation that leads only one place. Bribes have been offered, and accepted.

Also discovered. The same situation is present in many embassies: Argentine, Liberian, Guatemalan – Jews are turning up as citizens of virtually everywhere. There are also instances where passport officers just give in to compassion when confronted with the unbearable condition of certain applicants – the horrors of this thing simply multiply the more you look at it. But forgery and bribery and whatever else occurs to you do not begin to create the numbers we need. What we have in mind is quite different, a private arrangement that produces real certificates.'

'Difficult. And sensitive.'

De Montfried smiled. 'Monsieur Bloch has great faith in you.'

'Theoretically, in what way would a Soviet journalist involve himself in such matters?'

'Who can say? It's been my experience of life that one does not try to control influential people. One can only present one's case and hope for the best. If on reflection you find yourself in agreement with what has been said here this evening, you'll find a way, I suspect, to bring your abilities to bear on the situation. I myself don't know the solution, so I seek people out and pose the problem. But if I could believe that you would go home tonight and think about these matters I would be frankly overjoyed.'

Gently, and by mutual agreement, the conversation was allowed to drift off into pleasantries and, just in time for de Montfried to attend his 'beastly charity thing,' they parted. Outside the little library, a club member with a bright red face and white hair greeted de Montfried effusively, pretending to pull an engineer's whistle cord and making the French sound for *toot, toot*. De Montfried laughed heartily, the most amiable fellow imaginable. 'We've known each other forever,' he said to Szara. They shook hands in the downstairs hall and the steward returned Szara's umbrella, which had apparently been dried with a cloth.

January 1939.

08942 57661 44898

And so on, which turned out to mean *S novym godom* and *S novym schastyem* – happy new year and the best to you all – cold and formal wishes from the Great Father Stalin. During his week in Berlin, Szara had found himself in the neighbourhood of the storage building that held the painting with the DUBOK dossier secreted behind the canvas. It had seemed to him remote, and very much beside the point. *This is a lesson about time*, he thought. With the surge of German power into Austria and Czechoslovakia, Russia assumed the role of counterweight, and if Stalin had been vulnerable when he decimated the military and intelligence services, he wasn't now. Hitler was driving the world to his door. Stalin's murders were achieved in basements; Hitler's work was photographed for the newspapers. Russia was weak, full of starving peasants. Germany built superb locomotives. The Okhrana dossier had best remain where it was.

In early January, Szara suddenly ran a terrible fever. He lay amid soaked sheets; saw, when he closed his eyes, the splashing in the moonlit river Havel and heard, again and again, the scream for mercy. It was not delirium, it was a sickened memory that refused to heal. He saw Marta Haecht dancing in the yard of a thatched-roof cottage in some Ukrainian ghetto village. He saw the eyes of people who had stared at him in Berlin, a long tile hall, the broken face of a Wittenau policeman, the room in the narrow house. It had no name, this sickness; that was its secret, he thought; it fed deep, where words and ideas didn't reach.

He tried the writer's time-honoured cure: writing. Unshaven, in wrinkled pyjamas, he spent a few mornings at it, producing journalistic short stories in pursuit of the German character. Brutal, nasty stuff. He attacked hypocrisy, cruelty, fulminous envy, an obsessive sense of having been wronged, grievously, and misunderstood, eternally. Rereading, he was both horrified and pleased, recalled Lenin's wondrously sly dictum that 'paper will stand for anything you write on it,' and thought for a moment he might actually seek publication. But it was not, he came to realize, the blow he needed to strike. All it would do was make them angry. And they already were that, most of the time. It was not something he'd accused them of, yet in some ways he saw it as their dominant characteristic – he had no idea why, not really. One morning, as a fall of thick, wet snowflakes silenced the city, he tore the stories up.

Schau-Wehrli was his January angel, crisscrossed the icy streets of Paris and made his *treffs* with Valais, paid the concierge to bring him bowls of thick, amber soup, and sat on the edge of his bed when she had a spare moment. He came to understand, eventually, that the possibility of feverish babbling made them nervous – they didn't want him in the hospital. Nobody quite said anything about it, but a doctor from the medical faculty at the Sorbonne, a sympathizer, suddenly made house calls to a man with a bad fever. A professor with a grand beard, peering down at him from the heights of professional achievement to say 'Rest and keep warm and drink plenty of hot tea.'

When Schau-Wehrli stopped by they'd gossip – like himself, she really had no one to talk to. After the meeting in the Berlin theatre, she told him, Tscherova had apparently redoubled her efforts, joining the rather lively circles of young, Nazi party intellectuals and thus manoeuvring her subagents into extremely productive relationships. 'What did you do to her?' Schau-Wehrli would ask, teasing him as a great lover. He would smile weakly. 'Really nothing. She is just so . . . so Russian,' he would say. 'A little sympathy, a kind word, and a flower suddenly blooms.'

The fever broke after ten days and slowly Szara began to work again. In the last week of January, Abramov ordered a third-country meeting to pursue certain details regarding a reorganization of the OPAL network. This time it was to be in Switzerland, near the town of Sion, a couple of hours up the Rhône valley from Geneva, on the night of 7 February. The transmission took its time coming in and Kranov was annoyed. 'They've changed W/T operators again,' he said, lighting a cigarette and sitting back in his chair. 'Slow as mud, this new one.'

Goldman wired the following day, ordering – as he had when Szara had gone to Berlin – a piggyback courier delivery. Sixty thousand French francs were to be taken to Lausanne on the day after his meeting with Abramov and passed, using a complicated identification/parol procedure, to an unnamed individual. This was a lot of money, and it caused a problem. Couriers were limited to a certain level of funds; after that Moscow, evidently in fear of temptation, dictated the presence of a second courier, specifically a diplomatic or intelligence officer and not just a network agent like Odile.

So Maltsaev told him, anyhow.

Szara was eating dinner at his neighbourhood bistro, *Le Temps* folded in half and propped up against the mustard pot, when a man materialized across the table and introduced himself. 'Get in touch with Ilya Goldman,' he said by way of establishing his bona fides. 'He'll confirm who I am – we were in Madrid together. At the embassy.' He was now in Paris, he continued, on temporary assignment from Belgrade, where he'd been political officer for a year or so.

Szara immediately disliked him. Maltsaev was a dark, balding young man with a bad skin and a sour disposition, a man much given to sinister affectations, a man who spoke always as though he were saying only a small fraction of what he actually knew. He wore tinted eyeglasses and a voluminous black overcoat of excellent quality.

Maltsaev made it clear that he found courier work boring and very much beneath him – the order to accompany Szara to Switzerland offended him in any number of ways. 'These little czars in Moscow,' he said with a sneer, 'throw roubles around as though the world were ending tomorrow.' He had a pretty good idea what went on in Lausanne, he confided, typical of the deskbound comrades to try and solve the problem with money. Typical also that some unseen controller in the Dzerzhinsky Square *apparat* was using the occasion to make Maltsaev's life miserable, screwing him with some witless assignment that could be handled by any numskull operative. 'Another enemy,' he grumbled. Somebody jealous of his promotions or his assignment in Paris. 'But next we'll see if he gets away with it. Maybe not, eh?' He pointed at Szara's plate. 'What's that?'

'Andouillette,' Szara said.

'What is it? A sausage? What's in it?'

'You won't want it if I tell you,' Szara said.

'Probably the chef's mistress,' Maltsaev said with a laugh. 'Order me a steak. Cooked. No blood or back it goes.' His eyes were animated behind the tinted lenses, flicking around the room, staring at the other customers. Then he leaned confidentially toward Szara. 'Who is this Abramov you're going to see?' He looked triumphant and pleased with himself – *surprised I know that?*

'Boss. One of them, anyhow.'

'A big shot?'

'He sits on one Directorate, certainly. Perhaps others, I don't know.'

'Old friend, I'll bet. The way things go these days, you don't last long without a protector, right?'

Szara shrugged. 'Everybody's got their own story – mine's not like that. It's all business with Abramov.'

'Is it.'

'Yes.'

'Hey!' Maltsaev called as a waiter went past and ignored him.

It snowed on the night of the sixth, and by the time Szara and Maltsaev left the Gare de Lyon on the seventh of February the fields and villages of France were still and white. *The nineteenth century*, Szara thought with longing: a pair of frost-coated dray horses pulling a cart along a road, a girl in a stocking cap skating on a pond near Melun. The sky was dense and swollen; sometimes a flight of crows circled over the snow-covered fields. But for the presence of Maltsaev, it would have been a time for dreaming. The frozen world outside the train window was unmoving, cold and peaceful, smoke from farmhouse chimneys the only sign of human life.

Following the rules, they had booked the compartment for themselves, so they were alone. Szara kept a hand or a foot in permanent contact with the small travelling case that held the sixty thousand francs, each packet of hundred-franc notes bound by a strip of paper with Cyrillic initials on it. But even though they were alone, Maltsaev spoke obliquely: *your friend in Sion, the man in Brussels*. A glutton's appetite for gossip, Szara thought. Who do you know? How do the loyalties work? What's the real story? Maltsaev was the classic opportunist, probing for whatever you might have that he could use. Szara parried him on every point, but felt that eventually the sheer weight of the attack might wear him down. To escape, he feigned drowsiness. Maltsaev sneered with delight: 'Going to dreamland with our dear gold on your lap?'

They'd left at dawn, and it was again dark when they

reached Geneva. They walked three blocks from the railway station and found the Opel Olympia that had been left in front of a commercial travellers' hotel, the ignition key taped to the base of the steering wheel column. Szara drove. Maltsaev sat beside him, smoking his cardboard-tipped Belomor cigarettes, a road map spread across his lap. They circled the north shore of Lake Leman on good roads in intermittent light snow, then, after Villeneuve, began to climb over the mountain passes.

Here the weather cleared and there was a bright, sharp moon, its light sparkling on the ice crystal in the banked snow at the sides of the road. Sometimes, on the curves, they could see down into the valleys spread out below: clusters of stone villages, ice rivers, empty roads. The sense of deep silence and distance at last reached Maltsaev, who ceased talking and stared out of the window. By ten o'clock they had descended to Martigny and turned north on the narrow plain by the Rhône, here an overgrown mountain stream. There was hardpack snow on the roads and Szara drove carefully but steadily, encountering only one or two cars along the way.

Sion was dark, no lights anywhere, and they had to hunt for a time until they found the gravel road that went up the mountainside. Five minutes later the grade flattened out and they rolled to a stop in front of an old hotel, tyres crunching on newly fallen snow. The hotel – a carved sign above the arched doorway said Hôtel du Vaz – was timber and stucco capped by a steep slate roof hung with icicles. It stood high above the road, at the edge of a shimmering white meadow that sloped gently toward the edge of an evergreen forest. The ground-floor shutters were closed; behind them was a faint glow, perhaps a single lamp in what Szara presumed to be a reception area in the lobby. When he turned off the ignition and climbed out of the Opel, he could hear the sound of the wind at the corner of the building. There were no other cars to be seen; perhaps it was a summer hotel, he thought, where people came in order to walk in the mountains.

Maltsaev got out of the car and closed the door carefully. From an upper window, Szara heard Abramov's voice. 'André Aronovich?'

'Yes,' Szara called. 'Come down and let us in. It's freezing.'

'Who is with you?'

Looking up, Szara saw one shutter partly opened. Before he could respond, Maltsaev whispered, 'Don't say my name.'

Szara stared at him, not understanding. 'Answer him,' Maltsaev said urgently, gripping him hard at the elbow. Abramov must have seen the gesture, Szara thought. Because a moment later they heard the sound, eerily loud in the still, cold air, of a heavy man descending an exterior staircase, perhaps at the back of the hotel. A man in a hurry.

Maltsaev, coat flapping, started to run, and Szara, not knowing what else to do, followed. They were immediately slowed when they moved around the side of the hotel because here the snow was deeper, up to their knees, which made running almost impossible. Maltsaev swore as he stumbled forward. They heard a shout from the trees and to their left. Then it was repeated, urgently. A threat, Szara realized, spoken in Russian.

They came around the corner at the back of the hotel and stopped. Abramov, in a dark suit and homburg hat, was trying to run across the snow-covered meadow. It was absurd, almost comic. He struggled and floundered and slipped, went down on one hand, rose, lifted his knees high for a few steps, fell again, then lurched forward as he tried to reach the edge of the forest, leaving behind him a broken, white path. The homburg suddenly tilted to one side and Abramov grabbed it frantically, instinctively, and held the brim tightly as he ran, as though, late for work, he were running to catch a tram in a city street.

The marksmen in the forest almost let him reach the trees. The first shot staggered him but he kept on a little, only slower, then the second shot brought him down. The reports echoed off the side of the mountain, then faded into silence. Maltsaev walked into the meadow, Szara followed, moving along the broken path. It was slippery and difficult, and soon they were breathing hard. Just before they reached him, Abramov managed to turn on his side. His hat had rolled away and there was snow caught in his beard. Maltsaev stood silently and tried to catch his breath. Szara knelt down. He could see that Abramov had bled into the snow. His eyes were closed, then they flickered open for a moment, perhaps he saw Szara. He made a single sound, a guttural sigh, 'Ach,' of exhaustion and irritation, of dismissal, and then he was gone.

The Renaissance Club

At the Brasserie Heininger, at the far corner table where you could see everyone and everyone could see you, seated below the scrupulously preserved bullet hole in the vast and golden mirror, André Szara worked hard at being charming and tried to quiet a certain interior voice that told him to shut up and go home.

A newcomer to the crowd of regulars at the corner table, and so the centre of attention, he proposed a toast: 'I would like us to drink to the love . . . to the hopeless loves . . . of our childhood days.' Was there a split second of hesitation – my God, is he going to weep? – before the chorus of approval? But then he didn't weep; his fingers combed a longish strand of black hair off his forehead and he smiled a vulnerable smile. Then everyone realized how very right the toast was, how very right *he* was, the emotional Russian long after midnight, in his grey tie and soft maroon shirt, not exactly drunk, just intimate and daring.

That he was. Beneath the tablecloth, his hand rested warmly on the thigh of Lady Angela Hope, a pillar of the Paris night and a woman he'd been specifically told to avoid. With his other hand, he drank Roederer Cristal from a gold-rimmed champagne flute which, thanks to the attentions of a clairvoyant waiter, turned out to be perfectly full every time he went to pick it up. He smiled, he laughed, he said amusing things, and everyone thought he was wonderful, everyone: Voyschinkowsky, 'the Lion of the Bourse'; Ginger Pudakis, the English wife of the Chicago meat-packing king; the Polish Countess K —, who, when properly intrigued, made ingenious gardens for her friends; the terrible Roddy Fitzware, *mad, bad, and dangerous to know*. In fact the whole pack of them, ten at last count, hung on his every word. Was his manner perhaps just a shade more Slavic than it really needed to be? Perhaps. But he did not care. He smoked and drank like an affable demon, said, 'For a drunkard the sea is only knee deep!' and other proverbial Russianisms as they came to him, and generally made a grand and endearing fool of himself.

Yet – he was more Slavic than they knew – the interior voice refused to be still. *Stop*, it said. *This is not in your best interest; you will suffer, you will regret it, they will catch you*. He ignored it. Not that it was wrong, in fact he knew it was right, but still he ignored it.

Voyschinkowsky, inspired by the toast, was telling a story: 'It was my father who took me to the Gypsy camp. Imagine, to go out so late at night, and to such a place! I could not have been more than twelve years old, but when she began to dance . . .' Lady Angela's leg pressed closer under the table, a hand appeared through the smoky air, and a stream of pale Cristal fizzed into his glass. What other wine, someone had said of champagne, can you hear?

Like Lady Angela Hope, the Brasserie Heininger was notorious. In the spring of '37 it had been the site of, as the Parisians put it, '*une affaire bizarre*': the main dining room had been sprayed with tommy guns, the Bulgarian maître d' had been assassinated in the ladies' WC, and a mysterious waiter called Nick had disappeared soon after. Such violently Balkan goings-on had made the place madly popular; the most desirable table directly beneath the golden mirror with a single bullet hole; in fact the only mirror that survived the incident. Otherwise, it was just one more brasserie, where moustached waiters hurried among the red plush banquettes with platters of crayfish and grilled sausage, a taste of *fin-de-siècle* deviltry while outside the February snow drifted down into the streets of Paris and cabmen tried to keep warm.

As for Lady Angela Hope, she was notorious among two very different sets: the late-night crowd of aristocrats and parvenus, of every nationality and none at all, that haunted certain brasseries and nightclubs, as well as another, more obscure perhaps, which followed her career with equal, or possibly keener, interest. Her name had been raised in one of Goldman's earliest briefings, taken from a file folder kept in a safe in the Stefan Leib shop in Brussels. Both Szara's predecessor and Annique Schau-Wehrli had been 'probed' by Lady Angela, who was 'known to have informal connections with British intelligence stations in Paris.' She was, as promised, fortyish, sexy, rich, foul-mouthed, promiscuous, and, in general, thoroughly accessible; an indefatigable guest and hostess who knew 'everybody.' 'You will meet her certainly,' said Goldman primly, 'but she has entirely the wrong friends. Stay away.'

But then, Goldman.

Szara smiled to himself. Too bad Goldman couldn't see him now, the forbidden Lady Angela snugly by his side. Well, he thought, this is fate. This had to happen, and so now it is happening. Yes, there may have been some kind of alternative, but the one person in his life who really understood alternatives, knew where they hid and how to find them, was gone.

That was Abramov, of course. And on 7 February, in a meadow behind the Hôtel du Vaz in Sion, Abramov had resigned from the service. Exactly how that came to happen Szara didn't know, but he'd managed to unwind events to a point where he had a pretty good idea of what had gone on.

Abramov, he suspected, had attempted to influence Dershani by use of the photographs taken in the garden of the house at Puteaux. It hadn't worked. Realizing his days were numbered, he'd at last taken Szara's advice offered on the beach at Aarhus and planned one final operation: his own disappearance. He'd arranged the meeting at the Hôtel du Vaz in Sion (owned, Szara was told that night, by a front corporation operated by the NKVD Foreign Department), which gave him a legitimate reason to leave Moscow. He'd then created a notional agent in Lausanne who needed sixty thousand *French* francs. This made Goldman in Brussels a logical source and Szara's scheduled trip to Sion a convenient method of delivery. The money was meant to give Abramov a running start in a new life; the operation was dovetailed and simple, but it hadn't worked.

Why? Szara could see two possibilities: Kranov, already thought to spy on the OPAL network for the Directorate, might have alerted security units when an untrained and uncertain hand operated the wireless key in Moscow. Every operator had a characteristic signature, and Kranov, trained to be sensitive to change of any kind, had probably reacted to Abramov's rather awkward keying of his own message.

To Szara, however, Goldman was the more interesting possibility. Network gossip suggested the *rezident* had previously had a hand in a special operation, something well outside the usual scope of OPAL's activities, in which a young woman was kidnapped from a rooming house in Paris. And when Szara described to Schau-Wehrli the operatives he'd met later that night at the Hôtel du Vaz – especially the one who used the work name Dodin, a huge man, short and thick, with the red hands and face of a butcher – she had reacted. In the next instant she was all unknowing, but he'd felt a shadow touch her, he was sure of it.

Through Kranov or Goldman – or both – the special

section of the Foreign Department had become involved, dispatched Maltsaev to Paris to keep watch on Szara as he went to meet Abramov and to find out if he was an accomplice, or even a fellow fugitive. Szara realized that his instinctive distaste for Maltsaev's personality had provoked him into a blank and businesslike response to the man's offensive needling, and that in turn had quite probably saved his life.

They'd buried Abramov at the edge of the meadow, under the snow-laden boughs of a fir tree, chipping at the frozen ground with shovels and sweating in the cold moonlight. There were four of them besides Maltsaev; they took off their overcoats and worked in baggy, woollen suits, swearing as they dug, their Swiss hunting rifles propped against a tree. They spread snow over the dirt and returned to the empty hotel, building a fire in the fireplace downstairs, sitting in handmade pine chairs and smoking Maltsaev's Belomors, talking among themselves. Szara was part of every activity, taking his turn with the shovel, struggling with Abramov's weight as they put him in the ground. He had no choice; he became a temporary member of the unit. They talked about what they could buy in Geneva before they went back to Kiev, they talked about other operations; something in Lithuania, something in Sweden, though they were oblique with a stranger in their midst. The only ceremony for Abramov was Szara's silent prayer, and he made very sure his lips did not move as he said it. Yet, even at that moment, in the dark meadow, he planned further memorials.

Early in the morning, standing on the platform of the railway station in Geneva and waiting for the Paris train, Maltsaev was blunt: 'The usual way in these affairs is to send the accomplice along on the same journey, innocent or not doesn't matter. But, for the moment, somebody considers you worth keeping alive. Personally I don't agree

– you are a traitor in your heart – but I just do what they tell me. That's a good lesson for you, Szara, come to think of it. Being smart maybe isn't so smart as you think – you see where it got Abramov. I blame it on the parents, they should have made him study the violin like all the rest of them.' The train pulled in. Maltsaev, after a contemptuous bow and a sweep of the hand toward the compartment door, turned and walked away.

Staring at Voyschinkowsky across the table, pretending to listen as the man told a story about his childhood, Szara for the first time understood the chain of events that had led to the night of 7 February. It had started with Lötte Huber's romance with Sénéschal and from there moved, seemingly driven by fate, to its conclusion. *Inevitable*, he thought. The champagne was cunning; the opposite of vodka in that it didn't numb, it revealed. One could say, he realized, that a Nazi official's appetite for red berry sauce had two years later led to the death of a Russian intelligence officer in a Swiss meadow. He shook his head to make such thoughts go away. *Remember*, he told himself silently, *this must be done with a cold heart*.

Voyschinkowsky paused to take a long sip of champagne. 'The Lion of the Bourse' was in his early sixties, with a long, mournful face marked by the chronically red-rimmed eyes and dark pouches of the lifelong insomniac. He was reputed to be one of the richest men in Paris. 'I wonder whatever became of her?' he said. He had a thick Hungarian accent and a heavy, hoarse voice that seemed to come from the bottom of a well.

'But Bibi,' Ginger Pudakis said, 'did you make love?'

'I was twelve years old, my dear.'

'Then what?'

One side of Voyschinkowsky's mouth twisted briefly into a tart grin. 'I looked at her breasts.'

'Finis?'

'Let me tell you, from one who has lived a, a rich and varied cosmopolitan life, there was never again a moment like it.'

'Oh Bibi,' she breathed. 'Too sad!'

Lady Angela whispered in Szara's ear, 'Say something clever, can you?'

'Not sad. Bittersweet,' he said. 'Not at all the same thing. I think it is a perfect story.'

'Hear, hear,' said Roddy Fitzware.

They went on to a nightclub to watch Apache dancing. A young dancer, her skirt bunched up around her waist, slid across the polished floor into the audience and accidentally drove a spike heel into Szara's ankle. He winced, saw a momentary horror on her face amid the black and violet makeup, then her partner, in the traditional sailor's shirt, whisked her away. *Now I am wounded in the line of duty*, he thought, *and should receive a medal, but there is no nation to award it*. He was very drunk and laughed out loud at the thought.

'Were you stabbed?' Lady Angela asked quietly, evidently amused.

'A little. It's nothing.'

'What a very, very nice man you are.'

'Hah.'

'It's true. Next week, you're to have supper with me, tête-à-tête. Can you?'

'I shall be honoured, dear lady.'

'Mysterious things may happen.'

'The very thing I live for.'

'I expect you do.'

'You're right. Will there be a violinist?'

'Good God no!'

'Then I'll come.'

* * *

The dinner was at Fouquet's, in a private room with dark green curtains. Gold-painted cherubs grinned from the corners of the ceiling. There were two wines, and langoustines with artichokes and turbot. Lady Angela Hope was in red, a long, shimmering silk sheath, and her upswept hair, a colour something like highly polished brass, was held in place by two diamond butterflies. He thought her presentation ingenious: glamorous, seductive, and absolutely untouchable – the culmination of the private dinner was . . . that one would have dined privately.

'What *am* I to do with my little place in Scotland? You must advise me,' she said.

'Could anything be wrong?'

'Could anything be wrong – could anything be right! This dreadful man, a Mr *MacConnachie* if you will, writes that the northwest cornice has *entirely* deteriorated, and . . .'

Szara was, in a way, disappointed. He was curious, and the street imp from Odessa in him would have liked the conquest of a titled English lady in a private room at Fouquet's. But he'd understood from the beginning that the evening was for business and not for love. While they dawdled over coffee, there was a discreet knock on the doorframe to one side of the curtain. Lady Angela playfully splayed her fingers at the centre of her chest. 'Why, whoever can that be?'

'Your husband,' Szara said acidly.

She suppressed a giggle. 'Bastard,' she said in English. Her upper-class tone made a poem of the word and he noted that it was absolutely the most honestly affectionate thing she had ever said, or likely ever would say, to him. Underneath it all, he thought her splendid.

Roger Fitzware slipped between the curtains. Something in the way he moved meant he was no longer the slightly effeminate and terribly amusing Roddy that the Brasserie Heininger crowd so adored. Short and quite handsome, with thick reddish-brown hair swept across a noble forehead, he was wearing a dinner jacket and smoking a little cigar. 'Am I *de trop?*' he said.

Szara stood and they shook hands. 'Pleased to see you,' he said in English.

'Mm,' Fitzware said.

'Do join us, dear boy,' Lady Angela said.

'Shall I have them bring a chair?' Fitzware said, just to be polite.

'I think not,' said Lady Angela. She came around the table and kissed Szara on the cheek. 'A very, very nice man,' she said. 'You must ring me up – very soon,' she called as she vanished through the curtain.

Fitzware ordered Biscuit cognac and for a time they chatted about nothing in particular. Szara, a student of technique, found considerable professional satisfaction in watching Fitzware work; intelligence people, no matter their national origin, always had a great deal in common, like people who collected stamps or worked in banks. But the approach, when it came, was no surprise, since it turned out to be the same one favoured by the Russian services, one that created an acceptable motive and solicited betrayal in the same breath.

Fitzware conducted the conversation like a maestro:

The concierge situation in Paris – and here he was quite amusing: his apartment house groaned beneath the heel of a ferocious tyrant, *un vrai dragon* in her eighties with a will of iron – led gracefully to *the political situation in Paris* – here Fitzware implicitly acknowledged the concerns of his guest by citing, with a grim expression, the slogan chalked on walls and bridges, *Vaut mieux Hitler que Blum*, a fascist preference for the Nazis over Léon Blum, the Jewish socialist who'd led the government a year earlier. Then it was time for *the political situation in France*, followed closely by *the political situation in Europe*. Now the table was set and it only remained for dinner to be served.

'Do you think there can be peace?' Fitzware asked. He lit a small cigar and offered Szara one. Szara declined and lit a Gitane.

'Of course,' Szara said. 'If people of good will are determined to work together.'

And that was that.

Fitzware had hoisted a signal flag of inquiry, and Szara had responded. Fitzware took a moment to swirl his cognac and exhale a long, satisfied plume of cigar smoke. Szara let him exult a little in his victory; for somebody in their line of work, recruitment was the great, perhaps the only, victory. Now it was settled, they would *work together for peace*. As who wouldn't? They both knew, as surely as the sun rose in the morning, that there would be war, but that was entirely beside the point.

'We're terribly at sea, you know, we British,' said Fitzware, following the script. 'I fear we haven't a clue to the Soviet Union's intentions regarding Poland – or the Baltics, or Turkey. The situation is complex, a powder keg ready to go up. Wouldn't it be dreadful if the armies of Europe marched over a simple misunderstanding?'

'It must be avoided,' Szara agreed. 'At all cost. You'd think we would have come to understand, in 1914, the price of ignorance.'

'Sorrowfully, the world doesn't learn.'

'No, you're right. It seems we are destined to repeat our mistakes.'

'Unless, of course, we have the knowledge, the information, that permits us to work these things out between diplomats – in the League of Nations, for instance.'

'Ideally, it is the answer.'

'Well,' said Fitzware, brightening, 'I believe there's still a chance, don't you?'

'I do,' Szara said. 'To me personally, the critical information at this time would concern developments in Germany. Would you agree with that?'

Fitzware did not respond immediately; simply stared as though hypnotized. He'd led himself some way down a false trail, assuming that Szara's information concerned Soviet operations – intelligence; political or otherwise. Now he had to shift to a completely different area. Quickly, it dawned on him that what he was being offered was, on balance, even better than he'd realized. Offers of Soviet secrets were, in many cases, provocations or dangles – attempts to involve a rival service in deluding itself or revealing its own resources. One had to wear fire-proof gloves in such cases. Offers of *German* secrets, on the other hand, coming from a Russian, would very likely be hard currency. Fitzware cleared his throat. 'Emphatically,' he said.

'To me, the key to a peaceful solution of the current difficulties would be a mutual knowledge of armaments, particularly combat aircraft. What would be your view on that?'

In Fitzware's eyes Szara glimpsed the momentary light of elation, as though an inner voice cried out, *I'd dance naked on me fookin' birthday cake!* In fact, Fitzware permitted himself a civilized grunt. 'Hm, well, yes, of course I agree.'

'With discretion, Mr Fitzware, it's entirely possible.'

An unspoken question answered: Fitzware was not in communication with the USSR, was not being drawn into the occluded maze of diplomatic initiatives achieved by intelligence means. He was in communication with André Szara, a Soviet journalist operating on his own. That was the meaning of the word *discretion*. Fitzware considered carefully; matters had reached a delicate point. 'Your terms,' he said.

'I have great anxiety on the question of Palestine, particularly with the St James's Conference in session.'

At this, Fitzware's triumphant mood slightly deflated. Szara could not have raised a more difficult issue. 'There *are* easier areas in which we might work,' he said.

Szara nodded, leaving Fitzware to tread water.

'Can you be specific?' Fitzware said at last.

'Certificates of Emigration.'

'Real ones?'

'Yes.'

'Above the legal limit, of course.'

'Of course.'

'And in return?'

'Determination of the Reich's monthly bomber production. Based on the total manufacture of the cold-process swage wire that operates certain nonelectronic aircraft controls.'

'My board of directors will want to know the reason you say "total."'

'*My* board of directors believes this to be the case. It is, whatever else one might say, Mr Fitzware, a very good, a very *effective*, board of directors.'

Fitzware sighed in agreement. 'Don't suppose, dear boy, you'd consider taking something simple, like money.'

'No.'

'Another Cognac, then.'

'With pleasure.'

'We have a good deal of work yet to do, and I can't promise anything. All the usual, you understand,' Fitzware said, pressing the button on the wall that summoned a waiter.

'I understand perfectly,' Szara said. He paused to finish his Cognac. 'But you must understand that time is very important to us. People are dying, Great Britain needs friends, we must make it all work out somehow. If you will save lives for us, we will save lives for you. Surely that's world peace, or damn close to it.'

'Close enough,' Fitzware said.

In the violent, changeable weather of early March, Szara and Fitzware got down to serious negotiation. 'Call it what you like,' Szara was later to tell de Montfried, 'but what it was was pushcart haggling.' Fitzware played all the traditional melodies: it was his board of directors that wanted something for nothing; the mandarins in Whitehall were a pack of blind fools; he, Fitzware, was entirely on Szara's side, but making headway through the bureaucratic underbrush was unspeakably frustrating.

Much of the negotiating was done at the Brasserie Heininger. Fitzware sat with Lady Angela Hope and Voyschinkowsky and the whole crowd. Sometimes Szara joined them, other times he took one of his café girls out for dinner. He would meet Fitzware in the men's WC, where they would whisper urgently back and forth, or they would go out on the pavement for a breath of fresh air. Once or twice they talked in a corner at the social evenings held in various apartments. Over the course of it, Szara realized that being a Jew made bargaining difficult. Fitzware was eternally proper, but there were moments when Szara thought he caught a whiff of the classical attitude: why are you people so difficult, so greedy, so stubborn?

And of course Fitzware's board of directors tried to do to him what his own Directorate had done to Dr Julius Baumann. Who are we really dealing with? they wanted to know. We need to have a sense of the process; where is the information coming from? More, give us more! (And why are *you people* so greedy?)

But Szara was like a rock. He smiled at Fitzware tolerantly, knowingly, as the Englishman went fishing for deeper information, a smile that said, *We're in the same business, my friend*. Finally, Szara made a telling point: this negotiation is nothing, he admitted ruefully to Fitzware, compared to dealings with the French, who had their own Jewish communities in Beirut and Damascus. That seemed to work. Nothing, in love and business, quite like a rival to stimulate desire.

They struck a deal and shook hands.

Baumann's figures, from 1 January 1937 to February 1939, brought an initial payment of five hundred Certificates of Emigration – up from Fitzware's offer of two hundred, down from Szara's demand for seven hundred. One hundred and seventy-five certificates a month would be provided as the information was exchanged thereafter. The White Paper would produce seventy-five thousand legal entries through 1944, fifteen thousand a year, one thousand two hundred and fifty a month. Szara's delivery of intelligence from Germany would increase that number by a factor of fourteen per cent. *Thus the mathematics of Jewish lives*, he thought.

He told himself again and again that the operation had to be run with a cold heart, told himself to accept a small victory, told himself whatever he could think of, yet he could not avoid the knowledge that his visits to the corner *tabac* seemed much more frequent, his ashtrays overflowed, he took more empty bottles to the garbage can in the courtyard, his bistro bills rose sharply, and he ate aspirin and splashed gallons of cold water on his eyes in the morning.

There was too much to think about: for one, unseen Soviet counterintelligence work that was meant to keep people like him from doing exactly what he was doing; for another, the potential for blackmail come the day when Fitzware wanted a view of Soviet operations in Paris and threatened to denounce him if he refused to cooperate; for a third, the strong possibility that Baumann's information was in fact supplied by the Reich Foreign Office intelligence unit and would in time poison the British estimate of German armaments. What, he wondered, were they hearing on the subject from other sources? He was to find that out, sooner than he thought.

During this period, Szara found consolation in the most unlikely places. March, he discovered, was good spying weather. Something about the fierce skies full of racing clouds or the spring rains blowing slantwise past his window gave him courage – in a climate of turbulence one could put aside thoughts of consequences. The political parties of the left and the right were to be seen daily on the boulevards, bellowing their slogans, waving their banners, and the newspapers were frantic, with thick black headlines every morning. The Parisians had a certain facial expression: lips compressed, head canted a little to one side, eyebrows raised: It meant *where does all this lead*? and implied *no place very good*. In Paris that spring of 1939, one saw it hourly.

De Montfried, meanwhile, had appointed himself official agent runner. He was no Abramov and no Bloch, but he had long experience as a commercial trader and believed he understood intuitively how any business agent should be handled. This assumption produced, in the hushed railway library of the Renaissance Club, some extraordinary moments. De Montfried offering money – 'Please don't be eccentric about this, it is only the means to an end' – which Szara did not care to take. De Montfried in the guise of a Jewish mother, pressing smoked fish sandwiches on a man who could barely stand to look at a cup of coffee. De Montfried handed a stack of five hundred Certificates of Emigration, clearing his throat, playing the stoic with tears of pleasure in his eyes. None of this mattered. The days of Abramov and Bloch were over; Szara had been running

OPAL operations for too long not to run his own when the time came. That included making sure he didn't know too much about details that did not directly concern him.

But de Montfried said just enough so that Szara's imagination managed the rest. He could see them, perhaps an eye surgeon from Leipzig with his family or a tottering, old rabbi from Berlin's Hasid community, could see them boarding a steamer, watching the coastline of Germany disappear over the horizon. Life for them would be difficult, more than difficult, in Palestine. What the Nazi Brown Shirts had started the Arab raiding bands might yet finish; but it was at least a chance, and that was better than despair.

The British operatives provided all the usual paraphernalia: a code name, CURATE, an emergency meeting signal – the same 'wrong number' telephone call the Russians sometimes used – and a contact to be known by the work name Evans. This was a rail-thin gentleman in his sixties, from his bearing almost certainly a former military officer, quite possibly of colonial service, who dressed in chalk-stripe blue suits, carried a furled umbrella, cultivated a natty little white moustache, and stood straight as a stick. Contacts were made in the afternoon, in the grand cinemas of the Champs-Élysées neighbourhood: silent exchanges of two folded copies of *Le Temps* placed on an empty seat between Szara and the British contact.

Silent but for, on one occasion, a single sentence, spoken by Evans across the empty seat and suitably muffled by the clatter of a crowd of Busby Berkeley tap dancers on the screen: 'Our friend wants you to know that your numbers have been confirmed, and that he is grateful.' He was not to hear Evans speak again.

Confirmed?

That meant Baumann was telling the truth; his information had been authenticated by other sources reporting to the British services. And that meant, what? That Dr Baumann was betraying a German *Funkspiele* operation, all by himself and just because? That Marta Haecht's boss had been mistaken: it wasn't Von Polanyi having lunch with Baumann at the Kaiserhof? Szara could have gone on and on; there were whole operas of possibilities to be drawn from Fitzware's message. But there was no time for it.

Szara had to hurry back to his apartment, hide a hundred and seventy-five certificates under the carpet until they could be delivered to de Montfried that evening, make a five P.M. meeting in the third arrondissement, the Marais, then head out to the place d'Italie for a *treff* with Valais, the new group leader of the SILO network, a little after seven.

The meeting in the Marais took place in a tiny hotel, at an oilcloth-covered table in a darkened room. A week earlier, Szara had been offered his very own emigration certificate to Palestine. 'It's a back door out of Europe,' de Montfried had said. 'The time may come when you'll have no other choice.' Szara had politely but firmly declined. There was no doubt a reason he did this, but it wasn't one he wanted to name. What he did ask of de Montfried was a second identity, a good one, with a valid passport that would take him over any border he cared to cross. His intention was not flight. Rather, like any efficient predator, he simply sought to extend his range. De Montfried, his favours refused again and again, was eager to oblige. 'Our cobbler,' he'd said, using the slang expression for forger, 'is the best in Europe. And I'll arrange to have him paid, you're not even to discuss it.'

The cobbler was nameless; a fat, oily man with thinning curls brushed back from a receding hairline. In a soiled white shirt buttoned at the sleeves, he moved slowly around the room, speaking French in an accent Szara could place only generally, somewhere in Central Europe. 'You've brought a photograph?' he said. Szara handed over four passport pictures taken in a photo studio. The cobbler chuckled, chose one, and handed the rest back. 'Myself, I don't keep records – for that you'll have to see the cops.'

He held a French passport between thick forefinger and thumb. 'This, *this*, you don't see every day.' He sat down and flattened the passport out on the table and began removing its photograph by rubbing on chemical solvent with a piece of sponge. When he was done he handed the damp picture to Szara. 'Jean Bonotte,' he said. The man looking back at him was vain, with humorous dark eyes that caught the light and a devil's beard that ran from sideburn tight along the jawline and then swept up to join the moustache, the sort of beard kept closely pruned, trimmed daily with scissors. 'Looks smart, no?'

'He does.'

'Not so smart as he thought.'

'Italian?'

The cobbler shrugged eloquently. 'Born Marseille. Could mean anything. A French citizen, though. That's important. Coming from down there you can always say you're Italian, or Corsican, or Lebanese. It's whatever you say, down there.'

'Why is it so good?'

'Because it's real. Because Monsieur Bonotte will not come to the attention of the Spanish Guardia just about the time you get off the ferry in Algeciras. Because Monsieur Bonotte will not again come to anyone's attention, excepting Satan, but the police don't know anything about it. He's legally alive. This document is legally alive. You understand?'

'And he's dead.'

'Very. What's the sense to talk, but you can have confidence he has left us and will not be dug up by some French farmer. That's why I say it's so good.'

The cobbler took the photo back, lit the corner with a match, and watched the blue-green flame consume the paper before he dropped it in a saucer. 'Born in 1902. Makes him thirty-seven. Okay with you? The less I have to change the better.'

'What do you think?' Szara asked.

The cobbler drew his head back a little, evidently farsighted, and looked him over. 'Sure. Why not? Life's hard sometimes and we show it in the face.'

'Then leave it as it is.'

The cobbler began to glue Szara's photo to the paper. When he was done, he waddled over to a bureau and returned with a stamper, a franking machine that pressed paper into raised letters. 'The real thing,' he said proudly. He placed the device at a precise angle to the photo, then slid a scrap of cardboard atop the part of the page already incised. He pressed hard for a few seconds, then released the device. 'This prevents falsification,' he said with only the slightest hint of a smile. He returned the franking device to the bureau and brought back a rubber stamp and a pad, a pen, and a small bottle of green ink. 'Government ink,' he said. 'Free for them. Expensive for me.' He concentrated himself, then stamped the side of the page firmly. 'I'm renewing it for you,' he said. He dipped the pen into the ink and signed the space provided in the rubber-stamped legend. 'Prefect Cormier himself,' he said. He applied a blotter to the signature, then looked at it critically and blew on the ink to make sure it was dry. He handed the passport to Szara. 'Now you're a French citizen, if you aren't already.'

Szara looked through the pages of the passport. It was well used, with several recorded entries into France and visits to Tangier, Oran, Istanbul, Bucharest, Sofia, and Athens. The home address was in the rue Paradis in Marseille. He checked the new date of expiry, March of 1942.

'When the time comes to renew again, just walk into any police station in France and tell them you've been living abroad. A French embassy in a foreign country is even better. You know the man who sent you to me?'

'No,' Szara said. De Montfried wouldn't, he knew, make such a contact directly.

'Just as well,' the cobbler said. 'You're a gentleman, I'd say. You're happy?'

'Yes.'

'Use it in good health,' said the cobbler. 'Me I'd go and pick up a *carte d'identité* – say you lost it – and a health card and all the rest of it, but that's up to you. And don't put your hand in your pocket, it's all taken care of.'

It was after six when he left the hotel. The St-Paul Métro platform was packed solid. When the train rolled in, he had to force his way on, jamming himself against the back of a young woman who might have been, from the way she was dressed, a clerk or a secretary. She said something unpleasant that he didn't quite catch as the train pulled away, but he got a good strong breath of the sausage she'd eaten for lunch. He could see the place on her neck where her face powder stopped. 'Sorry,' he muttered. She said something in slang he didn't understand. When the crowd surged on at the Hôtel-de-Ville station he was pressed against her even harder; her stiff, curly hair rubbing against his nose. 'Soon we'll be married,' he said, trying to make light of the situation. She was not amused and pointedly ignored him.

After a change of trains he reached his stop, Sèvres-Babylone, and went trotting up the rue du Cherche-Midi toward his apartment. No matter how hard he might be pressed, he could not meet with Valais while a second passport was in his pocket. The concierge said good evening through her little window as he rushed toward his entryway in the dark courtyard. He pounded up three flights of stairs, jiggled the lock open with his key, tucked the Bonotte passport under the carpet with the certificates, then took off downstairs. The concierge raised an eyebrow as he hurried past – very little bothered or surprised her, but in general she did not approve of haste.

Back to the Sèvres Métro, dodging housewives returning from the markets and hurdling a dog leash stretched between an aristocratic gentleman and his Italian greyhound squatting at the kerb.

The Métro was even worse as the hour of seven approached. Valais was forbidden to wait more than ten minutes for him; if he were any later they'd have to try for the fallback meeting the following day. The first train that stopped revealed an impenetrable wall of dark coats when the door opened, but he managed to force his way onto the next. After a change at Montparnasse, with almost no time to make sure he wasn't being followed, he left the station a minute after seven, ran around the first corner, then went tearing back the way he'd come. It was primitive, but the best he could manage under the pressure of time.

With thirty seconds to spare, he entered a women's clothing shop – long racks of cheap dresses and a dense cloud of perfume – just off the place d'Italie. The shop was owned by Valais's girlfriend, a short, buxom woman with a hennaed permanent wave and crimson lipstick. What Valais, a contemplative, pipe-smoking lawyer, and she saw in each other he couldn't imagine. She was a few years older than Valais and hard as nails. Szara was breathless as he strode toward the back of the store. The curtain at the entrance of the dressing room hung open, and a woman in a slip was thrashing her way into a pea green dress that was tangled about her head and shoulders.

Valais was waiting in a small workroom where alterations were done. When Szara entered he was about to leave, his overcoat buttoned and his gloves on. He looked up from his watch, clenched his pipe in his teeth, and shook hands. Szara collapsed in a chair in front of a sewing machine and put his feet up on the treadle.

Valais launched into a long, determined, cautiously phrased description of his activity over the past ten days. Szara pretended to pay attention, his mind returning to what Evans had said in the cinema that afternoon, then found himself thinking about the woman he'd stood with on the Métro. Had she pressed back against him? No, he thought not. 'And then there is LICHEN,' Valais said, waiting for Szara to respond.

Who the hell is LICHEN? Szara experienced a horrible moment of dead memory. At last it came: the young Basque prostitute Hélène Cauxa, virtually inactive the past two years but collecting a monthly stipend nonetheless. 'What's she done now?' Szara asked.

Valais put a black briefcase on the sewing machine stand. 'She, ah, met a German gentleman in the bar of a certain hotel where she sometimes has a drink. He proposed an arrangement, she agreed. They went off to a cheaper hotel, nearby, where she sometimes entertains clients. He forgot his briefcase. She brought it to me.'

Szara opened the briefcase: it was stuffed with a package of pamphlet-size booklets, perhaps two hundred of them, bound with string. Clipped to the cover of the one on top was a slip of paper with the word WEISS printed in pencil. He worked one of the booklets loose and opened it. On the left-hand side of the page were German phrases, on the right the same phrases in Polish:

Where is the mayor (head) of the village?
Tell me the name of the chief of police.
Is there good water in this well?
Did soldiers come through here today?
Hands up or I'll shoot!
Surrender!

'She demanded additional money,' Valais said.

Szara's hand automatically went to his pocket. Valais told him how much and Szara counted it out, telling himself he'd surely remember later how much it was and forgetting almost instantly. 'WEISS must be the name of the operation,' he said to Valais. The word meant white.

'The invasion of Poland,' Valais said. He made a sucking noise, and a cloud of pipe smoke drifted to the ceiling of the dress shop. From the front of the store, Szara heard the ring of the cash register. Had the woman in the slip bought the pea green dress?

'Yes,' he said. 'These are intended for Wehrmacht officers who will be transferred from attaché duty in Paris, a few of them anyhow, back to their units in Germany before the attack. Then some for the Abwehr, military intelligence. Still, seems quite a few. Maybe he was on his way to other cities after Paris.'

'More Polish sorrow,' Valais said. 'And it puts Hitler on the frontier of the Soviet Union.'

'If he's successful,' Szara said. 'Don't underestimate the Poles. And France and England have guaranteed the Polish border. If the Germans aren't careful they're going to take on the whole world again, just like 1914.'

'They are confident,' Valais said. 'They have an unshakable faith in themselves.' He smoked his pipe for a time. 'Have you read Sallust? The Roman historian? He speaks of the Germanic tribes with awe. The Finns, he says, in winter find a hollow log to sleep in, but the Germans simply lay down naked in the snow.' He shook his head at the thought. 'I am, perhaps you don't know, a reserve officer. In an artillery unit.'

Szara lit a cigarette and swore silently in Polish – *psia krew*, dogs' blood. Now everything was going straight to hell.

Back on the Métro with the briefcase. Running up the stairs on the rue du Cherche-Midi. Looking in the mirror and combing his hair back with his fingers, he discovered a white streak of plaster dust on the shoulder of his raincoat – he'd rubbed up against a wall somewhere. He brushed at it, then gave up, put the briefcase in the back of his cupboard, and went out the door. Raced halfway down the stairs, reversed himself, and climbed back up. Reentered his apartment, snatched the pile of emigration certificates from under the carpet, put them in his own briefcase, and went out a second time.

The streets were crowded: couples going out for dinner, people coming home from work. The wind was ferocious, swirling up dust and papers. People held their hats on and grimaced; waves of chalk-coloured cloud were speeding across the night sky. He'd take the Métro to Concorde, then change to the Neuilly line. From there it was a half-hour walk at least if he couldn't find a taxi. It would certainly rain. His umbrella was in the cupboard. He'd arrive at the Cercle Rénaissance late, looking like a drowned rat, with a white streak on his shoulder. He held tightly to the briefcase with its hundred and seventy-five certificates inside. Had she pressed back against him? A little?

When Szara entered the library de Montfried was reading a newspaper. He looked up, his face flushed with anger. 'He's going into Poland,' he said. 'Do you know what that will mean?'

'I think so.' Uninvited, Szara sat down. De Montfried closed the paper emphatically and took off his reading glasses. His eyes seemed the colour of mud in the half light of the small room.

'All this ranting and raving about the *poor, suffering* German minority in Danzig – that's what it means.'

'Yes.'

'My God, the Jews in Poland are living in the ninth century. Do you know? They're . . . when the Hasid hear of the possible invasion they dance to show their joy – the worse it gets, the more they are certain that Messiah is coming. Meanwhile, it's already started, the Poles themselves have started it. No pogroms just yet but beatings and knifings – the gangs are running free in Warsaw.' He glared angrily at Szara. His face was twisted with pain but, at the same moment, he was an important man who had the right to demand explanations.

'I was born in Poland,' Szara said. 'I know what it's like.'

'But why is he alive, this man, this Adolf Hitler? Why is he permitted to live?' He folded the newspaper and put it down on a small marquetry table. The club's dinner hour was approaching and Szara could smell roasting beef.

'I don't know.'

'Can nothing be done?'

Szara was silent.

'An organization like yours, its capacities, resources for such things . . . I don't understand.'

Szara opened his briefcase and passed the stack of certificates to de Montfried, who held them in his hands and stared at them vacantly. 'I have another engagement,' Szara said, as gently as he could.

De Montfried shook his head to clear it. 'Forgive me,' he said. 'What I feel is like an illness. It will not leave me.'

'I know,' Szara said, rising to leave.

* * *

Back to the rue du Cherche-Midi. Briefcases exchanged. Szara headed out into the windy night and slowly made his way to the rue Delesseux house. The Directorate, he thought, would want physical possession of the pamphlets, would have a special courier bring them to Moscow. Still, he believed it was best to transmit the contents and the WEISS code name as soon as possible. He began to switch from Métro line to Métro line, now following procedures closely; rue Delesseux was not to be approached by a direct route. At the La Chapelle station there was fighting. Perhaps communists and fascists, it was hard to tell. A crowd of workingmen in caps, all mixed together, three or four of them down on the floor with blood on their faces, two holding a third against a wall while a fourth worked on him. The motor-man didn't stop. The train rolled slowly through the station with white faces staring from the windows. They could hear the shouts and curses over the sound of the train, and one man was hurled against the side of the moving carriage and bounced hard, the shock felt by the passengers as he hit – several people gasped or cried out when it happened. Then the train returned to the darkness of the tunnel.

Schau-Wehrli was at work in the rue Delesseux. Szara handed her a pamphlet and stood quietly while she looked it over. 'Yes,' she said reflectively, 'everything points to it now. My commissary people in Berlin, who work for the German railway system, say the same thing. They've heard about requests for a traffic analysis on the lines that go to the Polish border. That means troop trains.'

'When?'

'Nobody knows.'

'Is it a bluff?'

'No, I think not. It most certainly was with the Czechs,

but not now. The Reich industrial production is meeting quotas, the war machinery is just about in place.'

'And what will we do?'

'Stalin alone knows that,' Schau-Wehrli said. 'And he doesn't tell me.'

It was well after midnight when Szara finally got home. He'd never managed to eat anything, but hunger was long gone, replaced by cigarettes and adrenaline. Now he just felt cold and grimy and used up. There was a large tin bathtub in the kitchen, and he turned on the hot water tap to see what might be left. Yes, there was one good thing in the world that night, a bath, and he would have it. He stripped off his clothes and threw them on a chair, poured himself a glass of red wine, and turned the radio dial until he found some American jazz. When the tub was ready he climbed in and settled back, drank a little wine, rested the glass on the broad part of the rim, and closed his eyes.

Poor de Montfried, he thought. All that money, yet he could do little, at least that was the way he saw it. The man had virtually humiliated him in the library, had been so angry that the certificates, bought at a cost he could not imagine, seemed a small and insufficient gesture. Oh the rich. Would any of the café girls still be about? No, that was hopeless. There was one he could telephone – full of understanding, that one, she loved what she called *adventures of the night*. No, he thought, sleep. The music ended and a man began to announce the news. Szara reached for the dial, his arm dripping water on the kitchen floor, but the radio was just a little too far. So he had to hear that the miners were on strike in Lille, that the minister of finance had denied all allegations, that the little girl missing in the Vosges had been found, that Madrid continued to hold out, factions fighting each other in the besieged city. Stalin had issued an important political statement, referring to the current crisis as 'the Second Imperialistic War.' He stated he would 'not allow Soviet Russia to be drawn into conflicts by warmongers who are accustomed to having others pull their chestnuts out of the fire,' and attacked those nations who wanted 'to arouse Soviet anger against Germany, to poison the atmosphere, and to provoke a conflict with Germany without visible reason.'

Then the music returned, saxophones and trumpets from a dance hall on Long Island. Szara rested his head against the tub and closed his eyes. Stalin claimed that England and France were plotting against him, manoeuvring him to fight Hitler while they waited to pounce on a weakened winner. Perhaps they were. Aristocrats ran those countries, intellectuals and ministers of state, graduates of the best universities. Stalin and Hitler were scum from the gutters of Europe who'd managed to float to the top. Well, one way or another, there would be war. And he would be killed. Marta Haecht as well. The Baumanns, Kranov, the operative who'd driven him away from Wittenau on Kristallnacht, Valais, Schau-Wehrli, Goldman, Nadia Tscherova. All of them. The bath was cooling much too fast. He pulled the plug and let some of it gurgle out, then added more hot water and lay back in the steam.

In London, on the fourth floor at 54 Broadway – supposedly the headquarters of the Minimaz Fire Extinguisher Company – MI6 officers analysed the CURATE product, packaged it alongside information from a variety of other sources, then shipped it off to intelligence consumers in quiet little offices all over town. It travelled by car and bicycle, by messenger and pneumatic tube, sometimes down long, damp corridors, sometimes to panelled rooms warmed by log fires. The product came recommended. Confirming data on German swage wire manufacture was independently available, and German bomber production numbers were further supported by factory orders, in Britain itself, for noninterference technology that protected aviation spark plugs, and by engineers and businessmen who had legitimate associations with German industry. The material arrived, for example, at the Industrial Intelligence Centre, which played the key role in analysing Germany's ability to fight a war. The centre had become quite important and was connected to the Joint Planning subcommittee, the Joint Intelligence subcommittee, the Economic Pressure on Germany subcommittee, and the Air Targets committee.

The CURATE story also floated upwards, sometimes unofficially, into the precincts of Whitehall and the Foreign Office, and from there it wandered even further. There was always somebody else who really ought to hear about it; knowledge was power, and people liked to be known to have secret information because it made them seem important: *secret*, but not secret from them. Simultaneously, in a very different part of the civil service, the bureaux that dealt in colonial affairs had been stirred up like hornets' nests when the espionage types had come poaching on their territory. British Mandate Palestine was their domain and – love the Arabs or love the Jews or hate them all – the brawl over legitimate Certificates of Emigration had been bloody and fierce. And it was discussed.

So people knew about it, this CURATE, a Russian in Paris feeding the odd morsel to the British lion in return for a subtle shift of the paw. And some of the people who knew about it were, privately, rather indignant. To begin with, their hearts' passion lay elsewhere. From the time of their undergraduate days at Cambridge they'd thrown in their lot with the idealists, the progressives, the men of conscience and good will at the Kremlin. Precisely who did the work it would be difficult to say – Anthony Blunt or Guy Burgess, Donald MacLean or H. A. R. Philby, or others unknown; they all traded on the information exchanges of the intelligence and diplomatic bureaucracies – but one or more of them thought it worthwhile to let somebody know, and so they did. Spoken over supper at a private club or left in a dead-drop in a cemetery wall, the code name CURATE and the very general outline of what it meant began to move east.

It did not move alone – many other facts and all sorts of gossip needed to be passed along – and it did not move with great speed; alarms were not raised. But it did, in time, reach Moscow and, a little later, the proper office in the appropriate department. It fell among cautious people, survivors of the purge who lived in a dangerous, undersea twilight of predators and their prey, people who moved carefully and with circumspection, people who knew better than to catch a fish that might be too big for their nets – that way one might wind up at the bottom of the ocean; it had happened. In the beginning, they contented themselves with pure research, with trying to find out who it was, where it was, and why it was. Action would follow at the appropriate time and in the appropriate way. It has been said that counterintelligence people are by nature voyeurs. They like to watch what goes on because when the moment finally comes to rush out of the shadows and kick down the doors, the fun is really over, the files are taken away, the wheels begin to grind, and then it's time to start all over again.

One morning in early May the Paris newspapers soberly reported a change of Soviet foreign ministers: M. M. Litvinov replaced by V. M. Molotov.

Some went on to read the article beneath the headline; many did not. These were the redemptive hours of spring – Paris was leafy and soft and full of girls, life would go on forever, the morning light danced on the coffeecup and the bud vase, and sun streaming into a room turned it into a Flemish painting. Russian diplomats came and went. Who, really, cared.

André Szara, true to his eternally divided self, did both: read on and didn't care. He judged the story rather incomplete, but that was nothing new. M. M. Litvinov was in fact Maxim Maximovich Wallach, a pudgy, Jewish, indoor gentleman of the old school, a thorough intellectual, myopic and bookish. How on earth had he lasted as long as he had? V. M. Molotov, in fact Vyacheslav Mikhaylovich Skryabin, had changed his name for a rather different reason. As Djugashvili became Stalin, Man of Steel, so Skryabin became Molotov, the Hammer. *So*, thought Szara, *between them they'll make a sword*.

Szara's flip commentary turned out to be just the truth, but he had a lot to think about that day. He contemplated a good deal of rushing about here and there, and he was no less receptive to spring breezes than any other man or woman in Paris, so the weight of the news didn't quite reach him – he didn't hear the final piece of a complex machine snap into its housing. He heard the birds singing, the neighbour flapping her bedding before she hung it over the windowsill to air, the scissors grinder ringing his bell out on the rue du Cherche-Midi – but that was all.

Adolf Hitler heard it, certainly, but then he had very sharp ears. He was later to say 'Litvinov's dismissal was decisive. It came to me like a cannon shot, like a sign that the attitude of Moscow towards the Western powers had changed.'

The French intelligence services heard it, though probably not so loud as a cannon shot, reporting on 7 May that unless great diplomatic effort was exerted by England and France, Germany and the USSR would sign a treaty of nonaggression by the end of the summer.

* * *

Szara was summoned to Brussels on the tenth of May.

'We're going to have to make an arrangement with Hitler,' Goldman said with sorrow and distaste. 'It's Stalin's own damn fault – the purges have weakened the military to a point where we simply cannot fight and expect to win. Not now. So time is going to have to be bought, and the only way to buy it is with a treaty.'

'Good God,' Szara said.

'Can't be helped.'

'Stalin and Hitler.'

'The European communist parties aren't going to be happy, our friends in America aren't going to like it, but the moment has come for them to learn a little realpolitik. The hand-wringers and the crybabies will go off in a great huff. Them we'll have to kiss good-bye. And good riddance. The ones who decide to remain faithful will be true friends, people who can be depended on to see things the way we see them, so maybe all is for the best. We've been sweating and bleeding since 1917 to build a socialist state; we can't let it all go down the river in the service of starry-eyed idealism. The factories, the mines, and the collective farms; those are the reality – and to protect that investment we'll make a deal with the devil himself.'

'We're evidently to do just that.'

'Can't be helped. Most of the intelligence services have already got it figured out, the public will know by the summer, July or August. That gives us a few weeks to do the work.'

'Not much time.'

'It's what we have, so we'll manage. First, and most important, the networks themselves. Don't waste your time on the mercenaries, work with the believers. You're letting them in on the secret life at the top, where strategic decisions are made. The Nazis will never be anybody's friends, and not ours either, but we need time to arm for the confrontation and this is the way to buy it. Anybody who doesn't accept this line – I am to be informed. Is that understood?'

'Yes.'

'With our German informants nothing changes. In war we fight our enemies, in peace we fight our friends. So now we'll have a form of peace, but operations continue as before. We want, now more than ever, to know what goes on with the Germans – their thinking, their planning, their capacities, and their military dispositions. Times are perilous and unstable, André Aronovich, and that is when networks must operate at their maximum capability.'

'If we have a, a misfortune. If somebody gets caught, what does that do?'

'God forbid. But I don't expect Referat VI C will send everybody home to tend their rose gardens, so neither will we. The way to handle what you call "a misfortune" is to make sure it doesn't happen. Does that answer your question?'

Szara made a wry face.

'Second, get busy with your personal connections. Oh-me oh-my the world is a terrible place, whatever is to be done? However *shall* we find peace? There must be a compromise, someone must be willing to budge an inch and let the other fellow see he means no harm. Only the USSR is strong enough to do that. Let the British and the French rattle their swords and wheel their cannons about; we mean to relieve the pressure on Hitler's eastern border, we mean to sign trade agreements and cultural exchanges – let the folk dancers fight this out between them – we mean to find a way we can all live together in a world where not everything is as we'd wish it to be. No more mobilizations! No more 1914!'

'Hurrah!'

'Don't be clever. If you don't believe it, nobody else will. So find a way.'

'And the Poles?'

'Too stubborn to live, as usual and as always. They'll stand on their honour and make pretty speeches and wake up one morning speaking German. There is nothing to be done for the Poles. They've chosen to go their own way. Good, now let them.'

'Should they give up Danzig?'

'Give up your *sister*. We sit here in this little shop and we happen to know that once the German bombers get busy, Warsaw will turn into a blazing hell. That's the reality. Now, for number three, pick up your ingenious pen and go to work. Try one of those intellectual French journals guaranteed to give you a headache and start shaping the dialogue. If there were some way to coopt the argument itself – you know, by stating the initial questions – life would be perfect. To that we can't aspire – every writer under the sun is going to have a say on this, but at least you can give them a nudge. As in: what must world socialism do to survive? Must we all die, or is there an alternative? Is diplomacy truly exhausted? Could the bloodbath in Spain have been avoided if everybody had been a little more willing to negotiate?

'You'll be crucified by the doctrinaire Marxists, of course, but so what. The important thing is to get the discussion rolling by claiming some territory. There's bound to be somebody who'll rush to defend you – there always is, no matter what you say. And if, no, *when* people come up to you at parties and tell you that Lenin's spinning in his display case, you'll have the right answers: remember, the USSR is the hope of progressive mankind and the only ongoing remedy to fascism. But it must survive. Stalin is a genius, and this pact will be a work of genius, a diplomatic side step to avoid the crippling blow. And the minute the pact becomes public, that's what I want to read under your byline, without hauling you all the way up to Belgium. Is everything clear?'

'Oh yes,' Szara said. 'England and France want war to satisfy their imperialist aspirations, Russia stands alone in seeking peace. Subtext, with a wink and a poke in the ribs, that sly old fox from the Caucasus is doing what he has to in order to gain time. We'll settle with Hitler when *we're* ready. Is that about it?'

'Exactly. You're not alone in this, of course. All the Soviet writers will take a hand – they'll likely have a play onstage in Moscow in ninety days. Your participation was directly ordered, by the way: "You've got Szara over there, put him to work!" is exactly how it was said. It's a broad effort now – they've brought Molotov in to negotiate with Ribbentrop, the German foreign minister, in case you wondered about that. We can't be sending a chubby little Jewish man off to deal with the Nazis, you agree?'

'Realpolitik, as you said.'

'That is the word. By the way, I suggest you pack a bag and keep it by the door. If the situation evolves the way we think it might, there's a possibility you may be travelling on short notice.'

'On OPAL business?'

'No, no. As the journalist Szara, the voice of Russia speaking out from foreign lands. You really ought to treat yourself to a grand dinner, André Aronovich, I see great professional advancement in your future.'

The Molotov appointment – on the surface no more than a piece of diplomatic business during a time when there was more than an ample supply of it – induced in Paris, and evidently in other European capitals, a change of chemistry.

André Szara found himself doing things he didn't quite understand but felt compelled to do anyhow. As Goldman had suggested, he prepared to travel on a moment's notice. Climbed up on a chair, took his suitcase down from the top of the armoire, blew some of the dust off it, and decided he needed something else. His twelve-year-old suitcase, its pebbled surface a soiled ochre colour with a maroon stripe, had seen hard service in his *Pravda* days. It was nicked and scratched and faded and made him look, he thought, like a refugee. All it needed was the knotted rope around the middle. So he went off to the luggage stores, but he didn't really like what he found – either too fashionable or too flimsy.

He passed a custom leathergoods shop one day in the seventh arrondissement – saddles and riding boots in the window – and, on the spur of the moment, went inside. The owner was a Hungarian, a no-nonsense craftsman in a smock, his hands hard and knotted from years of cutting and stitching leather. Szara explained what he wanted, a kind of portmanteau like a doctor's bag, an old-fashioned but enduring form, made of long-wearing leather. The Hungarian nodded, produced some samples, and quoted an astonishing price. Szara agreed nonetheless. He hadn't wanted an *object* so badly for a long while. Oh, and one last thing: from time to time he carried confidential business papers, and what with the sort of people one finds working in hotels these days . . . The Hungarian was entirely understanding and indicated that Szara was not the only customer to express such concerns. The traditional false bottom was as old as the hills, true, but when properly crafted it remained effective. A second panel would be fashioned to fit precisely on the bottom; papers could be safely stored between the two layers. 'It is, sir, naturally safest if you were to have it sewn in place. Not so much for light-fingered hotel staff, you understand, for the bag will be provided with an excellent lock, but more a matter of, one might say, frontiers.' The delicate word hung in the air for a moment, then Szara made a deposit and promised to return in June.

A week later he decided that if he was to travel, he didn't want to leave the Jean Bonotte passport in his apartment. Robberies were rare but they did occur, especially when people went away for an extended period. And from time to time the NKVD might send a couple of technicians around, just to see whatever there was to see. So he opened an account in the Bonotte name, using the passport for identification, at a Banque du Nord office on the boulevard Haussmann, then rented a safe deposit box for the passport itself. Three days later he returned, on a perfect June morning, and put an envelope holding twelve thousand francs on top of the passport. *What are you doing?* he asked himself. But he really didn't know; he only knew he was uncomfortable, in some not very definable way, like a dog that howls on the eve of a tragedy. Something, somewhere, was warning him. His ancestry, perhaps. Six hundred years of Jewish life in Poland, of omens, signs, portents, instincts. His very existence proved him to be the child of generations that had survived when others didn't, perhaps born to know when the blood was going to run. *Hide money*, something told him. *Arm yourself*, said the same voice, a few nights later. But that, for the moment, he did not do.

A strange month, that June. Everything happened. Schau-Wehrli was contacted by a group of Czech émigrés who lived in the town of Saint-Denis, in the so-called Red Belt north of Paris. They were communists who'd fled when Hitler took over the remainder of Czechoslovakia in March, and the contact with OPAL was made through the clandestine apparatus of the French Communist party. The group was receiving intelligence by means of secret writing on the backs of bank envelopes, which contained receipts for funds mailed to Prague and Brno for the support of relatives. They were using an invisible ink concocted in a university chemistry laboratory. Like the classics, lemon juice and urine, application of a hot iron brought up the message. The information itself was voluminous, ranging from Wehrmacht order of battle, numbers and strengths of German units, to financial data, apparently stolen by the same bank employees who prepared the envelopes, as well as industrial information – almost all the renowned Czech machine shops were now at work on Reich war production.

This group required a great deal of attention. There were eight of them, all related by blood or marriage, and though motivated by a passionate loathing of the Nazis, they perceived their contribution as a business and knew exactly what this kind of information was worth. Three of the Saint-Denis members had intelligence experience and had created a network in Czechoslovakia, after Hitler took the Sudetenland, with the goal of supporting themselves and their families when they resettled in France. The two bank employees were the daughters of sisters, first cousins, and their husbands worked at acquiring information through friendships maintained at men's sports clubs. Such an in-place network, already functioning efficiently, was almost too good to be true, thus the Directorate in Moscow was simultaneously greedy for the product and wary of Referat VI C counterintelligence deception. This ambivalence created a vast flow of cable traffic and exceptional demands on the time of the deputy director, Schau-Wehrli, so that Goldman eventually ordered the RAVEN network transferred to Szara's care.

He nodded gravely when given the new assignment, but the idea of working with Nadia Tscherova did not displease him. Not at all.

At the rue Delesseux he read his way through the RAVEN file, which included Tscherova's most recent reports in their original format: an aristocratic literary Russian printed in tiny letters, on strips of film that had been carried over the border in Odile's shoulder pads, then developed in an attic darkroom. Previous reports had been retyped, verbatim, and filed in sequence.

Szara read with pure astonishment. After the tense aridity of Dr Baumann and the lawyer's precision of Valais, it was like a night at the theatre. What an eye she had! Penetrating, malicious, ironic, as though Balzac were reborn as a Russian émigrée in 1939 Berlin. Read serially, RAVEN's reports worked as a novel of social commentary. Her life was made up of small roles in bad plays, intimate dinners, lively parties, and country house weekends in the Bavarian forest, with boar hunting by day and bed hopping by night.

Szara had tender feelings for this woman, even though he suspected she was a specialist in the provocation of tender feelings, and he would have expected himself to read of her never-quite-consummated *liaisons intimes* with a leaden heart. But it just wasn't so. She'd told him the truth that night in her dressing room: she protected herself from the worst of it and was unmoved by what went on around her. This casual invulnerability was everywhere in her reports, and Szara found himself, above all else, amused. She had something of a man's mind in such matters, and she characterized her fumbling, half-drunken, would-be lovers and their complicated *requests* with a delicate brutality that made him laugh out loud. By God, he thought, she was no better than he was.

Nor did she spare her subagents. Lara Brozina she described as writing 'a kind of ghastly, melancholy verse that Germans of a certain level adore.' Brozina's brother, Viktor Brozin, an actor in radio plays, was said to have 'the head of a lion, the heart of a parakeet.' And of the balletmaster Anton Krafic she wrote that he was 'sentenced every morning to live another day.' Szara could positively see them – the languid Krafic, the leonine Brozin, the *terribly* sensitive Brozina – amusing frauds making steady progress along the shady underside of Nazi society.

And Tscherova did not spare the details. During a weekend in a castle near the town of Traunstein, she entered a bathroom after midnight 'to discover B. [that meant BREWER, Krafic] drinking champagne in the bathtub with SS Hauptsturmführer Bruckmann, who was wearing a cloche hat with a veil and carmine lipstick.' What in heaven's name, Szara wondered, had the Directorate made of *this?*

Referring to the file of outgoing reports he discovered the answer: Schau-Wehrli had reprocessed the material to make it palatable. Thus her dispatch covering RAVEN's description of the jolly bath said only that 'BREWER reports that SS Hauptsturmführer BRUCKMANN has recently been with his regiment on divisional manoeuvres in marshy, swamplike terrain near the Masurian Lakes in East Prussia.' Another pointer, Szara noted, toward the invasion of Poland, where such conditions might be encountered.

A rich, rewarding file.

He worked his way through the last of it on the afternoon of the summer solstice, *the day the sun is said to pause*, he thought. Pleasing, that idea. Something Russian about it. As though the universe stopped for a moment to reflect, took a day off from work. One could sense it, time slowing down: the weather light and sunny, rather aimless, a bird twittering away on a neighbouring balcony, Kranov coding at his desk, humming a Russian melody, the little bell on the door of the ground-floor *tabac* tinkling as a customer entered.

Then the warning buzzer went off beside Kranov's table – a danger signal operated from beneath the counter in the *tabac*. This was followed, a moment later, by a knock on the door at the bottom of the stairs, a door shielded by a curtain on the back wall of the shop.

Szara had absolutely no idea what to do, neither did Kranov. They both froze, sat dead still like two hares caught in a winter field. They were literally surrounded by incrimination – files, flimsies, stolen documents, and the wireless telegraph itself, with its aerial run cleverly up the unused chimney by way of the attic. There was no getting rid of anything. They could have run down the stairs and rushed out the back door, or jumped the three storeys and broken their ankles, but they did neither. It was three-thirty on a bright summer afternoon and not a wisp of darkness to cover their escape.

So they sat there and presently heard a second knock, perhaps a bit more insistent than the first. Szara, not knowing what else to do, walked down the stairs and answered it. To find two Frenchmen waiting politely at the door. They were Frenchmen of a certain class, wore tan summerweight suits of a conservative cut, crisp shirts, silk ties not terribly in fashion but not terribly out. The brims of their hats were turned down at precisely the same angle. Szara found himself thinking in Russian, *My God, the hats are here*. The two men had a particular coloration that a Frenchman of the better sort will assume after lunch, a faint, rose-tinted blush on the cheeks which informs the knowledgeable that the beef was good and the wine not too bad. They introduced themselves and presented cards. They were, they said, fire inspectors. They would just have a brief look around, if it wasn't terribly inconvenient.

Fire inspectors they were not.

But Szara had to go along with the game, so he invited them in. By the time they'd climbed to the third floor,

Kranov had pulled the blanket off the window and flung it over the wireless, turning it into a curious dark hump on an old table from which a wire ran up the corner of the wall and disappeared into the attic through a ragged hole in the ceiling. Kranov himself was either in a closet or under the bed in Odile's apartment on the second floor – one of those truly inspired hiding places found amid panic – but in the event he was unseen. The Frenchmen didn't look, they didn't strip the blanket off the wireless, and they didn't even bother to enter Odile's apartment. One of them said, 'So much paper in a room like this. You must be careful with your cigarettes. Perhaps a bucket of sand ought to be placed in the corner.'

They touched the brims of their hats with their forefingers and departed. Szara, his shirt soaked at the armpits, collapsed in a chair. Somewhere on the floor below he heard a bump and a curse as Kranov extricated himself from whatever cranny he'd jammed himself into. *A comedy*, Szara said to himself, *a comedy*. He pressed his palms against his temples.

Kranov, swearing under his breath, threw the blanket into a corner and flashed Goldman a disaster signal. For the next two hours messages flew back and forth, Kranov's pencil scratching out columns of figures as he encoded responses to Goldman's precise questions. Somewhere, Szara was certain, the French had a receiver and were taking note of all the numbers crackling through the summer air.

By the end of the exchange Szara realized that the game was not actually over, the network was not blown. Not quite. They had, evidently, been warned, probably by the Deuxième Bureau – diplomatic and military intelligence – using agents of the Paris Prefecture of police or the Direction de la Surveillance du Territoire, the DST, the

French equivalent of the American FBI. The warning came in two parts:

We know what you're doing, went the first.

This was no great surprise, when Szara had a moment to think about it. The French police had always insisted, since Fouché served Napoleon, on knowing exactly what went on in their country, and most particularly in their capital. Whether they actually did anything about what they knew was treated as a very different matter – here political decisions might be involved – but they were scrupulously careful in keeping track of what went on, neighbourhood by neighbourhood, village by village. So their knowledge of the existence of OPAL was, finally, no great surprise.

From their point of view it did not hurt them that the Russians spied on Germany, the traditional enemy of France. They may have received, at a very high level, compensation for allowing OPAL a free hand, compensation in the form of refined intelligence product. Always, there were arrangements that did not meet the eye.

But the second part of the warning was quite serious: if you truly mean to become an ally of Germany, we may decide that your days here are numbered, since such an alliance might damage French interests, and that will not be permitted to happen. So here, gentlemen, are a pair of fire inspectors, and we send them to you in a most courteous and considerate fashion, which is to say before anything actually starts burning.

We're sure you'll understand.

In July, the OTTER operation ended. They would hear from Dr Baumann no more. So that month's exchange of information for emigration certificates was the last. Szara signalled de Montfried for a meeting, he responded immediately.

De Montfried was driven in from his country house, a

château near Tours. He was wearing a cream-coloured suit, a pale blue shirt, and a little bow tie. He carefully placed his straw hat on the marquetry table in the library, folded his hands, and looked expectantly at Szara. When told the operation was over, he covered his face with his hands, as though in great fatigue. They sat for some time without speaking. Outside it was oppressively quiet; a long, empty, summer afternoon.

Szara felt sorry for de Montfried but could find no words of consolation. What was there to say? The man had discovered himself to be rather less powerful than he'd thought. Yet, Szara realized, how little would change for him. He would present the same image to the world, would live beautifully, move easily in the upper realms of French society; the haughty Cercle Rénaissance would still be the place where a library of railway books was maintained for his pleasure. Certainly he was to be envied. He had simply found, and rather late in life, the limits of his power. Perceiving himself to be a wealthy and important man, de Montfried had attempted to exert influence on political events and, based on Szara's understanding of this world, had succeeded. He simply did not understand how well they'd done. He simply did not understand that he'd imposed himself on a world where the word *victory* was hardly to be heard.

Together, he and Szara had been responsible for the distribution of one thousand three hundred and seventy-five Certificates of Emigration to Mandate Palestine. As these covered individuals and their families, and were so precious that marriages and adoptions were arranged, sometimes overnight, the number of salvaged lives was perhaps three thousand. What, Szara wondered, could he say? *You bloody fool, you want to save the world – now you know what it takes to save three thousand lives!* No, he could not say that. And had he said it he would have been wrong. The true price of those lives was yet to be paid and would turn out to be higher, for Szara and others, than either of them could have realized at that moment.

De Montfried dropped his hands heavily to the arms of his chair and sat back, his face collapsed with failure. 'Then it's finished,' he said.

'Yes,' Szara said.

'Can anything be done? Anything at all?'

'No.'

Szara had certainly thought about it – *thought* wasn't really the word; his mind had spun endless scenarios, reached desperately for a solution, any solution at all. But to no avail.

It was Szara's opinion that Evans had told him the truth that afternoon in the cinema: the British services *were* able to confirm the figures from other sources. That meant he could not simply lie, offer numbers that would appear to be logical. They would know. Not at first – for a month or two it might be managed, and a month or two meant another three hundred and fifty certificates, at least seven hundred lives. Seven hundred lives were worth a lie – in Szara's calculus they certainly were. But it was worse than that.

When he'd first gone to the British, he'd believed his figures to be false, part of a German counterintelligence attack. It had not mattered, then. But the world had shifted beneath his feet; Germany would take Poland, and Russia would agree to a treaty that left Britain and France isolated. False figures delivered now might deform the British armament effort in unforeseen ways, false figures could well help the Nazis, false figures could cost thousands of lives, tens of thousands, once the Luftwaffe bombers flew. So those seven hundred lives were lost.

'Have you told them?' de Montfried asked.

'Not yet.'

'Why not?'

'On the possibility that you and I, sitting here, might invent something, discover something, find another way. On the possibility that you have not been forthcoming with me and that you have resources I don't know about, perhaps information of some kind that can be substituted.'

De Montfried shook his head.

They sat in silence.

'What will you tell them?' de Montfried said at last.

'That there has been an interruption at the source, that we wish to continue until a new method can be worked out.'

'And will they accept that?'

'They will not.'

'Not even for one month?'

'Not even that.' He paused for a moment. 'I know it's difficult to understand, but it's like not having money. Lenin said that grain was "the currency of currencies." That was in 1917. For us, it might now be said that information is the currency of currencies.'

'But surely you know other things, things of interest.'

'For the people I deal with directly, that might very well work. But we are asking for something I'm certain they – MI6 – had to fight for, and only the magnitude of what we were offering made it possible for them to win that battle. I don't think they'll go back to war for other material I might offer. I'm sure they won't. Otherwise, believe me, I would try it.'

Slowly, de Montfried gathered himself to face the inevitable. 'It is very hard for me to admit to failure, but that is what's happened, we've failed.'

'We've stopped, yes.'

De Montfried withdrew a leather case and a fountain pen from the inside pocket of his jacket, unscrewed the top of the pen, and began to write a series of telephone numbers on the back of a business card. 'One of these will find me,' he said. 'I am almost never out of touch with my office – that's the number you've been using – but I've included several other numbers, places where I'm to be found. Otherwise we'll leave it as it's been, simply say *Monsieur B. is calling*. I'll leave instructions for the call to be put through to me directly. Day or night, any time. Whatever I have is at your disposal should you need it.'

Szara put the card in his pocket. 'One can never be sure what might happen. One has to hope for the best.'

De Montfried nodded sadly.

Szara stood and offered his hand. 'Good-bye,' he said.

'Yes,' de Montfried said, rising to shake hands. 'Good luck.'

'Thank you,' Szara said.

The card joined the money and the Jean Bonotte passport that afternoon.

The OTTER operation had ended suddenly and badly.

Odile must have activated an emergency signal available in Berlin, because Goldman called a special meeting, to take place just after she got off the train. Szara and Schau-Wehrli were summoned to a place called Arion, in Belgium, an iron mining town just over the Luxembourg border a few kilometres north of the French city of Longwy. It was hot and dirty in Arion. Coal smoke from the mills drifted through the soot-blackened streets, the sunset was a dark, sullen orange, and the night air was dead still. The meeting was held in a worker's tenement near the centre of town, the home of a party operative, a miner asked to spend the night with relatives. They sat in the cramped parlour with the shutters closed amid the smells of sweaty clothes and boiled food.

Odile was shaken – her face an unnatural white – but determined. She had got off a local train from the German border only a few minutes before they arrived. Goldman was there with another man Szara did not know, a short, heavy Russian in middle age, with wavy fair hair and extremely thick glasses that distorted his eyes. At first Szara thought he might be asthmatic: his breath rasped audibly in the little room. After they'd settled down, Szara noticed that the man was staring at him. Szara met his glance but the man did not look away. He put an oval cigarette between his lips, creased the head of a wooden match with his thumbnail, and lit the cigarette from the flare. Only then did he turn to face Odile. As he shook the match out, Szara saw that he wore a large gold watch on his wrist.

By the time Szara and Schau-Wehrli arrived, Odile had told her story to Goldman and the other man and produced Baumann's message. Goldman handed it to Szara. 'Have a look,' he said.

Szara took the slip of paper, read quickly over the production numbers, then discovered a terse sentence scrawled along the bottom of the sheet: *You should be aware that rumours of a rapprochement between Germany and the USSR have angered members of the diplomatic and military class*.

'What is your opinion?' Goldman asked.

'My opinion,' Szara said. 'It seems he's trying to supply additional information. We've been after him for months to do that. Do such rumours exist?'

'Perhaps. In the class of people he refers to, they could easily be more than rumours,' Goldman said. 'But how would Baumann know such things? Who is he talking to?'

Szara said he didn't know.

Goldman turned to Odile. 'Please tell us again what happened.'

'I always clear the drop early in the morning,' Odile said, 'when the maids go to work in the neighbourhood. I went to the wall by the little wood, made certain I was not observed, reached over the wall and felt around until I found the loose rock, then withdrew the paper and put it in the pocket of my raincoat. There was no message from the network, so I was next going to the telephone pole to acknowledge reception by turning the bent nail. I went about ten steps when a woman came out of the woods. She was approximately fifty years old, wearing a house-dress, and extremely agitated and nervous. "He has been taken," she said to me in German. I pretended not to understand what it was all about. "He is in a camp, in Sachsenhausen," she said, "and his friends can't help him." I stared at her and started to hurry away. "Tell them they must help him," she called after me. I walked very fast. She came a few steps after me, then stopped and went back into the woods. I did not see her do this, but I looked over my shoulder a few seconds later and she was gone. I heard a dog barking, a little dog, from the woods somewhere. I made my way to the Ringbahn station at Hohenzollern-Damm, went into the public toilet, and hid the message in my shoulder pad. I was out of Berlin on a local train about one hour later. I saw nobody unusual on the train, had no other experience out of the ordinary.'

'Friends?' Schau-Wehrli said. 'His *friends* can't help? Did she mean the Jewish community? Lawyers, people like that?'

'Or work associates,' Szara mused. 'People at the German companies he deals with.'

'The point is,' Goldman said, 'has he been arrested as a Jew? Or a spy?'

'If they caught him spying, they would have taken her as well,' Schau-Wehrli said. 'And the Gestapo would have him – that means Columbia House, not Sachsenhausen.'

'Perhaps,' Goldman said. 'It's hard to know.'

'Can he be helped?' Szara asked.

'That's a question for the Directorate, but yes, it has

been done before. For the time being, the Berlin operatives are going to try and contact him in the camp and let him know we're aware of what's happened and that we're going to get him out. We're trying to help him to resist interrogation. Do you think he can?'

Szara sensed that Baumann's life hung on his answer: 'If anyone can, he will. He's a strong man, psychologically. His physical condition is another matter. If the interrogation is extreme, he may die on them.'

Goldman nodded at the answer. 'At your meeting in Berlin, was anything said that can help explain either his message, the "members of the diplomatic and military classes" business, or his wife's reference to "friends"? Are those, perhaps, the same people?'

'They could be,' Szara lied. 'I can't say.'

'Is that your answer?' the man in the glasses asked.

Szara faced him. The eyes behind the thick lenses were watery and lifeless. 'My answer is no. Nothing was said that would explain either of those statements.'

Travelling back to Paris on a succession of local trains they had to sit in separate compartments. That gave Szara time to think while the sombre towns of northeastern France rolled past the window.

He felt old. It was the business with Nadia Tscherova again, only worse. He was tormented by what had happened to Baumann, and by his own part in the man's destruction, yet what he had seen on Kristallnacht went a long way toward justifying what they had done together. A sacrifice of war. A machine gun position left to delay an enemy's progress down a road while the rear guard retreats. All very well, he thought, until you're the machine gunner. In his not so secret heart he thought it might be for the best if Baumann were to die. Peacefully. A death of mercy. But his instinct told him that would not happen.

Baumann was frightened, exhausted, beaten down and humiliated, but also strong. A hard soul lived in that old grey man.

Of course the Russian-German treaty explained it all. From the beginning, Von Polanyi's intelligence unit in the German Foreign Office had fathered Baumann's approach to the Soviet *apparat*: a communications channel had been opened up. Baumann's production figures were probably being traded for information coming back the other way, but moving along an entirely different path. At this very moment, he speculated, some Russian in Leningrad was being told to have no further contact with a certain Finnish ferry captain. That's how things were done, agreements made and kept. *We will keep you informed*, they'd said to somebody in 1937, *of our bomber production*. Secretly, by intelligence means, because neither our countries, nor our leaders, Hitler and Stalin, may be seen by the world to accept each other's existence. We are officially mortal enemies, yet it is to our mutual advantage to have certain understandings. Thus, Szara realized, Baumann's numbers were confirmed by the British because he was *not* being run by Nazi counterintelligence, Schellenberg's office in the Referat VI C.

In another month the pact between Hitler and Stalin would be revealed to the world. Thus they'd shut down the Baumann operation because they no longer needed to communicate in this way. Henceforth such figures would travel by telex from foreign office to foreign office. Meanwhile somebody – *not* Von Polanyi, based on what Frau Baumann had said to Odile – had decided to throw Baumann into Sachsenhausen. Their way of saying thank you, evidently.

No, Szara told himself, you may not think that way. Germans do things for reasons. It was more likely their way of saying *now get out of Germany, Jew*. And here's a little taste of something unpleasant to help you remember to keep your mouth shut.

Maybe, Szara told himself. Just maybe. Something in Goldman's statement about Sachsenhausen had been hopeful, as though Baumann's extrication could be achieved and he knew it.

Oh, but that clever little bastard was smart! He'd sniffed all around the truth. Which was that the 'friends' and the 'diplomats' were one and the same and that 'you' meant Szara and nobody else. What had Baumann actually intended? That would bear thinking about, but there was a nugget to be mined somewhere in those formal words, something he wanted to give to Szara – a present to his case officer. Why? Because he knew Szara, and, despite endless orders and urgent requests for more information – requests unheeded, orders ignored – Szara had not abandoned him or threatened him. Now he said: Please help me, and I'll help you.

Meanwhile that other one, with the glasses, who was he?

Oh Russia, he said to himself, what strange humans you grow.

And now he had to follow Goldman's orders, given a month ago in Brussels and repeated as he left Arion: *write something*. Now he had to go home and do it. Of all the things in the world he didn't want to do, that was near the top of the list. *In these turbulent days, people of good will ought to be asking themselves certain difficult questions. Close the window, shut out the noise of the crowds marching in the streets, and face the issue squarely and without emotion: What can be the future of socialism in today's world? How shall it best survive?*

At somebody's intellectual soirée he'd met an editor. What was his name? A proud little rooster crowing on his own little dunghill of a magazine. 'Come and see me,

André Aronovich,' the man had crooned. Now aren't you, Szara thought at the time, just the most clever fellow to address me by my patronymic, you oily little bore. Ah, but look here, here's fate with a swift kick in the backside – the rooster was going to get what he wanted, a fat scoop of corn tossed into his yard. Would Szara perhaps get paid? Hah! A meagre lunch maybe – 'I always order the daily special here, André Aronovich, I recommend it.' Do you? Well, myself I think I'll have the peacock in gold sauce.

He'd better get it done, he thought. He'd collected his port-manteau from the Hungarian in the seventh arrondissement and expected to get his travel orders any day. Where, he wondered, would they send him.

He woke as in a dream. For a moment he wasn't anywhere at all, adrift in no place he knew but, as in a dream, it did not matter, there was nothing to fear. He lay on top of his raincoat in the loft of a barn, the smell of the hay beneath him sweet, freshly cut. High above him was a barn roof, silvery and soft with age, early light just barely glowing between the cracks where the boards had separated. Sitting up, he faced a broad, open window – it was what they used, standing on their wagons, to pitch forkfuls of hay into the loft. He crawled across the hay in order to look out and saw that it was just after dawn: a shaft of sunlight lay across a cut field, strands of ground mist rising through it. Beside a narrow road of packed, sandy soil stood a great oak; its leaves rattled softly in the little wind that always comes with first light.

There were three men on the road. Men from a dream. They wore black shoes and black leggings and long black coats and black hats with broad brims. They were bearded, and long sidelocks curled from beneath the brims of their hats. Hasidim, he thought, on their way to *shul*. Their faces were white as chalk. One of them turned and looked at him, a look without curiosity or challenge; it took note of a man watching from the window of a barn, then it turned away, back toward the road. They made no sound as they walked, and then, like black and white ghosts in a dream, they vanished.

Poland.

His mind came to life very slowly. The previous day, when he tried to recall it, had broken into fragments, blurred images of travel. He had flown to an airfield near Warsaw on an eight-seater plane that bumped across a ridged tar surface after it landed. There was deep forest on three sides of the airfield, and he'd wondered if this were the main field that served the city. All day he'd never really known exactly where he was. There was a taxi. A train. No, two trains. A ride in a wagon on a hot day. A dog who growled deep in his throat yet wagged his tail at the same moment. A pedlar met on a road. The slow apprehension that he would not arrive anywhere in particular any time soon, that he was where he was, that travellers slept in barns. An old woman, a kerchief tied around her seamed face, said that he was welcome. Then there was a mouse, a moon, the slow, swimming dreams of sleep in an unknown place.

He leaned against the worn barnwood and watched the day break. There was still a quarter moon, white against the blue-black morning sky. A band of storm clouds moved east, edges stained red by the rising sun. Here and there light broke through the clouds, a pine wood appeared on the horizon, a rye field took colour, a sharp green, as he watched. This ghostly, shifting light, wet smell of morning earth, crows calling as they flew low along the curve of a field, he could remember. He had once lived in this part of the world, a long time ago, and sometimes they had ventured beyond the winding streets of Kishinev and he'd witnessed such mornings, when he was a little boy who woke up long before anyone else did in order not to miss any of the miracles. He could see himself, kneeling on a bed in front of a window, a blanket around his shoulders. He could see the sun climbing a hill on a morning in late summer.

'Hey up there, *pan*, are you asleep still?'

He leaned out the window and peered down to find the old woman looking up at him from the yard. She stood, with the aid of a stick, like a small, sturdy pyramid, wearing sweaters and jackets on top, broad skirts below. Her dogs, a big brown one and a little black and white one, stood by her side and stared up at him as well. 'Come along to the house,' she called up to him. 'I'll give you coffee.'

She hobbled away without waiting for an answer, the dogs romping around her, sniffing the bushes, lifting a leg, pressing the earth with their extended forepaws to have a morning stretch.

On the way to the farmhouse, Szara saw that she'd left two large, wooden buckets by the well and, like any tramp worth his salt, he knew she wanted him to bring the water in. First he took off his Paris shirt, worked the squeaky pump handle, and splashed himself with surges of icy water from the spout. He shivered in the early morning air and rubbed himself dry with the shirt, then put it back on and combed his wet hair back with his fingers. When he rinsed his mouth, the cold water made his teeth ache. Next he filled the buckets and staggered into the kitchen, absolutely determined not to slop water on the floor. The farmhouse was an old drystone building with a low ceiling, a tile stove with a large crucifix on the wall above it, and glass windows. The smell of the coffee was strong in the close air of the kitchen.

She brought it to him in a china cup – the saucer was apparently no more – that must have been a hundred years old. 'Thank you, *matrushka*,' he said, taking a sip. 'The coffee is very good.'

'I always have it. Every morning,' she said proudly. 'Except when the wars come. Then you can't get it for any money. Not around here, you can't.'

'Where am I, exactly?'

'Where are you? Why you're in Podalki, that's where!' She cackled and shook her head at such a question, made her way to the stove, and, using her skirt as a potholder, withdrew a pan of bread from the oven. This she placed by the side of his coffee, went off to the pantry and returned with a bowl of white cheese covered with a cloth. She put a knife and a plate before him, then stood by the stove while he ate. He wanted to ask her to sit with him, but he knew that such a request would offend her sense of propriety. She would eat when he was done.

He sawed off the heel of the loaf and covered the steaming slab with white cheese. 'Oh, this is very good,' he said.

'You must be on your way to the city,' she said. 'To Czestochowa.'

'I'm on my way to Lvov.'

'Lvov!'

'That's right.'

'Blessed Mother, Lvov. You're a long way from there,' she said with awe at the distance he contemplated travelling. 'That's a Ukrainian place, you know,' she told him.

'Yes. I know.'

'They say it's in Poland, but I don't think so, myself. You'll want to watch your money, over there.'

'Have you been there, *matrushka?*'

'Me?' She laughed at the idea. 'No,' she said. 'People from Podalki don't go there.'

When he was done with the breakfast he put a few zlotys under the rim of the plate. Back in the barn loft he spread his map out on the hay, but the village of Podalki wasn't to be found. One of the Tass men from Paris who'd been on the plane with him had a much more detailed map, but they'd become separated at the railway station in Warsaw. He found Czestochowa easily enough. If that was the next town of any size, he'd crossed the river Warta the day before. The man driving the cart had called it something else, and it was just a wide expanse of water, sluggish and shallow at summer's end. The man in the wagon had driven up a tiny path, and Szara was taken across the river by an old Jewish ferryman with a patch over one eye. He had a wooden raft and pulley system, hauling on a rope until they were on the other bank. The ferryman told him that the little road would, if he were patient and lucky, eventually take him to Cracow. 'From there you can go anywhere at all, if you want,' the man had said, pocketing the tiny fare with a shrug that questioned why anybody bothered going anywhere at all.

Szara folded the map, returned it to his satchel, put his soft felt hat on, and slung his jacket over his shoulder. When he came out of the barn, the old lady and her dogs were taking the cow out to pasture. He thanked her again, she wished him a safe journey, made the sign of the cross to protect him on his way, and he headed down the narrow, sandy road in the direction of Podalki village.

Twenty minutes later he was there. It wasn't much. A few log houses scattered on both sides of a dirt street, a man with shaven head and cavalry moustache, sleeves rolled up on the hot day, thumbs hooked in braces as he lounged in the doorway of what Szara took to be the Podalki store. There was a tiny, Jewish ghetto on the other side of the village: women in wigs, a Hasid, yarmulke pinned to his hair, chopping wood in the little yard of his house, pale children with curly sidelocks who watched him, cleverly, without actually staring, as he went past. Then Podalki was no more, and he was alone again on the broad Polish steppe, amid endless fields that ran to the forest on the horizon.

He walked and walked, the sun grew hotter, the valise heavier; he started to sweat. The fields on either side of the narrow road were alive; insects buzzed and whirred, the black, moist earth had a certain smell to it, rotting and growing, sweet and rank at once. Sometimes a clump of white birch stood by a small stream, the delicate leaves flickering in the slightest breeze. From this perspective, his life in the city looked frantic and absurd. The intensity of his work, the grating, fretful anxiety of it, seemed utterly artificial. How strange to care so deeply about such nonsense – codes and papers, packages exchanged in cinemas, who had lunch with who at a hotel in Berlin. It was madness. They spun around like the blindfolded It in a children's game. In early August someone had broken into a dry cleaning plant on the outskirts of Paris and stolen the uniforms of the Polish military attaché's staff. A great hubbub ensued: meetings, wireless messages, questions without answers, answers without questions.

But that was nothing compared to what came next: on the twenty-third of August the Hitler/Stalin pact was announced. Oh and hadn't there been just every sort of hell to pay! Weeping and moaning and gnashing of teeth. It had been just as Goldman had predicted – the idealists wringing their hands and beating their breasts. Some people were quite literally stunned – walked about the streets of Paris and were heard to make doleful and solemn declarations: 'I have determined to break with the party.' There were even suicides. What, Szara wondered, had they thought they were playing at? Philosophy?

He heard the creak of cart wheels behind him and the clop of hooves. A wagon driven by a young boy overtook him, a vast load of hay mounded in the bed. Szara moved to one side of the road to let it pass, stepping between furrows at the edge of a field. 'Good morning, *pan*,' said the boy as the cart drew up beside him. Szara returned the greeting. The smell of the old horse was strong in the heat of the day. 'A pretty morning we have,' said the boy. 'Would you care to ride a way?' The wagon didn't actually stop, but Szara hauled himself up and perched on the wooden rim next to the driver. The horse slowed perceptibly. 'Ah, Gniady, now you mustn't be like that,' said the boy, clucking at the horse and flapping the reins. They rode for a time in silence; then a tiny track, two ruts wide, opened up between fields and the boy chucked the left rein to turn the horse. Szara thanked the boy and dismounted. Walking once again, he thought, *Now there's the job for me*. Sometimes he saw men and women at work in the fields. The harvest was only just beginning, but now and then the flash of a scythe would catch the light. The women worked with skirts tucked up, their bare legs white against the wheat or rye stalks.

Somebody, Szara realized, was going to be very annoyed with him for dropping out of sight like this, but that was just too bad. Let them go to hell and rage at the devils. He was tired of their threats – he had rejoined reality, as it happened, and they would have to get along in their dream world as best they could. Above him, the sky spread out to heaven, the morning blue growing pale and hazy as the day wore on. Well to the south there rose a low, dark shape, a distant mountain range, with white cloud building slowly above it, a thunderstorm for the humid evening to come. *This* was what existed: the steppe, the enormous sky, the wheat, the packed sand of the little road. For a moment he was part of it, simply a fact of nature, no more, no less. He didn't even know what day it was. He'd left Paris on the thirtieth of August, though he'd thought of it as the twenty-ninth, since it was three o'clock in the morning, still 'last night,' when he'd taken a taxi to Le Bourget airport. The long day of meandering through eastern Poland had been, in fact, the thirtieth. That made it the very end of summertime.

Summer would actually continue, he realized, for a long while yet, well into September, when the harvest would occupy almost everybody in the countryside, when people would sleep in the fields in order to start work at first light. At night they'd sit around and talk in low voices, they'd even have a small fire once a field was cleared, and couples would go off into the shadows to make love. Still, for him, the summer had just about run its course. He had a schoolboy's sense of time, and the end of August was the end of liberty, just as it had been in childhood, just as, he supposed, it always would be. Strange, he thought, that he found himself once again free as the summer ended. 31 August 1939 – that was the official date. He reckoned once again and made sure. Yes, that was it. By tomorrow he'd likely be 'himself' again, the official himself, the journalist André Szara, riding on trains, writing things down, doing what everyone expected of him.

But for the moment he was a lone traveller on the tiny road to Czestochowa, enjoying a perfect freedom on the last day of summer.

He reached Czestochowa by late afternoon, thanks to a ride in an ancient lorry delivering cucumbers to the markets in the city. A tram ride took him to the railway station and he bought a ticket to Cracow, where he could get another train to Lvov. 'We call it the midnight train to Lvov,' said the dignified ticket seller. 'We also say, however, that dawn in the city of Lvov is very beautiful.' Szara smiled with appreciation at the characteristically Polish bite of the description. The cities were a hundred and eighty miles apart. That meant the train from Cracow was not expected to leave on time, that the locomotive was very slow, or both.

At the restaurant across the street from the station he prepared for the journey, eating cold beet soup, rye bread with sweet butter, a piece of boiled beef accompanied by fresh red horseradish that made tears inevitable, and several glasses of tea. He was sore from sleeping in a hayloft and from miles of walking and was covered with a fine, powdery dust from the road, but the dinner was curative, and he dozed in the first-class compartment until the 6:40 for Cracow chugged away from the station a little after eight. In the gathering dusk of the Czestochowa countryside he saw a lightning storm, great, white bolts of it, three and four in a row, on the southern horizon. Two hours later they were in Cracow.

He had long ago been a student at the university, but he elected to remain at the station until the 'midnight train to Lvov' actually departed. The ticket seller in Czestochowa had told him the truth – the train was very late leaving; some of the people who joined him in the compartment arrived after two in the morning. He watched the night streets of Cracow go by under flaring gas lamps, the Zydowski cemetery, the railway bridge across the Vistula, and then he dozed once more until the muttered comments of his fellow travellers woke him up. The train was barely moving on what seemed to be a branch track, people in the compartment were trying to peer out the window, and then, suddenly, they lurched to a halt. Such a stop was apparently quite unusual. One or two groans of fury were heard, others attempted to solve the mystery by lowering the window and squinting into the darkness outside. A man in a railway uniform came down the track carrying a lantern, passengers called out to him, asked him what the problem was, but he ignored them all. The compartment was dark; Szara lit a cigarette, sat back against the worn plush fabric of the seat, and set himself to wait. Other passengers followed his example. Newspaper crackled as a sandwich was unwrapped, a young couple spoke confidentially in low voices. From the third-class car, a violin started up. Some minutes later a troop train went past, moving very slowly. Soldiers could be seen hanging out the windows and standing packed in the aisles, some dangling their feet from open doorways. Szara could see the glow of their cigarettes. 'They go north,' said the young woman across from him. 'Away from the border. Perhaps the crisis with Hitler has been settled.'

A man sitting next to her lit a match and pointed to the front page of the evening newspaper. 'Shooting in Danzig,' he said. 'You see? I would have to say they're headed up there.'

The conductor came down the passageway, opened the door of the compartment, and said, 'Ladies and gentlemen, I fear I must ask you to get off the train. Please.'

This statement was greeted with general indignation. 'Yes, yes,' the conductor sympathized, 'but what's to be done? I'd tell you the problem if I knew, I'm sure it will all be fixed quickly.' He had a drooping moustache and rather doleful eyes that gave him the look of a spaniel. He went off to the next compartment and the young man called after him, 'Do we take our baggage?'

'Why no,' the conductor said. 'Or maybe yes. I'm not sure. I leave it up to you, good ladies and gentlemen.'

Szara took his valise down from the rack above the window and helped the other passengers with their luggage. 'I tell you . . .' the man with the newspaper said forcefully, but then seemed not to have anything to tell. Slowly the train emptied and the passengers half-slipped, half-jumped, down a grassy embankment and stood about on the edge of a field of weeds. 'Now what?' Szara said to the man with the newspaper.

'I'm sure I don't know,' he said. Then he bowed slightly and extended his hand. 'Goletzky,' he said. 'I'm in soap.'

'Szara. Journalist.'

'Ah, well. Here's someone who'll know what's going on.'

'Not at all,' Szara said.

'Do you write for the Cracow papers?'

'No,' Szara said. 'I've been in Paris the last few months.'

'You're a lucky fellow, then. I count myself fortunate if I get to Warsaw once a year. Mostly I call on the southern provinces – perfumed soaps for the gentry, the old-fashioned yellow bar for the farmer, Dr Grudzen's special formula for young ladies. There isn't much I don't offer.'

'What do you suppose they're going to do with us?' Szara asked. He glanced at his watch. 'It's well after four.' He looked to the east and saw a faint glow on the horizon, then he yawned.

Up the track, the engine released a long hiss of steam, then the slow march of pistons could be heard as it moved off. A cry went up from the assembled passengers: 'Oh no! It's leaving!' Some people started to climb aboard the coaches; then everybody realized that the train was standing still, only the locomotive was moving away.

'Well, that's very nice I must say,' said Goletzky angrily. 'Now they've uncoupled the engine and left us sitting here in the darkness between Cracow and Lord only knows where!'

The passengers began to realize that nothing was going to happen very quickly, and sat gloomily on their suitcases to wait for someone in the railway system to remember them. Fifteen minutes later their locomotive reappeared – they had the conductor's word that it was theirs – now pulling the troop train in the opposite direction. The engineer waved his cap: a gesture taken variously as cruelty, compassion, or an arcane signal known only to railwaymen; and the soldiers were singing, their voices strong in the early morning air. The troop train's original locomotive appeared last, ignominiously towed backwards. 'So,' Goletzky commented, 'it's army manoeuvres that have got us stranded.'

Szara didn't like what he saw, but he didn't know why. He wrote the feeling off to the sort of pointless irritation that comes with fatigue. Some of the passengers returned to their seats in the coaches. The conductor made no very great attempt to stop them. 'Really, ladies and gentlemen,' he said sadly, shaking his head at the anarchy of it all. Others remained outdoors, trying to make a holiday of it. Somebody got a fire going and the garlicky aroma of roasting sausage filled the air. Another group gathered about the violin player. Still others could be seen wandering into the fields, some in search of privacy, others taking the opportunity to observe the countryside.

The drone of an aeroplane caught everyone's attention. It was flying somewhere above them in the darkness, circling perhaps. Then the noise of its engine grew suddenly stronger, a drawn-out mechanical whine that climbed the musical scale and grew louder in the same instant. 'It's going to crash,' said the young woman from Szara's compartment, her voice shrill with fear, her face lifted anxiously towards the sky. She crossed herself as her lips moved. Goletzky and Szara both stood at the same instant, as though drawn to their feet by an invisible force. Somebody screamed. Goletzky said, 'Shall we run?' Then it was too late to run – the noise swelled to an overwhelming shriek that froze the passengers in place. The plane materialized from the darkness for only a fraction of a second. Szara saw swastikas on its wings. Something made him flinch away, then the bomb exploded.

The blast wave took him off his feet – for an instant he

was adrift in the air – then threw him into the embankment. He felt the force of impact shift the teeth and bones on one side of his face and his hearing stopped, replaced by a hissing silence. When he opened his eyes they didn't work: the right half of the world was higher than the left, as though a photograph had been cut in two and pasted back together with the halves misaligned. This terrified him, and he was frantically blinking his eyes, trying to make his vision come right, when bits and pieces of things began to rain down on him and he instinctively protected his head with his forearm. Then something moved inside his face and his vision cleared. He forced himself to sit up, searching his clothing, frightened of what he might find but compelled to look. He found only dirt, bits of fabric and leaves, and a stain on the lapel of his jacket. Nearby, Goletzky sat with his head in his hands. At the bottom of the embankment the conductor lay still, face down in the earth. His feet were bare and a red line ran down one heel. Szara looked for the young woman but could not see her anywhere. An older woman he did not recognize – hair wild, tears streaming from her eyes, dress half blown away – was screaming at the sky. From the way her mouth worked and the sickened anger on her face Szara could tell she was screaming, but he could not hear any sound at all.

He was taken first to a hospital in the city of Tarnów. There he sat in a corridor while the nursing sisters cared for the injured. By then, most of his hearing had returned. By then his valise had miraculously reappeared, brought down the corridor by a soldier asking if anyone knew who it belonged to. By then he had heard that Germany had attacked Poland sometime after four in the morning. Polish soldiers, the Germans claimed, had overrun a German radio station at Gleiwitz, killed some German soldiers, and broadcast an inflammatory statement. This was no more than a classic staged provocation, he believed. And now he knew what had become of the Polish uniforms stolen in Paris. When his turn finally came, he was seen by a doctor, told he'd possibly had a concussion. If he became nauseated he was to seek medical assistance. Otherwise, he was free to continue his journey.

But that was not quite the truth. Outside the examining room a young lieutenant politely informed him that certain authorities in Nowy Sacz wished to speak with him. Was he under arrest? Not at all, the lieutenant said. It was only that someone at the hospital had notified the army staff that a Soviet journalist had been injured in the attack on the Cracow-Lvov line. Now a certain Colonel Vyborg earnestly wished to discuss certain matters with him at the Nowy Sacz headquarters. The young lieutenant had the honour of escorting him there. Szara knew it was pointless to resist, and the lieutenant led him to an aged but functional Czechoslovakian motor car and had him safely in Nowy Sacz an hour later.

Lieutenant Colonel Anton Vyborg, despite his Scandinavian surname, seemed a vestige of the old-fashioned Polish nobility. Szara fancied the name might date from the medieval wars between Poland and Sweden, when, as in all wars, families found themselves living on the wrong side of the lines. Whatever the story, there was something of the Baltic knight in Vyborg; he was tall and lean and thin-lipped, in his forties Szara thought, with webbed lines at the corners of his narrow eyes and pale hair cut short and stiff in the cavalry officer style. Like a cavalry officer, he wore high boots of supple leather and jodhpur-cut uniform trousers. Unlike a cavalry officer, however, his uniform jacket was hung over the back of his chair, his collar was unbuttoned and tie pulled down, and his sleeves were folded back. When Szara entered his office he was smoking a cigar, and a large metal ashtray held the stubs of many others. He had a handshake like steel, and looked hard at Szara with very cold blue eyes when they introduced themselves. Then, having made a rapid and intuitive judgment of some kind, he grew courtly, sent his orderly scurrying for coffee and rolls, and presented what was likely, Szara thought, the genial half of a sharply two-sided personality.

While he waited for his orderly to return, Colonel Vyborg smoked contentedly and stared into space, apparently at peace with the world. He was alone in this, however, since officers were rushing past the open door with armloads of files, telephones were jangling continuously, and the sense of the place was frantic motion, just barely below the level of panic. At one point, a young officer stuck his head in the door and said, 'Obidza' – which could only have been the name of a small town. Colonel Vyborg made the merest gesture of acknowledgment, a polite, almost ironic inclination of the head, and the man wheeled and trotted off. Szara heard him somewhere down the hall, 'Obidza,' telling someone else the news. Vyborg blew a long stream of cigar smoke into the air, rose abruptly, walked to the window, and stared down into the courtyard. The office – obviously temporary; the sign on the door read Tax Assessor – was in the Nowy Sacz city hall, an imposing monstrosity dating from the days of the Austro-Hungarian Empire, when Galicia had been a province of Austria. Vyborg stared onto the courtyard for a long time. 'Now we burn files,' he said.

He looked meaningfully at Szara and cocked an eyebrow, but did not seem to want to hear what a journalist might think about such events. He settled himself back at the desk and said, 'I think perhaps we ought to start our discussion without the coffee – nothing is really going to go smoothly today, and that includes my orderly's trip to the bakery. Do you mind?'

'Not at all,' Szara said.

'Now a Soviet journalist, if he's survived the last two years, can be no fool. You certainly know who you're talking to.'

Szara had assumed from the beginning that Vyborg was the director or the deputy of a military intelligence unit. 'An, ah, information bureau,' he said.

'Yes. That's right. You're legally a neutral, Mr Szara, since last week, 23 August. As a Soviet citizen you are officially neither a friend nor an enemy of Poland, so I'm going to offer you an accommodation of mutual interest. For our part, we'd like to know what you're doing here. Your papers are all in order, we assume you've been assigned a specific task. We'd like to know what's of such interest that *Pravda* would send you here a week after the USSR has signed a treaty that's going to turn out to be this country's obituary. In return, I'll make certain that you are provided with transportation out of this region – we're forty miles north of the border, by the way – and will in general make sure you get to Lvov, if that's where you want to go.

'That's the offer. You can certainly refuse to accept it. The Germans' promise of nonaggression no doubt extends to you personally, and you may feel you want to take them up on it. If so, you needn't move very far, you may stay right here in Nowy Sacz – in two or three days they'll come to you. Or even sooner. On the other hand, you may want to leave right away. In that case I'll have my aide drive you to the railway station – or as close to it as the crowd will permit. Thousands of people are milling around down there, trying to get out any way at all, and the trains don't seem to be running. Still, you can take your chances if you like. So, how shall it be?'

'Seems a fair offer,' Szara said.

'You'll tell me, then, the nature of your assignment in Lvov.'

'They want to know something of the daily life of national minorities in eastern Poland: Byelorussians, Ukrainians, Jews, Lithuanians.'

'*Persecuted* national minorities, you mean. In a former Russian province.'

'The assignment, Colonel Vyborg, is not that. I'd like to point out that I was asked to make this journey some weeks before any pact was announced between the USSR and Germany. They did not, in other words, send me into the middle of a war to write a story about the lives of tailors and farmers. I don't really know what my editors had in mind – they send me somewhere and I do what I'm told to do. Maybe they didn't have very much in mind at all.'

'Jolly anarchic old Russia – the right hand never knows what the left hand is doing. Something like that?'

'What can't be said about Russia? Everything is true, eventually.'

'You are, in fact, a Pole.'

'A Jewish family from Poland, in Russia since I was a teenager.'

'Then I'll revise my statement – a typical Pole.'

'Some would say not.'

'Some certainly would. But others would answer them by saying horseshit.'

Vyborg drummed his fingers on the table. A studious-looking man in an exceptionally rumpled uniform, a sort of shambling professor with spectacles, appeared in the doorway and stood there hesitantly, eventually clearing his throat. 'Anton, excuse me, but they are in Obidza.'

'So I'm told,' Vyborg said.

'Well then, shall we . . .'

'Pack up our cipher machines and go? Yes, I suppose.

I've asked Olensko to organize it. Tell him to begin, will you?'

'With you commanding?'

'I'll find you in Cracow. First I'm going to take our Russian war correspondent to see the front.'

'Russian war correspondent?' The man was amazed. 'So soon?' He stared at Szara without comprehension. 'Will they print a dispatch from this war?' the man finally asked, disbelief in his voice. 'Fifty German divisions attack Poland? My, my, no. Perhaps "Some German units bravely defend their borders thirty miles inside Poland."'

Vyborg laughed bitterly by way of agreement. 'Who knows,' he said with resignation, 'it may give old Kinto something to think about.' The word he used for Stalin meant a kind of singing bandit, a merry figure from Georgian folklore. Szara grinned at the remark. 'You see?' Vyborg said triumphantly. 'He's on our side.'

Speeding southwest in an open military command car, Szara and Vyborg sat grimly in the back seat. Vyborg's driver was a big sergeant with close-cropped hair, a lion tamer's moustache, and a veinous, lumpy nose that was almost purple. He swore under his breath without pause, swinging the big car around obstacles, bouncing through the fields when necessary, hewing a path through the wheat stalks. The road was a nightmare. Refugees walked north, their possessions on their backs or in little carts. Some drove their farm animals before them or led them on a rope halter. Four people carried a sick man in a bed. Meanwhile, Polish military units – marching infantry, horse-drawn artillery and ammunition wagons – attempted to move south. The car passed a burnt-out wagon with two horses dead in the traces. 'Stukas,' Vyborg said coldly. 'A terror weapon.'

'I know,' Szara said.

They were climbing steadily on the rutted dirt road that worked its way through the hills that led to the Polish side of the Carpathian mountains. The air was cooler, the rolling countryside softening as the daylight began to fade. Szara's head ached horribly; the bouncing of the hard-sprung car was torture. He'd not survived the bomb attack as well as he'd thought. His mouth tasted like brass, and he felt as though a path of tiny pins had been pushed into the skin along one side of his face. The car turned west, into a sunset coloured blood red by smoke and haze, the sort of sky seen in late summer when the forests burn. Their road followed the path of a river, the Dunajec, according to Colonel Vyborg.

'We still hold the west bank,' he said. 'Or we did when we left Nowy Sacz.' He produced a large pocket watch and gazed at it. 'Perhaps no longer,' he mused. 'We haven't much hope militarily. Perhaps diplomatically something can be done, even now. We face a million and a half Germans, and tanks and planes, with perhaps two thirds that number – and we haven't any air force to speak of. Brave pilots, yes, but the planes . . .'

'Can you hold?'

'We must. The French and the British may come to help – they've at least declared war. Time is what we need. And, whatever else happens, the story must be told. When people are ground into the dirt that is always what they say, isn't it, that "the story must be told."'

'I'll do what I can,' Szara said softly. In the people on the road he saw sometimes sorrow, or fear, or anger, but mainly they seemed to him numb, lost, and in their eyes he could find only perplexity and exhaustion beyond feeling. He had no immunity to these refugees. His eyes held each one as the car wove among them, then went on to the next, and then the next.

'An effort,' Vyborg said. 'It's all I ask of you.' He was

silent while they passed a priest giving last rites by the side of the road. 'More likely, though, it will wind up with my getting us both killed. And for what. Russia will not be sorry to see the last of Poland.'

'Was a treaty possible?'

'Not really. As one of our leaders put it, "With the Germans we risk losing our freedom, with the Russians we shall lose our soul." Still, it may be in the Politburo's interest for attention to be called to what the Germans are doing. It's not impossible.'

When Szara heard the drone of the aeroplane he clenched his fists. Vyborg's eyes searched the sky and he leaned forward and put a hand on the sergeant's shoulder. 'Slow down, Sergeant,' he said. 'If he sees a staff car he'll attack.'

The Stuka came out of a sun-broken cloud, and Szara's heart began to beat hard as he heard the accelerating whine of the engine. 'Stop,' Vyborg said. The driver jammed on the brakes. They leaped out of the car and ran for the ditch by the side of the road. Szara pressed himself into the earth as the plane closed. *God save me*, he thought. The noise of the dive swelled to a scream, he heard horses neighing with terror, shouts, screams, chattering machine guns, a whipcrack above his head, then the ground rocked as the bomb went off. When the sound of the engine had disappeared into the distance he sat up. There were red ridges across his palms where his fingernails had pressed into his hands. Vyborg swore. He was picking broken cigars out of his breast pocket. On the road a woman had gone mad; people were running after her into a field, yelling for her to stop.

At dusk the column of refugees thinned, then stopped altogether. The land was deserted. They sped through a village. Some of the houses had been burned; others stood with doors wide open. A dog barked at them frantically as they drove by. Szara opened the valise, took out a small notebook, and began to write things down. The driver swung around a bomb crater and cursed it loudly. 'Quiet!' Vyborg commanded. Szara appreciated the gesture, but it didn't really matter. *Germans bomb civilians*, he wrote. No, they would not publish that. *Poles suffer after government refuses compromise*. He scribbled over the words quickly, afraid Vyborg could see what he was writing. *A new kind of war in Poland as Luftwaffe attacks nonmilitary targets*.

No.

It was hopeless. The futility of the journey made him sad. Typical, somehow. Killed on Polish soil while making a useless gesture – an obituary that told the truth. Suddenly he knew exactly who Vyborg was: a Polish character from the pages of Balzac. Szara stole a glance at him. He'd lit the broken stump of a cigar and was pretending to be lost in thought as his writer wrote and they travelled to the lines. Yes, the defiant romantic. Pure courage, cold to the dangers of whatever passion took the present moment for its own. Such men – and the women were worse – had destroyed Poland often enough. And saved it. Either could be true, depending on the year you chose. And the great secret, Szara thought, and Balzac had never tumbled to it, was that the Polish Jews were just as bad – in their faith they were unmovable, no matter what form faith took: Hasidism, Zionism, communism. They were all on fire, and that they shared with the Poles, that they had in common.

And you?

Not me, Szara answered himself.

The driver braked suddenly and squeezed to the right on the narrow road. A convoy of three horse-drawn ambulances was making slow progress in the other direction. 'Getting close to it now,' Vyborg said.

The car made its way up a wooded mountainside. Szara could smell the sap, the aroma sharp and sweet after the long heat of the day. The night air was cooling quickly, a wall of dark pines rose on either side of the road. They had very little light to drive by, the headlamps of the car had been taped down to slits. The sergeant squinted into the darkness and braked hard when, with a sudden twist or turn, the road simply disappeared. Nonetheless, their progress was observed. On two occasions a Wehrmacht artillery observer spotted the light moving on a mountain road and tried his luck: a low, sighing buzz, a flash in the forest, a muted *crump* sound, then the muffled boom of the German gun bouncing among the hills. 'Missed,' Vyborg said tartly as the echo faded away.

Once again, he was awake at dawn.

Wrapped in a blanket on the dirt floor of a ruined shepherd's hut, kerosene splashed on his neck, wrists, and ankles against the lice. From the hut, an artillery observer's position in support of the battalion holding the west bank of the Dunajec, they could see a narrow valley between the water and the wooded hillside, a village broken and burned by German shelling, a section of the river, the wooden pilings that had served as stanchions for a blown bridge, and two concrete pillboxes built to defend the crossing. The observer was no more than eighteen, a junior lieutenant who'd been mobilized only three days earlier and still wore the suit he'd had on in an insurance office in Cracow. He'd managed to scrounge an officer's cap and wore officer's insignia on the shoulders of a very dirty white shirt – his jacket neatly folded in a corner of the little room.

The lieutenant was called Mierczek. Tall and fair and serious, he was somebody's good son, an altar boy no doubt, and now a soldier. A little overawed at first by the presence of a colonel and a war correspondent, he'd made them as comfortable as he could. A harassed infantry major had greeted them the night before and brought them up to the post. Szara had described him in his notebook as *1914 war vintage or earlier; ferocious, bright red face; complaining he hasn't sufficient ammunition, field guns, etc. He gave us bread and lard and tea and a piece of a dense kind of currant cake his wife had baked for him before he left for the front. He wears a complicated – Masonic? noble? – ring. Not happy to see us. 'There's no knowing what will happen. You will have to take your chances as best you can.' They are facing elements of the XVIII Corps of the Wehrmacht Fourteenth Army under Generaloberst List. Advances from northern Slovakia have already been made through the Jablunkov and Dukla passes. Some German units advanced more than fifteen miles the first day. We may, no matter what happens here, be cut off. A delightful prospect. Polish air force bombed on the ground in the first hours of the war, according to Colonel V.*

The tiny river valley in the Carpathians was exquisite at dawn. Streaky red sky, mist banks drifting against the mountainside, soft light on the slate blue river. But no birds. The birds had gone. Instead, a deep silence and the low, steady rumble of distant gunnery. Mierczek stared for a long time through a missing section of roof at the back of the hut, searching the sky for clouds, praying silently for rain. But Hitler's timing had been perfect: the German harvest was in – the population would not suffer deprivation because farmhands were suddenly called to serve in the army. The infamous Polish roads, which would turn to mud of a diabolical consistency once the autumn rains began, were dry; and the rivers, the nation's only natural defence positions, were low and sluggish.

The German attack started at 05:00. Szara and Vyborg both looked at their watches as the first shells landed in the village. Mierczek cranked his field telephone and made contact with the Polish counterbattery at the edge of the forest above the town. Gazing through binoculars, he located the muzzle flashes at a point in the wood on the other side of the river, then consulted a hand-drawn map with coordinates pencilled on it. 'Good morning, Captain, sir,' Mierczek said stiffly into the telephone. Szara heard the earpiece crackle with static as a voice shouted into it. 'They're in L for Lodz twenty-four, sir,' Mierczek responded. He continued to stare through the binoculars, then consulted his map again. 'To the southeast of the grid, I think. Sir.' Vyborg passed his binoculars to Szara. Now he could see the village in sharp focus. A fountain of dirt rose into the air. Then a housefront fell into the little street, a cloud of dust and smoke rolling out behind it. A few small flames danced along a broken beam. He swung the binoculars to the river, then to the German side. But he could see very little happening there.

The Polish field guns began to fire, the explosions leaving dirty brown smoke drifting through the treetops. Now Szara saw an orange tongue of flame in the German-occupied woods. 'Two points left,' Mierczek said into the phone. They waited but nothing happened. Mierczek repeated his instructions. Szara could hear an angry voice amid the static. Mierczek held the phone against his chest for a moment and said confidentially, 'Some of our shells do not explode.' As the Polish guns resumed firing, Szara saw the orange flash again, but this time in a different place. Mierczek reported this. Two men in dark shirts with their sleeves rolled up went running from house to house in the village. They disappeared for a time, then emerged from a back door with a grey shape on a stretcher.

It was getting harder and harder for Szara to see anything; the pall of smoke thickened until solid objects faded into shapes and shadows. The flashes from the German artillery seemed to change position – there simply, he decided, couldn't be that many of them in the forest. Then a Polish machine gun opened up from one of the pillboxes. Szara moved the binoculars towards the far bank of the river and saw hundreds of grey shapes, men running low, come out of the woods and dive flat on the ground. Polish rifle fire began to rattle from the houses in the village. A Polish ammunition dump was hit by a shell; the sound of the blast was ragged, a huge billowing cloud swirled upward, brilliant white stars trailing smoke arched over the river. Mierczek never stopped reporting, but the Polish counterfire seemed ineffective. Finally Colonel Vyborg spoke up. 'I believe, Lieutenant, you're trying to pinpoint a tank battery. It seems they've cut passages into the woods for the tanks to move around.'

'I think you're right, sir,' Mierczek said. In the midst of communicating this information his face tensed, but he carried his report through to the end. Then he unconsciously held his lower lip between his teeth and closed his eyes for an instant. 'The battery's been hit,' he said. Szara traversed the Polish woods but could see little through the smoke. Vyborg was staring out the low, uneven rectangle cut into the logs that served as a window. 'Give me the binoculars,' he said to Szara. He watched for a few seconds, then said, 'Pioneers,' and handed the binoculars back to Szara. German troops were in the river, shielded by the wooden stanchions where the bridge had stood, firing machine pistols at the portals of the pillboxes. The German Pioneer closest to the Polish side was shirtless, his body pink against the grey water. He swam suddenly from behind a stanchion with a rope held in his teeth. He took long, powerful strokes, then he let go of the rope, which floated away from him when he turned on his back and moved downstream with the current. Behind him, soldiers hauled themselves along the rope as far as the stanchion he'd just left. Some of them floated away also but were replaced by others.

'Hello? Captain? Hello?' Mierczek called into the phone. He cranked the handle and tried again. Szara could no longer hear the static. 'I think the line has been severed,' Mierczek said. He took a pair of electrician's pliers from a khaki bag, moved quickly to the low doorway, and disappeared. His job was, Szara knew, to follow the line until he found the break, repair it, and return. Szara saw a flash of the white shirt to his left, toward the battery, then it vanished into the dense smoke hanging amid the trees.

Szara swept his binoculars to the village. Most of the houses were now on fire. He saw a man run from one of them toward the woods, but the man fell on his knees and pitched forward after a few steps. Back on the river, the Pioneers had gained two more stanchions, and crowds of Germans were firing from the ones they held. The fire was returned. White chip marks appeared magically in the old, tarred wood and sometimes a German trooper fell backwards, but he was immediately replaced by another man working his way along the line. A little way down the river there were flashes from the front rank of trees and, concentrating hard, Szara could see a long barrel silhouetted against the trunk of a shattered pine tree. He could just make out a curved bulk below the barrel. Yes, he thought, Vyborg had been right, it was a tank. A group of Polish infantrymen moved out of the forest below him, three of them carrying a machine gun and ammunition belts. They were trying to take up a position with a field of fire that would enfilade the stanchions. They ran bent over, rushing forward, one of them lost his helmet, but then all three made it to a depression in the sand between the edge of the water and a grove of alder trees. He could see the muzzle flash of the machine gun. Swept the binoculars to the stanchion and saw panic as several of the Germans fell away from the pilings. He felt a rush of elation, wanted to shout encouragement to the Polish machine gunners. But by the time he had again located their position, only one man was firing the gun and, as Szara watched, he let it go, covered his face with his hands, and slumped backwards. Slowly, he got himself turned over and began to crawl for the edge of the woods.

The field telephone came suddenly to life, static popping from the earpiece. Vyborg grabbed it and said, 'This is your observer position.' A voice could be heard yelling on the other end. Then Vyborg said, 'I don't know where he is. But he repaired the line and until he returns I will direct your fire. Is there an officer there?' Szara heard the negative. 'Very well, Corporal, you're in charge then. There are tanks in the woods to your north, at the edge of the forest. Can you fire a single round, short? Even in the river will work.' There was a reply, then Vyborg stared at the map Mierczek had left behind. 'Very well, Corporal,' he said. 'My advice is quadrant M28.' Szara moved the binoculars to see the impact of the ranging fire Vyborg had directed but was distracted by a group of Germans who had reached the west bank of the river and were running into the woods. 'They're across,' he said to Vyborg. Vyborg said, 'You're too short, come up a couple of degrees.'

Szara glanced at the doorway, wondering where Mierczek was, then realized he was not going to return. Szara could now see muzzle flashes from positions in and above the village as Polish troopers fired at the Germans who had established a flank attack in the woods. Five Panzer tanks moved out of the woods onto the sandy shore of the river, rumbling forward to the edge of the water and forming an angle that allowed them to fire directly into the Polish forces in the village. Szara's binoculars found the Polish machine gunner who'd tried to crawl away from the beach.

He lay still in the sand. 'Corporal?' Vyborg said into the phone.

By late afternoon, they were near the town of Laskowa, not far from the river Tososina – uncertain where to go next, possibly cut off by Wehrmacht encirclement, but, narrowly, alive.

They had escaped from the scene of the German bridgehead over the Dunajec – a matter of minutes. Colonel Vyborg had taken the precaution of leaving the staff car, with the sergeant to guard it, up the road from the village. Had it been in the village itself they would now be captured or, more likely, dead. As Polish resistance had worn down, the German infantry had negotiated the river on wooden rafts, isolated the remaining Poles in a few positions at the far end of the village, and demanded surrender. The Poles, from the look of it, had refused. Vyborg had watched the beginning of the final attack through his binoculars, then, unwilling to witness the end, had carefully restored them to their leather case and deliberately pressed both snaps shut. Working their way through the hillside brush they had come under fire several times, German rounds singing away through the branches, but the forest itself had protected them from the German marksmen.

For a time, the road crossing the Carpathian foothills was clear, then they came upon the remnants of a retreating Polish regiment driven back from the border: exhausted soldiers, faces and uniforms grey with dust, wagonloads of bandaged, silent men, walking wounded leaning on their rifles or helped by friends, officers who gave no orders. It was, for Szara and evidently for Vyborg as well, worse than the battle at the Dunajec. There they had seen courage in the face of superior force; this was the defeat of a nation's army. A group of peasants harvesting wheat in a field stopped working, took their caps off, and watched silently as the troops walked past.

For a time, the sergeant drove slowly, at the pace of the regiment. Then, around noon, the forward units were engaged. According to a lieutenant questioned by Vyborg, a German corps that had fought its way across one of the Carpathian passes from northern Slovakia had now turned east – with extraordinary, unheard-of speed; a completely motorized force that moved in trucks and tanks – to close the pocket and cut off Polish forces attempting to retreat along the road. When the mortar and machine gun exchanges started up and the regiment began to organize its resistance, Vyborg directed the sergeant to take a tiny cart track – two wagon ruts in the dirt – that cut through a wheat field.

Thus they spent the day. 'We will get you to a telegraph or a telephone somewhere,' Vyborg said, his mind very much on Szara's presumptive dispatch to *Pravda*. But the tiny path wound its way among the hills, in no hurry to get anywhere, over numberless little streams that watered farm cattle, past the occasional peasant settlement deep in the Polish countryside, far, far away from telegraph wires or much of anything. Deeper and deeper, Szara thought, into the fourteenth century – a land of high-sided hay carts with enormous wooden wheels hewed by axes, farm women in aprons, the rooty smells of dry September earth flavoured with pig manure, sweet hay, and woodsmoke. 'See what we have lost,' Vyborg said.

They stopped in midafternoon at a dusty farmyard and bought bread and sausage and freshly brewed beer from a frightened peasant who called them '*pan*,' sir, with every other breath. A man with the fear of armies running in his very blood – getting him to take money almost required force. *Just go*, said his eyes while he smiled obsequiously. *Just go*. Leave me my wife and daughters – you already have my sons – spare my life, we've always given you whatever you asked. Take it. Note that I'm a humble, stupid man of no interest. Then go away.

They stopped in a wood to eat. The sergeant drove the car far enough in so that German spotter aircraft would not see it. When the engine was turned off a deep silence descended, broken only by the low, three-note song of a single bird. The forest reminded Szara of a cathedral; they sat beneath tall oak trees that filtered and darkened the light until it was like the cool shadow of a church. One worshipped simply by being there. But it seemed to do Vyborg more harm than good; his mood grew darker by the moment, and the sergeant finished his bread and sausage and took his canteen of beer over to the car, folded the bonnet back, and began to tinker with the engine. 'He disapproves,' Vyborg said. 'And shows it in his own way.' But for courtesy, Szara would have joined him. He knew this black depth that lived in the Polish soul and feared it – the descent to a private hell where nothing could ever be fixed, or better, or made right often ended badly. He'd seen it. He noticed that the flap on Vyborg's holster was unbuttoned. An innocuous detail, but this was not the sort of officer who would be casual about such things. He knew that if Vyborg determined his honour lay in the single shot fired in a forest there was nothing he could say or do to stop it. 'You cannot take this on yourself, Colonel,' Szara finally said to break the silence.

Vyborg was slow to answer. Considered not bothering to say anything at all, finally said, 'Who else, then?'

'Politicians. Not least, Adolf Hitler.'

Vyborg stared at him in disbelief, wondering if perhaps he'd adopted the most hopeless fool in the world to tell his nation's story. 'Sir,' he said, 'do you believe that what you saw forcing the Dunajec was the Nazi party? What have I missed? If there was a lot of drunken singing and pissing on lampposts I somehow didn't see it. What I saw was Deutschland, Poland's eternal enemy. I saw Germans. "C'mon fellows, there's a job to be done here and we're the ones to do it, so let's get busy." I saw the Wehrmacht, and I would have been, any officer worth his salt would have been, proud to command it. Do you believe that a bunch of shitbag little grocers and naughty schoolboys, led by Himmler the chicken farmer and Ribbentrop the wine salesman, would have overcome a Polish battalion? Do you?'

'No. Of course not.'

'Well then.'

Vyborg had raised his voice. The sergeant, sleeves rolled up to his elbows, working at the engine of the car, began whistling. 'And,' Vyborg went on, now in control of himself, 'I do take this on myself. Is there somewhere, in some filing cabinet in Warsaw, a report signed A. S. Vyborg, lieutenant colonel, that says the Stuka divebomber may be expected to do such and such? That says the Wehrmacht is able to cover fifteen miles of countryside a day, using tanks and motorized infantry? There is not. We are going to lose this war, we are going to be subjugated, and the fault lies with diplomacy – you're not entirely wrong – but it also lies with me and my colleagues. When a country is conquered, or subdued by political means, the secret services are always to blame – they, who are supposedly allowed to do *anything*, should have done *something*. In political life it is the cruellest equation there is, but we accept it. If we do not accept it we cannot continue with the work.'

He paused, drank the remaining beer in his canteen, and wiped his lips delicately with his fingers. The sergeant had stopped whistling, and the three-note bird had started to sing again, low and mournful. Vyborg settled his back against a tree trunk and closed his eyes. He was very pale, Szara realized, tired, perhaps exhausted. The strength of his personality was deceptive. The lost light of the forest muted the colour of his uniform – now it seemed heavy wool fabric, cut by a tailor, not a uniform at all, and his sidearm became a bulky nuisance on a belt. The colonel forced himself to return from wherever he'd been, leaned forward, searched his breast pocket for a cigar, and showed a brief anger when he couldn't find any. When he spoke again his voice was quiet and resolved. 'Every profession defines its own failures, my friend. The doctor's patient does not recover, the merchant closes his shop, the politician leaves office, the intelligence officer sees his country dominated. Surely, on the level you've lived in Russia, you know that. You've had, so to speak, at least contacts with your own services.'

'Rarely,' Szara said. 'To my knowledge, at any rate. You're referring not to the secret police – of course one sees them every day in some form or another – but to those who concern themselves with international issues.'

'Exactly. Well, I'll tell you something, you've missed a historic era, a phenomenon. We know the Soviet services, we oppose them after all so we had better know them, and what most of us feel, alongside the appropriate patriotic wrath, is perhaps just a little bit of envy. Seen together it is a curious group: Theodor Maly – the former Hungarian army chaplain, Eitingon, Slutsky, Artuzov, Trilisser, General Shtern, Abramov, General Berzin, Ursula Kuczynski – called Sonya, that bastard Bloch, all the Latvians and Poles and Jews and what have you – they are, or perhaps one ought to say, in most cases, *were*, the very best that ever did this work. I don't speak to their morals, their personal lives, or their devotion to a cause in which I do not believe, no, one really can't see them in that light. But in the business of espionage there have never been any better, possibly won't ever be. I suppose it could be considered a pity; all of them slaughtered to some strange, enigmatic purpose known only to Stalin, at least a pity you never came to experience their particular personalities.'

'You've met them?'

'Not in the flesh, no. They are paper men who live in file folders, but perhaps it is, for them, their truest manifestation. What, after all, is there to see? A little fellow with glasses reading a newspaper in a café. An overweight Jewish gentleman choosing a tie, charming the sales clerk. A man in shirtsleeves and suspenders, berated by his wife for some small domestic stupidity.' Vyborg laughed at the thought of it, his gallery of rogues muddling through their daily lives. 'Ah, but on paper, well, that's another story. Here an ambassador is compromised, there a powerful émigré group simply disintegrates, plans for an ingenious ciphering machine are copied and no one knows it has happened. An incident in Brussels, a disappearance in Prague – one must surmise that a fine hand is at work. As the stage magician says: now you see it, now you don't. Ah, but dear ladies and gentlemen you must forgive me, I cannot tell you how the trick is done.'

The sound of an approaching aircraft made Vyborg glance up through the trees. For a time, while the plane wandered invisible somewhere in the clouds above the forest, neither of them spoke. At last, it faded away into the distance. Vyborg stood and brushed himself off. 'One thing we certainly do know: it isn't one of ours.' Szara stood up. Vyborg glanced back up at the sky. 'We'd better be moving,' he said, 'or one of these clever Wehrmacht pincer manoeuvres is going to close around us and we'll wind up as prisoners. In the last war the officer class respected the gentleman's code, but this time around I'm not so certain.'

They drove on, the countryside shimmering a thousand shades of green and gold in the haze of the waning afternoon. Three wagons came towards them and the sergeant, at Vyborg's direction, pulled over to let them use the twin ruts of the path. Polish Jews, men, women, and children, eyes downcast for the occasion of passing army officers, headed east, away from the advancing Germans. When the car was again in motion, Szara said to Vyborg, 'No gentleman's code for them, evidently.'

'I fear not. If we are to be occupied by German forces, I am afraid our Jews will suffer. Those who just passed us believe that, and I have to agree. They, however, are headed east. Will Russia have them?'

'Russia does what it has to do,' Szara said. 'Life won't be good for them there, but most of them will survive. Stalin will find some use for them in the end.'

'In the camps?'

'Perhaps in labour battalions. They won't be allowed to settle down and live their lives.'

'Don't you love your adopted land, Mr Szara?'

'It doesn't love me, Colonel, and in an affair of any sort that tends to make life uncomfortable.'

'But you could go away, yet you don't.'

'Who hasn't thought of it? And I'm just as human as the rest of them. But something about this part of the world makes it hard to leave. It's not to be explained in the ordinary ways, and poetic yearnings for the sky and the earth seem awfully meagre when the Chekists come around. Yet one stays. One decides to leave, puts it off a week, then something happens, so then it's Thursday for certain, but on Thursday it can't be done, then suddenly it's Monday but the trains aren't running. So you wait for March, and some new decree gives you hope, then spring comes in April and your heart is suddenly strong enough for anything. Or so you think.' He shrugged, then said, 'You wake up one morning; you're too old to change, too old to start again. Then the woman in your bed snuggles up because her feet are cold and you realize you're not that old, and after that you start to wonder what shattering horror or peculiar pleasure the rest of the day might bring, and by God your heart has grown Russian and you didn't even notice.'

Vyborg smiled. 'I should read your writing,' he said. 'But what kind of a Russian speaks this way yet lives in Paris? Or do I have it wrong?'

'No. You have it right. And all I can say in my defence is, what poet doesn't praise the love that loves from afar?'

Vyborg laughed, first politely, then for real as the notion tickled him. 'What a shame,' he said, 'that we're about to lose this beautiful, heartbreaking country of ours. If that weren't the case, Mr Szara, I assure you I would recruit you to the very corner of hell simply for the pleasure of your company.'

That night he lay on a blanket beside the car and tried to will himself to sleep. That was the medicine he needed – for exhaustion, sore spirit, for survival – but when it came, for a few minutes at a time, it wasn't the kind that healed. An area around his right temple throbbed insistently, seemed swollen and tender, and he feared something far worse than he'd imagined had gone wrong inside him. The night was starless and cool. They'd driven and driven, managing only a few miles an hour over the wagon ruts, then given it up just at the last moment of dusk.

Leaving the oak forest, they'd suddenly entered a seemingly endless wheat field that ran uninterrupted for miles. There were no villages, no people at all, only ripe wheat that rustled and whispered in the steady evening wind. The last jerrycan of fuel had been poured in the gas tank; somehow they would have to find more. Szara had frightening dreams – the genial irony that had sustained their morale during the day disappeared in darkness – and when he did manage to sleep he was pursued and could not run. The ground beneath him was hard as stone, but turning on his other side made his head swim with pain and forced him back to his original position. Long before dawn he awakened to the roll of thunder, then saw on the horizon that it was not thunder: a pulsing, orange glow stained the eastern edge of the night sky. For a few minutes he was the only one awake; rested his head on his arm and watched what he knew to be a burning city under artillery barrage.

When the sergeant and the colonel awoke, they too watched the horizon. For a long time nobody spoke, then the sergeant took both canteens and went off to try and find water. They'd had nothing to eat or drink since afternoon of the previous day, and thirst was becoming something it was hard not to think about. Vyborg lit a match and tried to study the map, not at all sure where they were.

'Could it be that Cracow is on fire?' Szara asked.

Vyborg shook his head that he didn't know and lit another match. 'Our little wagon track is not on the map,' he said. 'But I've estimated we'll hit the north-south rail line at a switching station somewhere north and east of here.'

Szara took the last crushed Gitane from a battered pack. He had two more in his valise, rolled up in a clean shirt. He thought about changing clothes. He had sweated and dried out many times and was everywhere coated with a fine, powdery dust that made him feel itchy and grimy. Too much Parisian luxury, he thought. Baths and cigarettes and coffee and cold, sweet water when you turned on the tap. From his perspective of the moment it seemed a dream of a lost world. France had declared war, according to the colonel, and so had England. Were the German bombers flying over their cities? Perhaps Paris was an orange glow in the sky. Vyborg looked at his watch. 'There must not be water anywhere near,' he said.

Szara sat against the tyre of the staff car and smoked his cigarette.

An hour later the sergeant had not returned, and dawn was well advanced. Colonel Vyborg had twice walked a little way up the path – with no results. Finally he seemed to make a decision, opened the trunk and took out an automatic rifle. He detached the magazine from its housing forward of the trigger guard and inspected the cartridges, then snapped it back into place and handed the weapon to Szara. From the markings it was a Model ZH 29 made in Brno, Czechoslovakia, a long, heavy weapon, not quite clumsy; the hand grip just behind the barrel was protected by a ribbed metal alloy so the shooter didn't blister his fingers when the gun fired automatically. Vyborg said, 'There are twenty-five rounds, and one in the chamber. The setting is for single shots, but you can move the lever behind the magazine to automatic.' He reached over and worked the bolt. 'I've armed it,' he said. He drew his weapon, a short-barrelled automatic, from its holster, and inspected it as he had the Czech rifle. 'Best we stay a few yards apart but side by side – a field is a bad place for walking about with armed weapons.'

For a time they moved along the path, the colonel stopping every now and then and calling out softly. But there was no answer. The track curved upwards around a low hill and, as the sun came above the horizon, they found the sergeant on the other side, some three hundred yards away from the car, at a place where the wheat stalks had been crushed and broken. His throat had been cut. He lay stretched on his stomach, eyes wide open, a look of fierce worry settled on his face. A handful of dirt was frozen in each fist. Vyborg knelt and brushed the flies away. The sergeant's boots were gone, his pockets were turned out, and, when Vyborg reached inside his uniform jacket, a shoulder holster worn just below the armpit was empty. There was no sign of the canteens. For a time, Szara and Vyborg remained as they were: Szara standing, the rifle heavy in his hands, Vyborg kneeling by the body, which had bled out into the earth. The silence was unbroken – only the distant rumble and the sound of the wheat stalks brushing against each other. Vyborg muttered an obscenity under his breath and went to take a religious medal from around the sergeant's neck, but if he'd worn one it had also been stolen. At last the colonel rose, the pistol held loosely in his hand. He kicked at the ground experimentally with the toe of his boot, but it was hard and dry as rock. 'We have no shovel,' he said at last. He turned and walked away. When Szara caught up with him he said, 'This always starts here when there's war.' His voice was bitter, disgusted and cold. 'It's the peasants,' he said. 'They've decided to look out for themselves.'

'How did they know we were here?'

'They know,' Vyborg said.

By full daylight they could see columns of black smoke where the city was burning and the sound of the barrage had grown more distinct, could be heard to crackle like wet wood in a fire. Vyborg drove, Szara sat beside him. They did not speak for a long time. Szara watched the needle on the petrol gauge, quivering just below the midpoint on the dial. Now, when they encountered a rise or a low hill, Vyborg stopped the car just below the top, took his binoculars, and climbed the rest of the way. Szara stood guard, rifle in hand, back protected by the metal side of the car. On the fourth or fifth scouting expedition, Vyborg appeared just below the brow of a hill and waved for Szara to join him. When he got there Vyborg said, 'They're on the other side. Go slowly, stay as close to the ground as you can, and do not speak; make gestures if you have to. People notice motion, and they hear human sounds.'

The sun was blazing. Szara crawled on his elbows and his knees, breathing dust, the rifle cradled across his arms. Sweat beaded in droplets at his hairline and ran down the sides of his face.

When they crested the hill, Vyborg handed him the binoculars, though he could see the valley very well without them. They'd reached the railway switching station – as Vyborg had predicted – which lay by a dirt road at the foot of a long gentle grade. A single set of rails curved to the west, coming together by the switching station with a double-track north-south axis. A switchman's hut and a set of long iron levers housed in a wooden framework stood to one side of two laybys, lengths of track where one train could be held while another used the right-of-way.

The little valley, mostly weeds and scrub trees, was alive with Wehrmacht grey. The hut and the switching apparatus had been protected by a sandbagged machine gun position; a number of Wehrmacht railway officers, identifiable by shoulder patches when he used the binoculars, were milling about with green flags in hand. From the position of the long row of goods wagons parked on the western track, Szara inferred that the troop train had arrived directly from the German side of the border. There was further evidence of this. Across the wooden boards of one of the wagons was a legend printed with chalk: *Wir fahren nach Polen um Juden zu versohlen*, We are riding to Poland to beat up the Jews. Insignia indicated that he was witnessing the arrival of elements of the Seventeenth Infantry Division; about a thousand of them had already formed up while hundreds more continued to jump down from the open doors of the goods wagons.

With the binoculars, details of faces were very clear to Szara. He saw them through a smoky haze that lay over the valley, with foreground weeds cutting across his field of vision and with the eerie detachment of observation at long range – mouths move yet no sound is heard – but he could see who they were. Farm-boys and idlers and mechanics, street toughs and clerks, factory workers and students – an army of young faces, dark and fair, some laughing, some anxious, some full of bravado, some silent and withdrawn, some handsome and some ugly, others entirely unremarkable – an army like all others. A group of officers, generally in their thirties and forties (as the troopers were in their teens and twenties), stood to one side and smoked and talked quietly in little groups while the inevitable confusion of a military force on the move was sorted out by the NCOs, the sergeants and corporals.

Szara observed this particular group with interest. They were all of a type: big, strong, competent, full of easy authority but without swagger. They were, he knew, the soul of an army, supervisors and foremen rather than executives, and upon their abilities would ultimately rest defeat or victory. They worked with their units almost casually, sometimes taking a stray by a handful of uniform and heading it where it belonged, usually without any comment at all, simply pointing it in the direction it ought to go and giving it a bit of a shove to get it moving.

From a group of cattle trucks farther down the track, the division's horses were being led to the staging area. They were great, muscular beasts, bred for army life on the horse farms of East Prussia. They would pull the divisional artillery, the provisioning and ammunition wagons, and some of the better ones would be ridden by officers: the German army, like most other European armies, moved by horsepower. There would be a few open staff cars, like the one Szara and the colonel were using, for senior officers and the medical staff, but it was horses who did all the heavy work, four thousand of them for each division of ten thousand soldiers. The spearhead of the German offensive was armoured – divisions of tanks and trucks, and their speed had so far entirely outmanoeuvred the Polish defence – but the units moving up now would hold the territory that the fast-moving armoured groups had captured.

Szara shifted his binoculars up the road that led north, where several companies were already on the move. It was no parade, they were walking not marching, weapons casually slung – as always the giants carried rifles while small, lean men lugged tripod machine guns and mortar tubes – in a formation that was ragged but functional. The machine was, for the moment, running in low gear. Szara saw that a field gun had tipped over into a ditch, the horses tangled up in their reins and skittering about to get their balance – the accident had evidently just happened. The situation was quickly put right: a sergeant shouted orders, several troopers soothed the horses, others freed the reins, a group organized itself to lift the gun back onto the road. It took only a moment, many willing hands – *heave!* – and the job was done, the advance continued.

Vyborg touched him on the shoulder to get his attention and made a hand motion indicating they'd spied long enough. Szara slithered backwards for a time, then they rose and walked toward the car. Vyborg spoke in an undertone – even though they were well away from the Germans, something of their presence remained. 'That,' he said, 'was the road to Cracow. Our reckoning was, after all, correct. But, as you can see, the road is presently in use.'

'What can we do?'

'Swing around behind or try to sneak through at night.'

'Are we cut off, then?'

'Yes. For the time being. What was your impression of the Wehrmacht?'

They reached the car; Vyborg started the engine and slowly backed down the track until a curve took them out of the direct sightline of the hill they'd climbed. 'My impression,' Szara said after Vyborg had backed the car into the wheat and turned it off, 'is that I do not want to go to war with Germany.'

'You may have no choice,' Vyborg said.

'You believe Hitler will attack Russia?'

'Eventually, yes. He won't be able to resist. Farmlands, oil, iron ore; everything a German loves. By the way, did you take note of the horses?'

'Handsome,' Szara said.

'Useless.'

'I'm no judge, but they seemed healthy. Big and strong.'

'Too big. The Russians have tough little horses called *panje*, they can live on weeds. These big German beasts will disappear in the Russian mud – that's what happened to Napoleon, among other things. They're strong enough, powerful, but too heavy. And just try and feed them.'

'Hitler knows all about Napoleon, I'd imagine.'

'He'll think he's better. Napoleon came out of Russia with a few hundred men. The rest remained as fertilizer. Hundreds of thousands of them.'

'Yes, I know. What the Russians call General Winter finally got them.'

'Not really. Mostly it just wore them down, then finished the job. What got them was spotted fever. Which is to say, lice. Russia defends herself in ways that nobody else really thinks about. The peasant has lived with these lice all his life, he's immune. The Central European, that is the German, is not. Far be it from me to intrude on old Kinto's information *apparat*, but if Hitler starts making hostile noises, somebody ought to go and have a look at what sort of salves and preventatives the German pharmaceutical houses are turning out. That could, in the long run, matter a great deal. Of course, why on earth would I be telling you such things? It will hardly do for *Pravda*. Still, if you do get out of here alive, and should you chance to meet one of the operatives you've never known, there's a little something to whisper in his ear.'

The night was exquisite, starlight a luminous silver wash across the black of the heavens. Szara lay on his back and watched it, hands clasped to make a pillow beneath his head, simultaneously dazzled by the universe and desperate for water. It was now almost too painful to talk; his voice had gone thick and hoarse. Just after dark they had crept once more to their point of vantage, sensing, like thirsty animals, that somewhere near the switchman's hut there was a stream or a well. But a new train idled on the western track and, by the light of several roaring bonfires, units organized themselves and moved off north on the road to Cracow.

At midnight they made a decision: abandoned the car and worked their way south through the countryside, carrying weapons, canteens, and hand baggage. The first two hours were agony, groping and stumbling through thick brush that bordered the wheat field, halting dead still at every miscellaneous sound of the night. What helped them, finally, was a German railway patrol; a locomotive, its light a sharp, yellow cone that illuminated the track, moved cautiously south pushing a flatcar manned by soldiers with machine pistols. Following the light, they walked for another hour, saw the silhouette they wanted, then simply waited until the engine disappeared over the horizon.

The tiny railway station had a water tower. They twisted open a valve at the bottom and took turns drinking greedily from the stream sluicing onto the ground. It was foul water, bad-smelling and stale, and Szara could taste dirt and rotting wood and God knew what else, but he lapped at it avidly, drinking from cupped hands, not caring that the stream soaked his shirt and trousers. A man and a woman came out of a little cottage that backed up to the station;

he was likely a sort of stationmaster, flagman, switchman, or whatever else might be required.

Vyborg greeted the couple politely and told the man he would require new clothing, whatever might be available. The woman went off and returned with a faded shirt and pants, broken-down shoes, a thin jacket, and a cap. Vyborg took a wallet from his jacket and offered the man a sheaf of zloty notes. The man looked stubbornly at his feet, but the woman stepped forward and accepted the money silently. 'What will become of us now?' the man asked.

'One can only wait and see,' Vyborg said. He bundled up the clothing, took charge of the rifle and the canteens, and said, 'I will take these off and bury them.' The man found him a coal shovel, and Vyborg vanished into the dark fields away from the track.

'To bury fine boots like those . . .' said the woman.

'Best forget them,' Szara told her. 'The Germans know what they are and who wears them.'

'Yes, but still,' said the woman.

'It's bad to see such a thing,' the man said sharply, angry that the woman saw only fine boots. 'To see a Polish officer bury his uniform.'

'Is there a train?' Szara asked.

'Perhaps in a few days,' the man said. 'From here one goes to Cracow, or south to Zakopane, in the mountains. In normal times every Tuesday, just at four in the afternoon.'

They stood together awkwardly for a time, then a workman came out of the field and stepped across the track. 'It's done,' Vyborg said.

There was no train. Szara and Vyborg determined to go east, on a road that ran well to the south of the railway station, skirting the Slovakian border, winding its way through the river valleys of the Carpathians. They joined an endless column of refugees, on foot, in carts drawn by farm horses, in the occasional automobile. German units were posted at the crossroads, but the soldiers did not interfere with the migration; they seemed bored, disinterested, slouching against stone walls or bridge abutments, smoking, watching without expression as the river of humanity flowed past their eyes. No papers were demanded, no one was called out of line or searched. Szara noticed what he took to be other soldiers in the column who, like Vyborg, had shed their uniforms and obtained civilian clothing. Among the refugees there were various points of view about the German attitude, ranging from attributions of benevolence – 'The Fritzes want to win our confidence' – to pragmatism – 'The less Poles in Poland, the happier for them. Now we'll be Russia's problem.' The road east became a city: babies were born and old people died, friends were made and lost, money was earned, spent, stolen. An old Jew with a white beard down to his waist and a sack of pots and pans clanking on his back confided to Szara, 'This is my fourth time along this road. In 1905 we went west to escape the pogroms, in 1916 east, running away from the Germans, then in 1920, west, with the Bolsheviks chasing us. So, here we are again. I don't worry no more – it'll sort itself out.'

It took them six days to reach the small city of Krosno, some eighty miles east of the Cracow-Zakopane line. There, Szara saw with amazement that the Polish flag still hung proudly above the entrance to the railway station. Somehow, they'd managed to outdistance the German advance. Had the Wehrmacht permitted the column of refugees to enter Polish-held territory in order to overload supply and transport systems? He could think of no other reason, but that seemed to him dubious at best. Vyborg left Szara at the station and went off to look for an intelligence unit and a wireless telegraph among the forces manning the Krosno defences. Szara thought he'd seen him for the last time, but two hours later he reappeared, still looking like a dignified, rather finely made workman in his cap and jacket. They stood together by a beam supporting the wooden roof of the terminal, restless crowds of exhausted and desperate people shifting endlessly around them. The noise was overwhelming: people shouting and arguing, children screaming, a public address system babbling indecipherable nonsense. They had to raise their voices in order to make themselves heard. 'At last,' Vyborg said, 'I was able to reach my superiors.'

'Do they know what's going on?'

'To a point. As far as you're concerned, Lvov is not currently under attack, but that is a situation which may change quickly. As for me, my unit was known to have reached Cracow, but there they vanished. Communication is very bad – several Polish divisions are cut off, mostly trying to break out and fight their way to Warsaw. The capital will be defended and is expected to hold. Personally I give it a month at most, probably less. I'm afraid there isn't much hope for us. We do have miracles in this country, even military ones from time to time, but the feeling is that there's not much that can be done. We've appealed to the world for help, naturally. As for me, I have a new assignment.'

'Outside the country?'

Vyborg's thin-lipped mouth smiled tightly for a moment. 'I can tell you nothing. You may wish me well, though, if you like.'

'I do, Colonel.'

'I would ask you, Mr Szara, to write about what you've seen, if you can find a way to do that. That we were brave, that we stood up to them, that we did not surrender. And I would say that the next best thing, for us, if you can't do that, is silence. I refer to your assignment from *Pravda*. Stories about our national minorities have already appeared in London and Paris, even in America. Perhaps you will decline to add your voice to the baying chorus.'

'I'll find a way.'

'I can only ask. That's all that officers of defeated armies can do, appeal to conscience, but I ask you anyhow. Perhaps you still feel yourself, at heart, a Pole. People of this nation are far-flung, but they often think of us, it would not be inappropriate for you to join them. Meanwhile, as to practical matters, I'm told that a train for Lvov will be pulling in here within the hour. I'd like to think that you'll be on it – you have your work cut out for you, I can see – but at least that way I'll have kept my part of the bargain, albeit by an unexpected route.'

'Journalists are very good at forcing their way onto trains, Colonel.'

'Perhaps we'll meet again,' Vyborg said.

'I would hope so.'

Vyborg's handshake was strong. 'Good luck,' he said, and slipped away into the milling crowd of refugees.

Szara did get on the train, though not actually inside it. He worked his way to the side of a coach, then moved laterally until he came to the extended iron stair. There was a passenger already in residence on the lowest step, but Szara waited until the train jerked into motion, then forced his way up and squeezed in beside him. His fellow traveller was a dark, angry man clutching a wicker hamper in both arms and, using his shoulder, he attempted to push Szara off the train – the step belonged to him, it was his place in the scheme of things.

But Szara availed himself of a time-honoured method and took a firm grip on the man's lapel with his free hand so that the harder the man pushed, the more likely he was to leave the train if Szara fell off. The train never managed to pick up any speed; there were people hanging out the windows, lying flat on the roof, and balancing on the couplings between cars, and the engine seemed barely capable of moving the weight forward. For a long time the two of them glared at each other, the man pushing, Szara hanging on to him, their faces separated only by inches. Then, at last, the pushing and pulling stopped and both men leaned against the bodies occupying the step above theirs. The train made the eighty miles to Lvov in six agonizing hours, and if the station at Krosno had been a hell of struggling crowds, Lvov was worse.

Attempting to cross the platform, Szara literally had to fight. The heat of the crowd was suffocating, and he shoved bodies out of his way, tripped over a crate of chickens and fell flat on the cement floor, then struggled desperately among a forest of legs in order to rise before he was trampled to death. Someone punched him in the back, hard – he never saw who did it, he simply felt the blow. Once he got to the waiting room, he fell in with a determined phalanx using their combined weight to move toward the doors. They'd almost got there when a crowd of frantic, terrified people came sweeping back against them. Szara's feet left the ground, and he was afraid his ribs might break from the pressure; he flailed out with one hand, hit something wet that produced an angry yelp, and with enormous effort got his feet back on the floor.

Somewhere, only barely touching the edge of his consciousness, was a drone, but he made no attempt to connect it with anything in the real world, it was simply there. He moved sideways for a few seconds, then some mysterious countercurrent picked him up and sent him sprawling through the doors of the station – he kept his balance only by jamming one hand against the cement beneath him, gasping at the air as he came free of the crowd.

He found himself not in the main square of Lvov, but at a side street entrance to the railway station. People were running and shouting, he had no idea why. Several carts had been abandoned by their drivers, and the horses were galloping wildly up the cobbled street to get away from whatever it was, loose vegetables and burlap sacks flying off the wagons behind them. The air was full of tiny, white feathers, from where he did not know, but they filled the street like a blizzard. The drone grew insistent and he looked up. For a moment he was hypnotized. Somewhere, in some file in the house on the rue Delesseux, was a silhouette, as seen from below, identified in a careful Cyrillic script as the Heinkel-111; and what he saw above him was a perfect match of the darkened outline among the pages of what he now realized was the Baumann file. This was one of the bombers controlled by the swage wire manufactured on the outskirts of Berlin. There was a second flight approaching, at least a half-dozen of them in the clouds above the city, and he remembered, if not precise facts and figures, at least the certain conclusion: they were known to produce the virtual annihilation of every stick and stone and living thing once they released their bombs. As the planes flew in slow formation, a series of black, oblong cylinders floated away beneath them and tumbled, in a crooked line, toward the earth.

The first explosion – he felt it in his feet and heard it in the distance – startled him, then several more followed, each time growing louder. He ran. Blindly and without purpose, in panic, then tripped and fell at the base of a doorway. He lashed out at the door, which swung open, and he crawled frantically into a room. He smelled sawdust and shellac, spotted a large, rough-hewn work table, and rolled beneath it. Only then did he discover he was not alone – there was a face close to his, a man with a scraggly beard, half glasses, and a stub of pencil wedged between his temple and the hem of his cap. The man's eyes were enormous and white, blind with terror. Szara squeezed himself into a ball as a shattering roar rocked the table above him, perhaps he howled, perhaps the man curled up next to him did – he no longer had any idea who he was or where he was, the world exploded inside his head and he forced his eyes shut until he saw brilliant colours in the darkness. The floor bucked and sang with the next explosion and Szara tried to claw his way through it into the safe earth below. Then there was another, and then another, receding, and, finally, a silence that rang in his ears before he realized what it meant.

'Is it over?' the man said in Yiddish.

The air was thick with smoke and dust; they both coughed. Szara's throat felt as though it had caught fire. 'Yes,' Szara said. 'They've gone.' Together, and very slowly, they crawled from beneath the table. Szara saw that he was in a carpentry shop, and the man with the half glasses was apparently the carpenter. The windows were gone, Szara had to look for a long time before he discovered tiny sparkles of glass embedded in the back wall. But he could find no other damage. What had dissolved the windows had also slammed the door, and the carpenter had to pull hard before it sprang open.

Cautiously, they looked out into the street. To their left was a gap where a house had been – only a pile of board and brick remained – and the house next to it was on fire, black smoke boiling out of the upper windows. Somebody nearby shouted, 'Help' – perhaps a woman's voice. The carpenter said '*Mein Gott*' and pressed his face between his hands.

At the opposite end of the street from the burning house a vast crater had been torn open. They walked over to it and peered down; a broken pipe gushed water from a ragged end. 'Help,' said the voice again. It came from a shop directly across from the hole in the street. 'It's Madame Kulska,' said the carpenter. The door of the shop had disappeared and the interior, a dressmaker's workroom, had been swirled by a typhoon, bits and pieces of material were everywhere. 'Who's there?' said the voice. 'Nachman,' said the carpenter. 'I'm under here,' said the voice. *Under here* was covered by a jumbled layer of fallen bricks. Szara and the carpenter quickly cleared the rubble away, revealing the dusty back of a huge armoire and a small woman pinned beneath it. Szara took one corner, the carpenter the other. '*Ein, zwei, drei*,' said the man, and together they raised the cabinet until it fell back into the smashed brick wall, the door swinging open to reveal a row of dresses, of various shapes and colours, suspended from wooden hangers.

'Give me your hand, Mr Nachman,' said the woman. They both helped her to sit upright. Szara could see no blood. The woman looked curiously at her hand, then wiggled the fingers. 'Are you hurt?' the carpenter said. 'No,' said the woman, her voice faint and giddy with astonishment. 'No. I don't think so. What happened?'

He heard the sound of a bell clanging. Leaving the carpenter with the woman, Szara went to the door. A fire engine had driven up to the burning building, and firemen were uncoiling a hose connected to a tank of water on the back. Szara wandered out of the shop and down the street. Two men hurried by, carrying an injured boy on a stretcher improvised from a quilt. Szara's heart sickened. What was the point of dropping bombs on this neighbourhood? To murder? Simply that? A man on a ladder was helping a young woman out of a window from which smoke drifted in a pale mist. She was weeping, hysterical. A crowd of neighbours, gathered at the foot of the ladder, tried to call out soothing words.

The next street was intact. So was the one after that. A man ran up to him and said, 'There are eight people dead at the railway station.' Szara said, 'It's terrible. Terrible.'

Then the man ran off to tell somebody else. Another fire engine drove past. The driver was a rabbi with a bloody handkerchief tied around his forehead; sitting next to him a small boy conscientiously rang a bell by pulling on a rope. Szara sank to the cobble stones. Looking down, he saw that his hand still clutched the valise. He had to use his free hand to pry the fingers open. People wandered by, dazed, in shock. Szara put the valise between his feet and held his head in his hands. *This is not human*, he thought, *to do this is not human*.

But there was something else in his mind, a ghost of a thought caught up among everything he felt. The city of Lvov had been bombed by a flight of Heinkel-111s. People had been killed, houses blown up, and there were fires that had to be put out and wounded who had to be treated.

But the city was still there. It had not been reduced to a mound of smoking ashes, not at all. He suddenly understood that a dark shape he'd seen half buried in a neighbouring alley was a bomb that had failed to explode. Others had fallen in the streets, between houses, in courtyards and parks, while some had destroyed rooftops but left the occupants of the building miraculously unharmed. Slowly, a realization worked its way into his consciousness. He could not believe it, at first, so he spoke the words out loud. 'My God,' he said. 'They were wrong.'

Poste Restante

In the dappled, aqueous dusk of the hydrotherapy room, the journalist Vainshtok cleaned his spectacles with a soiled handkerchief. He screwed up his eyes and wrinkled the bridge of his nose, producing the ferocious scowl of the intellectual momentarily separated from his glasses. '*Chornaya grayaz*,' he said with contempt, squinting through each lens in turn. 'That's all it was.' The slang phrase was peculiar to journalists – literally it meant grey mud – and described a form of propaganda intended to obscure an issue and cover up reality. '"The *pathetic* state of Poland's national minorities,"' Vainshtok quoted himself with a sneer. 'Boo-hoo.'

'Why?' Szara asked.

Vainshtok settled the spectacles back on his nose and thought a moment. 'Well, whatever the reason, they certainly did want it – they gave me the front page, and a fat byline.'

They were six miles from Lvov, at the Krynica-Zdroj, one of the more elegant spas in Poland, where the privileged had gathered to have their exhausted livers, their pernicious lumbago, and their chronic melancholia cured by immersions and spritzes, dousings and ingestions, of the smelly sulphurous waters that bubbled up from deep within the earth. And if simultaneously they chanced to do a little business, to find a husband or a wife, to consummate a love affair, well so much the better. Currently the spa's clientele was limited to a handful of Soviet journalists and a horde of foreign diplomats and their families who'd fled east from the fighting in Warsaw. 'As to why they wanted it, really why,' Vainshtok went on, 'that seems fairly obvious.' He inclined his head and gave one of his wild eyebrows a conspiratorial twitch.

Szara almost laughed. Vainshtok was one of those people who are forever impervious to their physical presence, but he looked, at that moment, extraordinarily strange. His skin shaded green by the rainy-day gloom of the basement pool, he wriggled in discomfort on the skeleton of a garden chair – the cushions had disappeared, along with the white-smocked attendants who'd laid them out every morning – and wore, the strap crushing a hand-painted tie, a shoulder holster with the grip of an automatic protruding from it. On the wall behind him, the foam green tile gave way to a Neptune riding a sea horse in ultramarine and ochre. 'It is certainly not the truth,' he said. 'Those starving Ukrainians and sorely persecuted Byelorussians groaning under the heel of Polish tyranny are, in fact, as we sit in this godforsaken grotto, attacking army units as they try to set up defensive positions in the marshland. What you have are the same old Ukrainian outlaw bands behaving in the same old ways, yet Moscow requires a sympathetic view. So, what do they want with it? You tell me.'

'They're preparing an action against the Poles.'

'What else?'

Szara stared into the pool. It was green and still. At either end stood imposing water machines, nickel-plated monsters with circular gauges and ceramic control knobs, their rubber hose-works strung limply from iron wheels. He imagined a long line of naked, bearded aristocrats awaiting treatment – there was something nineteenth century, and slightly sinister, about the apparatus, as though it were meant to frighten madmen back to sanity.

'Meanwhile,' Vainshtok said, 'the highly regarded André Szara goes off on a tour of the battlefields of southern Poland, misses his chance to write the big national minorities story, and in general causes great consternation.'

Szara grinned at Vainshtok's needling. 'Consternation, you say. Such a word. Why not *alarms and excursions*, as the English put it. In fact, with all this chaos, I doubt anybody even noticed.'

'They noticed.'

A certain tone in Vainshtok's voice caught Szara's attention. 'Did they?'

'Yes.'

Again the note, this time a monosyllable. Not at all typical of Vainshtok. Szara hesitated, then leaned forward, a man about to ask frank and difficult, possibly dangerous, questions.

'Oh, you know how they are,' Vainshtok said hurriedly. 'Just any little thing and they turn bright red and throw a few somersaults, like the king's ministers in a children's book.' He laughed a little.

'Someone here?'

The question was dismissed with a shrug and a frown. 'Three Jews meet in heaven, the first one says –'

'Vainshtok . . .'

'"The day I died, the whole city of Pinsk–"'

'Who asked?'

Vainshtok sighed and nodded to himself. 'Who. The usual who.'

Szara waited.

'I didn't ask him his name. He already knew mine, as he no doubt also knew the length of my *schvontz* and the midwife who took me from my mother. Who indeed! A Cossack in a topcoat. With the eyes of a dead carp. Look, André Aronovich, you're supposed to show up in Lvov. Then you don't. You think nobody's going to notice? So they come around looking for you. What am I supposed to say? Szara? He's my best pal, tells me *everything*, he just stopped off in Cracow to buy rolls, don't worry about him. I mean, it was almost funny – if it wasn't like it was it would be funny. Mind you, it was the same day the Germans finally broke into Lvov: buildings on fire, people weeping in the streets, tanks in the marketplace, that fucking swastika flying over the town hall, a few diehards sniping from the windows. And suddenly some, some *apparat* type appears from nowhere and all he wants to know is where's Szara. I almost said, "Pardon me, you're standing in my war," but I didn't, you know I didn't. I crawled on my belly until he went away. What do you want? Remorse? Tears? I don't really know anything about you, not really. So I told him nothing. It just took some time to get it said.'

Szara sat back in the garden chair. 'Don't worry about it,' he said. 'And I was in the city that day. I saw the same things you did.'

'Then you know,' Vainshtok said. He took off his glasses and looked at them, then put them back on. 'All I want is to stay alive. So I'm a coward, so now what.'

He could see that Vainshtok's hands were shaking. He took out a cigarette and silently offered it, then lit a match and held it while Vainshtok inhaled. 'Have the Germans been out here?' he asked.

Vainshtok blew smoke through his nose. 'Only a captain. The day after they took the city he came around. A couple of the ambassadors went out to meet him, they all put their heads together, then he came in and drank a cup of tea in the lobby. A diplomatic crisis was averted, as the old saying goes, and the SS never showed up. Myself, I didn't take any chances.' He patted the automatic affectionately. 'Somehow I get the feeling that in certain situations the Non-Aggression Pact doesn't quite cover somebody who looks like me. "Oops! Sorry. Was that a *Russian* Jew? Oh, too bad."'

'Where'd you get it?'

'You met Tomasz? The caretaker? Big white eyebrows, big belly, big smile – like a Polish Santa Claus?'

'When I arrived. He told me where you were.'

'Tomasz will get you, for a small fee, whatever you want.' Vainshtok took the pistol out of the holster and handed it to Szara. It was a blued-steel Steyr automatic, an Austrian weapon, compact and heavy in his hand.

'You get to play with it for three minutes,' Vainshtok said. 'But you have to give me five marbles and a piece of candy.'

Szara handed it back. 'Is there anything to eat in this place?'

Vainshtok looked at his watch. 'In an hour or so they serve boiled beets. Then, at dinnertime, they serve them again. On the other hand, the china is extremely beautiful, and they're actually very good beets.'

Szara slept on a wicker couch on the sunporch. The hotel was jammed with people and he was lucky to find anything at all to sleep on. At a right angle to the couch, a Spanish consular official had claimed the porch swing for a bed, while a Danish commercial attaché, one of the last to arrive from Warsaw, curled up on the floor next to a rack of croquet sets. The three of them had managed a conversation in French, talking in low voices after midnight, cigarettes glowing in the dark, in general trying to sort out rumours – the prime topic of conversation at the spa. Elements of the Polish army were said to have withdrawn to the Pripet marshes with the idea of holding out for six months while French and British expeditionary forces were organized to come to Poland's defence. A Norwegian diplomat was believed to have been interned. This was curious because Norway had declared neutrality, but perhaps the Germans intended the 'mistake' as a warning. Or perhaps it hadn't happened at all. The United

States, the Dane was certain, had declared neutrality. A special train would be organized to remove diplomats from Poland. But many diplomats from Warsaw, having taken refuge in the town of Krzemieniec, in western Poland, had been casualties of a heavy bombing attack by the Luftwaffe. The Polish government had fled to Romania. Warsaw had surrendered; Warsaw still held; Warsaw had been so obliterated by bombing that there was nothing left *to* surrender. The League of Nations would intervene. Szara faded away without realizing it; the quiet voices on the porch and a light patter of rain lulled him to sleep.

It was a particularly golden dawn that woke him. The distant forest was alive with light. How hard summer died here, he thought. It made him wonder what day it was. The seventeenth of September, he guessed, making what sense he could of the jumble of days and nights he'd wandered through. The lawns and gravelled paths sparkled with last night's raindrops as the sun came up and it was, but for a faint buzz of static somewhere in the hotel, immensely quiet. A rooster began to crow; perhaps a village lay on the other side of the forest. He looked at his watch – a few minutes after five. The Spaniard on the porch swing was lying on his back, coat spread over him like a blanket and pulled decorously up to his chin. Beneath a lavish moustache his mouth was slightly open, and his breath hissed in and out daintily as he slept. Szara caught, for just a moment, the barest hint of coffee in the air. Was it possible? Just wishful thinking. No, he did smell it. He wrestled free of the jacket tangled about him and sat upright – *oh, bones* – checking to make sure the valise was under the couch where he'd put it the night before. His beard itched. Today he would find some way to heat up a pot of water and have a shave.

Some campaigner he'd turned out to be. Not anymore. He was a creature of hotels now. Someone was making coffee – he was sure of it. He stood and stretched, then walked into the lobby. Anarchy. Bodies everywhere. A woman with two chins was snoring in a chair, a Vuitton suitcase tied securely to her finger with a shoelace. What did she have in there? he wondered. The silver service from some embassy? Polish hams? Wads of zlotys? Little good they'd do her now; the Germans no doubt had occupation scrip already printed and ready to spend. He moved toward the staircase and lost the scent, then backtracked into the dining room. Cautiously, he pushed open one of the swinging doors to the kitchen. Only a cat sleeping on a stove. The static was louder, however, and the coffee was close. At one end of the kitchen, another swinging door opened onto a small pantry and two women looked up quickly, startled at his sudden appearance. They were hotel maids, he guessed, pretty girls with tilted noses and cleft chins, one dark, the other fair, both wearing heavy cotton skirts and blouses, their hands red from scrubbing floors. A zinc coffeepot stood on a small parlour stove wedged into one corner, and an old-fashioned radio with a curved body sat on a shelf and played symphonic music amid the static. The maids were drinking coffee from the hotel's demi-tasse cups. After Szara said good morning he pleaded for coffee. 'Just tell me how much,' he said. 'I would be happy to pay.'

The blond girl coloured and looked down at her shoes. The dark one found him a tiny cup and filled it with coffee, adding a shapeless chunk of sugar from a paper sack. She offered him a piece of twig to use as a stirrer, explaining, 'They have locked up the spoons somewhere. And of course there is nothing to pay. We share with you.'

'You are kind,' he said. The coffee was sharp and hot and strong.

'There is only a little left,' the dark girl said. 'You won't tell, will you?'

'Never. It's our secret.' He drew an *X* over his heart with one finger and she smiled.

The symphonic music faded away, replaced by a voice speaking Russian: 'Good morning, this is the world news service of Radio Moscow.'

Szara looked at his watch. It was exactly five-thirty, that made it seven-thirty Moscow time. The announcer's voice was low and smooth and reasonable – one need not concern oneself too much with the news it broadcast; somewhere in the Kremlin all was being carefully seen to. There was a reference to a communiqué, to a meeting of the Central Committee, then the news that some forty divisions of the Red Army had entered Poland along a five-hundred-mile front. In general they had been welcomed, there was no fighting to speak of, little resistance was expected. Foreign Minister Molotov had announced that 'events rising from the Polish-German war have revealed the internal insolvency and obvious impotence of the Polish state.' There was great concern that some 'unexpected contingency' could 'create a menace to the Soviet Union.' Molotov had gone on to say that the Soviet government 'could not remain indifferent to the fate of its blood brothers, the Ukrainians and Byelorussians inhabiting Poland.' The announcer continued for some time; the phrasing was careful, precise. All had been thought out. War and instability in a neighbouring state posed certain dangers; the army was simply moving up to a point where the occupation of contested territory would insulate Soviet citizens from fighting and civil disorders. The announcer went on to give other foreign news, local news, and the temperature – forty-eight degrees – in Moscow.

Later that morning word came from Lvov that the Germans were preparing to leave the city. A great wave of excitement and relief swept over the population of the

Krynica-Zdroj, and it was determined that a column would be formed – Ukrainian bands continued their offensive; several travellers were known to have disappeared – to make the journey into town. A light but steady rain was deemed to be of no importance; the spa had an ample supply of black umbrellas and these were distributed by the smiling caretaker, Tomasz. The diplomatic corps made every effort to appear at its best – men shaved and powdered, women pinned up their hair, formal suits were dug out of trunks and suitcases. The procession was led by Tomasz, wearing an elegant little hat with an Alpine brush in the band, and the commercial counsellor of the Belgian embassy in Warsaw, carrying a broomstick with a white linen table napkin mounted at one end, a flag of neutrality.

It was a long line of men and women beneath bobbing black umbrellas that advanced down the sandy road to Lvov. The fields were bright green and the smell of black earth and mown hay was sharp and sweet in the rainy air. The spirit of the group was supremely optimistic. Prevailing views were concentrated on the possibility of a diplomatic resolution of the Polish crisis as well as on cigarettes, coffee, soap, perhaps even roast chicken or cream cake; whatever might be had in newly liberated Lvov.

Szara marched near the end of the column. The people around him were of various opinions about the Soviet advance, news of which had spread like wildfire. Most thought it good news: Stalin informing Hitler that, despite their expedient pact, enough was enough. It was felt that a period of intense diplomacy would now take place and, no matter the final result of the German invasion, they could go home. To Szara there was something infinitely Polish about the scene, these people in their dark and formal clothing marching along a narrow road in the rain beneath a forest of umbrellas. Towards the end of the six-mile walk, some of the diplomats were tiring, and it was determined that everybody should sing – 'The Marseillaise' as it turned out, the one song they all knew. True, it was the national anthem of a recently declared belligerent, but they were advancing under a white flag, and for raising the spirits on a rainy day there simply wasn't anything better. Vainshtok and Szara marched together; the former, his shoulder holster abandoned for the journey, thrust his clenched fist into the air and sang like a little fury in a high, wavering voice.

Szara didn't sing. He was too busy thinking. Trying to sort a series of images in his mind that might, if he found the organizing principle, come together to form a single, sharp picture. Beria's ascension, Abramov's murder, the suicide of Kuscinas, the Okhrana dossier, Baumann's arrest: it all ended with forty Russian divisions marching into Poland. *Stalin did this*, he thought. Stalin did what? Szara had no name for it. And that made him angry. Wasn't he smart enough to understand what had been done? *Maybe not*.

What he did know was that he had been part of it, witness to it, though mostly by accident. He didn't like coincidence, life had taught him to be suspicious of it, but he was able to recall moment after moment when he'd seen and heard, when he'd known – often from the periphery but known nonetheless – what was going on. *Why me, then?* he demanded of himself. The answer hurt: *because nobody took you very seriously. Because you were seen to be a kind of educated fool. Because you were useful in a minor but not very important way, you were permitted to see things and to find out about things in the same way a lady's maid is permitted to know about a love affair: whatever she may think about it doesn't matter*.

What he needed, Szara thought, was to talk it out. To say the words out loud. But the one person he could trust,

General Bloch, had disappeared from his life. Dead? In flight? He didn't know.

"'*Aux armes, citoyens!*'" Beside him, Vainshtok sang passionately to the cloudy Polish heavens.

No, Szara thought. *Let him be*.

In the city, people stood soberly in the square that faced the ruined station and watched in silence as the Wehrmacht marched west, back toward Germany. It was so quiet that the sound of boots and horses' hooves on the cobblestones, the creak of leather and the jangle of equipment, sounded unnaturally loud as the companies moved past. Some of the infantrymen glanced at the crowd as they went by, their faces showing little more than impersonal curiosity. The diplomats stood under their umbrellas alongside the Poles and watched the procession. To Szara they seemed a little lost. There was nobody to call on, nobody to whom a note could be handed; for the moment they had been deprived of their natural element.

The normal progress of the withdrawal was broken only by a single, strange interlude in the grey order of march: the Germans had stolen a circus. They were taking it away with them. Its wagons, decorated with curlicues and flourishes in brilliant gold on a dark red field, bore the legend Circus Goldenstein, and the reins were held by unsmiling Wehrmacht drivers, who looked slightly absurd managing the plumed and feathered horses. Szara wondered what had become of the clowns and the acrobats. They were nowhere to be seen, only the animals were in evidence. Behind the bars of a horse-drawn cage Szara saw a sleepy tiger, its chin sunk on its forepaws, its green-slit eyes half closed as it rolled past the crowd lining the street.

Toward evening, the diplomats walked back down the sandy road to the spa. Two days later, a Russian tank column rolled into the city.

* * *

Behind the tanks came the civil administration: the NKVD, the political commissars, and their clerks. The clerks had lists. They included the membership of all political parties, especially the socialists – Polish, Ukrainian, Byelorussian, and Jewish. The clerks also had the names of trade union members, civil servants, policemen, forestry workers, engineers, lawyers, university students, peasants with more than a few animals, refugees from other countries, landowners, teachers, commercial traders, and scores of other categories, particularly those, like stamp dealers and collectors, who habitually had correspondence with people outside the country. So the clerks knew who they wanted the day they arrived and immediately set to work to find the rest, seizing all civil, tax, educational, and commercial records. Individuals whose names appeared on the lists, and their families, were to be deported to the Soviet Union in trains, eventually to be put to work in forced labour battalions. Factories were to be disassembled and sent east to the industrial centres of the USSR, stores stripped of their inventories, farms of their livestock.

Special units of the NKVD Foreign Department arrived as well, some of them turning up at the spa, their black Pobedas spattered with mud up to the door handles. The diplomats were to be sorted out and sent on their way home as soon as the western half of Poland conceded victory to Germany. 'Be calm,' the operatives said. 'Warsaw will surrender any day now, the Poles can't hold out much longer.' The Russians were soft-spoken and reassuring. Most of the diplomats were relieved. A registration table was set up in the dining room with two polite men in civilian clothes sitting behind it.

Szara and Vainshtok waited until five o'clock before they joined the line. Vainshtok was philosophical. 'Back to dear old Berlin.' He sighed. 'And dear old Dr Goebbels's press conferences. How I've lived without them I don't know. But, at least, there'll be something for dinner besides beets.'

Vainshtok was skinny and hollow-chested, with thin, hairy arms and legs. He reminded Szara of a spider. 'Do you really care so much what you eat?' Szara asked. The line moved forward a pace. 'You certainly don't get fat.'

'Terror,' Vainshtok explained. 'That's what keeps me thin. I eat plenty, but I burn it up.'

The man in front of them, a minor Hungarian noble of some sort, stepped up to the table, stood at rigid attention, and, announcing his name and title, presented his diplomatic credentials. Szara got a good look at the two operatives at the table. One was young and alert and very efficient. He had a ledger open in front of him and copied out the information from documents and passports. The other seemed rather more an observer, in attendance only in case of some special circumstance beyond the expertise of his partner. The observer was a short, heavy man, middle-aged, with wavy fair hair and extremely thick glasses. As his junior questioned the Hungarian in diplomatic French – 'May I ask, sir, how you managed to find your way to this area?' – he put an oval cigarette in the centre of his lips, creased the head of a wooden match with his thumbnail, and lit the cigarette from the flare.

Where? Szara asked himself.

The Hungarian's French was primitive. 'Left Warsaw on late train. Night in eight September . . .'

Where?

The observer glanced at Szara, but seemed to take no special notice of him.

'Stopping in Lublin . . .' said the Hungarian.

'I don't feel well,' Szara said confidentially. 'You go ahead.' He turned and walked out of the dining room. Manoeuvred his way through the crowded lobby, excusing himself as he bumped into people, and took the passageway that led to the hydrotherapy pool and the treatment areas in the basement. The spiral staircase was made of thin metal, and his footsteps clattered and echoed in the stairwell as he descended. He took the first exit, walking quickly through a maze of long tile halls, trying doors as he went. At last one opened. This was a water room of some sort; the ceiling, floor, and walls were set with pale green tiles, hoses hung from brass fittings, and a canvas screen shielded a row of metal tables. The screen had a series of rubber-rimmed apertures in it – for arthritic ankles to be sprayed with sulphurous water? He hiked himself up onto a metal table, took a deep breath, tried to calm down.

Where, he now realized, was in some lost Belgian mining town the night that Odile was debriefed after she got off the train from Germany. The observer was the man with the gold watch; Szara remembered him lighting a cigarette off a match flare, remembered him asking a single question: 'Is that your answer?' Some such thing. Intimidation. A cold, watery stare.

And so? So he'd turned up at the Krynica-Zdroj, sitting behind a table with a ledger on it. So? That's probably what he did with his life. Szara resisted a shiver. The little room was clammy, its air much too still, a cavern buried in the earth. What was wrong with him, running away like a frightened child? Was that all it took to panic him, two operatives sitting at a table? Now he'd have to go back upstairs and join the line; they'd seen him leave, perhaps it would make them suspicious. *See how you incriminate yourself!* No, there was nothing to fear. What could they do, surrounded by a crowd of diplomats. He hopped off the table and left the room. Now, which hallway led where?

He wandered a little distance toward where he thought the exit was, stopped dead when he heard footsteps on the staircase. Who was this? A normal, deliberate descent. Then Vainshtok, nasal and querulous: 'André Aronovich? André Aronovich!'

Vainshtok, from the sound of it, was walking down the corridor at right angles to where he stood. 'I'm over here,' Szara said.

Coming around the corner, Vainshtok signalled with his eyes and a nod of the head that someone was behind him, but Szara could see no one. 'I've come to say good-bye,' he said, then reached out suddenly and took Szara in his arms, a powerful hug in the Russian style. Szara was startled, found himself pulled hard against Vainshtok's chest, then tried to return the embrace, but Vainshtok backed away. Two men turned the corner into the hallway, then waited politely for farewells to be said. 'So,' Vainshtok said, 'let those who can, do what they must, eh?' He winked. Szara felt the bulging weight between his side and the waistband of his trousers and understood everything. Vainshtok saw the expression on his face and raised his eyebrows like a comedian. 'You know, Szara, you're not such a snob after all. You'll come and see me when you get to Moscow?'

'Not Berlin?'

'Nah. Enough!'

'Lucky for you.'

'That's it.' His eyes glistened.

He turned abruptly and walked away. When he reached the end of the corridor, he turned towards the staircase, followed by one of the men. A moment later Szara heard them climbing the stairs. As the other man came to join him, Szara saw that it was Maltsaev, dark and balding, wearing tinted eyeglasses and the same voluminous overcoat wrapped about him, his hands thrust deep in the pockets. He nodded at Szara with evident satisfaction. 'The wandering troubadour – at last!' he said merrily.

Szara looked puzzled.

'You've given Moscow fits,' Maltsaev explained. 'One moment you're landing at Warsaw airfield, the next, nothing, air.'

'A detour,' Szara said. 'I was, how shall I put it, *escorted* by Polish military intelligence. They picked me up at a hospital in Tarnow, after a bombing on the rail line, and drove me to Nowy Sacz. Then we couldn't get through the German lines. Eventually, I managed to cling to the platform of a train that was going to Lvov. Once I got there, a policeman sent me out here to the spa, with the diplomats.'

Maltsaev nodded sympathetically. 'Well, everything's going to be fine now. I'm up here on some liaison assignment with the Ukrainian *apparat*, but they wired me in Belgrade to keep an eye out for the missing Szara. I'm afraid you'll have to go into the city and tell some idiot colonel the whole saga, but that shouldn't trouble you too much.'

'No, I don't mind,' he said.

'Your friend Vainshtok's going back to Moscow. Probably you won't have to. I would imagine you'd prefer to stay in Paris.'

'If I can, I'd like to, yes.'

'Lucky. Or favoured. Someday you'll tell me your secret.'

Szara laughed.

Maltsaev's mood changed, he lowered his voice. 'Look, you didn't mind, I hope, the last time we spoke, at the station in Geneva . . .'

Szara remembered perfectly, a remark about Abramov: *his parents should have made him study the violin like all the rest of them.* 'I understand completely,' he said. 'A difficult time.'

'We're none of us made of iron. What happened with Abramov, well, we only wanted to talk with him. We were certainly prepared to do more, but it would never have come to that if he hadn't tried to run. We couldn't, you understand these things, we couldn't let him disappear. As it was, I got a thorough roasting for the whole business. Any hope of getting out of the embassy in Belgrade – there it went. Anyhow, what I said at the station . . . I hadn't slept, and I knew I was in trouble, maybe a lot of trouble. But I shouldn't have taken it out on you.'

Szara held up a hand. 'Please. I don't hold a grudge.'

Maltsaev seemed relieved. 'Can we go back upstairs? Maybe get you a decent dinner in Lvov before you have to see the colonel? I'd rather not try the Polish roads in the dark if I don't have to. Driving through the Ukraine was bad enough, especially with Soviet armour on the roads.'

'Let's go.'

'It smells awful down here.' Maltsaev wrinkled his nose like a kid.

'Sulphur. Just like in hell.'

Maltsaev snorted with amusement. 'Is *that* how they cure you! Sinner, cease your drinking and depravity or here's how it will be.'

They walked together along the corridor toward the stairway. 'Your friends are waiting for us?' Szara asked.

'Fortunately, no. Those guys make me nervous.'

They came to the spiral staircase. 'Is there a subbasement?' Maltsaev asked, peering down.

'Yes. There's a pool in it, and the springs are there somewhere.'

'Just every little thing you'd want. Ah, the life of the idle rich.' He gestured for Szara to precede him up the steps.

'Please,' said Szara, standing back.

'I insist,' Maltsaev said, a parody of aristocratic courtesy.

They both hesitated. To Szara, a long moment. He waited for Maltsaev to climb the stairs but the man stood there, smiling politely; apparently he had all the time in the world. Szara took the gun out and shot him.

He expected a huge, ringing explosion in the confined space of the stairwell but it did not happen that way. The weapon snapped, something fizzed – it was as though he sensed the path of the bullet – and he could smell burned air.

Maltsaev was furious. 'Oh you didn't,' he said. He started to take one hand out of his pocket but Szara reached over and grasped him by the wrist. He was curiously weak; Szara held him easily. Maltsaev bit his lip and scowled with discomfort. Szara shot him again and he sat down abruptly, his weight falling back against an iron rung of the stairway. He died a few seconds later. By then he just looked melancholy.

Szara stared at the weapon. It was the blued-steel Steyr that Vainshtok had carried. Why had he given it up? Why had he not defended himself? Szara found the safety device, then put the automatic in the side pocket of his jacket. He listened hard, but there was no running, no commotion above him. The shots had not been heard. Perhaps the powder load in the bullet was minimal; he really didn't understand. He pulled Maltsaev's hand free of his pocket and went looking for the weapon he knew was there, but he didn't find it. Nor could he find it anywhere else. That meant Maltsaev's crew, perhaps the same one that had finished Abramov, was nearby. Maltsaev wasn't a murderer, Szara reminded himself, he was an arranger of murders. Szara found a car key in an inside pocket and a set of identity papers. Running his hands down the overcoat, he discovered a flap sewn into the sleeve that held a sword and shield NKVD pin in a soft pigskin bag with a drawstring. There was also a wallet packed with roubles, zlotys, and reichsmarks. Szara put everything in his own pockets. Next he grabbed Maltsaev's ankles and pulled. It was difficult, he had to use all his strength, but once he got the body moving, the smooth wool overcoat slid easily across the floor. It took at least two minutes to drag Maltsaev down the hall and into the unlocked room, and the trip left a long maroon streak on the tile. The lock on the door was simple enough, it worked on a lever. Szara thumbed it down and pulled the door closed until he heard it click.

At the foot of the iron stairway he paused, retrieved both ejected cartridges, then climbed, shoes in one hand, gun in the other; but there was no one waiting for him on the landing and he dropped the weapon into his pocket and hopped on one foot to put his shoes back on. The lobby was as he'd left it; people milling about, affable confusion, a line working its way up to the table. 'Well,' said the Spanish official who'd shared the sunporch with him, 'your friend has finally made it out of here. It's given us all hope.'

'He's known to be clever – and lucky,' Szara said, clearly a bit envious.

The Spaniard sighed. 'I'll be going back to Warsaw eventually. As you know, Germany is exceptionally sympathetic to our neutrality. Perhaps it won't be too long.'

'I hope not,' Szara said. 'Such disorder helps nothing.'

'How true.'

'Perhaps we'll dine together this evening.'

The Spaniard inclined his head, an informal bow of acceptance.

Szara used a wall mirror to assure himself that the observer was still at the table, then avoided his line of vision by taking a back door, walking behind the kitchen area where the two young Polish women were preparing beets over a wooden tub, saving every last peeling in a metal pan. They both smiled at him as he went past, even the shy one. He entered the sunporch by a side door and looked out through the screen. There were two black Pobedas parked in the gravel semicircle. One was coated with road dust and grime, the other spattered with mud and clay. Recalling what Maltsaev had said about Soviet armour on the roads, he decided to try the latter. He picked up his valise, took a deep breath, and walked off the sunporch onto the lawn. He nodded to a few diplomats strolling along the paths, then slid into the front seat of the muddy Pobeda as though it were the most natural thing in the world for him to do.

The car's interior smelled strongly: of pomade, sweat, cigarettes, vodka, mildewed upholstery, and petrol. He put Maltsaev's key into the ignition and turned it, the starter motor whined, died, whined on a higher note, produced a single firing of the engine, sank to a whisper, suddenly fired twice, and at last brought the engine to sputtering life. He wrestled with the gear-lever – mounted on the steering column – until it went into one of the gears. Through the streaked panel window on his left he could see the diplomats staring at him: who was he to simply climb into a car, valise in hand, and drive away? One of them started to walk toward him. Szara lifted the clutch pedal – the car lurched forward a foot and stalled. The diplomat, a handsome, dignified man with grey wings of hair that rested on his ears, had raised an interrogatory index finger – *oh, just a moment*. Szara turned the ignition key again and the starter motor whined up and down the musical scale as it had before. When the engine at last fired he blinked the sweat out of his eyes. '*Un moment, s'il vous plaît*,' the diplomat called out, only a few feet away. Szara gave him a tight smile and a shrug. The gears meshed and the car rolled forward, crunching over the gravel. Szara looked in the rearview mirror. The diplomat was standing with hands on hips, the caricature of a man offended by simply unspeakable rudeness.

* * *

There wasn't a road sign left in Poland – Vyborg's colleagues had seen to that – only a maze of dirt tracks that ran off every which way. But he had walked the route to Lvov and that was the one direction he knew he had to avoid. Maltsaev's assistants could well be waiting for him there, by the side of the road, just conveniently out of sight of the diplomatic corps at the spa.

There was a much-used map of eastern Poland on the floor of the car, and the sun, at six-twenty on an afternoon in late September, was low in the sky. That was west. Szara kept the sun on his left side and headed north, managing some ten miles before dusk overtook him. Then he backed off what he believed to be a main road onto a smaller road and turned off the engine. Next he took a careful inventory: he had plenty of money, no water, no food, the best part of a tank of petrol, six rounds in the Steyr. It was, he now saw, an M12, thus a Steyr-Hahn – Steyr-with-hammer – stamped o8 on the left-hand surface of the slide, which had something to do with the absorption of the Austrian army into the German army after 1938, a mechanical retooling. Exactly what this was he could not remember; a rue Delesseux circular unread, who cared about guns? He also had three sets of identity papers: his own, Maltsaev's, and the Jean Bonotte passport in the false bottom of the valise, bound with a rubber band to a packet of French francs and a card with telephone numbers written on it. In the trunk of the Pobeda was a full can of petrol and a blanket.

Enough to start a new life. Many had started with less.

'The wind and the stars.' Whose line was that? He didn't remember. But it perfectly described the night. He sat on the blanket at the foot of an ancient linden tree – the road was lined with them, creating an avenue that no doubt wound its way to some grand Polish estate up the road.

The night grew chilly, but if he pulled his jacket tight he stayed warm enough.

He had thought he'd sleep in the car, but the smell of it sickened him. Not that he wasn't used to what he took to be its various elements. Nothing new about vodka or cigarettes, his own sweat was no better than anyone else's, and all Russian cars reeked of petrol and damp upholstery. Something else. To do with what they'd used the Pobeda for, perhaps a lingering scent of the taken, the captured. Or maybe it was the smell of executioners. Russian folklore had it that murder left its trace: the vertical line at the side of the mouth, the mark of the killer. Might it not change the way a man smelled?

A former Szara would have turned such light on himself, but not now. He had done what he had to do. 'Let those who can, do what they must.' Thus Vainshtok had saved his life. Because he would not, or could not, use the weapon himself? No, that was absurd. Szara refused to believe it. There was some other reason, and he had to face the possibility that he might never find out what it was.

There was a great deal he didn't understand. Why, for instance, had they sent Maltsaev after him? Because he'd disappeared from view for several days? Had they found out what he'd done in Paris with the British? No, that was impossible. Of all the world's secret services it was the British the Soviets truly feared. Their counterintelligence array – Scotland Yard, MI5 – was extremely efficient; Comintern agents trying to enter Great Britain under false identities were time and again discovered, for the British maintained and used their files to great effect. As for MI6, it was, in its way, a particularly cold-blooded and predatory organization. A consequence of the British national character, with its appetite for both education and adventure, a nasty combination when manifested in an intelligence service. Szara could not imagine the problem lay in that direction. Fitzware, for all his peculiarities of style, was a serious, a scrupulous officer. The courier, then, Evans. No. It was something else, something in Russia, something to do with Abramov, Bloch, the Jewish *khvost*. Perhaps Beria or his friends just decided one morning that he'd lived long enough. But André Szara had made his own decision, at some point, that he would not be one of those who went meekly into captivity, carving *za chto* into the stone of a cellar wall. Now a single act, the pulling of a trigger, had freed him. Now – a Jew, a Pole, a Russian – he had no country at all.

'The wind and the stars.' Strange how he couldn't stop thinking it. He wondered how long he might live. Probably only a little while longer. Just after dark a car had rumbled down the road he'd left. Then, an hour later, another. Was it them? They would certainly be looking for him. And they'd never stop until they found him; that was the rule of the game and everybody understood it. Ah but if this were to be his last night on earth how he would treasure it. A little breeze blowing steady across the Polish farmland, the grand sky – that immense and perfect and glittering mystery. There were frogs croaking in the darkness, life all around him. He didn't have much of a plan, only to try and get across the Lithuanian border to the north. After that he'd see. Possibly Sweden, or Denmark. So far he'd stolen seven hours of existence; every hour was a victory, and he had no intention of going to sleep.

Szara was later to put it this way:

'If ever the hand of God guided my path it was when, from the twentieth to the twenty-third of September, 1939, I drove from southern Poland to Kovno, Lithuania, in a stolen NKVD car. Clearly there was a tragedy taking place in Poland; I saw the signs of it, I walked in its tracks, and I fear that it may have contributed to my escape, for it absorbed the energies of all Soviet security forces. Finally I do not know for certain, and I can only say that I survived. This was, equally, an accident of geography. Had I been thirty miles to the west, NKVD officers or political commissars serving on the front line surely would have arrested me. I believe they knew who I was, what I had done, and had a description of the car I was driving. In the same way, had I been thirty miles to the east, I would have been arrested by the NKVD of the Soviet Ukraine or murdered by the Ukrainian bands, who were then very active. But I was in the middle, in an area behind the lines but not yet secured by the *apparat*. Those who may have experience of a zone in which Soviet troops are manoeuvring, not fighting, will know what I mean. I moved among lost units hampered by poor communications, amidst confusion and error and inefficiency, and it was as though I were invisible.'

Well yes, true as far as it went, but not the whole story by any means. He was able, for instance, to choose an identity suitable to the moment. Confronted by a Soviet patrol at dawn on the twenty-second, he produced Maltsaev's NKVD badge, and the officer waved him ahead and cursed his troopers when they didn't get out of the road quickly enough. But in a *shtetl* village in the middle of nowhere, he became Szara the Polish Jew, was given a bench in the study house to sleep on, and fed by the rabbi's wife. Meanwhile, the remarkable fact of the Pobeda was ignored by the villagers. He drove it into a muddy, unfenced yard full of chickens and there it sat, safe and invisible from the road, while he slept. Later, when it suited his purpose, he presented himself as André Szara, Soviet journalist, and, later still, Jean Bonotte of Marseille, a French citizen.

It took him some twenty hours to negotiate almost three hundred miles to a point just short of the border with Lithuania. The first night, moved by some obscure but very powerful instinct – 'the hand of God'? – he drove away from his refuge at midnight and continued on the same road, north he hoped, for some six hours. He feared he would be unable to cross the many rivers that lay across his path but, as it turned out, the Poles had not blown the bridges. So the Pobeda rattled over the loose boards of the narrow structures spanning first the Berezina, then the Belaja. Just beyond the former he came to a cobbled road, heading east and west, flanked by birch trees. He knew, just for that moment, precisely where he was, for those cobblestones had been laid by the Emperor Napoleon's Corsicans in 1812, a solid foundation for wheeled guns and ammunition carts, and it led off in the direction of Moscow. Szara drove across it, heading due north.

Somewhere near Chelm, just before dawn, his path was blocked by a train of cattle trucks standing idle at a crossing. Uniformed NKVD soldiers were guarding the train, and in the darkness he could just make out the barrel of a machine gun, mounted on top of a goods wagon, as it swung to cover the Pobeda. One of the sentries unslung his rifle and walked over to ask him who he was and what he was doing there. Szara was about to reach for the badge, then didn't. Something told him to leave it where it was. Just a Pole, he said. His wife had gone into labour and he was off to fetch the midwife. The soldier stared. Szara could hear voices inside the cattle trucks, speaking Polish, pleading for water. Without further conversation, Szara put the car in reverse and backed up, his heart pounding, while the soldier watched him but did nothing – a potential problem was simply removing itself. When he was out of sight of the train, he rested his head on the steering wheel for a time, then turned the car around, backtracked a few miles, picked a road at random, and, an hour later, after several turnings, drove over the tracks at a deserted crossing.

Passing a farm early in the morning, he heard the drawn-out lowing of unmilked cattle and the frantic barking of deserted dogs left at the end of their chains. At another level crossing there was a wooden cattlegate blocking the road and when he got out to open it he saw something yellow on the ground and bent down to see what it was: it turned out to be a scrap of paper bound to a small stone with yellow wool, perhaps unravelled from a shawl. Unwinding the wool, he found a note: *Please tell Franciszka Kodowicz that Krysia and Wladzia have been taken away in a train. Thank you.* The wind blew at the piece of paper in his hand. He stood by the car for a long time, then carefully wrapped the paper around the stone and rebound it with the yellow wool, placing it back on the ground where it had landed when the girls had thrown it from the moving train. He was, he noted dispassionately, now beyond vows or resolutions. He slid into the front seat of the car, holding his breath as the musky scent of pomade and sweat assaulted him, forced the gear lever down, and drove north. That was his resolution, that was his vow: to exist.

On the third night, having swung west to avoid the market town of Grodno, he saw from the map that he'd entered the country of the Pripet marshes. He suspected the Russian line of advance had not yet reached the area, its northern flank held up for some reason, for he could find no evidence of an occupying force. He stopped the car and waited for morning, telling himself to remain awake and alert. He woke, again and again, when his chin hit his chest, finally fading away altogether into the blank sleep of exhaustion. The next time he came to it was daybreak, and he saw that he was surrounded by marshland that ran to the low horizon, a plain of swaying reeds and long reaches of flat water coloured by a grey, wind-swept sky. The land was ancient, desolate, its vast silence punctuated by the distant cries of waterfowl.

He walked around for a time, trying to get his bearings, washing his face and hands in the chill, dark water of the marsh. He searched the sky but there was no sun – he had no idea where he was, or which way was north. And he didn't care. That was the worst part, he truly did not care. His resolve had flowed away like sand on the outgoing tide. He sat on the running board of the Pobeda, slumped against the door, and stared out over the grey ponds and blowing reeds. He had somehow come to the end of his journey, the future he'd held out to himself no more than a trick of the illusionist, the self-deluded survivor. Against the vast background of the deserted land he saw his insignificance only too clearly – a vain, petty man, envious and scheming, an opportunist, a fraud. Why should such a man remain alive? *Get in the car*, he told himself. But the wilful interior voice sickened him – all it knew was greed, all it did was want. Even here, at the end of the world, it sang its little song, and any gesture, no matter how absurd, would satisfy it. But the only act he could imagine called for removing the Steyr from beneath the driver's seat of the car and relieving the earth of an unneeded presence – at least an act of grace. Did he have the courage to do it? Surprisingly, he did. What had he done with his life – other than seek a transient peace between the legs of women. He had, in order to live another day, and then another, served the people who now did what they did and who would, he knew for a certainty, do what they would do. And to put a good finish on the history of his particular life, the time and place were perfect: *ironically, he was only a few miles from the safety of the Lithuanian border*. He looked at his watch, it was sixteen minutes after nine. The sky shifted across his vision, a hundred shades of grey, drifting and rolling like battlesmoke blown by a wind off the sea.

* * *

What saved him – for he was very, very close to it – was a vision. Of this he was not to write; it was not germane, and there may have been other reasons. Well down the long, straight road ahead of him appeared the silhouette of a hunter; a man stepped out of the reeds, a shotgun, the barrel broken safely from the stock, riding his forearm. A spaniel followed, stood at the side of the hunter and shook a fine spray of marshwater from its coat. Then the man walked across the road, the dog trotting ahead, and both vanished.

Then, almost the next thing he knew, he was driving. Through a great labyrinth of roads and paths that could have led anywhere or nowhere. Sometimes, with tears in his eyes, he drove into a blur, but never lifted his foot from the accelerator. He drove, fiercely, angrily, toward the wind. Took any road on which the churning skies hurried toward him, their speed heightened by the rush of the car in the opposite direction. He passed, and barely noticed, an empty guard tower, barbed wire strung away in both directions, a wire gate hanging crazily on one hinge as though brushed aside by a giant. At last he saw an old man by the side of the road, poking listlessly at a garden patch with a primitive hoe. Szara stamped on the brake. 'Where in God's name am I?' he called out.

'*Vas?*' said the man.

Szara tried again and got the same answer. They stared at each other, deadlocked, Szara angry, the old man more confused than frightened and saying finally, with politely controlled irritation, 'What is the matter with you, sir, that you shout so?' The man was speaking German, Szara finally realized, the common second language in that country. He let out a single cry of absurd laughter, slammed the car into gear, and roared on into Lithuania.

* * *

He arrived in Kovno a fugitive. And stayed to become a refugee.

Two cities anchored the northern and southern extremes of the Pale of Settlement, Kovno and Odessa. Szara, who had grown up in the latter, soon came to understand the former. These were border cities, Odessa on the Black Sea across from Istanbul, Kovno at the conjunction of Russia, Poland, and Lithuania, and border cities lived by a particular set of instincts: they knew, for instance, when war was coming, because when there was war they were not spared. They knew the people who showed up before the wars. Immigrants, refugees, whatever you called them, they had a way of arriving just ahead of the armies and were taken to be an omen of difficult times, as migrating birds portend winter.

But Kovno's long and complicated history had marked its citizens with the very characteristics that enabled them to survive it. Actually, by the time Szara arrived in the city known in his childhood as Kovno, it was called by the Lithuanian name Kaunas. Its nearby neighbour, however, remained Wilno, since it had been declared Polish territory, rather than Vilna, the Russian name before 1917. The Lithuanians themselves preferred Vilnius, but at that particular moment this alternative was running a poor third.

The people of Kovno, now Kaunas, were obviously multilingual. Szara had spoken German, Polish, and Yiddish in the city before he ever slept there. They were also virtually immune to politics, not strange for a city that has known Teutonic Knights and Bolshevik lawyers and everything in between. And they were, in their own quiet way, deeply obstinate. In all things but particularly in matters of nationality. The Lithuanians knew they were home, the Poles knew what they stood on was Polish soil no matter what anybody said, the Jews had been there for hundreds of years, faring about as well as they did anywhere, while the better part of the German population looked west, with longing hearts and the occasional song, to the Fatherland.

Nonetheless, obstinate though the citizens of Kovno might have been, it seemed, in the autumn of 1939, that quite a considerable number of them were intent on being somewhere else.

Szara rented a third of a room in a boardinghouse, actually a boarding apartment, at the top of seven flights of stairs, sharing with two Polish Jews, cameramen in the Polish film industry who'd fled Warsaw by riding cross country on a motorcycle. One of the men worked nights as a sweeper at the railway station, and Szara had his bed until he arrived home at six-thirty in the morning. That got Szara up early. After breakfast he haunted the steamship offices, willing to leave from any of the Baltic ports – Liepāja, Riga, Tallinn – but there were simply too many people with the same idea. Ships and ferries to Denmark – his first choice – in fact to anywhere on earth, were booked well into 1940. Cabins, deck space, every available inch. Undaunted, he took a train up to Liepāja and tried to bribe his way onto a Norwegian timber freighter, but only a precipitate exit from a waterfront café saved him from arrest. And the incident was witnessed – there were two vaguely familiar faces at the same café, seen perhaps at the steamship offices. No matter where he went or what he tried it was the same story.

Even at the thieves' market, where the Pobeda caused low whistles of appreciation but very little financial interest. Sublime realists, Kovno's thieves – where could one drive? South was occupied Poland, north the Baltic, east the USSR. To the west, the port of Memel had been snaffled up by the Reich in March, Königsberg was German, now Danzig as well. Szara took what was offered for the Pobeda and fled. Trust the NKVD, he thought, to have eyes and ears at the Kovno thieves' market.

Attempts at currency conversion got him precisely nowhere. He couldn't sell his zlotys; German marks were being introduced in Poland and nobody was going there anyhow. The roubles weren't even supposed to be outside the USSR – those he burned. The French francs, by far the greatest part of his little treasury, would have moved very briskly on the kerbside foreign exchange markets, but he refused to part with them; they could be used anywhere and everybody else wanted them for the same reason he did.

The first few days in Kovno Szara was extremely cautious; he knew the Soviet intelligence *apparat* in Lithuania to be well established and aggressive. But, in time, he abandoned the principles of clandestine practice and became one more nameless soul whose principal occupation was waiting. He sat in the parks and watched the chess games with all the other refugees as the leaves turned gold in the slow onset of autumn. He frequented the cheapest cafés, dawdled endlessly over coffees, and soon people began to nod good morning: he was part of their day, always at the table in the corner.

He made one friend, an unlikely one, a gentleman known as Mr Wiggins, who was to be found at the Thomas Cook steamship and travel office. Mr Wiggins came from the pages of Kipling; he had a waxed moustache, parted his hair in the middle, and wore an old-fashioned collar, formal, uncomfortable, and reassuring. He was, in his way, a terribly decent man who served the Thomas Cook company with conviction and chose to see, in the refugee flood that swept through his office from dawn to dusk, not the flotsam of Europe but a stream of clients. Szara seemed to be one of his favourites. 'I am so sorry,' he'd say, very real regret in his voice. 'No cancellations today. But you will try tomorrow, I hope. One can't ever tell. People do change their minds, that's one thing I have learned in this business.'

Mr Wiggins, and everyone else, knew that war was coming to Lithuania – or, if not war, at least occupation. The country had been freed of Russian rule in 1918 – of Lenin's dictum 'Two steps forward and one step back,' this had been a step back – and had got rather to enjoy being a free nation. But its days were numbered and nothing could be done about it. Szara, as always encountering familiar faces, bought the local and foreign newspapers early in the morning and took them back to his lair, in the common kitchen of the apartment, for intensive study, sharing the bad news with his fellow boarders as they drank thin, warmed-up coffee and tried not to say anything compromising.

The future became clearer as the days passed: a great shifting of population was to take place in Estonia and Latvia and simultaneously in Germany. Slavs east, Germans west, it was just about that simple. The Germans, more than a hundred thousand of them, were to be taken aboard Baltic passenger steamers and shipped back to Germany, whence their great-great-grandfathers had migrated hundreds of years earlier. Meanwhile, various Slavic nationalities resident in Germany were headed east to join their long-lost brothers in the Soviet Union. This shuffling of populations was intended to reestablish the racial purity of Germany and to relieve the pressure on German settlers in Eastern Europe. They suffered horribly, according to Goebbels, because they retained their language and customs and dress in the midst of alien cultures and nobody liked them, being principally envious of their success. *One could call them blond Jews*, Szara thought.

But the fact of the migration hung over the breakfast table like a pall: if the Germans were leaving the Baltic states, who was coming?

There was only one candidate nation, and it wasn't France. To Szara, schooled in a certain way of thinking since 1937, it had even a deeper resonance: if the division of Poland was one of the secret protocols in the Hitler-Stalin pact, what were the others? 'Terribly sorry,' said Mr Wiggins. 'There simply isn't a thing.'

Like all refugees, Szara had too much time to think. He sat on a park bench and smoked a cigarette while the leaves drifted down. He had supposed, in escaping from Poland, that either death or glory awaited him, and so he'd taken his chances. With Maltsaev murdered he really had nothing to lose. But he had never for a moment imagined it might end up as a penurious life spent in dim cafés and shabby apartments, waiting for the Red Army to reach the gates of the city. He thought of trying to put a call through to de Montfried, to ask for help, but what kind of help could he offer? Money? More money that wouldn't buy what Szara needed? Some of the prosperous Jews in Kovno were spending literally fortunes to buy their way out before the Russians arrived, and there were stories going around that some of them wound up losing everything, forbidden to board steamers by cold-eyed pursers with armed seamen at their side. Other rumours – and Szara knew at least one of them to be true – told of desperate refugees putting to sea in rowboats, sometimes guided by self-proclaimed smugglers, never to be seen again. Drowned? Murdered? Who knew. But the confirming postal card never arrived in Kovno and friends and accomplices could draw only one conclusion from that.

In the end, Szara realized that the trap opened in only one direction and he determined to try it.

'From Hamburg? Copenhagen from Hamburg, you say?' Mr Wiggins, for just an instant, permitted himself to be startled. Then he cleared his throat, once again the traveller's perfect servant. 'No trouble at all, I'd think. Plenty of room. First-class cabin, if you like. Shall I book?'

* * *

It should have worked.

There were, of course, improvisations, as there had to be, but he managed those well enough and, in the end, it wasn't his fault that it didn't work. Fortunes of war, one might say.

He began with the hospitals. Wiggins helped him – the wealthy members of the German community went here, those of lesser means went there. Szara went there. A sad, brown brick structure, according to the name a Lutheran institution, in an innocuous neighbourhood away from the centre of the city. In a day or two of watching he'd determined how the hospital worked. In need of coffee or something stronger, the doctors, in accordance with their standing, patronized the Vienna, a dignified restaurant and pastry shop. The orderlies, janitors, clerks, and the occasional nurse used a nearby rathskeller for the same purposes. Szara chose the rathskeller. The hospital's day shift ended at four in the afternoon, so the productive time at the rathskeller ran for an hour or two after that. He spent three days there during the busy hours, just watching, and he spotted the loners. On day four he picked his man: sulky, homely, no longer young, with large ears and slicked-back hair, always one of the last to leave, not in a hurry to go home to a family. Szara bought him a beer and struck up a conversation. The man was a native Lithuanian, but he could speak German. Szara found out quickly why he drank alone: there was something a little evil about this man, something he covered up by use of a sneering, suggestive tone that implied there was something a little evil about everybody. Asked just what it was that *he* did, Szara admitted he was a dealer in paper. He bought and sold paper, he said, adding a sly glance to show the man what a smart fellow he thought he was.

The orderly, as he turned out to be, understood immediately. He knew about such matters. He even winked. This one, Szara guessed, had seen the inside of a jail, perhaps for a long time, perhaps for something very unpleasant.

And what kind of paper was the gentleman buying these days?

German paper.

Why?

Who could say. A client wanted German paper. Not from Germany, mind you, and not from Lithuania. Paper from Poland or Hungary would do. Yugoslavia was even better.

The orderly knew just the man. Old Kringen.

Szara ordered another round, the best they had, and a discussion of money ensued. A bit of bargaining. Szara pretended to be shocked, leaned on the price, didn't gain an inch, looked grumpy, and gave in. Would old Kringen, he wanted to know, get much older?

No. He was finished, but he was taking his time about it, didn't seem to be in much of a hurry.

Szara could understand, but his client couldn't afford any, ah, embarrassment.

The orderly snickered, a horrible sound. Old Kringen wasn't going anywhere. And lying where he was he didn't need his passport, which was kept in the hospital records office. The orderly had a friend, however, and the friend would see him right. It was going to cost a little more, though.

Szara gave in on the price a second time.

And a third, visiting the rathskeller two days later. But he had what he needed. Old Kringen was a Siebenbürger, from the Siebenbürgen – Seven Hills – district of Romania, an area long colonized by German settlers. Szara had no idea why he'd come to Kovno, perhaps to take advantage of the emigration offer in neighbouring Latvia, perhaps for other reasons. He was much older than Szara, from his photo a grumpy, hard-headed fellow, his occupation listed as swine breeder. Szara bought what he needed and, in search of privacy, found a hotel room in the tenement district that could be rented by the hour. He eradicated the birth date with lemon juice, wrote in an appropriate year for himself, smeared the page with fine dust to coat the damage to the paper, and changed the photograph, signing something illegible across the corner. Then he held it up to the light.

The new Kringen.

He had disposed of the Maltsaev papers while still in Poland; now it was the turn of the Szara papers. The walls of the tiny room were thin, and various groans and shouts to either side of him indicated that Friday night was in Kovno much as it was everywhere else. There was a woman – he imagined her as an immensely fat woman – with an enormous laugh on the other side of the wall. Something went thud and she shrieked with mirth, making whooping noises and pausing, he guessed, only to wipe her eyes. To such accompaniment, André Szara died. He sat on a straw mattress with a soiled sheet spread over it, his only light a candle, and scratched at whatever was biting his ankle. He'd borrowed a coffee cup from his afternoon café and used it as a fireplace, ripping a page at a time from his passport, setting the corner aflame, and watching the entry and exit stamps disappear as the paper curled and blackened. The red cover resisted – he had to tear it into strips and light match after match – but finally it too was dropped, its flame blue and yellow, into the cup of ashes. Farewell. He wondered at such soreness of heart, but there was no denying what he felt. It was as though André Szara, his raincoat and smile and a clever thing to say, had ceased to exist. *Troublesome bastard just the same*, Szara thought, stirred the ashes with his finger and poured them out the window into a courtyard full of cats.

A small canal ran through that part of Kovno. The NKVD badge sank like a stone. So did the Steyr.

The dock in Riga was packed with Germans – their baggage, their clocks, their dogs, and a band to play while it all marched up the gangplank. German newsreel cameramen were much in evidence, Szara kept his face averted. By a curious tribal magic he could not divine, the crowds had organized themselves into castes – the prominent and the wealthy in front, pipe-smoking farmers next, and workmen and other assorted types to the rear. Everybody seemed content with the arrangement.

His papers had received only the most cursory check – who in God's name would want to sneak under the tent of this circus? In fact, though it did not occur to Szara, the NKVD took full advantage of the Baltic migration to infiltrate agents into Germany: such returns to the homeland had always suggested interesting possibilities to intelligence services.

Szara was fully prepared for exposure. Any determined Gestapo officer would spot the crudely altered passport, and five minutes of interrogation was all it would require for the certain knowledge that he was an imposter. He planned to admit it, long before they ever went to work on him. The Jean Bonotte passport was sewn into his jacket, the French francs hidden in the false bottom of the valise, just where a type like Bonotte, a man from Marseille, no doubt a Corsican, no doubt a criminal type, would hide them. Germany and France were legally at war, though it had not yet come to any serious fighting. Mostly talk. German diplomacy was continuing, an attempt to smooth things over with the British and the French – why should the world be set on fire over a bunch of Poles? Szara expected he would, if discovered, be interned as a citizen of France. At worst a war spent in excruciating boredom in a camp somewhere, at best exchanged for a German citizen who happened to be on the wrong side of the line when the first cannon was fired. On the bright side, a German internment camp was probably the last place in the world the NKVD would think to look for André Szara.

Still, he did not wish to be caught. He was no German, not even a Romanian swine-breeding German from the Seven Hills, and he did not wish to be beaten up by this crowd. There was a deep and patient anger in them. For the newsreel cameras they were glad to be 'going home,' but among themselves they promised that they would soon enough be 'going back.' At which time, evidently, certain scores would be definitively settled. And worst of all, he knew, if they had cause to single him out and concentrate on his features, they were not above having a look to see if he were a Jew. No, he did not wish to be caught, and he had determined to avoid direct contact in every possible way.

To this end he played the part of a man ruined by sorrow, a victim of anti-German hostility. Practised saying a single sentence in the sort of *Volksdeutsch* accent common to a man like Kringen: 'They took . . . everything.' He had to use it almost immediately. A burly fellow, standing next to him on the dock, wanted to strike up a conversation and offered a greeting. Szara stared at him, as though he were intruding on a world of private anguish, and delivered his line. It worked. As Szara watched, the man's expression went from surprise to pained sympathy, then tightened with anger. Szara bit his lip; he could not say any more without losing control. He turned his face away, and the man laid a great paw of a hand on his shoulder, the honest human warmth of the gesture very nearly shaming him into real tears.

A bright day. A calm sea.

Life aboard the passenger steamer was tightly organized. There were numerous officials in attendance but they seemed to Szara benign, meant to ease the transition of the emigrants into German life. He was processed – a matter of saying yes and no – given a temporary identity card, and told to report to the proper authorities wherever he settled and permanent residence documents would be provided at that time. Had he any notion of where he wished to live? Family in Germany? Friends? Szara hid behind his catastrophe. 'Don't worry, old fellow, you're in good hands now,' said one official.

The public address system was constantly at work: a schnauzer discovered in the crew quarters, an uplifting message of welcome from Dr Goebbels, the Winterhilfe charity was stationed at a table on the afterdeck, those with last names beginning A to M should report to the dining room for mid-day dinner promptly at one P.M., N to Z at two-thirty. To promote the appetite, a songfest would begin in fifteen minutes on the foredeck, led by the well-known contralto Irmtrud Von something from the Munich State Opera Company and the well-known countertenor SS Untersturmführer Gerhard something else of the Bavarian Soldiers' Chorus, two inspirational artists who had volunteered to accompany the voyage and join their fellow *Volk* in singing some of the grand old songs.

For one ghastly moment Szara thought he might have to sing, but saw to his relief that a sufficient number of people remained at the perimeter so that he could safely avoid it. He stood for the rousing performance of 'Deutschland über Alles' that began the programme, watched the breasts of the contralto swell mightily with patriotism, then moved to the railing and became part of the small audience.

Almost all the passengers took part, and they were deeply affected by the singing; there were unashamed tears on the cheeks of both the men and the women and a kind of joyous agony on their faces as they raised their voices together. The mass rendition of 'Silent Night' – Christmas carols were familiar to all – was extraordinary, sung with great and tender feeling as the ship rumbled through the flat Baltic waters.

Szara maintained his cover, nodding in time and seeming to mumble the old words to himself, but his internal reaction to the performance was something very nearly approaching terror. It was the instinctive and passionate unity of the singers that frightened him; the sheer depth of it was overwhelming. You couldn't, he thought, find three Jews in the world who would agree on what it meant to be Jewish, yet there were apparently fifty million of these people who knew exactly what it meant to be German, though many of those on deck had never set foot in Germany.

Something was wrong, what was it? Obviously they suffered injustice without end – that certain look was plain on their faces. They swayed and sang, seemingly hypnotized, held hands – many wept – and together formed a wall of common emotion, a wall of nostalgia, regret, self-pity, sentimentality, resentment, hatred, ferocity. The words bounced around inside him, none of them right, none of them wrong, none of them mattered. What he did know for certain at that moment was that they were poisoned with themselves. And it was the rest of the world that would suffer for it.

He avoided lunch, knowing it would be impossible to escape conversation over a table laden with food. A short, fleshy woman, with the tiny eyes of pure malice, sought him out – he could tell she'd been watching him – and silently presented a generous wedge of *Bundt* cake in a napkin. The group had understood him, accepted him; he was damaged goods, to be left alone yet not neglected. She turned and walked away, leaving him to eat his cake in peace, while he suppressed a violent shiver that seemed to come from the very centre of his being.

As the sun set, the voice on the public address system grew suddenly whispery with reverence and awe. A fortuitous change of plans: the ship would be met at Hamburg by a train of first-class coaches, all passengers would proceed to Berlin, there to be addressed by the Führer himself. Please do not be concerned for the friends and family who will come to the dock to meet you, there will be plenty of room for everybody. Heil Hitler!

And if Szara had a passing notion that he could slip away in the confusion of landing and find his way to the Copenhagen ferry, the reality of the arrival, two days later, put a firm lid on such nonsense. A wall of cheering Germans stood to either side of the disembarking passengers, an aisle of welcome, as effective as barbed wire, that lined the way to the railway station.

So he went to Berlin.

To Szara, the city seemed dark and solemn. Stiff. Brooding. Whatever he scented in the streets was worse, much worse, than Kristallnacht in November of '38. Now the nation was at risk; this business was no longer some political manoeuvre of the Nazi party. France and England had declared war – the gall, the presumption of them! – and the people had coalesced in the face of such an astonishing development. That civilized nations – the British at any rate, not the unbathed French – would side with the Poles and the Jews and the other Slavic trash was simply beyond comprehension, but it was a fact of life and it had to be faced. They were equal to it.

At the Potsdam terminal a fleet of buses waited to transport the returning *Volksdeutsch* to the Olympic Stadium, where a crowd of seventy-five thousand people awaited their arrival. A special section toward the front was reserved for the Baltic emigrants, and Adolf Hitler would address them later in the evening. Szara had no intention of going anywhere near the place; security measures would be intensive wherever a national leader was expected and in this instance would include the Gestapo, Berlin plainclothes detectives, identity checks – an imposter's nightmare. Though his thin cover had worked on the docks of Latvia, it would never stand up under that level of scrutiny.

But there was an accursed absence of confusion as the buses were boarded; the *Volksdeutsch* were infuriatingly patient and malleable, organizing themselves into neat lines – who, Szara tried to remember, had called the Germans *carnivorous sheep?* – and when he tried to disappear between two buses a young woman wearing an armband chased him down and courteously headed him back in the proper direction. In desperation he doubled over, his free hand clutching his belly, and ran groaning back into the station. *That* they understood and they let him go. He found a different exit, now simply a traveller with a valise. He spotted a sign for the number 24 tram, the Dahlem line, that would take him to Lehrter Bahnhof, where he could catch the late train to Hamburg. Things were looking up.

But it was not to be. He walked about on the streets near the station for a half-hour or so, giving the busloads of *Volksdeutsch* time to depart, then reentered Potsdam station. But he saw a uniformed policeman and a Gestapo functionary checking identification at every gate that led to the tramways and realized that without the protective coloration of the emigrants he was in some difficulty. He stood out, he could sense it. Who was this rather aristocratic looking man in soiled clothing and a soft felt hat worn low over the eyes? Why did he carry a fine leather valise?

Resisting the urge to panic, he walked away from the station and found himself in even worse trouble. Now he was alone, on deserted streets.

The Berlin he'd known a year earlier still had its people of the night, those who liked darkness and the pleasures it implied. But no longer. The city was desolate, people stayed home, went to bed early; Hitler had chased decadence indoors. Szara knew he had to get off the streets. He felt it was a matter of minutes.

He walked quickly west, to the Leipzigerplatz, where he knew there was a public telephone. He'd memorized several telephone numbers, in case he lost the valise, and the receiver was in his hand before he realized he had no German coins. He'd obtained reichsmarks from Poles who'd fled into Lithuania, enough to buy a ticket on the Copenhagen steamer, but he'd not foreseen the need to use a telephone. *Not like this, not for such a stupid miscalculation*, he pleaded silently. He saw a taxicab and waved it down. The driver was offended, declared himself 'no travelling change purse,' but Szara bought two ten-reichsmark coins for fifty reichsmarks and the driver's attitude turned instantly to grave decency. 'Can you wait?' Szara asked him, thumbing through his remaining bills. The driver nodded politely. Anything for a gentleman.

The telephone rang for what seemed like a long time, then, unexpectedly, a man answered. Szara mentioned a name. The man's voice was terribly languid and world-weary. 'Oh, she's not *here*,' he said. Then: 'I suppose you'll want the number.' Szara said he did, fumbling in his pocket for a pencil and a matchbox. The man gave him the number and Szara hung up. Out of the corner of his eye he saw the driver scowling at his watch. There was a police car on the other side of the Leipzigerplatz. 'Another minute,' he called out. The driver noticed his odd German and stared.

Szara dialled the new number and a maid answered. Szara asked for 'Madame Nadia Tscherova.' Relief flooded over him when he heard her voice.

'I find myself in Berlin,' he said. 'Would it be terribly inconvenient . . .?'

'What? Who is it?'

'A backstage friend. Remember? The terrible play? I brought you . . . a present.'

'My God.'

'May I come and see you?'

'Well,' she said.

'Please.'

'I suppose.'

'Perhaps you'll tell me where.'

'How can you not know?'

'The fact is I don't.'

'Oh. Well, it's a villa. Facing the Tiergarten, just at the edge of Charlottenburg, on Schillerstrasse. The third from the end of the street. There's a . . . I'll have the coach lamps put on. When will you come?'

'I have a taxi waiting for me.'

'Soon then,' she said and hung up.

He got into the cab and gave the driver directions. 'What part of Germany do you come from?' asked the driver.

'From Italy,' Szara said. 'From the Tyrol. Actually, we rarely speak German.'

'So you're Italian.'

'Yes.'

'For an Italian you don't speak so badly.'

'*Grazie*.'

The driver laughed and pulled away as the police car began to circle slowly around the Leipzigerplatz.

'Dearest!' She cried out in Russian. This was a different Nadia – affected, brittle. She threw an arm around his shoulders – her other hand held a glass – drew him close, and kissed him full on the lips. The kiss tasted like wine. '"What ingenious devil has cast you on my doorstep?"' she said. The maid who'd shown him in curtseyed, her starched uniform rustling, and left the room.

'And go iron yourself,' Tscherova muttered to her back as she drew the tall door closed.

'What sort of devil?' Szara asked.

'It's from Kostennikov. *The Merchant's Bride*. Act Three.'

Szara raised an eyebrow.

'Come upstairs,' she said.

He followed her through rooms of oiled walnut furniture and towering emerald draperies, then up a curving marble staircase with gilded banisters. 'Well you've certainly –'

'Shut up,' she whispered urgently. 'They listen.'

'The servants?'

'Yes.'

Sweeping up the stairs in ice-coloured silk shirt and pants, voluminous lounging pyjamas, she called out, 'Last one up is a monkey!'

'Aren't you making it awfully obvious?' he said quietly.

She snorted and danced up the last few steps. Her gold slippers had pompoms on them and the soles slapped against the marble. She paused for a sip of wine, then took his hand and towed him into a bedroom, kicking the door shut behind them. A fire burned in a marble fireplace, the wallpaper was deep blue with white snowdrops, the cover on the huge bed was the same blue and white, and the carpet was thick, pale blue wool.

'Oh, Seryozha,' she said, her voice full of woe. A borzoi crept guiltily off a blue and white settee and slunk over to the fireplace, settling down on his side with the mournful sigh of the dispossessed and a single swish of his feathery tail. Then he yawned, opened his long, graceful jaws to the limit, and snapped them shut with a brief whine. *What settee?*

'Won't they suspect I'm your lover?' Szara asked.

'Let them.'

Szara looked confused.

'I can have all the lovers, and generally strange guests, that I want. What I can't have is spies.'

'They know Russian?'

'Who knows what they know? From my émigré friends they expect Russian, shouting and laughter. Anything political or confidential, keep your voice down or play the Victrola.'

'All this. It's yours?'

'I will tell you everything, my dear, but first things first. Forgive me, but I do not know your name. That's going to become awkward. Would you like me to make something up?'

'André,' he said. 'In the French spelling.'

'Good. Now I must ask you, André in the French spelling, if you have any idea what you smell like.'

'I'm sorry.'

'I've been through hard times in Russia: little rooms, long winters, everybody terrified, and no privacy. I'm no shrinking violet, believe me, but . . .'

She opened a door with a full mirror on it and gestured toward the clawfoot tub within. 'I lack nothing. You will find a sponge, bath salts, lavender soap or almond, facecloth, back-brush, shampoo from Paris. You may give yourself a facial, if you like, or powder yourself like a cruller from the Viennese bakery. Yes? You're not insulted?'

'A long journey,' he said, walking into the bathroom.

He undressed, horrified at the condition of his clothing. In the scented air of the bathroom his own condition became, by contrast, all too evident. Still, when he looked in the mirror, he could see that he'd survived. A day's growth of beard – was one side of his face still slightly swollen from the dive-bombing? – hair quite long, newly grey here, and here, and here, eyes yellowish with fatigue. Not old. Yet. And very lean and sharp, determined.

He ran the steaming water into the tub and climbed in. The heat woke up various nicks and scrapes and bruises he'd acquired in his travels and he grimaced. It felt as though he had a hundred places that hurt, each in a different way. He watched the water darken, added a handful of crystals from a jar and stirred them about. 'That's the spirit!' she called through the open door, smelling the bath salts. She hummed to herself, opened a bottle of wine – he heard the squeak of the cork being drawn – and put a record on the Victrola. Italian opera, sunny and sweet: *on market day, peasants gather in the village square*.

'I like this for a bath, don't you?' she said from the bedroom.

'Yes. Just right.'

She sang along for a few bars, her voice, lightly hoarse, hunting shamelessly for the proper notes.

'May I have a cigarette?'

A moment later her hand snaked around the door with a lit cigarette. He took it gratefully. 'Smoking in the bath,' she said. 'You are truly Russian.'

The borzoi came padding in and lapped enthusiastically at the bathwater.

'Seryozha!' she said.

With his index finger Szara rubbed the dog between the eyes. The borzoi raised its head and stared at him, soapy water running from its wet muzzle. 'Go away, Seryozha,' he said. Surprisingly, the dog actually turned and left.

'Yes, good dog,' he heard her say.

'When I'm done . . . I don't have anything clean, I'm afraid.'

'I'll get you one of the general's bathrobes. Not the old

rag he actually wears. His daughter gave him one for his birthday – it's still in the box. Red satin. You'll look like Cary Grant.'

'Is he your lover?'

'Cary Grant? I thought we'd been discreet.'

He waited.

'No. Not really. Nobody is my lover. When the general and I are together the world thinks otherwise, but we don't fool ourselves or each other. It takes some explaining, but I can't imagine you're going anywhere else tonight, so there's time. But for one thing I can't wait. You really have to tell me why you came here. If you are going to ask me to do all sorts of wretched things, I might as well hear about it and have it done with.' She turned the record over. There was a certain resignation in her voice, he thought, like a woman who dreads a squabble with the butcher but knows it can't be avoided.

'The truth?'

'Yes. Why not?'

'I've . . . Well, what have I done? I haven't defected. I guess I've run away.'

'Not really. You have?'

'Yes.'

She was silent for a moment, thinking it over. 'Run away to Berlin? Is, uh, that where one generally goes?'

'It was a rat's maze. I ran down the open passage.'

'Well, if you say so.' She sounded dubious.

He put his cigarette out in the bathwater, rested the butt on the edge of the tub, then pulled the plug and watched the grey water swirl above the drain. 'I'm going to have to fill up the tub again,' he said.

'I'll bring you a glass of wine if you like. And you can tell me about your travels. If it's allowed, that is.'

'Anything's allowed now,' he said. He burst out laughing.

'What?'

'Really nothing.' He laughed again. It was as though a genie had escaped.

It was well past midnight when they tiptoed down the stairs to the kitchen, a narrow room with a lofty ceiling and porcelain worn dark on its curves by years of scrubbing. They made absurdly tall sandwiches of cheese and pickles and butter and stole back across the Baluchi carpets like thieves. Szara caught a glimpse of himself in a mirror: shaved, hair combed, wearing a red satin bathrobe with a shawl collar, a giant sandwich teetering on a plate – it was as though in headlong flight he'd stumbled through a secret door and landed in heaven.

Back in Nadia's sanctuary, they settled on the carpet close to the dying fire while Seryozha rested on crossed forepaws and waited alertly for his share of the kill. Szara watched her tear into the sandwich, a serious Russian eater, her hair falling around her face as she leaned over the plate. He simply could not stop looking at her. She apparently ignored it, was perhaps used to it – after all, the job of an actress was to be looked at – still, he did not want to seem a goggling, teenage dolt and tried to be subtle, but that was a hopeless tactic and he knew it. *This is God's work*, he thought: drifting hair the colour of an almond shell and the fragile blue of her eyes, the lines and planes and light in her. There weren't words, he realized. Only the feeling inside him and the impulse to make sure, again and again, that he saw what he saw. Suddenly, she looked up and stared back at him, blank-eyed, jaw muscles working away as she chewed, until he sensed that she'd composed her expression into a reasonable imitation of his own. He turned away. 'Yes?' she said, raising an eyebrow.

'It's nothing.'

She poured wine into his glass.

'Do we expect the general home at any moment?' he asked. 'Do I hide in a closet?'

'The general is in Poland,' she said. 'And if he were here you would not have to hide. Krafic comes to see me with his boyfriends. Lara Brozina and her brother. You know them, in what we'll call a different setting. Others also. A little Russian colony, you see: émigré intellectuals, free thinkers, batty painters, and what-have-you. The general refers to us as "an antidote to Frau Lumplich."'

'Who is she?'

'A character he made up. "Madame Lump," one would say in Russian.'

'An enlightened general. An enlightened German general.'

'They exist,' she said. She brushed crumbs from her hands and held a bite of sandwich out to Seryozha, who arched his neck forward and took it daintily between his small front teeth for a moment, then inhaled it. She rose and brought over a framed photograph from the night table next to her bed. 'General Walter Boden,' she said.

A man in his late sixties, Szara thought. Fleshless, ascetic face below a bald head, deep care lines, mouth a single brief line. Yet the look in his eyes told a slightly different story. At some point, in a life that left his face like stone, something had amused him. Permanently.

'Extraordinary,' Szara said.

'It pleases me you see that,' she said with feeling.

'When I put this picture together with what you've told me, I would have to guess that this is not a man well loved by the Nazis.'

'No. They know how he feels about them; in the general's world, the notion of *beneath contempt* is taken quite literally. He is rich, however. Very, very rich. They do respect that. And his position with the General Staff is not unimportant, though he speaks of it as "the maid's room in the lion's den." His friends include the old aristocracy, the Metternichs and Bismarcks, princes and counts, the Prussian landholders. Hitler hates them, foams at the mouth because he can't get at them; they occupy two powerful fortresses in Germany, the army and the foreign ministry.'

'Fortresses. Will they hold under siege?'

'We shall see.'

You don't, Szara reminded himself, *have to think about such things anymore*. 'Is there another log for the fire?' he asked. The embers were dark red.

'No. Not until the morning. One is a prisoner of servants, in some ways.'

'A long way from Rosenhain Passage, though, and that awful theatre.'

She nodded that it was. He stared at her, forced himself to look away. She yawned, took a foot out of her slipper, and propped it inside her opposite knee. 'How did you meet?' Szara said.

'At a reception. We went to dinner a few times. Talked into the night – he speaks passable Russian, you yourself know what that feels like, especially when you have no country to go home to. A strange romance. I waited for the inevitable offer, *a relaxing weekend in the country*, but it never came. One night at a restaurant he simply said "Nadia, my girl, generals and actresses are nothing new in Berlin. A cliché of the nightclubs. But come along to my house, even so, and see how you like it." I did. And in this room I asked, "Whose bedroom is this?" for I'd already seen his, and everything was obviously new. "I believe it is yours, if you like," he said. I had expected anything but this, and I was speechless. That strip of Persian carpet, the one by your hand? He'd meant it for Seryozha. Suddenly I started to cry – inside, I didn't want him to see. And that was the end of the discussion. I came to live here and it was a kind of salvation; I stopped doing all those other things, seeing those vile people. Now this is my life. When he wants to see me, I'm here. I sit across from him at dinner, we converse, my job is to be exactly who I am. Any affectation, to become what I imagine he might want, would break his heart. We have a life together, we go – what is the phrase? – we go out in society. To his friends. Sometimes to the country, to grand estates. In Germany, civilized life continues in such places, much as it does in the basements of Moscow. But no matter where we go, I am always at his shoulder. I take his arm. Now I could – and of course I would, nothing would be easier – make the world believe that he was a sublime lover. A few small signals and the tongues begin to wag. If he desired that, it would be little enough to ask. But he does not. He does not care what people think of him. I'm not here for his vanity, for his reputation. I'm here because it gives him pleasure to have me here.'

Her face was flushed; she drank the last of the wine in her glass. When she met his eyes he saw anger and sorrow, and all the courage and defiance she could possibly summon. Not that it was overwhelming, it wasn't, but for her it was everything she possessed. 'And God damn you if you've come here to make me work again. No matter *what* you've said. For I won't. Won't betray this man in the way you want. I'll go where even your power does not reach. And we both know where that is.'

Szara took a deep breath and let the air between them cool a little. Then he said, 'I've told only the truth' – he looked at his watch – 'since ten-thirty last night. Almost six hours. The way things are for me lately, I have a right to be proud of even that.'

She lowered her eyes. He stood, the carpet soft beneath his bare feet, and walked to a mirrored cabinet with glasses and a silver ice bucket on it. He opened the door and found a bottle of Saint-Estèphe, took a corkscrew and worked it open, then filled both their glasses. She had meanwhile found a newspaper, was bunching up wads of it and feeding it to the fire. 'It looks warm, anyhow,' she said.

'I was wondering,' he said, 'what had become of the people in Paris in all this. Because if you'd let them know about an intimacy with a senior staff officer they would have been – inquisitive. To say the least.'

'And something terrible would have happened. Because even if I'd tried to conceal everything, I don't trust my little friends in Berlin. They've had to improvise their lives for too long – not all humans are made stronger by that.'

'Very few.'

'Well, for me there is only one escape, and I was prepared to take it. I'd made my peace with the idea. In the beginning, when I stole away from Russia and came to live in Berlin, these people approached me. Threatened me. But I gave them very little, only bits of gossip and what they could read in the newspapers if they wanted. Then they played a second card. Your brother Sascha is in a camp, they said, where he deserves to be. But he's as comfortable as he can be under the circumstances; he works as a clerk in a heated room. If you want his situation to continue, you must be productive. It's up to you.'

'And you did what you had to do.'

'Yes. I did. In exile, I cared very little what I made of my life because I discovered I wasn't touched by it. Perhaps Russia has something to do with that – to be sensitive yet not at all delicate, a curious strength, or weakness, or whatever you want to call it. But then I met this man, and suddenly it was as though I'd woken from a long sleep. Every small thing now mattered – the weather, the way a vase stood on a table, meeting someone and wanting them to like me. I had built walls – now they crumbled. And this I knew I could not survive. Not for long. I could no longer do what I'd done for the people who came around with money, and once they began to press I knew there would be only one way out. So I hadn't, as I saw it then, very long to live. Yet each day was vivid, and I trembled with life. They say it is the only gift, and now I came to understand that with all my heart. I never cried so hard, and never laughed so much, as I did in those weeks. Perhaps it was a form of prayer, because what came next was a miracle, I know of no other word to describe it.

'It was in early August. A man came to see me. Not here. At the theatre, in the same way you did. Clearly he knew nothing of the general. A dreadful man, this one. Fair, wavy hair, thick glasses, a vile little chunk of a thing with no mercy anywhere in him. None. And what he mostly wanted to talk about was you. Something had gone wrong, something extremely serious, for nothing has happened since. No money, no demands, no couriers, nothing.'

She twisted the glass about in her hands, watching the light of the burning newspaper reflected in the red surface of the wine. 'I've no idea what happened,' she said. 'I only know it saved my life. And that you seemed to be the cause of it.'

He woke up in a kind of heaven. He had no idea how he'd happened to wind up on her bed but there he was, his face against the soft coverlet, his side a little sore from sleeping on the knot in the twisted belt of the bathrobe. He was in heaven, he decided, because it smelled exactly the way heaven, or his heaven at any rate, ought to smell: the perfume she wore – which reminded him of cinnamon – and scented soap, as well as wine, cigarette smoke, the ashes of a dead fire, and the sweetish odour of a well-washed borzoi. He could, he thought, detect Nadia herself, sweet in a different, a human way. For a time he simply lay there, suspended in a perfect darkness, and inhaled. When he felt himself slipping back into unconsciousness, he forced his eyes open. A knitted quilt was tossed carelessly on the settee – so that's where she'd slept. His suit – apparently the maids had cleaned it – hung from a hanger on the knob of the bathroom door, and the rest of his clothing was piled neatly on a dresser. Miraculously clean and dry.

He struggled to sit up. Returning from the dead, it felt like. All those nights in Poland, lying on the ground on a blanket; followed by restless hours on a thin mattress in the Kovno apartment, people around him awake, coughing, talking in low voices. Now he hurt for every minute of it. He unhooked the white shutter that covered the lower half of the window and pushed it aside. An autumn garden. Surrounded by high walls. Dead leaves had drifted across the paths and mounded at the foot of a hedge. Nadia sat at a weathered iron table – she was reading, he could not see her face – one hand dangling above the wolfhound stretched out at her side. *Am I in Russia?* Wrapped in a long black coat and a red wool scarf she was lost in her book. The wind lifted her autumn-coloured hair, leaves spun down from the trees and rattled along the garden paths; the sky was at war, broken towers of grey cloud, blown and battered, swept past a pale sun. Certainly it would rain. His heart ached for her.

Later he sat in a garden chair across from her and saw that she was reading Babel's *Red Cavalry*. The wind was cool and damp and he pulled his jacket tightly about him.

For a long time they did not say anything.

And she did not look away, did not deny him her eyes: *if this is what you wish*, she seemed to say, *I will pose for you*. She touched nothing, changed nothing, and did not defend herself. The wind blew her hair across her face, Seryozha sighed, the light shifted as the clouds crossed the sun, she never moved. Then he began to understand that he'd misread her. This stillness was not simply poise – what he saw in her eyes was precisely what was in his own. Could she be that deluded? To want somebody so lost and useless? Was she blind?

No.

From the moment he'd walked through the door of the dressing room he had been in love with her. That it might be the same for her had never occurred to him, simply had not crossed his mind. But maybe it worked that way – women always knew, men never did. Or maybe not, maybe it all worked some other way. He didn't really care. Now he understood that everything had changed. And now he understood what, just exactly what, he had been offered.

Sad, he thought, that he couldn't take it. They were castaways, both of them, marooned together on an exotic island – as it happened, the garden of a Florentine villa on the Schillerstrasse. But somewhere beyond the high walls a military band was playing a march and, he thought, the general will soon return from the wars. Only for a moment did he imagine a love affair in flight: the unspeakable hotel rooms, the secret police, the predators. No. She belonged in his imagination, not in his life. A memory. Met in the wrong way, in the wrong place, in the wrong year, in times when love wasn't possible. One remembers, and that's all. Something else that didn't happen in those days.

'When will you leave?' she said. 'Today?'

'Tomorrow.'

Just for an instant he was clairvoyant: he could watch the question as it took shape in her mind. She leaned across the table until she was very close, he could see that her lips were dry from the wind, a red mark on the line of her jaw – suddenly she was out of perspective, too near to be beautiful. And when she spoke it was a voice he didn't know, so soft he could barely hear what she said. 'Why did this happen?'

'I don't know,' he said. 'I don't.'

She pressed her lips together and nodded a little. She agreed. There was no answer.

'There isn't anything we have to do, you know,' he said.

Her face changed, gracefully but completely, until he was confronted by the single great inquisitive look of his life. 'No?'

He had never in his life been the lover he was with her.

They waited for nightfall – only the first in a series of common consents that flowed to meet the occasion. Szara could not safely go out in the street, and Nadia knew it, so there was no point in raising the issue. They simply passed a rather nineteenth-century sort of day; they read, they talked, they cut clusters of autumn berries from a shrub to make a table decoration, avoided the servants, played with the dog, touched only accidentally and only now and then, and neither of them let on how it affected them. If living in the days of war demanded a love affair measured in hours and not in months, they discovered that a love affair was something that could be compressed in just that way.

They could have looked, from any of the windows in the front of the three-storey villa, out on the Tiergarten and observed that day's life in Berlin: strollers and idlers, officers and couples, old men reading newspapers on a park bench. But they declined to do so. The private world suited them. They did not, however, build sand castles, did not pretend the present was anything other than what it was, and they tried to talk about the future. Difficult, though. Szara's plans focused vaguely on Denmark; from there he would extemporize. He had no idea how he might be able to earn a living; his writing languages, Russian and Polish, would not serve him very well anywhere he could think of. Émigré intellectuals lived in penury – sometimes the little journal paid, sometimes it didn't. The former aristocrats gave parties, everyone ate as much as they could. But even that tenuous existence was denied him – he was a fugitive, and the émigré communities were the first places they would look for him. Of course he could not go back to Paris, much too dangerous. Sad, because to be there with her . . .

Sad, because even to know him put her in danger. This he did not say. But she knew it anyhow. She'd seen enough of Soviet life to apprehend vulnerability in every one of its known forms. So she understood that one did what one had to do. This real politik was very alchemical stuff. It started with politicians and their intellectuals, all this doing what had to be done, but it had a tendency to migrate, and the next time you looked it was in bed with you.

Still, they agreed, one had to hope. Humans survived the most awful catastrophes: walked away from the inferno with singed hair, missed the train that went over the cliff. Both felt they might just be owed a little luck from whatever divine agency kept those books. There were still places on earth where one could get irredeemably lost, it only took finding one. And how exactly did one go about herding sheep? Could it be all that difficult?

In the end, they refused to let the future ruin their day, which made them heroes of a low order but heroes nonetheless. And they had the past to fall back on, realizing almost immediately that the sorts of lives they'd led created, if they did nothing else, long and luxuriant anecdotes. They discovered that they had, on several occasions, been within minutes of meeting each other, in Moscow, in Leningrad. Had been in the same apartments, known some of the same people; their trails through the snowy forest crossed and recrossed. What would have happened had they met? Everything? Nothing? Certainly something, they decided.

They weren't very hungry, as the day wore on toward

evening, and just after dark they toyed with a light supper. Their conversation was somewhat forced, slightly tense, in the dining room with a ticking grandfather clock that made every silence ring with melodrama. Nadia said, 'If it weren't for the general's feelings, I'd have poured soup in that monster long ago.'

They retired early. He, for form's sake, to a guest room, she to her blue and white sanctuary. When the noise in the kitchen subsided and the house grew quiet, Szara climbed the marble staircase.

They lit a fire, turned out the lights, played the Victrola, drank wine.

She surprised him. The way she moved through the daily world, fine boned, on air, made her seem insubstantial – one could hold her only cautiously. But it wasn't so. With a dancer's pointed toe she kicked the bottoms of her silk pyjamas fully across the room, then melted out of the top and posed for him. She was full and lovely and curved, with smooth, taut skin coloured by firelight. For a moment, he simply looked at her. He'd supposed their joined spirits might float to some unimagined romantic height, but now he fell on her like a wolf and she yelped like a teenager.

And what a good time they had.

Much later, when they simply hadn't the strength to go on any longer, they fell sound asleep, still pressed together, the sheets tangled around their legs, drifting away in the midst of the most charming and vile conversation.

It was not yet dawn when they woke up. He reached for her, she flexed with pleasure, slowly, like stretching, and sighed. He watched her from cover, a pale shape in the darkness, eyes closed, mouth open, breasts rising and falling. Suddenly he understood that sometimes there was no reaching the end of desire, no satisfying it. They simply would not, he realized, ever quite get enough of each other. Nonetheless, he thought, they could hope for the best. They could try. They could make a beginning.

He could have crawled out of bed at dawn and set out into the cold world, but he didn't. They stole another day, and this time they didn't wait for nightfall. They disappeared in the middle of the afternoon. At eight in the evening a servant set out a tureen of soup at the long table in the dining room with the ticking grandfather clock. But nobody showed up. And at eight-thirty she took it away.

He left in the middle of the following day. A taxi was called. They stood in the vestibule together until it came. 'Please don't cry,' he said.

'I won't,' she promised, tears running everywhere.

The taxi honked twice and he left.

The Gestapo had him an hour later. He never even got out of Berlin.

To his credit, he sensed it. He did not enter the Lehrter Bahnhof immediately but walked the streets for a while, trying to calm himself down – simply another traveller, a little bored, a little harassed, a man who had to take the train up to Hamburg on some prosaic and vastly uninteresting errand.

But the passport control people at the staircase that led down to the platform didn't care what he looked like. A Berlin policeman took the Kringen identity papers and compared them to a typewritten list, looked over Szara's shoulder, made a gesture of the eyes and a motion of the head, and two men in suits closed in on either side of him. Very correct they were: 'Can you come with us for a moment, please?' Only willpower and raw pride kept him from collapsing to his knees, and he felt the sweat break out at the roots of his hair. One of the men relieved him of his valise, the other frisked him, then they marched him, to the great interest of the passing crowd, toward the station police post. He wobbled once and one of the detectives caught him by the arm. They took him down a long corridor and through an unmarked door where a uniformed SS officer was sitting behind a desk, a file open in front of him. Reading upside down, Szara could see a long list of names and descriptive paragraphs on a yellow sheet of teletype paper. 'Stand at attention,' the man said coldly.

Szara did as he was told. The officer concentrated on the Kringen identity documents and left him to stew, the standard procedure. 'Herr Kringen?' he said at last.

'Yes.'

'Yes, *sir*.'

'Yes, sir.'

'What did you use to obliterate the birthdate? Lemon? Oxalic acid? Not *urine* – I hope for your sake I haven't touched your piss.'

'Lemon, sir,' Szara said.

The officer nodded. He tapped the Kringen name with the eraser at the end of a pencil. 'The actual Herr Kringen went into the Lutheran hospital to have a bunion removed from his foot. And while this poor man lay in a hospital bed, some little sneak made off with his papers. Was that you?'

'No, sir. It wasn't me. I bought the passport from an orderly at the hospital.'

The officer nodded. 'And you are?'

'My name is Bonotte, Jean Bonotte. I am of French nationality. My passport is hidden in the flap of my jacket.'

'Give it to me.'

Szara got his jacket off and with shaking hands tried to rip the seam open. It took a long time but the heavy thread finally gave. He placed the passport on the desk and put his jacket back on, the torn flap of lining hanging ludicrously down the back of his leg. Behind him, one of the detectives snickered. The officer picked up the telephone and requested a number. He turned the pages of the Bonotte passport with the pencil eraser. While he waited for his call to go through he said, 'What reason have you for your visit to Germany? A mad impulse?' The detective laughed.

'I fled Poland, but could not find a way out of Lithuania.'

'So you obtained Kringen's passport and came out with the *Volksdeutsch* from Riga?'

'Yes, sir.'

'Well, aren't you clever?' said the officer, looking at Szara carefully for the first time and meaning what he said.

They drove him to Columbia House, Gestapo headquarters in Berlin, and locked him in an isolation cell. Small but clean, a cot and a bucket, a heavily grilled window nine feet up and a light bulb in the ceiling. They weren't entirely sure what they had, he guessed, not the sort of poor fish at whom they screamed, *Spy! You will be executed!* but, just maybe, the real thing, and that had to be handled at length and in a very different way. Perhaps with delicacy, perhaps not. If the decision was 'not,' the next step was no secret. Szara could hear the screaming from distant parts of the building, and it sickened him and weakened his will to resist, as it was intended to.

Abramov, with evident distaste, had covered this possibility during the time of his training: nobody resists torture, don't try. Tell them what you have to, it's our job to keep you from knowing too much. There are two goals you must try to accomplish: one, the less you say in the first forty-eight hours the better – that gives us time – but in any event, feed them the least important material you can. You are just a low-level opportunist forced to work for the government – contemptible, but not important. And two, try to signal us that you've been caught. That's crucial. We can protect a network from damage, close down everything you touched, and rescue your associates while we work through channels to get you free or at least to keep you from harm. The signals will change based on circumstance: a technical variation in wireless telegraphy or simply vanishing from our sight while working in hostile territory. But there will certainly be a signal established and an appropriate way to deliver it. Remember, in this organization there is always a chance, we can do almost anything. 'If you are taken,' Abramov had said, 'you must cling to hope as a sailor cast into the sea clings to a spar.'

Szara closed his eyes and rested his head against the cold cement wall. *No, Sergei Jakobovich* – he addressed Abramov's departed soul – *not this time*. Hope, despair – all such fancies were now entirely beside the point. He'd at last made the error that could not be overcome. Had not sufficiently understood the capability, the magnitude, of the German security machine – not until he'd seen the long sheet of yellow teletype paper with the name KRINGEN in the left-hand column. The identity that had been purchased in Paris would not hold up, not once they went to work on it, it wouldn't. When he worked his way back through the last two years of his life – Khelidze, Renate Braun, Bloch, Abramov, the OPAL network, then de Montfried and the British, finally the assignment in eastern Poland – he saw himself as a man willing to do almost anything in order to stay alive. He'd not done badly, had lasted a long time compared to the others – the intellectuals, Old Bolsheviks, Jews, foreign communists. Had outlived almost all of them, twisted and turned, lied and schemed, survived.

But it was not meant to be, and this he faced.

He suspected that what he'd almost done to himself in

the Pripet marsh, the day he'd crossed into Lithuania, had been a shadow of the future – somehow he'd sensed that he was living out his last few days. But he had slightly misread the omen; he wasn't done with life, that wasn't it. Life was done with him. And in his deepest heart, he wondered if he hadn't come to Berlin knowing that he would find a way to Tscherova, an unconscious appeal to fate to let him passionately love a woman once more before he left the earth. If so, his wish had been granted, and now it was time to accept the inevitable cost of the bargain. He marvelled at the coldness of his heart. The time of dreams and delusions was ended; he saw the world, and himself, in perfect clarity. Certain obligations remained – to protect Tscherova, principally – but there were others, and he would now plan how to sacrifice himself in the most effective way. How late, he thought, strength comes to some people.

The interrogator was called Hartmann. An SS Obersturmbannführer, a major, a well-fed man with a placid face and small, carefully groomed hands, who addressed him politely. Hartmann was nothing more, Szara realized, than the intake valve of an information machine. He existed to acquire facts – perhaps a lawyer, or some functionary in a judicial system, before being called to his present duty by the Nazi party. He did not process the information. That happened elsewhere, far above him in the hierarchy, where an administrative panel, a directorate, made decisions.

To begin with, Hartmann pointed out that if they were straightforward with each other, all would turn out for the best. He implied, without actually saying it, that his job was best done if Szara did not have to be taken to the cellars; they were, together, men who could proceed with their obligations – Szara's to confess, Hartmann's to certify the quality of that confession – while remaining innocent of such measures. That sort of thing was for another sort of person.

Szara did not resist. He cooperated. By the afternoon of the first day he had to admit he was not Jean Bonotte. Hartmann had provided paper and pencil and asked him to write a biography, beginning with his childhood in Marseille – names and places, schools and teachers. 'I cannot write such a biography because I did not grow up there,' Szara said. 'And I am not named Jean Bonotte.'

'This passport is a forgery, then,' Hartmann said.

'Yes, Herr Obersturmbannführer, it is.'

'Then will you tell me your true name? And your nationality, if it is not French?'

'I will,' Szara said. 'My real name is André Aronovich Szara. As for my nationality, I was born a Polish Jew when Poland was a province of Russia. By 1918 I was living in Odessa, and so remained a citizen of the Soviet Union, eventually becoming a journalist for the newspaper *Pravda*.'

Hartmann was puzzled. 'Is it a newspaper that sent you to Berlin? With false identity? I wonder if you could clarify this.'

'I can. I obtained the false identity myself, and the newspaper has known nothing of me since I left Poland.'

Hartmann paused. Szara sensed discomfort. The interrogator took refuge in the notes he'd made to himself to guide him in the interview, but they were all wrong now. His Frenchman, trapped on the wrong side of the lines, had disappeared. In his place stood a Russian, a rather prominent one he suspected, captured while in flight from the USSR, Germany's nominal ally. Hartmann cleared his throat, for him a gesture of irritation. He had to question his competence to work in such areas. All sorts of intimidating issues suddenly made themselves felt; the prisoner's culpability under German law, possible extradition, others he could not even imagine. All of them grave, difficult, complex, and ultimately to be resolved in a political, not a legal, context. This was obviously not going to be a case he would be allowed to pursue; he could put himself in a good light only by presenting to his superiors the most precise information. Hartmann took up his pen and turned to a fresh page in his writing tablet. 'Slowly and clearly,' he said, 'and beginning with your surname, you will please spell.'

It rained hard that night, for Szara a blessing. It reminded him that there was a world outside his cell, and the steady splash on the high, grilled window muted, if it could not quite obliterate, the sounds of a Gestapo prison. His plan was successfully launched; Hartmann had ended the interview with the utmost correctness. Szara suspected they would not see each other again, and in the event this turned out to be the case.

Szara's strategy of revelation without defiance had proceeded from one basic assumption: he could not be sure he would withstand what was euphemistically known as intensive interrogation. He feared he would first give up the existence of the OPAL network, and that would lead inexorably to the exposure of Nadia Tscherova. He had to avoid the cellars in Berlin and then, if it came to that, the cellars in Moscow.

The conventions of the German character first specified efficiency – thus they'd arrested him. A crucial component of that efficiency, however, was thoroughness, and this he perceived to be his possible ally. Now that they knew who he was, he expected they would want from him all they could get, essentially political intelligence. Who did he know? What were they like? How, precisely, was the political line of *Pravda* determined? What personalities were at play? For his part, he meant to make use of what he called the Scheherazade defence: as long as he intrigued them with stories, they would not execute him or send him back to Russia. In the normal interrogation process, where every statement raised questions, a cooperative subject might continue the discussion for a period of months. Szara's hope lay in the fact that Germany was at war, and in war it was a given that unpredictable things happened, including catastrophes of all sorts – invasions, raids, bombings, mass escapes, even negotiations and peace. Any or all of it might be to his advantage. And if they should reach the end of the line with him and determine to ship him back to Russia, he then had one last move to make: he could contrive to take his life by attempted escape, from the Germans or the Russians, whoever gave him the barest edge of an opportunity.

It wasn't much of a plan, he knew, but in his circumstances it was all he had. It might have worked. He was never to find out, because there was one convention of the German character he'd neglected to include in the equation.

They came for him after midnight, when the sounds of the Gestapo interrogations were impossible not to hear and sleep was out of the question. First there was the clang of a gate, then approaching footsteps in the corridor. Szara gripped the frame of the cot with all the strength in his hands, but the footsteps halted outside his cell and the door burst open. Two SS troopers stood in the spill of strong light, recruiting poster SS, tall and fair and sallow in their black uniforms. Then it was '*Raus!*' and all that, toothy grins, the silent sharing of the great joke that only they understood. Holding his beltless trousers up with his hands, he hurried along the corridor as best he could, shuffling because they'd taken his shoelaces as well. His mind had gone numb, yet his senses seemed to operate independently: the troopers smelled like a gymnasium, a man in an isolation cell moaned as though in a dream. They went down several flights of stairs, at last arriving in a brightly lit office filled with desks, the walls covered with beautifully drawn charts and lists.

A little gnome of a man waited for him at a railing; in his hands a wet hat dripped onto the linoleum. Eyes down, Szara thought he saw an edge of pyjama bottom peeking out from one leg of the man's trousers. 'Ah,' said the man in a soft voice. 'It's Herr Szara.'

'You'll have to sign for him,' said the taller of the two SS.

'It's what I do,' said the man, almost to himself.

Papers were produced and laid on a desk. The gnome carefully unscrewed the cap of a silver fountain pen. He began to scratch a well-flourished signature at the bottom of each page. 'Have we all his things?' he asked as he wrote.

The SS man pointed to the door, where Szara's valise stood to one side with several envelopes stacked on top of it. When the last signature was executed, the gnome said, 'Come along, then.' Szara held the envelopes under one arm, picked up the valise, and used his free hand to hold his trousers up. 'Do you have an umbrella we can use?' the gnome asked the SS trooper.

'A thousand apologies, *mein Herr*, it's something we don't have.'

The gnome sighed with resignation. 'Good night, then. Heil Hitler. Thank you for your kind assistance.'

In the floodlit courtyard stood a small green Opel, its bonnet steaming in the rain. The man opened the door and Szara climbed in and leaned back against the leather seat. Water sluiced down the windscreen and blurred the floodlights to golden rivers. The little man slid behind the wheel, turned on the ignition, said, 'Excuse me,' and, leaning across Szara, retrieved a Luger automatic pistol from the glove compartment. 'Your forbearance,' he said formally, 'in not punching me will be appreciated. And please don't jump out of the car – I haven't run since childhood. Well, to tell you the truth, I didn't run then either.'

'May I ask where we're going?' Szara opened the envelopes, put his belt on and laced up his shoes.

'You certainly may,' said the gnome, peering through the rain, 'but it wouldn't mean anything even if I told you.' Uncertainly, he steered the Opel across the broad courtyard, flipped a leather card case open and showed it to a guard, then drove ahead when the iron gate swung open. There was a sudden shout behind them.

'What are they yelling about?'

'To turn on the windscreen wipers.'

'Yes, well,' the gnome grumbled, turning on the wipers, 'wake a man up at midnight and what do you expect.' The Opel turned the corner from Prinz-Albrecht-strasse to Saarland-strasse. 'So,' he said. 'You're the man who worked in Paris. You know what we Germans say, don't you. "God lives in France." Someday I would like to go.'

'I'm sure you will,' Szara said. 'I really must insist on asking you where we are going.' He didn't care if the man shot him. His fingers rested lightly on the door handle.

'We're going to a place near Altenburg. There. Now the secret's out.'

'What's there?'

'You ask entirely too many questions, if you'll permit me. Perhaps it's done in France – it isn't here. I can only say that I'm sure everything will be explained. It always is. After all, you're not handcuffed, and you've just left the worst place you could possibly be – now doesn't that tell you something? You're being rescued, so be a gentleman, sit quietly, and think up some entertaining stories about Paris. We'll be driving for a few hours.'

They drove, according to the road signs, south, through Leipzig, in the general direction of Prague. Eventually the car entered a network of small roads, the engine whining as they climbed. At the top of a hill, the Opel entered the courtyard of a small inn surrounded by woods. A single light could be seen, illuminating a yellow room at the apex of the steeply slanted roof.

The man who opened the door of the yellow room was not someone he'd met before, of that Szara was certain. Yet there was something strangely familiar about him. He was a tall, reedy fellow in his late thirties, balding, a few wisps of fragile blond hair combed neatly to one side. He was chinless, unfortunately so, with a hesitant, almost apologetic little smile that suggested ancient family and rigid breeding – as though a guest had just broken a terribly valuable vase while the host, fearing only that he would be seen to be discourteously brokenhearted, smiled anxiously and swore it was nothing. 'Please come in,' the man said. The voice was intelligent and strong, entirely at odds with his physical presence. He extended his hand to Szara and said, 'I am Herbert Von Polanyi.'

Now Szara understood, at least, his curious sense of recognition: Marta Haecht, describing Dr Julius Baumann's luncheon companion at the Hotel Kaiserhof, had drawn a perfect verbal portrait of him. Szara evidently stared. Von Polanyi canted his head a little to one side and said, 'You don't know who I am, of course.' The statement was not entirely sure of itself – a tribute, Szara guessed, to the NKVD's reputation for omniscience.

'No,' Szara said. 'I don't. But I am greatly in your debt, whoever you are, for getting me out of that very bad place. Apparently, you must know who I am.'

'Well yes, I do know who you are. You are the Soviet journalist Szara, André Szara. Connected, formerly connected I think, with a certain Soviet organization in Paris.' Von Polanyi gazed at him for a moment. 'Strange to meet you in person. You can't imagine how I studied you, trying to learn your character, trying to predict what you, and your directors, would do in certain situations. Sometimes I worried you would succeed, other times I was terrified you might fail. The time one spends! But of course you know that. We were connected through Dr Julius Baumann; I was his case officer, as were you. Two sides of the same game.'

Szara nodded, taking it all in as though for the first time.

'You didn't know?'

'No.'

Von Polanyi's face glowed with triumph. 'It is nothing.' He brushed victory away with a sweep of his hand. 'Come in, for God's sake. Let's be comfortable – there's coffee waiting.'

It was a spacious room with a few pieces of sturdy old furniture. Two small couches stood perpendicular to the window, facing each other over a coffee table. Von Polanyi, slightly awkward and storklike, arranged himself on one of the couches. He was dressed for the country, in wool pants and flannel blazer with a broad, quiet tie. A coffee service was laid out on the table, and Von Polanyi performed the various rituals with pleasure, fussing with sugar lumps and warm milk. 'This is something of an occasion,' he said. 'It's rare for two people like us to meet. But, here we are. You are physically well, I hope.' His face showed real concern. 'They didn't – do anything to you, did they?'

'No. They were very correct.'

'It isn't always so.' Von Polanyi looked away, a man who knew more than was good for him.

'May I ask,' Szara said, 'what has become of Dr Baumann and his wife?'

Von Polanyi nodded his approval of the question; that had to be cleared up immediately. 'Dr Baumann was, against the wishes of the Foreign Ministry which, ah, sponsored his relationship with the USSR, imprisoned in Sachsenhausen camp. Certain individuals insisted on this and we were unable to stop it. There he spent two months before we found a way to intercede. He was mistreated, but he survived. Physically and, I am certain, psychologically. You would find him today much the same as he was. He and his wife were expelled from Germany, having forfeited their possessions, including the Baumann Milling works, now owned by his former chief engineer. The Baumanns are at least safe and have established themselves in Amsterdam. As by now you are aware, all the information Dr Baumann passed on to you was controlled by an office in the Foreign Ministry. It was, however, and I will discuss this further in a moment, correct information. To the centimetre. So, in the end, you were not fooled. Did you suspect?'

Szara answered thoughtfully: 'Russians, Herr Von Polanyi, suspect everyone, always, doubly so in the espionage business. I can say Baumann's bona fides were permanently in question, but never seriously challenged.'

'Well then, it only means we did our job properly. Of course, he had no choice but to cooperate. Originally, we were able to offer him continued ownership of the business. Later, after Czechoslovakia was taken, the Nazi party gained confidence – the world's armies did not march, the American Neutrality Act was an inspiration – and the issue became life itself. I am not a sentimentalist, Herr Szara, but coercion on that level is disagreeable and in the end, I suspect, leads to betrayal, though Baumann, according to you, did keep his end of the bargain.'

'He did,' Szara said. *Unless*, he thought, *you count his hint in the final transmission and Frau Baumann's approach to Odile*.

'An honourable man. On the subject of Jews the Nazis are like mad dogs. They will not be reasonable, and such blindness may ultimately destroy us all. I believe that could actually happen.'

This was treason, pure and simple. Szara felt his guard drop a notch.

'On the same subject, I must say it's fortunate for you that you admitted your real identity – though not, I imagine, your vocation. When the information was disseminated to the various intelligence bureaux we took immediate steps to secure your release. We're a small office at the Foreign Ministry, simply a group of educated German gentlemen, but we have the right to read everything. I believed that the Gestapo might use you against us, and that is the reason we agreed to spend various favours and obligations in order to have you released. In bureaucratic currency, it was quite costly.'

'But there's more to it than that,' Szara said.

'Yes. There is. A great deal more. I hope you'll indulge me and let me come at this in my own particular way.' Von Polanyi glanced at his watch. 'You're to be taken across the border, but we have some few hours to ourselves. I've wanted to tell a certain story for a very long time, and what remains of this night may well be the only chance I'll ever have to tell it. So, do I have your permission to continue?'

'Yes, of course,' Szara said. 'I want to hear it.'

'While the coffee's still warm . . .' Von Polanyi said, filling Szara's cup, then his own. He settled back and made himself comfortable on the couch. The room, Szara realized, was very nearly a stage set, and not by accident. The light was low and confidential; in the woods outside the window there was only darkness and silence and the steady drip of the rain. The man in the green Opel had driven away; the sense of privacy was complete.

'This is,' Von Polanyi said, 'the story of a love affair. A love affair carried on at a distance, over a long period of time – six years, to date, and it continues – a love affair with roots in the personalities of two very different nations, a love affair in which you and I have both been intimately involved, a love affair, as it happens, between two powerful men. The reference is clear?'

'I would think so.'

'Love affair is a dramatic term, isn't it, but what else could one call a relationship based on a deep and sympathetic understanding, a shared passion for certain ideals, a common view of the human race? Love affair describes it. Especially when you include such elements as secrecy. There's always that in a love affair. Maybe one of the lovers is promised to somebody else, or it could be that the family doesn't approve. Or maybe it doesn't matter *why* – the two lovers want to meet but everything is in their way; they're misunderstood, even hated, and all they want to do is unite, to become as one. It's all so unfair.'

Von Polanyi paused, took a pack of Gitanes from a wooden box on the coffee table, and offered one to Szara. The same kind he'd smoked when he'd visited Dr Baumann, naturally. After he'd lit Szara's cigarette with a silver lighter, Von Polanyi continued. 'Now if we are writing a play, the logical ending for such a love affair is doom. But, if we leave the theatre and enter the world of politics, the doom may be for the world and not the lovers. Imagine that Shakespeare rewrote the final act of *Romeo and Juliet*: now the lovers poison the wells of Verona and, in the final scene, they're all alone and living happily ever after.

'Well,' Von Polanyi said, 'I suppose that's the end of my literary career. Because the reality, I'm afraid, is not so amusing. The lovers, of course, are Joseph Stalin and Adolf Hitler. In August, their secret love affair ended with the announcement of an engagement – the Non-Aggression Pact – and a lavish engagement present: Poland. And this is merely the engagement. One may well ask what splendours are planned for the wedding itself!

'But that's the future. For tonight, in the few hours we have, I want to talk about the past. But where to begin? Because this passion, this romance, does not confine itself to the lovers, it starts in the villages where they live and it starts a long time ago. Germany has always needed what Russia has: her oil, iron ore, rare metals and grain. And Russia has always needed what Germany has: our science and technology, our skills, the simple ability to get something done. A German sees a job that needs doing, he thinks a minute, rolls up his sleeves, spits on his hands, and – it's done! When we try to go it alone, alas, when we exclude the world outside our borders, things don't go so well. An example: our latest campaign is to get our people to eat rye bread, from grain we can grow ourselves, and to that end the Ministry of Propaganda is claiming that white bread weakened our soldiers in the 1914 war. Of course no one believes it.

'Now two countries like this, and practically next-door neighbours to boot – is it not a match that cries out to be made? It's been tried before, but somehow it never seems to take. Catherine the Great imported Germans by the wagonload; they helped, but nothing really changed. A more recent example: in 1917, the German General Staff put old Lenin on an armoured train and thus destroyed imperial Russia. Yet even so, the minute the world settled down, in 1922, they were at it again with the Treaty of Rapallo. Now we had the two most despised states in Europe rushing into each other's arms – if nobody else will love me, surely this ugly old thing will!

'Poor Rapallo. Another *treaty*, another date to torment the student suffering over his history text. But this marriage is a little more interesting if you look under the covers. The German War Ministry forms a development company called GEFO and funds it with seventy-five million gold reichsmarks. This allows the Junkers company to build three hundred fighter aircraft at a Russian town called Fili, just outside Moscow. Germany receives two hundred and forty of them, the USSR gets sixty and the technology. Next comes a joint stock company called Bersol – by now our poor, suffering student is surely reeling. Perhaps reeling in fact, since Bersol undertakes the manufacture of poison gas at Trotsk, in the province of Samara. In 1925, in Tambov province, near the town of Lipetsk, the Lipetsk Private Flying School comes into existence. Rather nebulous, though known today as the Luftwaffe. By September of 1926, Russian freighters deliver three hundred thousand shells plus gunpowder and fuses to Germany, disguised as pig iron and aluminium. Can the poor student stand any more of this? Once you add the fact that the Heavy Vehicle Experimental and Test Station near the town of Kazan is in fact a site for Krupp and Daimler and Rheinmetall to build light tractors – tanks is a better description – probably not. It's all so tiresome, unless of course the student goes to school in Prague. This goes on for twelve years. Germany rebuilds its forces; the two armies participate in exchanges of military officers, establishing facilities in both Berlin and Moscow. And that's just the secret part of Rapallo. In full view of the world, the Russian wheat and ore boats travel west, the German technicians pack their little black bags and head east.

'When Hitler came to power, though, in 1933, all had to end. Here was Germany's evil face, and the idealistic Soviet Union and its friends the wide world over had to be seen to turn away from it. Pity, because everything had been going so well.

'Any diplomat would say that such a moment, if nothing else can be done, is a time to keep a dialogue alive, but Hitler and Stalin shared a special and characteristic trait: they both believed that language was God's gift to liars, words existed only to manipulate those who thought otherwise. Both these men had risen from the gutters of Europe – here I am partial to a Russian saying: power is like a high, steep cliff, only eagles and reptiles may ascend to it – and they believed diplomacy to be the tool of those who had historically kept them down, the intelligentsia, professors, Jews, all such people. But then, a problem: how could any sort of communication be achieved? Solution: only by deeds, by gestures, by irrevocable actions that made one's intentions plain and clear. They certainly didn't invent this method. Since the first days of the newspaper, nations have communicated in this way – on the third page, on the second page, on the first page. We must admit, though, that Hitler and Stalin used the method with some particular flair.

'In 1933, Stalin wasn't quite sure what he was dealing with in Berlin. He'd read translations of Hitler's speeches, maybe even his book, but, as I've said, what did that mean? Then, in 1934, something even Stalin could understand. The Night of the Long Knives. Hitler had a rival, Ernst Röhm, who led the Brown Shirts. What did he do about it? Murdered them. All the important ones, and all in one night. And so much for rivals. Well, Stalin felt, apparently, the first stirrings of romantic passion, because by December of that year he answered in kind. The assassination of Kirov was organized, and Stalin's political rivals were eliminated in a purge that continued into 1936.

'Then it was Hitler's turn. In 1936 he marched into the Rhineland. He took *territory*. Once again, Stalin sat up and took notice. Found a way to express a kind of approval: the show trial of Kamenev and Zinoviev. That they were Jews is less important than Vyshinsky's *statement*, at the trial, that they were Jews. Here we see Stalin beginning to come to grips with his real problem, which was very simply this: the twelve years of Rapallo had taught both countries that they could cooperate; now, how was that cooperation to be reinstated? Because, with Hitler in power, those two countries could rule the world if they worked together. They were, like lovers, made whole each by the other, and thus invincibly strong.

'But Stalin had a difficult problem, the fact that communism had traditionally been a religion of idealists. On one side of him was Tukhachevsky, Trotsky's protégé, and the most powerful figure in the Red Army. Tukhachevsky was young, handsome, brilliant, and courageous, proven in battle, beloved by his officers. At a show trial, he would have made mincemeat of an oily little opportunist like Vyshinsky and Stalin knew it. Now he needed help, and help was at hand. You'll recall the officer exchanges that went on during the Rapallo period? Letters, orders, communications of various sorts, still existed in German files. At Stalin's behest, certainly through NKVD intermediaries of the most trusted sort, Reinhard Heydrich and the Gestapo SD intelligence service found Tukhachevsky's communications and remade them into forgeries proving that Tukhachevsky and four other Soviet marshals – two of them Jews! – had conspired with Hitler to overthrow the government of the USSR in a coup d'état. Exit the marshals and most of the leadership of the Red Army. What did the world, the *knowledgeable* world, civil servants and journalists, think of this? That the conspiracy was born in Germany, a brilliant manoeuvre by the intelligence services to weaken the military leadership of the USSR. Certainly, except for Stalin at the bottom of it, it could seem that way.

'That left Stalin with one final, but very grave, difficulty: the intelligence services themselves, the real levers of his power. The NKVD and the GRU were staffed by thousands of Old Bolsheviks and foreign communists, many of them Jews, every last one of them an ideologue. These people were concentrated in crucial positions – including the Foreign Departments of both services – and handled the most secret and sophisticated tasks. These were the people who'd bled in the revolution, these were the people who believed that whatever else might be wrong with the Soviet Union, at least it stood against Hitler's bullyboys and Jew baiters. Rapprochement with Germany under Nazi rule? Unthinkable.

'But, as I suspect you know, a man in love will do almost anything, and Stalin craved Hitler as ally, accomplice, and friend. Perhaps he thought, *There is one man in the world, and only one, with whom I could have a complete understanding, but here are all these stiff-necked romantics in my way. Will no one rid me of these meddlesome* – well, one can't say *priests*, but it isn't so far from true. And there was, there almost always is, someone at hand to take him up on it. On one level, the purge of 1936 to 1938 was seen as an elimination of those who knew too much, those who knew where the bodies were buried, the final act of a criminal securing his crime. To those with an inside view, however, it seemed principally a war for power in the intelligence services: the so-called Ukrainian *khvost*; Jews and Poles and Latvians versus the Georgian *khvost*, mostly those from Transcaucasia; Georgians, Armenians, Turks, with a few Jewish allies thrown in to muddy the issue. In fact, it was an extended pogrom, led by Beria, and when it was done the stage was set for a public consummation of the love affair.

'Hitler certainly knew what was going on, because Kristallnacht, the world's first real taste of what Germany had in mind for the Jews of Europe, was then allowed to take place, in late 1938. The former operatives of the NKVD would have assassinated him then and there, but they were either dead or working at the bottom of some gold mine in Siberia and soon to be. Stalin, eternally shrewd, left a few show pieces alive, to forestall the accusation that he'd done exactly what he did do – Lazar Kaganovich for instance, Maxim Litvinov for instance, some of the operatives in the European networks for instance, and a few prominent journalists, for instance Ilya Ehrenburg, for instance André Szara.'

Von Polanyi paused – perhaps he expected Szara to sputter and curse – and in a rather studied way chose that moment to discover that he wanted more coffee. Szara found himself dispassionate, nodding in polite affirmation, *yes, it could have been like that*, but he'd learned more about his own situation in that moment than he had about Joseph Stalin. He felt no anger at all. His mind was now ruled, he saw, by the suspended judgment of the intelligence officer. What he'd once pretended to be he had, by necessity, become, for his principal reaction to Von Polanyi's revelation was *perhaps*. It could be true. But, more to the point, why was he being told this? What role was Von Polanyi assigning him?

There had to be one. Von Polanyi had known about him for a long time, as far back as 1937, when he'd come to Berlin to recruit Dr Baumann – when the NKVD had agreed, far above his head, to receive strategic information by means of a clandestine network. Unwittingly, Szara had been an operative of the Reich Foreign Ministry's intelligence service – 'a small office . . . simply a group of educated German gentlemen' – and he had no very good reason to believe that Von Polanyi wanted the relationship to end. 'As far as I can tell,' Szara said carefully, 'everything you say is true. Can anything be done about it?'

'Not immediately,' Von Polanyi said. 'Tonight, the

centre of Europe runs on a line down the middle of Poland, and I believe the intention is to forge a Russo-German empire on either side of it. For Germany there is Western Europe: France, Scandinavia, the Low Countries, Great Britain; Spain and Portugal will come along when they see how things are, Italy remains a junior partner. Stalin will expect to acquire a substantial part of the Balkans, Lithuania, Latvia, Estonia, Turkey, Iran, and India – eventually a common border with a Japanese empire in the Pacific. The United States is to be isolated, slowly squeezed to death or invaded by a thousand divisions. Both Hitler and Stalin prefer political conquest to actual war, so the former alternative is the more likely.'

'For me,' Szara said, 'a world in which I could not live. But you are a German, Herr Von Polanyi, a German patriot. Is it possible you dislike the present leader so deeply that you would damage your country in order to destroy him?'

'I am a German, most certainly a German patriot. From that perspective, I will tell you that the damage has already been done, and a world has been created in which I refuse to live. If Germany loses this war it will be devastating, almost the worst thing that could happen but not the very worst. The very worst would be for Adolf Hitler and Joseph Stalin, and the people around them, to win such a war. That I cannot permit.'

Von Polanyi's arrogance was stunning; Szara forced himself to look puzzled and a little lost. 'You have something particular in mind, then.'

'At this moment, I frankly don't know what to do, not specifically. I do know, however, that a structure needs to be established, a structure with which Hitler's power may be damaged, perhaps destroyed, when the opportunity presents itself. Why would I want to create such a structure? I can only say: who will if I won't? I don't want to bore you with a history of the Von Polanyi family – in a sense you already know it. An old family, hundreds of years old. Never peaceful. A war family, if you like, but always honourable. Obsessed with honour. So, always, we die young. We also breed young, however, so the line continues despite the inevitabilities of such a heritage. For me, honour lies in the sort of action I am proposing. I am not unaware that this thorn in the German character is despised by some, but I think you can find a way to see the use of it.'

'Of course,' Szara said. 'But my own situation . . .' He didn't know where to begin.

Von Polanyi leaned forward. 'To do what I have in mind, Herr Szara, I need a man outside Germany, a man not only in a neutral country but in a neutral state of being. A man without affiliation, a man not obligated to any particular state or political creed, a man who understands the value of information, a man who can direct this information where it will do the most good – which is to say the most harm – and a man who can achieve that sort of liaison skilfully, in such a way that the source remains protected. Thus a man with the technical ability to support an act inspired by ethics, honour, call it by any name you like. Briefly put, I need a man who can do good and not get caught at it.'

So I am described, Szara thought, and a strange conspiracy is proposed: a Polish Jew and a German aristocrat shall work together to push Adolf Hitler over the edge of some yet unseen cliff. The presumption of the idea! That two rather ordinary men in an inn near Altenburg would even dare to dream of opposing a state of the magnitude of Nazi Germany, with its Gestapo, its Abwehr, SS divisions, Panzer tanks and Luftwaffe. Yet it was possible and Szara knew it – the power of intelligence was such that two ordinary men in an inn near Altenburg could destroy a nation if they used it properly.

'You are attracted to the idea,' Von Polanyi said, an edge of excitement in his voice.

'Yes,' Szara said. 'Perhaps it could be done. But I am officially a traitor to the Soviet Union, a network operative in flight, so my time on earth is very limited. Weeks, probably. Nothing can change that.'

'Herr Szara.' Von Polanyi's feelings were clearly hurt. 'Please try to think better of me than that. We have a friend in the SD who is, covertly, a friend of the NKVD. With your permission, we are going to have you leave this troubled world tonight, one of the many who did not survive Gestapo interrogation. You may, if all goes smoothly, read your own obituary should the Russians choose to proceed in that way. But you must not betray us, must not spring alive with your name at the foot of a newspaper column. Can you give me your word that it will be so – forever?'

'You have my word,' Szara said. 'But it cannot be that simple.'

'*Auf!*' Von Polanyi said in despair. 'Of course it isn't. Nothing is. You will live in mortal fear of chance recognition. But I do believe that a certain inertia will help to keep you safe. A Soviet officer will think a long time before insisting that an enemy declared dead by the NKVD is in fact still with us. To discredit the leadership of his own organization is something he will not do easily. Better to convince himself that he's seen a ghost, and that Moscow remains infallible.'

'They'll want proof.'

'The proof is that they've discovered the event by clandestine means, and that when a feeler is extended at some remote level – "Seen our man Szara anywhere?" – we'll deny we ever heard of you. Then they'll believe it. The real danger to you is gossip – a group of émigrés, for example, chattering about a Russian-speaking Frenchman who sneaks off to eat blini when he thinks no one's looking. You have a French passport, according to the Gestapo teletype. They describe it as "valid." Use it. Be that Frenchman. But you must alter your appearance as best you can and live the life of a Frenchman – a Frenchman who best not return to France, a Jew from Marseille, mixed up in who knows what unsavoury affair. Grow yourself a vulgar little moustache, grease your hair, gain weight. You won't fool the French; they'll know you're a fraud the minute you speak a word. But with luck they'll take you for nothing more than a creature of the gutter – just not their gutter. Put it about that you lived in Cairo and sold the wrong stocks to the chief of police. There is a bustling world at the margins of society; I'm sure you know it. It hides all sorts of people, it may possibly hide you. Well, what do you think?'

Szara didn't answer right away. He stared at his hands and finally said, 'Maybe.'

'The best deception is the one we ourselves believe in, and that is always the sort of deception that saves our lives,' Von Polanyi said, a bit of the philosopher's gleam in his eye. 'Survive, Herr Szara. I think it's your gift in this life. Trust in the fact that most people are never very sure of themselves – "Oh but you do remind me of him," they'll say. You must, however, become the legend you create for yourself, and you may not take vacations from it. For you, perhaps a little job of some sort might make all the difference – something not quite legitimate.'

Szara turned and looked out the window, but nothing had changed; a starless night, the steady rhythm of rain in a forest. Finally he said, 'How would we communicate?'

Von Polanyi let the silence rest for a moment; it meant they had reached an understanding, the sort that does not require words. Then he went through the procedures: a postal card to a certain drapery shop, a *poste restante* return address, then contact. His tone was casual, almost dismissive, implying it was the sort of thing that Szara had done a thousand times before. When he'd finished, Szara said, 'And if I simply vanish?'

'We are equals in this affair,' Von Polanyi said easily. 'If you don't want us, Herr Szara, then we don't want you. It's just that simple.'

They took him out of Germany in grand style, in a dark green Mercedes driven by a young man barely out of his teens, a naval officer, pink-cheeked, gangling, and endlessly solicitous. Every hour or so he would pull over, wait until the road was clear, then knock delicately on the lid of the boot and whisper loudly, 'All is well?' or some such thing.

All was well enough. Szara lay on a saddle blanket, his valise beside him, surrounded by assorted tack that smelled richly of old leather and horse. They had fed him sumptuously at the inn, a tray left in front of the door bearing poached eggs and buttered bread and jam tarts. And the naval officer – somewhere outside Vienna, he guessed – slipped him half a cold roast duck in a napkin and a bottle of beer. In the horsey-smelling darkness Szara felt a little seasick from the curves but picked at it for form's sake and drank the beer. There were three stops. Each time he imagined papers being presented to the accompaniment of Hitler salutes and a rough joke and a laugh. By nightfall they were rumbling up the avenues of a city and Szara was let out on a dark street in a pleasant neighbourhood. 'Welcome to Budapest,' said the young officer. 'The stamp is already in your passport. Good luck.' Then he drove away.

* * *

He was, in some sense, free.

Jean Bonotte was abroad in the world and lived much as Von Polanyi had suggested he might – in shabby hotels near railway stations or in the narrow streets by the harbour, where the air smelled like dead fish and diesel oil. He stayed nowhere very long. Joined a restless army of lost souls, men and women without countries, not so very different from his days in Kovno. He stood with them on the long lines for registration at the police stations – 'One more week, sir, then out you go' – ate at the same cheap restaurants, sat with them in the parks when the pale winter sun lit up the statue of the national hero. He changed. The cracked mirrors in the numberless hotel rooms told the story. He did not, as Von Polanyi had suggested, gain weight. He lost it, his face lean and haunted beneath his awkward, refugee haircut. He grew a natty moustache and trimmed it to perfection, the last vestige of self-respect in a world that had taken everything else away. A pair of faintly tinted eyeglasses gave him the look of a man who would be sinister if he dared, a weak, frightened man making a miserable pretence of strength. This message was not lost on the predators. Again and again the police of various cities took the little money he had in his pocket, and on two occasions he was beaten up.

The second day in Budapest, when he hadn't quite got the hang of life in the alleys, a little fellow with a cap down over his eyes and a stub of cigarette stuck to his lip demanded money for entry into a certain neighbourhood – or so Szara guessed from his gestures, for he understood not a word of Hungarian. Szara angrily brushed the impeding hand away and the next thing he knew he'd been hit harder than ever before in his life. He barely saw it happen, this dog didn't growl before it bit. Szara simply found himself lying in the street, ears ringing, blood running in his mouth, as he fumbled for money to offer. Fortunately he'd left his valise in a hotel or it would have been gone forever. The damage, when he saw it, was horrific. Both lips had been split to one side of his mouth, as well as the skin above and below. It healed poorly. A dark red scar remained. In his mismatched jacket and trousers, wearing a shirt bought purposely a size too large so that it stood out around his neck, he already looked like a man whose luck, if he ever had any, had run out a long time ago. The scar drew the eye, confirmed the image. If the NKVD was still hunting for André Szara, and he had to assume that they might be, they wouldn't look for him hiding inside this sad, battered fellow.

Budapest. Belgrade. The Romanian port of Constanţa. Salonika, where he sold lottery tickets in the streets of the large, prosperous Jewish community. Athens. Istanbul. The new year of 1940 he welcomed in Sofia, staring at a light bulb on a cord that dangled from the ceiling and thinking of Nadia Tscherova.

As he did every day, sometimes every hour. To the address in Schillerstrasse he sent postcards. Signed *B*. *A* would have been for André, *B* was what he was now. She would understand this immediately, he knew. This *B* was a wealthy sort of cad, travelling about southern Europe on business, who now and then gave a thought to his old girlfriend Nadia who lived in Germany. 'The sea is quite lovely,' said *B* from a town on the Black Sea coast of Turkey. In Bucharest he'd 'finally got over a beastly cold.' In Zagreb, where he worked for two old Jewish brothers who had a market stall where they sold used pots and pans, *B* detected 'signs of spring in the air.' *I am alive*, he told her in this way. *I am not in Germany, not in Russia, I am free*. But living a life – in Varna, Corfu, Debrecen – that she could not possibly share. 'Love always,' said *B*, mailing his card an hour before he left a city. What *love always* really meant, the ten thousand words of it, he could only hope she understood. In the ruined beds of a hundred rooms spread across the lost quarters of Europe, her ghost lay with him every night.

When he worked, it was almost always in Yiddish. Even in the Sephardic communities where they spoke Ladino, somebody was sure to know it. In the outdoor markets, in the back streets of almost any city, he found Jews, and they almost always needed something done. He didn't ask very much, and they'd nod yes with a tight mouth, *probably you'll rob me*. It wasn't exactly charity, just something in the way they were that didn't like to say no. Maybe he was hungry. He didn't look strong enough to load or unload wagons but he did it once or twice. Mostly he cleaned up, or ran errands, or sold things. The dented, blackened pots and pans in Zagreb. Secondhand suits in Bucharest. Used dishes, sheets, tools, books – even eyeglasses. 'No?' he'd say. 'Then try these. Can you see that girl over there? Perfect! That's silver in those frames – you look ten years younger.' It was easy to pick up – he had to wonder if it hadn't been there all the time – and it had to be done, a premium for the customer. Who wanted to buy from a stone? In these streets, money was earned and spent in the cheapest coin there was, a whole dinar, a lek or a lev, that you never saw. But life was cheap. He lived on bread and tea, potatoes and onions, cabbage and garlic. A little piece of dried-up meat was a banquet. If it had a rim of fat at the edge, a feast. His skin grew red and rough from being outdoors in the winter, his hands hard as leather. He'd beckon a customer to him confidentially, look both ways to make sure no one was listening, slip a subtle finger beneath a lapel and say, 'Listen, you got to buy from me today, you're not going to anybody else. So make a price, I don't care, I'm a desperate man.' The owner of a stall that sold buttons and thread said to him in Constanţa, 'David' – for so he called himself that week – 'you're the best *luftmensch* I ever had. Maybe you'll stay awhile.'

He became, that spring, the other kind of *luftmensch* as well, the man as inconspicuous as air, the operative. Privately, at first, in the way he began to remember his past. It came back like an old love affair, the ashes of his former life a little warmer than he'd thought.

He found himself in Izmir, the old Greek city of Smyrna, now Turkish. Just by the old bazaar, on Kutuphane street, was a restaurant owned by a swarthy little Sephardic lady with shining black eyes. For her he scrubbed pots. It turned his hands and forearms crimson, and he earned almost nothing, but she was a provident feeder – he lived on lamb and pine nuts and groats, dried figs and apricots – and she had an unused room in the cellar with a dusty straw mattress on an old door that he could sleep on. There was even a table, the edges marked by forgotten cigarettes, and a paraffin lamp. Through a half window at pavement level he could see Kadifekele, the Velvet Fortress, perched on top of its hill. He had a strong, intuitive feeling about the room: a writer had worked there. The old lady's son was something or other in the administrative section of the Izmir police, and for the first time in his travels Jean Bonotte had an actual work permit, though not under that name. 'Write down,' she'd said. And he'd laboriously scrawled some concoction on a scrap of paper. A week later, a permit. 'My son!' she explained of the miracle. Fortune smiled. Izmir wasn't a bad place: a sharp wind blew across the docks off the Aegean, the harbour was full of tramp freighters. The people were reserved, slightly inward, perhaps because, not so many years earlier, the blood had literally run in the streets here, Turks slaughtering Greeks, and the town couldn't quite put it in the past.

From his meagre wages Szara bought a notebook and pencils and, once the huge iron pots were dried and put away for the evening, began to write. This was night writing, writing for himself, with no audience in mind. It was March, a good writer's month, Szara felt, because writers like abundant weather – thunder and lightning, wind and rain, surging spring skies – not particularly caring if it's good or bad just so there's a lot going on. He wrote about his life, his recent life. It was hard, he was surprised at the emotional aches and pains it cost him, but evidently he wanted to do it because he didn't stop. On the near horizon was what Von Polanyi had said about the executions of the 1936 purge and the secret courtship of Hitler and Stalin. But it was life he wrote about, not so much politics. Izmir, he sensed, was not a place where you would want to write about politics. It was almost too old for that, had seen too much, lived somewhere beyond those kinds of explanations – here and there the marble corner of a tumbled-down ruin had been worn to a curve by the incessant brush of clothing as people walked by for centuries. In such a place, the right thing to do was archaeology: archaeology didn't have to be about the ancient world, he discovered; you could scrape the dirt away and sift the sand of more recent times. The point was to preserve, not to lose what had happened.

Working down through his life, beneath the common anarchy of existence, the misadventures, dreams, and passions, he found pattern. Rather, two patterns. If every life is a novel, his had two plots. He discovered he had, often at the same moment, both served and resisted the Hitler-Stalin *affaire*, had worked for two masters, both in the Soviet special services. Bloch and Abramov.

What General Bloch had done was both daring and ingenious and, Szara came to believe, driven by desperation. He knew what was going on, he fought against it. And in this war André Szara had been one of his soldiers. To

Szara, the depth of the operation and his part in it became clear only when he applied the doctrine of chronology – the exercise in a cellar in Izmir no different than the one he'd undertaken in a hotel room in Prague, when he'd worked through DUBOK's, Stalin's, history of betrayal.

Bloch had become aware of Stalin's move toward Hitler sometime before 1937 and had determined to prevent the alliance by naming Stalin as an Okhrana agent. He had somehow broken into Abramov's communication system and ordered Szara aboard the steamship taking Grigory Khelidze from Piraeus to Ostend. Khelidze was on his way to Czechoslovakia to collect the Okhrana file hidden sometime earlier in a left-luggage room in a Prague railway station. Szara had induced Khelidze to reveal his whereabouts in Ostend, then Bloch had ordered the courier's assassination. Then he'd used Szara as a substitute courier, used him to uncover Stalin's crimes in the Bolshevik underground, used him to publish the history of that treason in an American magazine. It had almost worked. The Georgian *khvost*, however, had somehow learned of the operation and prevented publication from taking place.

Here the chronology was productive: it revealed a mirror image of this event.

Szara, while in Prague, had written a story for *Pravda* about the agony of the Czech people as Hitler closed in for the kill. That story was suppressed. It was not in Hitler's interest for it to appear – evidently it was not in Stalin's interest, either. Ultimately, Britain and France were blamed for the loss of Czechoslovakia at Munich but, in the very same instant, Stalin and the Red Army stood quietly aside and permitted it to happen.

Abramov had then protected Szara, his old friend and sometime operative, by absorbing him directly into the intelligence *apparat* – what better place to hide from the devil than in a remote corner of hell? In Paris, Szara had become Baumann's case officer, in fact no more than one end of a secret communication system between Hitler and Stalin.

Then, a chance event that neither the Gestapo nor the NKVD could have foreseen.

The Paris OPAL network had broken through the screen of secrecy hiding their ongoing cooperation. Through Sénéschal's unwitting agent, the secretary Lötte Huber, Szara had discovered a meeting between Dershani, Khelidze's superior in the Georgian *khvost*, and Uhlrich, a known SD officer, and photographed it. Sénéschal had been murdered almost immediately because of this and Abramov had died for it a year or so later. Abramov, Szara now believed, had changed sides, attempted to use the photographs as leverage, and they had eliminated him as he attempted to escape.

There was more: Molotov's replacing Litvinov as the Hitler-Stalin courtship approached its moment of revelation, and Hitler's public approval of the change. Even Alexander Blok's poem 'The Scythians' seemed to have played a part in the operation. Here, the analysis depended on audience. If, on the night of the actor Poziny's recitation, the message was to the British and French diplomats in attendance, the poem served as a plea and a warning, which was how Blok had meant it: 'We ourselves henceforth shall be no shield of yours / we ourselves henceforth will enter no battle . . . Nor shall we stir when the ferocious Hun / rifles the pockets of the dead / Burns down cities . . .' To a German ear, however, at that particular moment in history, it might have meant something very different, something not unlike an invitation, from Stalin to Hitler, to do those very things. To bend Blok's poem to such a purpose was, to Szara, a particularly evil act, and it touched him with horror as nothing else had. He himself knew better, that compared to other evils the abuse of a poet's words oughtn't to have meant that much, yet somehow it did. Somehow it opened a door to what now happened in Europe, where, with Stalin's concurrence, the words became reality. The horror took place.

Late at night in Izmir, the spring wind blowing hard off the Aegean Sea, André Szara stared sightlessly out the window above his writing table. He would never understand the mysteries that these two peoples, the Russian and the German, shared between them. Blok had tried as only a poet could, applying images, the inexplicable chemistry at the borders of language. Szara would not presume to go deeper. He could see where answers might be hidden – somewhere in what happened between him and Marta Haecht, somewhere in what happened between Nadia Tscherova and her German general, somewhere in what happened between Hitler and Stalin, somewhere in what happened, even, between himself and Von Polanyi. Trust and suspicion, love and hate, magnetism and repulsion. Was there a magic formula that drew all this together? He could not find it, not that night in Izmir he couldn't. Perhaps he never would.

He could think only of Bloch's final act in the drama, in which he had manoeuvred Szara into the reach of de Montfried. It was as though Bloch, confronted by the certainty of failure – Beria ascendant, the murderers securely in power, a pact made with the devil – had sent one last message: *save lives*. Szara had done the best he could. And then the reality of circumstance had intervened.

And, soon enough, the reality of circumstance was that choices had to be made.

Szara filled a score of notebooks before he was done: messy, swollen things, pages front and back covered – entirely in disregard of the ruled lines – in pencilled Russian scrawl, erasures, scribbled-out words from moments when the great impatience was on him. In time, he began to live for the night, for the hours when the people of his life would come alive and speak. His memory astonished him: what Abramov said, the way Marta would put things, Vainshtok's sarcasms – and what may have been the final gesture of his life, which Szara never really did come to understand.

The potwasher's job took its toll. The skin of his hands dried out, cracked, and sometimes bled – occasionally he left a bloodspoor at the margin where his hand rested as he wrote. *Let them figure that out!* he thought. Them? He didn't know who that was. Russians had become secret writers, in camps and basements and cells and a thousand forms of exile, and they could only imagine secret readers. He was no different.

Otherwise, the world was unreasonably kind to him. The old lady developed a theory that his aptitude lay beyond scouring burned buckwheat crusts from the sides of pots and insisted, in the primitive one-word-at-a-time Yiddish they used between them, that he accompany her on the daily shopping expeditions – here she performed a fluent pantomime, lugging an invisible weight and blowing with fatigue – and when they attacked the markets, she took him to school. Onions were to be oblong and hard. You sniffed a melon here. With that thief you counted change twice. She had plans for him. He sensed a change of fortune, an improvement, a possible solution.

He was not the only one, that spring, who sought solutions. Far to the north of him, on Germany's western border, military intelligence officers were wondering exactly how they might penetrate France's Maginot Line or, if it could not be overrun, how to turn its flank. At first this seemed impossible. Even if the Wehrmacht were to violate Belgian neutrality, how were the Panzer tanks, so critical to the German attack scenario, to break through the dense Ardennes forest? To answer this question, the officers fixed lengths of pipe to the bonnets of their cars, making them the width of a tank, and drove through the forest. You had to go slow, they found, you had to weave in and out among the trees, you might have to knock down a few of them here and there, but it could be done.

It was done on 10 May. Along with glider and paratroop attacks to hold the Belgian bridges and subdue the Belgian forts. In the soft evening light on Izmir's seaside promenade Szara came upon a group of French people – perhaps commercial travellers or employees of French companies – gathered around a single copy of *Le Temps*. The Aeolus blew hard at that hour, and the men were holding their hats with one hand and the pages of the wind-whipped newspaper with the other. One of the women had tears on her face. Szara stood at the edge of the group and read over their shoulders. He understood immediately what had happened – he had seen Poland. One of the men was wearing a flat-brimmed straw boater. He let it go in order to flatten a recalcitrant page, the wind immediately blew it off and it rolled and skipped along the promenade.

Szara packed the notebooks that night, wrapping them carefully in brown paper and tying the package with string. An old sweater, a few novels – Balzac, Stendhal, Conrad in French – extra shirt and socks, a photograph of a Paris bistro torn from a magazine, a street map of Sofia; all of that went on top. It was time for the refugee to disappear, and a false-bottomed suitcase no longer served his purposes.

Early the following morning, sleepless and pale, he stood in a long line at the central post office. When he reached the grilled window he handed over a cable to be wired to de Montfried's office in Paris. He had an answer twenty-four hours later, was directed to a street of private banks where, beneath a vast, domed ceiling that assured a cool and perpetual dusk, a group of men in striped pants counted out thousands of French francs. Outside, Szara blinked in the hard sunlight and made his way to the office of the Denizcilik Bankasi, the Turkish Maritime Lines, a venerable institution that had been calling at the ports of the Mediterranean for over a century. The clerks were deeply understanding. This French patriot would return to his homeland, sailing in a first-class stateroom to face his destiny in war. Each in turn, they shook his hand and looked into his eyes, then pointed out a hallway that led to the baggage room. Here too he found sympathy. A supervisor stood with hands clasped behind his back and watched as his young assistant wrote out a claim ticket. With ritual care, a tag was tied to the handle, then the supervisor tapped a bell and a man in a blue uniform appeared and carried the valise away. Szara got a glimpse of the baggage room when he opened the door; sturdy, wooden shelves climbed to the ceiling. He saw old-fashioned Gladstones, steamer trunks, portmanteaus, wooden crates, even a few metal dispatch boxes with stencilled printing. The supervisor cleared his throat. 'Do not trouble yourself,' he said. 'The trust of our clients is sacred, and this we maintain, even in the most difficult times.' Then he added, 'Good luck. Godspeed.' News of the German attack on France had flowed through the city like a current; war was now certain, it would surely be worse than 1914. All the citizens of Izmir Szara encountered that day were very formal and dignified; it was their particular way with tragedy.

He sailed on 14 May and reached Marseille five days later. On the voyage he kept to his cabin and had his meals brought up by the steward. Even though future sailings had been suspended, there were few travellers on the ship, only those who felt they had to return to a country at war. By the time they docked, Antwerp had been captured and the Wehrmacht had taken Amiens. Szara's steward told him confidentially that some of the passengers felt it was already too late, and they had decided not to disembark in France. The customs and passport officials took care of the first-class passengers in their staterooms. They asked no questions of Jean Bonotte – there could be only one reason he was returning to France.

He was in Geneva a day later, travelling by hired car because the trains had become impossible, many of the locomotives and *wagons-lits* shifted north under French military control. Jean Bonotte was admitted to Switzerland on a five-day visa, in order to take care of banking business that had to be seen to in person. Again he wired de Montfried, again de Montfried responded immediately, and once again he was directed to a street of private banks. In this instance, the bankers were replaced, in an elaborately furnished sitting room, by lawyers. There were muted introductions, the fine weather was acknowledged, then the concept of *intervention* – a soft, subtle, even a graceful expression when purred a syllable at a time in French – was permitted to enter the conversation. Evidently it meant that certain officials would decide to intervene in Jean Bonotte's favour, for there could be no question but that he was the very sort of gentleman who should be resident in Switzerland. Szara said almost nothing; the Bonotte who sat at the table was virtually ignored, it was Bonotte the legal entity with whom they concerned themselves. These were gifted lawyers, with voices like cellos, who did not exactly ask questions; instead they provided answers, phrasing them for courtesy's sake in the interrogatory mood: 'Wouldn't it be much the best idea to inform the Prefecture that . . .' Szara followed along as best he could. Soothed by the distant clacking of typewriters, warmed by the sun pouring in a leaded-glass window, he might have fallen asleep if, every now and again, someone hadn't flourished a paper that needed signing. *This is how,* he thought, *you climb over barbed wire without cutting your hands*.

And so, it began again.

An eternal craft, Szara realized, in this warm and grey and placid city where the Rhône surged gently beneath stone bridges. Concessions were granted, money was earned, interest compounded, statements mailed in hand-addressed envelopes, and intelligence acquired, sold, traded, or simply locked away for later use. The city wasn't about secrecy, it was about privacy. Coat collars were worn flat. Szara found the usual small villa in the usual bland neighbourhood, on the chemin de Saussac, south of the city, and set aggressively about minding his own business, soon enough disappearing into the shadows of the daily and the expected. With his neighbours, he practised the single, stiff nod – no more, no less. He bought three brown suits, just barely different enough so the world might know he had more than one. Established a bank account, paid his bills, vanished. 'A most orderly and dignified city,' wrote the phantom *B* from Zürich. Something not unlike nostalgia attended Szara's hours on the train – all that effort to avoid a Geneva postmark while letting her know he was safe in Switzerland.

Safe was, of course, a relative term. He remained a fugitive. But somewhere, in his long odyssey through the back streets of southern Europe, Szara had learned to put aside his fear of inevitable retribution. Now he only hoped that if the NKVD discovered him he would not be kidnapped and interrogated. If they were going to kill him, let them get it over with quickly. He maintained some features of his previous disguise, in defence of chance recognition more than anything else. A woman journalist he knew, a Belgian, stared at him on a street one day. Szara acted like a man receiving an unexpected, though not at all unwelcome, sexual advance, and she hurried off. On another occasion an unknown man spoke to him, hesitantly, in Russian. Szara looked puzzled and asked, in French, if he needed assistance. The man apologized with a little bow and turned away.

What helped to protect him, Szara felt, was the attitude of the Swiss government toward the NKVD; the Soviet defector Ignace Reiss had been gunned down, quite openly, by NKVD operatives in Switzerland in 1937. The Swiss didn't like that sort of thing at all. What the Russians now maintained, he guessed, were quiet diplomatic affiliations and a few OPAL-style networks using former Communist party members as agents. Moscow thought it best to respect the limits of Swiss patience – any tolerance for revolutionary activity had long ago disappeared. The young Jews in flight from the Pale no longer argued the nights away – Hasidism! Socialism! Bolshevism! Zionism! – in Geneva cafés. Lenin, leaving exile in Switzerland in 1917, had left no statues of himself behind, and the Swiss seemed in no hurry to install them.

It would now be necessary to go to war.

This was his obligation, his heritage, it required no justification. 'I need,' Von Polanyi had said, 'a man who can do good and not get caught at it.' Very well, Szara was that man. In his desk drawer was the address of a certain drapery shop in Frankfurt. To complete the connection, he needed only a *poste restante* address, and this he obtained in Thonon, a pleasant train ride up the southern shore of Lac Leman. A communication line was now established out of Germany.

As to where Von Polanyi's information would go next, that depended on what he provided, and it was clearly Szara's choice to make: Geneva was rich with possibilities.

Carefully, quietly, Szara built an inventory of candidates. The obvious – French and British political officers – and the not so obvious. Szara made contact with organizations interested in progressive political causes. He used the library, read old newspapers, identified journalists with strong contacts within the diplomatic community. Through one of de Montfried's attorneys, he managed an introduction to one of them, now retired, who had written about the Swiss political world with extraordinary insight. He took a vanilla cake and a bottle of kirschwasser to the man's home and they spent the afternoon in conversation. Yes, information was considered a crucial resource in Switzerland, a good deal of buying and selling went on. A certain Swedish businessman, a French oil executive, a professor of linguistics at the university. On hearing the last, Szara feigned surprise. The old journalist grinned. 'A terrific communist in the old days, but I guess he saw the light.' The look on the man's face – cynical, amused – told Szara everything he needed to know. He'd turned up the corner of a network.

Paris fell on 14 June.

Szara saw the famous photograph of the Wehrmacht marching past the Arc de Triomphe. He had hoped desperately for a miracle, a British miracle, an American miracle, but none had been performed. Because all eyes were on France, the USSR chose that moment for the military occupation of Latvia and Estonia, then took the Romanian territories of Bessarabia and the northern Bukovina on the twenty-sixth. Szara mailed a postal card to a drapery shop in Frankfurt. 'My wife and I plan to return home on the third of July. Can new curtains be ready by that date?' Three weeks later, a letter to M. Jean Bonotte, Poste Restante, Thonon. In response to his inquiry, Herr Doktor Brückmann would arrive at the Hôtel Belvedere on the tenth of September. Patients wishing to consult with the doctor on neurological disorders should arrange appointments by reference from their local physicians.

'Dear, dear,' said the little man who'd driven him to the inn near Altenburg, 'you seem to have had a difficult time of it.'

Szara fingered the scar, now turned white. 'It could have been worse,' he said.

'We assume you are ready to cooperate with us.'

'I'm at your pleasure,' Szara said, and outlined how he wished to proceed, particularly in the matter of couriers. He implied that a certain individual in Berlin would regularly perform such services, but here he was deceptive. That individual, Szara swore to himself, once in Switzerland, would never leave it, not as long as war continued. *I will save that life at least*, he thought. Let them write it on his tomb. Von Polanyi would have to make other arrangements in the future.

'As you wish,' said the little man, accepting his choice. 'Now, I believe this will show our sincerity.' He handed Szara a brown envelope. 'Oh yes, one thing more. On turning over this document, Herbert asked me to say "Now lovers quarrel." I trust it makes some kind of sense to you.'

Until Szara, later that night, opened the envelope in his kitchen, it did not.

Then it took his breath away. In his hand he had two pages of single-spaced typewriting on plain white paper of indifferent quality. The first item concerned a Berlin photography studio on the Unter den Linden owned by a man named Hoffmann. Herr Hoffmann was Hitler's favourite photographer; he took portraits of Eva Braun, Hitler's mistress, and other Nazi dignitaries. The month before Hitler attacked Poland, Hoffmann had used a large map of that country to decorate his shop window. In April of 1940, he'd displayed maps of Holland and Scandinavia. Just one week before, the third of September, maps of the Ukraine, Byelorussia, and the Baltic countries had been posted.

The second item stated that the German transportation ministry had been ordered to make a study of east-west rail capacities leading to Germany's eastern border – the ministry had been told to assume that troops in excess of one million, plus artillery and horses, would have to be moved east.

The third item cited aviation fuel and maintenance requests for Luftwaffe reconnaissance aircraft operating over Liepāja, Tallinn, the island of Oesel, and the Moonzund archipelago – all Soviet defence lines in the Baltic – as well as the road network leading to Odessa, on the Black Sea.

The fourth item described the German General Staff's planning process for replacing border guard units in the region of the river Bug, the dividing line in Poland between German and Russian forces, with attack divisions. A study of evacuation plans for civilians in the area had been accelerated. Military staff was to replace civilian directors of all hospitals.

The final item stated simply that the operation was called Barbarossa: a full-scale attack on the Soviet Union, from the Baltic to the Black Sea, to take place in the late spring or early summer of 1941.

Szara had to go outside, into the air. He opened his front door cautiously, but all the houses on the street were dark, everyone was asleep. It was an overcast, warmish night, terribly still. He felt as though he'd been caught in amber, as though time had stopped dead on a wooded hill above Geneva. He had never in his life wanted so badly to walk, he realized. But he couldn't. He could not. To walk aimlessly up and down these empty streets would be to call attention to himself, and the paper lying on the yellow oilcloth that covered his kitchen table forbade such a thing; now more than ever he could not compromise the gentility that made him invisible. Just walking – it seemed so harmless. In fact he wanted more, much more. He wanted what he thought of as *life*, and by life he meant Paris, a crush of people in a narrow street, dusk, perfume, unwashed bodies, the sharp reek of Gauloises tobacco and frying potatoes. He wanted people, all kinds, laughing and arguing and posing, flirting, unconsciously touching their hair. He ached for it.

A lovers' quarrel, Von Polanyi called it. And wasn't he glib. No, that was wisdom speaking. A way of not exactly facing what it meant. It meant millions would die, and nobody, not anybody in the world, could stop it. *Madness*, he thought. Then corrected himself. He had seen a newsreel of Hitler dancing a jig outside the railway carriage in Compiègne, where the French had been forced to sign a peace treaty. A weird hopping little dance, like a madman. That was the line of the Western democracies – the man should be locked away somewhere. Szara had stayed to watch the newsreel a second time, then a third. The film had been altered, he was sure of it. One step of a jig had been turned into a lunatic's frenzy. Szara sensed an intelligence service at work. But Hitler wasn't mad, he was evil. And that was a notion educated people didn't like, it offended their sense of the rational world. Yet it was true. And just as true of his mirror image, Stalin. God only knew how many millions he had murdered. A decent, normal human being would turn away in sickness from either one of these monsters. But not Szara, not now. The luxury of damnation was not his. The accidents of time and circumstance demanded he rush to the side of one of the killers and hand him a sharpened axe. For now it had to be pretended that his crimes did not matter, and Szara, knowing the truth long before others, would have to be one of the first to pretend.

He did what had to be done. The linguistics professor was a short, angry man with a few brilliantined hairs pasted over a pink scalp. Szara understood him very well – combative, cocksure, vain, bathed in the arrogance of his theories. And, to be truthful, rather clever in his own devious way. The Communist party had always drawn such types, conferring importance on those denied it by their fellow humans. The man's eyes glittered with a sense of mission, and he was, Szara had to admit, terribly sly about what he was doing.

But Szara was the inheritor of a great tradition; Abramov's heir and Bloch's, one could trace it all the way back to the Okhrana officer and beyond, and he was more than a match for the professor. Szara wandered through the stacks of the university library, tracking his prey. Then he missed it the first time, but not the second. Just a slick little brush pass with a fortyish woman in a dark knit suit. Szara, nudging a Victorian study of phonemes out of his field of vision, saw a matchbox change hands, and that was enough for him. When the professor next visited his office, an envelope had been slipped beneath his door. Von Polanyi's second instalment was scheduled for October, and Szara knew there would be more to come. He took a rather malicious glee in all the variations he would visit upon the professor. Perhaps next time he would mail him a key to a storage locker.

But the professor would do his job, of that Szara was certain. Passing the information up the network until some Kranov would tap out code on his wireless in the dead of night. So it would come to Moscow. In Szara's imagination, a welcome was prepared for the Wehrmacht: Red Army units brought secretly to the border in goods wagons and covered trucks, tank traps dug in the dark hours when the Luftwaffe was blind, pillboxes reinforced, concrete poured. Until the lesser demon broke the greater, and the world could go on about its business.

18 October 1940.

André Szara stood among the autumn-coloured trees of a forest in the Alpine foothills and watched the waters of the Rhine curl white at the pillars of a bridge. On the other side of the river he could see the German village of Hohentengen; the red and black flag moved lightly in the wind above the town hall. A pretty place, at the southern extremity of the Black Forest, and quiet. On Szara's side of the Rhine, a few miles away, was the Swiss village of Kaiserstuhl, also pretty, also quiet. It was a peaceful border; not much happened there. At the German end of the bridge, two sentries stood guard over a wooden gate. A few log-and-barbed-wire barriers had been positioned at the edge of the village to thwart escape by a speeding car, but that was all.

He looked at his watch and saw that it was not yet four o'clock. Shifted his weight to lean against an oak tree, the dead leaves rustling at his feet as hc changed position. It was deserted here. Only fifteen miles from Zürich, but another world. In his imagination he tracked the courier: from Berlin south toward Munich, crossing the Danube in the province of Württemberg, heading for Lake Constance, then drifting toward Basel, where the Rhine turned north, at last a left at Hohentengen, and across the Hohentengen bridge. Again he looked at his watch; the minute hand hadn't moved. A wisp of smoke curled from the chimney of a woodsman's hut that housed the Swiss border guard. They, unlike their German counterparts across the bridge, did not have to stand guard with rifles in the chill mountain air.

Now it came.

Szara stiffened when he saw it. A huge, shiny black car with long curves up the front fenders and little swastika flags set above the headlamps. It moved carefully around the barriers, rolled to a stop at the gate. One of the guards leaned down to the driver's window, then stood to attention and saluted briskly. The other guard lifted the latch, then walked the gate open until he stood against the railing of the bridge. The car moved forward; Szara could just hear it bump across the uneven wooden boards of the surface. The door of the woodsman's hut opened, and a guard came halfway out and casually waved the car forward into Switzerland.

Szara, hands thrust in pockets, set off on a dirt path that ran along the hillside, then descended to the road at a point where it left the view of the border guards. He had surveyed all the little bridges along this part of the Rhine and finally chosen the Hohentengen, walking through the operation a week earlier. He was now certain the meeting would be unobserved. Skidding on wet leaves, he reached the surface of the road and moved toward the idling car which had stopped by a road marker showing the distance to Kaiserstuhl. Through the windscreen Szara could just make out – the October light was fading quickly and the oblique angle made it difficult to see – the silhouette of a driver in uniform and military cap. The glass of the passenger windows was tinted for privacy. He saw only a reflected hillside, and then his own image, a hand reaching to open the back door, a face cold and neutral, entirely at war with what went on inside him.

The door swung open smoothly, but he did not find what he expected. He blinked in surprise. These were not pale blue eyes, and there was no affection in them. Curiosity, perhaps. But not much of that. These were the eyes of a hunter, a predator. They simply stared back at him, without feeling, without acknowledgment, as though he were no more than a moving shape in a world of moving shapes. 'Oh, Seryozha!' she said, and pulled the borzoi back on his silver chain.

Szara must have looked surprised because Nadia said, 'Why are you staring? I couldn't very well leave him in Berlin, now could I?'

They leaned across the dog's back to embrace. Szara's heart glowed within him. Seryozha's presence meant she had no intention of going back to Berlin. For her, life in the shadows was over.

Of that he was absolutely certain.

Afterword

This novel is based on a conversation held in a private clinic in Paris in February of 1937. While recovering from an automobile accident, the Soviet intelligencc officer L. L. Feldbin – alias Alexander Orlov – was visited by his cousin Zinovy Katsnelson, a state security commissar for the Ukraine. Katsnelson claimed that members of the Ukrainian, principally Jewish, group within the special services intended to overthrow Stalin by denouncing him to the Communist party as a former agent of the Okhrana. Proof of the association lay in three copies of an Okhrana dossier held by the group. By March of 1937, Katsnelson had been recalled to Moscow and shot. Feldbin defected from an assignment in Spain in July of 1938, eventually reaching the United States. In the course of his debriefing, many years later, he reported what Katsnelson had told him.

Several characters in this book also appear in the novel *Night Soldiers*. I have tried to ensure that names, assignments, and locations are consistent in both books, with one exception: in *Night Soldiers*, the *rezident* Yadomir Ivanovich Bloch (Yaschyeritsa) is a colonel general, a rank of such high visibility that he would not have been able to operate as he does in *Dark Star*. Thus he has been demoted to lieutenant general in this novel.

Acknowledgments

I am grateful for the help of many individuals in the writing of *Dark Star:* historians of the period, librarians, booksellers, and friends – too many to name here. I would, however, like to thank Abner Stein and Anne Sibbald for their generous support and encouragement; manuscript editor Luise Erdmann for seeking clarity and precision in a chaotic world; and especially Joe Kanon, in particular for his confidence in my work, in general for making it possible for all sorts of writers to go on doing what they do best.